WOLVES RUNNING

THE SHAPESHIFTER SYMPHONIUM
BOOK ONE

DEBORAH JARVIS

Copyright © 2022 by Deborah Jarvis

ISBN -13 9798363619205

Cover Art by Etheric Designs

Editor: Sophia Kelly Shultz

All rights reserved.

No part of this book may be reproduced in any form or by any electronic or mechanical means, including information storage and retrieval systems, without written permission from the author, except for the use of brief quotations in a book review.

Any resemblance between characters and actual people living or dead is completely unintentional. No animals were harmed in the writing of this novel, though the dogs claimed they didn't get enough pats.

❦ Created with Vellum

CONTENTS

Foreword   v

1. The Cry of the Wolf   1
2. The Revelation of Nevermore   9
3. Home to the House   13
4. Pack Life   25
5. Night Swim   36
6. Unexpected Twist of Fate   49
7. Returning to Reality   67
8. The Burning of the Bridge   76
9. Moving Day   86
10. Ancient History   92
11. Future Days   104
12. Showdown   110
13. House Concerns   118
14. Moving Day   128
15. The Rescue   139
16. Aftermath   147
17. Lines Drawn   153
18. Stalking   161
19. Unexpected Support   168
20. The Cavalry   183
21. A New Twist   195
22. The School Board Meeting   204
23. Test Day   214
24. Playing with Matches   226
25. An Unexpected Turn of Events   234
26. Dinner with the Folks   248
27. Wedding Plans and a Cat   258
28. Deeper Concerns   264
29. The Hunted   271
30. Resolutions   304

About the Author	309
The Keyralithian Chronicles - Book 1	311
The Keyralithian Chronicles - Book 2	313
Forthcoming	315

FOREWORD

During the 2020 -2021 school year, I taught from home September through June, and it was during that time that I finished working on *The Crystal Pawn*. A few months after its release, while gearing up for the editing on *The Ivory Queen*, I had a dream one night at the end of Christmas vacation that didn't fade like most of my dreams do upon waking.

It was pretty intense – I was a shapeshifting wolf running through an urban neighborhood, wearing a red collar while pretending to be a dog. The dream then changed to finding out that one of my friends was also a wolf shapeshifter, and I had to bring him home to meet the rest of my pack and take him under my wing...er paw...so to speak. What followed was a jumble of confused fragments of me teaching him how to be a wolf, which ended when I woke the next morning with the dream still rattling around in my head.

The images hung on tenaciously as I fed the dogs and puttered around the house, and I ended up sitting on the couch to write the ideas down, figuring nothing would come of it. When school started back up a few days later, I was thirty-three pages in and not stopping.

For the next two and a half months, when I wasn't teaching or grading, I was writing. I would get up in the morning, write until I had to go up for my morning team meeting, teach during the day, get a lot of the grading done during my prep time, and then go back to writing as soon as I was done for the day. The muse had me in her grip pretty tightly, and she wasn't letting go.

During this time, I had absolutely no interest in working on the edits for *The Ivory Queen*. Not to put too fine a point on it, my editor was furious. She was all set to work on *Keyralithsmus,* and there I was, riding the wave of ecstasy that only the writing fervor can bring. When I finally came back down at the end of the book, she wanted nothing to do with it at all, and I didn't even broach it with her as we settled into the edits for *The Ivory Queen*. As we worked, however, she slowly came around to the idea of editing the new manuscript to be released, and a little while after *The Ivory Queen* came out, we began the process of editing *Wolves Running*.

What you hold in your hands is the original manuscript except for the ending. When we got to that part, I discovered it didn't really work, so instead of an August release, here we are in November. The ending is now much better, and I am thrilled that it is finally done.

Once again, I can't thank my editor Sophia Kelly Shultz enough for her tireless prodding and poking of the manuscript to make it better, not to mention not killing me! Thanks also go out to April Anamisis and Amanda Contildes for their beta reading and enthusiasm. I knew it was going well when April read the first chapter and couldn't put the rest down!

I can only hope that you, dear reader, feel the same!

As always, I want to thank my loving family - Rob, Will, and Rose - and my friends for their ongoing support. It means the world to me.

---Deb Jarvis, November 2022

P.S – Want to receive the fifty-nine page bonus story of Sasha and John's trip to Montana and their adventures there? Join my mailing list and get it for free! Email me at the.rael.coyote@gmail.com to be added to the list!

1
THE CRY OF THE WOLF

The secret was out. Three months ago, Sam Winston and a group of shapeshifters had gone public, then disappeared into some government protection program. The suddenness of the move left all of us speechless. Many of my people felt betrayed by this action; some were frightened, some excited, and all who lived within the city environs worried about what would happen next. There was no going back. The world now knew about shapeshifters. People knew about us.

When I heard the news, I groaned in disbelief and stared out of my apartment window. The city of Boulder and its buildings sprawled across the landscape, but beyond, the mountains called – home to my family, my pack. Oh, there were quite a few of us who lived here in Boulder; it was easy to exist in compared with other cities. I had chosen to live there because I wanted to be around people. I was one of the more gregarious wolves and, early in my twentieth year, had found my calling teaching biology. Now, ten years later, I was the proud owner of a master's degree diploma with my name — Sasha Wellington — emblazoned upon it, a group of wonderful current students in my classes, and quite a few former students who kept in touch long after their high school days had ended.

One of those students had become a good friend. I had met John Arndt while doing my practicum where I would eventually be hired. I was in charge of his last class of the day, AP Bio. John was a senior and somewhat of a loner. During the five months I worked with my cooperating teacher, John and I talked after the bell about anime, movies, and comics we were both passionate about, but I maintained a professional remove. When my time as a student teacher ended and John graduated, though, we evolved into close friends and started hanging out whenever we had time.

My boyfriend, a human named Rich, tolerated John coming over to watch movies at our apartment with good grace. Rich was pretty nice as humans went. He was courteous and made sure to include me in his group of friends when he found out I didn't really know many people in the city. I had spent several holidays with his family, and they all seemed like decent people. He also knew that John's friendship was important to me, and when I had reassured his male ego that John was not a threat in any way to our relationship, Rich even tried to engage him in conversations about football. These mostly fell flat because John had as little interest in sports as I did.

As for John, he never indicated any romantic inclination towards me. Oh, we talked about his interest in girls and the minimal success he'd had in dating; his quirkiness and intelligence were an off-putting combination for most women his age. With me, though, he was content discussing our joint fascination with the latest Marvel movie or Miyazaki film. I commiserated with him on his dating travails but focused more on our common interests. I think he appreciated it.

Not many outside of my family knew that I was a shapeshifter; after listening to Rich's comments about the revelation of the tribes, I knew I would never be able to tell him the truth. The fact that he had to work through my family's upcoming New Year's party was something of a relief to my whole clan. Rich's negative opinion was also held by a number of my co-workers, and many parents were suspicious that shapeshifters existed among the teaching staff. For a while, PTA meetings revolved around "saving the children from the monsters" and that sort of garbage. District administrators were adamant that none of their staff were shapeshifters; they didn't know about me or the corbie who taught English, and we both intended to keep it that way. As for John, I knew his thoughts were much kinder in that regard, but I didn't want to risk our friendship. I almost told him a number of times. Almost. In the end, I always chickened out.

Not long after Sam's reveal, I went to visit my family. They were of the opinion that being discovered was an inevitable consequence of society being so interconnected. My mother reiterated her desire for me to move home, but I just shrugged and stated that as long as no one knew, I was safe. I reminded her that there was a secluded place for me to run in the woods outside of the city. Most people couldn't tell a husky from a wolf at a distance, and I had a bright red collar that I wore when I ran just in case. It was rather large if human-me wore it, but when I became a wolf, it fit snugly enough. No problems for me that way, other than the occasional reported sightings of a large dog of unusual size running loose in the woods.

One afternoon during my Christmas break, John and I sat watching a new anime that both of us were into. It was the third episode of the *Gun Gale Online* series, and we were comparing it to the original *Sword Art Online*, loudly bickering about the differences in style and theme. I was a huge fan of the first season of *SAO*, but John was totally into the *Gun Gale* series.

"How much of that sushi are you going to eat?" I asked, watching him stuff another piece of an exotic maki roll into his mouth.

We had ordered a fairly substantial amount of maki rolls and sashimi to devour during his visit; at twenty-seven, he was still pretty gangly, and although he hadn't outgrown his appetite for copious amounts of food, he never seemed to gain a pound. As for myself, my metabolism ran fast, which tended to keep my weight down, but I had cut myself back a bit and was eating more fish and lean meats.

"What about you?" he countered after swallowing the rice-wrapped roll. "How much do *you* plan to eat? By my count, it's been, like what, an entire fish since we started?"

"And you're counting why?" I asked, menacing him with my chopsticks.

"No reason," he said. "Remember, fish are friends...not food!"

"Ha ha," I said, turning back to watch the episode. "Eat your seaweed salad and let me enjoy the show, will ya?"

He made a non-committal noise, and we went back to watching the cute little girl blow everything up with her giant gun. It was hilarious.

At about four o'clock that afternoon, though, John suddenly made an odd noise, and I looked over at him. He had turned very pale; his skin appeared clammy, and his eyes had taken on a glazed cast.

"John? You okay?" I asked.

"I'm not feeling at all well," he said, his voice shaky. "Mind if we finish this another day?"

"Of course," I said, rising as he moved unsteadily towards the hall closet to get his coat.

"I'll call you," he said, and almost ran out of the apartment into the darkening stairwell.

Rich poked his head out of the office after the door slammed.

"Sasha? What's up with him?"

"I'm not sure," I replied. "He said he didn't feel well. I'm going to go check on him. Be back in a little bit."

I grabbed my purse, jammed my feet into my boots, and left the apartment pulling my coat on as I went. Although my nose was not as sensitive as it was in my wolf form, I could tell that there was something off about John's scent. He didn't smell sick, not in an illness type of way, but he didn't smell like himself. The hallway of the apartment building held the odor long enough for me to dissect it. I blinked repeatedly when I registered what it was, then bolted out the door.

Now normally, when one of the wolf clan is born, at least one of our parents is well-aware that we have shapeshifter blood. More often, both parents are shifters or the human partner knows about it. Clan is super important to the wolves; family is everything. When we come to our time to change – and not all do – we have guides and plenty of instruction as to what is happening. Some come to it early, like at puberty. Some, though, don't come to it until very late, and it can be an unnerving surprise for the person who has come to accept they would never change.

On very rare occasions, however, a lone wolf will have a relationship with a human, which can result in a single human mother raising the child alone or, in the case of a female wolf, a child often left at an orphanage. I knew John was adopted at an early age with no claim to who his parents were, but he'd always smelled human. That was pretty typical for the late bloomers, too. I had to find John now. Fast. He had not been raised in a pack. He'd been raised by humans who were never quite sure of how to manage his startling intelligence. I knew from listening to him that he was not likely to get a lot of sympathy from his parents as he'd told me several times about their negative comments regarding shapeshifters.

Even though the outside air was very cold and bore the scent of the pending snowstorm, I could still catch his scent when I reached the street. There was also a tinge of fear to his smell, the beginnings of panic. I followed my nose as the first flakes began to fall, noticing that John had not taken his car, which was wise of him. If my own experience was any indication, he would most likely be feeling dizzy and nauseous right now. The world would seem like it was swimming, and he would be confused by the sudden assault to his senses. He would probably seek some dark, quiet place to hide. I know I did. I was ten when I first changed, and I hadn't wanted to come out of my closet for days.

His scent trail led to a dark alley between two of the festively-bedecked buildings a little way down the block. Full dark had come, and the alley was cloaked in shadows. My eyes adjusted quickly – another perk even in human form – and I saw that a large cardboard refrigerator box lay on its side next to the Dumpster behind the Convenient Mart. A dark shadow shuddered within, a low cry echoing out of the box.

I crouched down at the open end of the carton and peered in to see John curled in a fetal position at the back. His eyes had a feral gleam in the dim light, and he stared at me with something akin to terror.

"Get away!" he growled through clenched teeth. "Go! While you can. Go!"

I shook my head and crawled into the box on all fours.

"It's all right, John," I said. "Stop fighting it. It's going to be okay."

"No," he grated. "I'm not alright. I feel like I'm on fire!"

I made my way where he lay huddled against the back of the box and sat down next to him. I touched his forehead. He was right; he was burning hot. He reached up and grabbed my hand, clutching it in both of his own. He was shaking so hard I could hear his teeth rattle.

"I read...somewhere...that this was what it felt like before one became...a monster," he said, shuddering as if freezing the whole time. "You need to run, Sash. I don't want...to hurt you."

Great, I thought. Some moron shifter had given an interview to a journalist, and the media had blown the whole thing out of proportion. Typical.

"John," I said. "You have to trust me. You are not a monster. What is happening to you is normal. You have to stop fighting it, though, or it will just get worse."

"Normal?" he gasped out. "This is...normal?"

"For a shapeshifter, yes," I said, hesitating only a moment before saying, "I've been through it myself."

He glanced up at me with eyes like new crescent moons. A dawning realization grew within them, and I nodded to his unspoken question.

"Yes," I said. "So, you have to trust me now. You know me. You know who I am. Let the change take you. You will still be you. You, um, might have some problems with your clothes feeling confining, though, so try not to struggle when you change. I'll be right here."

He shuddered and, keeping his eyes on mine, stopped resisting. The change was so sudden it was almost explosive. One second there had been a frightened man huddled on the ground, the next a gangly black wolf dressed in baggy clothing, utterly spent, lay panting next to where I knelt. He continued to watch me, whining as he breathed, but he did not struggle and stayed still, head resting on the cardboard floor of the box.

"It's going to be a few before you can become human," I said. "You need to rest a little while. I first changed when I was ten, so it's been a decade or two, but I remember how exhausting it was. I also resisted my first change. My parents knew what I was, though, and had prepared me for it. I'm guessing one of your parents was also a shapeshifter, but you had no one to tell you about it except jerks on the internet who don't know anything."

He heaved a huge sigh and glanced up at me again, the question in his eyes plain.

"Well, of course, I am going to help you, idiot," I said, smiling. "What, you think I'm just going to let you go it alone? No way!"

He closed his eyes and let himself relax a bit more. I gently touched his forehead, and his eyes snapped open, unsure.

"Everything feels different with fur," I said. "Your whole body is going to be sensitive to just about anything. A light breeze, a dandelion seed...everything. Your nose tells you a hundred times more than it used to. This box isn't all that dark after all, is it? There's a rat behind the trash bags that you can hear much better than I can. But, you know," I joked, "with great power comes great responsibility."

John lifted his head to look at me and gave a sudden snort that visibly startled him and made me laugh.

"See?" I said. "You are still you, and I am still me. The essential you doesn't change. Just the external packaging, which occasionally likes to get all furry and go for a run in the forest."

John lowered his head back down, snorting through his nose.

"When you feel up to it, visualize yourself back in your own body. The change might be a little sluggish this soon, but you should be able to manage it. Take your time. This isn't a race."

A few minutes later, John managed to get back into human form.

He seemed exhausted and without warning, broke into huge sobs. He sat up, and I gathered him into my arms, holding him and comforting him as much as I could. We sat like that inside the box for a long time as the snow swirled down, hissing as it landed on the cardboard above our heads. John finally calmed himself enough to sit back a bit and dry his eyes. I handed him a clean tissue from my pocket as he tried to pull himself back together.

"So what do I do now?" he asked sniffing. "I feel like my life is over."

"It absolutely isn't. We are going to go see someone," I said, as I pulled out my phone. "She'll help put you to rights."

I called a number I kept on my favorites list, grinning as the line was picked up.

"Nevermore? Put on the tea kettle. I need a safe place for me and a new pup to talk."

"Student?" she asked.

"Prior," I said, grinning. "You'll never guess who."

"I'll put the kettle on," she said and hung up.

"Nevermore?" said John, raising an eyebrow.

"Well, yes," I said. "What else do you call a literary corbie?"

2

THE REVELATION OF NEVERMORE

I dialed Rich and told him that I was taking John to his parents' house and not to wait on me for dinner. Then we walked back to my car and drove through the snow across the city to where Katherine Corbeau lived. I hadn't told John who he was going to be meeting, and when Kathy opened the door, his face lit up. I knew that Kathy had been his favorite English teacher, and he trusted her more than any of the other full-time staff members. She had that effect on people.

"Come in, come in! So good to see you, John. Paul?" she called. "We're going to have company for dinner. Put on two extra potatoes when you start cooking."

"Right-o!" came a cheerful cry from the other room, and Paul Corbeau walked into the kitchen, looking over the rim of his round glasses and appearing every inch the stately raven from ancient times of yore. Paul was an IT expert and spent his days happily poking through bits of computer software. Most urban corbies were into the information field somewhere, and many of them loved computers, foreign languages, or composition and research. No few of the corbies I knew were teachers, too.

"So, who is this?" he asked, tilting one bright eye to examine John.

"One of our former students," said Kathy calmly. "He just discovered what he is, dear."

"Oh?" said Paul, eyebrows raising as he noticed the full tea tray on the kitchen table. "Well, then I'll leave you to your conversation and start dinner."

"Thank you, love," she said. "John, you can hang your coat up in the hall."

Kathy winked at me and carried the tea tray through the living room where a small Christmas tree was crammed next to an older television set announcing the dismal weather, through a short hall, then into the study towards the back of the house. John took off his jacket, hung it on one of several hooks in the little front hall, then followed me into the study. Kathy set the tray down on the table, motioning us to the huge, overstuffed chairs that crowded into the center of the tiny room. Once we were all seated, she poured us each a cup of tea, and turned to John.

"I would imagine you have questions," said Kathy.

"Mrs. Corbeau..."

"Kathy, dear. Call me Kathy."

"Kathy," said John, trying the name on his tongue. "How long have you been...?"

"A raven, John? I've been a raven all my life. I first changed at fourteen and met Paul when I was twenty. We've been together ever since. Raised three fine corbies of our own. They live a few hours away. The boys teach STEM, and my daughter is somewhat of a mad scientist. No grandchildren yet, but maybe someday."

John seemed to take a moment to digest this information, and then turned to me.

"And you? Is Rich a...?"

"Wolf? No. Rich is pretty human, I guess. No sudden surprises with him. I have four brothers, though. Three of them are like me, but one, Mark, never manifested the power to shapeshift. He has three kids though, and his oldest has already changed. She's twelve. The power comes when and if it will. You're kind of late to the game but not the latest I've heard of."

John's eyes grew moist like he was going to tear up, and Kathy saw him, taking his hands in hers.

"Shhh," she said. "Shh, it's okay. You have every right to feel bewildered and lost given what you've just been through. Everything has changed, but nothing has really. You'll never go through it that badly again. As long as you change a few times a month and go let yourself run it off, you'll never change when you don't want to."

"But I don't *want* to be a shapeshifter!" said John to Kathy. "I didn't ask for this! I mean, I always thought it must be neat to be able to be an animal, but I didn't actually wish for this. I just want my old life back."

"John," I said. "Your old life is still right where you left it. If you don't tell them, your parents will likely never know. I've met bears who lived with their human partners for decades without them ever finding out. That sometimes ends badly, though, so I don't recommend it; honesty is always best. The only thing that is different is that you are part of a whole new group of people. My pack will welcome you in without question."

"Your pack?" asked John. "You have a pack?"

"Well, yes," I said. "My family is a pack, and part of the larger wolf clan. Brothers, cousins, uncles, aunts, their mates, all their children. There's about twenty-five or thirty of us, I think."

"Thirty?" he asked.

"Or more," I shrugged. "I lose count with all the babies."

"Corbies are just as bad," chuckled Kathy, sipping her tea. "We have huge extended family groups. Huge gossips, all of us."

"I know," I laughed. "Remember that staff party?"

"Oh, how could I forget? Tad Collins will never live that down."

John sat, glancing back and forth between us, bewildered.

"So what do I do?" he asked, picking up his tea cup.

"For starters," I said, "You can come home with me tomorrow. Remember how I told you I am heading to my family for a few days?"

"Tomorrow is Thursday. I have work at the college," said John, and then his voice trailed off. "I guess I should call out, huh?"

"Yes," I said. "Tell your folks that you are doing something for the college, and you'll be back on Sunday night. Rich can't go with me this year. There's a huge end of the year report he has to file, so your timing couldn't have been better. Pack warm clothing."

"You can meet here and leave your car with us," said Kathy. "There's plenty of room in the driveway. That way, there are no questions from your parents."

"Look," began John, and then stopped, putting down his tea cup. He shifted uncomfortably in his chair. "I don't think I can go home right now and pretend that everything is normal. Can I stay with one of you tonight? I'll sleep on a couch or something. I just need to not be home."

"Of course," said Kathy. "You can stay here; we have a spare room. While dinner is finishing up, why don't you and Sasha get your car. You can go pack your things after we eat."

"I'll even ride over with you, if you want," I said. "I get not wanting to be alone."

"Thanks," said John, sounding relieved. "That would be great."

"Everything will be fine, John," I said as calmly as I could. "I promise."

He nodded hesitantly, and we left to go get his car.

3
HOME TO THE HOUSE

Early the next morning, I got up, pulled myself together, and kissed Rich goodbye. He had been up late working on his report, so when he rolled over, all I got was a sleepy farewell. The snowstorm had not amounted to much – maybe an inch – and the roads were already clear. I threw my bag into my car and drove over to Kathy's house.

Kathy was already up and made a full breakfast for us. Corbies are not light eaters either, and between the blueberry scones, scrambled eggs, rasher of bacon, oranges, yogurt, and sausages, the kitchen table was decked out like a feast. John had not yet woken, Kathy told me; when she had checked on him a short time ago, he was still sleeping solidly. From a conversation she had had with him the previous night, Kathy got the sense that he never rested comfortably at home.

"He doesn't fully trust them," she said. "They aren't cruel to him; they just don't understand him."

"This certainly doesn't make his problems any easier," I said. "I'll go wake him up."

"Go up as a wolf," laughed Kathy. "That might convince him that he's not alone."

"Tempting," I snickered. "He'll get enough of that this weekend. I think I'll stay human for the time being."

Kathy's laughter followed me out of the kitchen as I climbed the polished staircase to the second story of the old house. Reaching the top, I turned left to the room at the end of the short hall. The door was ajar, and I tapped before opening it enough to stick my head through. John blinked at me, bleary-eyed, his sleep-tousled hair sticking up at random angles, then peered at the clock on the bedside table.

"Shit," he said, rubbing his eyes. "I'm sorry. I know you wanted to leave early. I'll get right up."

"It's okay. Take a couple of minutes. Kathy just set out a ginormous breakfast, so come on down when you're dressed. There is hot coffee, too. I'll see you downstairs."

I left the room, shutting the door behind me, and returned to the kitchen. By the time John joined us, Paul had been in, grabbed two scones and some coffee, and left for the office. Kathy and I sat and nursed our coffees, needing more time to warm up to the day.

John said nothing as I handed him a cup and pointed to the fixings. He heaped four or five teaspoons of sugar into it, topped it off with a dollop of cream, and then began to load a plate. Kathy and I exchanged knowing glances. Newly-changed shapeshifters seemed to eat their weight in food the first year or so as they gained control of their powers. Us old fogey stogies didn't need to do that anymore. Kathy was nearing sixty, though she didn't look it, and my almost thirty-four years were enough that I could keep my mental balance most of the time.

It occurred to me then that the happiness I had heard in my mother's voice this morning when I told her I was bringing a newly-changed friend along with me this weekend was almost the same I had heard when I first told her about Rich. That enthusiasm faded after the first year. With Rich there, the clan had to be more reserved since we weren't "out" to him. Rich recognized their hesitant politeness, and I felt that part of the reason he wasn't going this year was due to the feeling that he wasn't really welcome anymore. To say that the clan was happy to not have him coming would be an understatement. My mother's reaction about my guest being someone she had heard of before was odd, however. There was almost an air of calculation to it that made me nervous.

I refocused my attention just in time to witness John realize, part way through his third plate, that he'd eaten half of the food on the table. He seemed mortified, but Kathy just laughed.

"Newly changed wolves and corbies are equally as ravenous," she said, passing him the orange juice. "My children ate everything in sight after they changed, so I am used to this. In a few years, you won't want to eat the world, I promise."

He rolled his eyes at me, and I nodded.

"It's like being seventeen again," I said, "but without acne."

His face lit with a grin, and he made a focused attempt to slow down a little bit. He still finished the whole plate of food, though.

I took a hand helping Kathy rinse the dishes before putting them into the dishwasher, and John belatedly came over to ask if he could help. We had pretty much finished by then, and I sent him to get his belongings so we could depart.

"Thank you for letting him stay here last night," I said to Kathy, giving her a hug. "I'll keep him safe."

"I am sure you will," said my friend. "Just remember how new all this is to him. Maybe some prep work before he meets the clan, hmm?"

"Oh, you know it," I laughed, as John reappeared carrying his backpack and coat. I donned my own coat and prepared to go.

"Thank you," John said to Kathy.

She smiled at him and pinched his cheek.

"Anytime, Kiddo. And I mean that."

I led the way out to my car, and John put his pack into the back seat. My duffle bag was already there, loaded with Christmas presents and gag gift squeaky toys for my brothers. I got in and glanced over at John. He was in the middle of fastening his seat belt and paused to give me an apprehensive glance.

"What?" he said.

"Nothing!" I said cheerfully. "Just thinking about what you have in store for you this weekend."

"Oh?" he said, his brow furrowing. "Should I be worried?"

"No, no," I said, and then grinned. "Okay, I know I shouldn't be so happy given that it is your second day as a wolf and it's weirding you out, but seriously, it is going to be so much fun to have you there."

"Why?" he asked as I began to back down the driveway.

"Because the last few years when Rich has been there, we haven't exactly been able to be ourselves. He really has no idea and, given his comments about the news reports about shapeshifters, I don't think I can ever tell him. Our family gatherings tend to be pretty loud normally, but with him there, they've been kind of subdued. No racing through the backyard as wolves and that sort of thing."

"Oh," John said. "I hadn't thought of that."

We drove for a few minutes while he digested this information.

"What is it normally like?" he finally asked. "Other than loud."

"Let's see. Races, hunting expeditions, midnight howls...I mean, let's face it, we're not human all the time. I also am going to warn you that nudity is not viewed as taboo there. It won't be flaunted, but someone streaking across the lawn to the hot tub is not unheard of."

"Ah," said John, uncomfortably. "I see."

He glanced at me and then away, his ears turning red. That said volumes.

"Relax," I said. "They'll likely be on good behavior because you weren't brought up within the culture of the clan."

"Oh," he said and lapsed into silence

I turned onto the interstate, and we began the long drive north. The lack of conversation was slowly becoming unbearable. I turned to him where he sat seemingly folding in on himself.

"Okay," I said. "Yes, this is going to be different. They will accept you, though."

"Sasha, this past day or so I thought I was going crazy, then I thought I might kill you by becoming a slavering beast. Instead, you admit to me that you are a shapeshifter and calmly talk me through transforming into a wolf, then back like it was no big thing to you. Which it apparently isn't. Then I bawl on your shoulder like a baby, get taken to my favorite English teacher's house, and find out she's a raven. Now I discover there is this whole other world out there like nothing I ever knew, and you act like I should just accept it?"

He stared straight ahead, not saying anything for a long moment.

"I have questions," he said. "A lot of them. And I need to know that you will stick by me through all of this, 'cause I sure as hell can't do it alone."

"Of course I will, John," I said. "I told you I would. I will be here with you the whole way."

"Okay," he said, visibly calmer. "First of all, why me? Who are my parents? The records were never very clear. They said I was found on a church step one morning with a note asking for me to be taken care of."

"You are probably the child of a loner wolf who got pregnant by one of her lovers and opted to leave you somewhere safe," I said. "It sucks, but it happens. Usually one of us tries to keep an ear out for such children, but we don't catch all of them."

"So my father...?"

"Probably doesn't even know you exist, I'm afraid," I answered. "In all likelihood, he never even knew he'd gotten your mother pregnant."

"Well, there goes that dream," said John bitterly, turning to stare out the window. I could tell that the revelation bothered him, and he was angry now.

The silence hung between us for a long moment. Then I sighed.

"Yeah," I said. "Next question?"

"Hmm," he said, looking back at me. "How did you know what was happening when I left your house yesterday evening? How did you find me?"

I raised an eyebrow at him and tapped my nose.

"Seriously?" he said. "You smelled me?"

"The nose knows," I said. "Wolves have a certain odor, and you never smelled that way before. I followed your scent to the alley. Good thing I did, or you would have had a seriously bad time of it."

"Yeah," he said. "The clothing was really uncomfortable."

"That's why we normally take it off before changing," I said dryly. "Last night, however, I didn't think you would be in the right mindset for me to make that rather awkward suggestion."

"Good point," said John, sighing.

The calm conversation was working. John was a very rational person and examining things logically would help steady him more than any reassurance I could ever give him. The friend I recognized was beginning to emerge from the panic and stress of the last eighteen hours. I kept going.

"Next?"

"What are you going to do about Rich?" he asked. "He's not exactly a shapeshifter fan."

I had not expected that question. I gripped the steering wheel tighter. It was not like I hadn't been asking myself that same question for some time now. Inevitably, either Rich would leave or I would. It made me incredibly sad, but that little difference between us had grown so much larger lately given his take on the shapeshifter news reports.

"I'll burn that bridge when I come to it," I said finally. "Nothing much I can do if he won't change his mind."

That seemed to satisfy his curiosity, and he leaned back in his seat a bit more. The conversation continued and wound its way through my cousins, aunts, uncles, parents, and the rest of the clan. He picked my brain for everything I knew about Sam Winston, which was a considerable bit more than the media knew, courtesy of the corbies.

"By all accounts, Sam and the others are safe and in hiding. They are working as liaisons to a governmental group formed to actually protect the shapeshifters, something akin to the Bureau of Indian Affairs, but more effective as there's no land involved other than what was in private hands, bought and sold."

"Are they ever able to visit home?" asked John.

"Periodically, but it's not publicized at all. Their role is to help the government find ways to protect shapeshifters. Unbelievably, it seems to be working. My mother said that they are close to making us a protected race."

John digested the information for a few moments.

"How did they get the government to accept them and not drag them off to a laboratory somewhere?" he asked.

"Apparently, there are some high-level officials who are either full shapeshifters or have family who are," I said. "I don't know all the details, but they had enough clout to make people actually pay attention."

"That's got to have been a shock to some people," he chuckled. "I can only guess what the Area 51 people are doing with this!"

"There were already conspiracy groups out there hunting for shapeshifters," I said. "This just gave them some actual validity. We still need to stay clear of them. Next question?"

About an hour into the drive, John seemed to run out of questions. He sat staring out the window while I listened to the radio, singing along to songs I knew, relaxing into the drive. My family lived about three hours out of Boulder on a large estate backed up to the Medicine Bow Routt National Forest. The drive was scenic, and after a while, John even began to sing along with songs he knew. It was very different from my last few drives up. Rich was good company, but he'd get going about politics or his job. I would counter with quips about the Biology honors kids and what they were doing. We didn't talk much about how we felt. It just wasn't our thing. He also never sang along with me.

In what seemed too short a time, we turned up the private road that wound its way to my family's house on the mountain. The tall pines loomed over the driveway before we'd gone a quarter of a mile, and it was much dimmer under the canopy of trees than on the highway. By reflex, I'd turned off the radio and drove in silence, listening for the first welcome home. A few minutes later, I heard it – a long, low howl that carried the mile or so we still had to drive through the forest.

Other voices joined it, and I glanced over at John to see him sitting up, listening intently. He didn't understand the song the way I did, but he recognized that it had meaning.

After the sound had faded, he turned to me, wide-eyed in amazement.

"How did they know we're here?" he asked. "Did they sense you somehow?"

"Video cameras in the trees along the road," I said smugly. "Howling is the only long-distance claim to fame we have. The rest is all tech."

"Do wolves have job types? I mean, like the corbies?"

"We tend to get into the sciences," I said. "Lab tech is really a hot field right now. Having a good sense of smell can really come in handy in forensics, too. Too many of us watched NCIS growing up. I swear my oldest brother is trying to be Abby."

"So, my college job is pretty much on par?"

"What, working in the laser lab? Ya think?"

He smiled and continued to watch out the window as we drove along. And then we were there.

The House hove into view as we rounded the last bend into the clearing, and I could hear John's intake of breath at the sheer size of the building. It had been modeled on an English manor, with wings and colonnades, topiary animals, and all the trimmings.

"This is your family's house?" he exclaimed. "Anything I should know about it? Mad women in the attic? Catacombs full of bricked-in skeletons? Secret passages leading from the lounge to the conservatory?"

"No mad women or rotting skeletons that I know of," I said. "And if there were any secret passages, I would have found them when I was a kid. I crawled and crept through every room in that house, peeked through every vent, and lifted every rug. The only room I didn't get into was the kitchen because our chef, Marseille, would have killed me. He's very particular about where things go."

"So who lives in the house?" he asked. "You have a chef, so there must be a lot of people there."

"Right now, no. The House is pack-owned," I said. "Everyone has a little share of it. It acts kinda like a bank; we all earn interest on our shares, and family members can draw extra against their share in lean times, as long as it is paid back. We all contribute what we can to the joint account each year, and the holding grows. The accountants are absolute geniuses and multiply finances regularly through various investments. In fact, they are so successful, houses are not uncommon as wedding presents."

I drove around to the side of the grounds where a gravel parking area had been tastefully hidden by hedges and parked next to what must have been the newest of a long line of Uncle Andrew's Mustangs. I knew nothing about cars, so only the horse logo told me what it was. John got out, his eyes fixed on the shining red auto, and I knew that I had completely lost him for at least the next few minutes.

"Do you know what this is?" he asked, his voice awed.

"A car?" I said.

"It's a 2020 Shelby GT500," he said, his voice hushed, staring fixedly at the car. "They just released them. They are the fastest Ford car ever made. Street-legal, that is. It can go 0-60 in…"

"Three seconds," came a voice from behind us.

I turned to see my favorite uncle walking over to us and gave him a huge hug as soon as he was in range. Andrew hadn't changed a bit. As always, he wore neatly pressed jeans and one of his trademark turtleneck winter sweaters, this one in a shade of heather green. He hugged me back, and then held me at arm's length to give me a once over.

"My dear, you are more radiant every day. Please tell me you got rid of that creature you have been hanging around with and that this is his replacement, hmmm?"

I rolled my eyes at him.

"No, Andrew, I have not yet gotten rid of "that creature" as you are fond of calling Rich. This is my friend John. He suddenly found himself in a sticky situation last night changing for the first time, so I dragged him home with me. He's an orphan."

"Oh? Shame that. Your mother should have known better and brought you to a pack. There's no accounting for good taste in some wolves. Well, you are more than welcome here, young man. Shall we go in? We can talk about cars later, but I know the rest of the family will be excited to meet you."

Andrew turned and led the way to the House. I gestured for John to follow my uncle, then grabbed our bags from the car. John noticed I had fallen behind and waited for me, accepting his luggage in passing. I gave him a reassuring smile, and we went inside.

Once though the huge double doors, we entered a room dominated by a sweeping staircase that arced up to meet the second floor. In the corner to the left stood this year's twelve-foot-tall Christmas tree, decorated tastefully with miniature white lights and antique glass ornaments. The silk-covered walls of the grand foyer were painted with *trompe l'oeil* floral designs, while marble statues stood in niches around the circumference. John stared about him in awe, and then back at me with unmistakable envy.

"This is amazing! Those flowers look so real! How come you never told me you grew up in a mansion?" he said.

"You never asked," I replied back. "That, and how many people do you know who go around saying, "Oh, yes, and I lived in a mansion when I was a kid?"

"Touché."

He went back to taking in the sights, from the gold leaf trim along the chair rail to the gilded plaster fresco on the edges of the ceiling. His eyes traveled up to the huge gilt chandelier hung with faceted crystals that depended from the roof two stories above with perilous ease. Three doors led off of the main room, and as my uncle stopped to address us, the one on the right opened, and my mother entered the room.

By tradition, the female head of the family is always accorded respect, but Mother had also earned it from all of us. A staunch supporter of all our endeavors, she was counselor, cheerleader, advocate, and comforting force in all her children's and grandchildren's lives. Unlike my father, who often was out in the world speaking at university lecture halls about the impacts of global warming, my mother had made the House a home for all pack members. That did not diminish from her role as the undisputed matriarch of the family. She was a force to be reckoned with, and no one dared set a foot wrong in her presence. I'd seen a few out-of-pack wolves try. The results were bloody. Literally.

When my mother entered, Andrew smiled in greeting to her. This act in the pack was considered non-threatening, and when Mother turned her gaze on me, I beamed at her, accepting her embrace. I'd missed her more than usual lately and was grateful for her reassurance given all that had been happening in our world. She dressed much like her brother, a crisp, white blouse the only real difference.

"It is wonderful to see you again, Sasha," she said, and walked over to John where he stood, seeming uncomfortable. "And this is the young man...John, is it...that you told me about?"

"Yes, Mother," I said. "John, this is my mother, Eloise."

"Pleased to meet you," said John, holding out his hand.

My mother shook it firmly, staring him in the eyes. He held her gaze, which was something I had not warned him about.

"John has much to learn of our ways," I broke in, hoping to remind my mother how new John was to the whole shifter situation.

"Indeed," said my mother, not backing down.

John finally had to drop his eyes under her penetrating stare, and the tension eased out of the room. He glanced at me, confused, and I mouthed to him that we would talk later.

"Well, why don't you take John upstairs and get him settled. I put him in the blue room next to yours. Take a few minutes to get yourselves oriented, then come down and join us in the living room. I will meet you both there."

She turned as if to go, then turned back to me.

"I am so glad that you are here, darling. It means a lot that you could come. Your father will be here tomorrow. I know he can't wait to see you, too."

She left the room with Andrew close behind in quiet conversation. I knew my mother very well; there was something going on that I was not privy to, though I suspected I knew given Andrew's comment about Rich.

"Come on," I said. "Up we go."

John followed me up the first section of the stairs that went to a small landing, and then up the left "wing" of the arc to the second floor. My room was two doors down the hall on the right, and John's was the next one past it. I showed John to his door, and then went into my own room to unpack. Four days with the family meant that I'd be able to unwind a little bit, so I'd brought a reading book, my bathing suit, and my gaming laptop. Other than that, I was just happy to be home. This was the room I'd grown up in, and while it was often used for guests now, it was still mine, and I always had claim to it whenever I was there.

After I put things away in the polished mahogany bureau, I went next door. John was sitting on his bed, texting, and he glanced up when I came in.

"Did you remember to bring a bathing suit?" I asked.

He nodded and went back to his text messages.

"What is it?"

"Just my dad," he replied. "He wanted to check in with me and see how I was doing. I told him I got invited up country for a few days. I didn't want to lie and involve the college. They are paranoid enough to call the department, and that would not be good for my career."

"So what'd you tell him?"

"I said a high school friend was having a New Year's Eve party and had invited me. I mean, I'm not lying, right?"

His eyes twinkled when he said this, and I grinned back at him.

"Totally not lying," I said. "Come on; we'll go meet the rest of my family."

4
PACK LIFE

When we entered the living room, we found ourselves surrounded by people. The House had felt empty before but apparently everyone had been outside. No one mentioned that they had been running as wolves; it would be assumed that I knew that. John was not graced with my expansive knowledge of pack terminology, however, and missed the subtext entirely. As the family came to greet me, I introduced John to them in a flurry of names, none of which he would likely remember. I barely did myself.

My brother David came over to talk with us about his new position at one of the research labs at a local college. He and John hit it off immediately, and before I knew it, my other three brothers had whisked me away and were plying me with cookies and questions about my friend.

"So, nothing?" asked Mark. "He seems nicer than Rich."

"Guys, no. He's my anime buddy. We nerd out together, okay? That's all."

"Shame," said Stephen, shaking his head.

"Guys, I was teaching during his senior year. It's bad form to poach one of your students."

"*Student* teaching," Bobby reminded me. "Technically not his teacher."

"Seriously? I would have never even brought him here if he hadn't basically turned into a wolf in my lap. He's my best friend. Not exactly boyfriend material."

"Fine, fine," said Stephen with a mock sigh of resignation. "Just be aware. Our cousin Melissa is here, and he should not get around her this weekend. She promised not to shift, but I'm not sure that she wouldn't try something with all the single males around here. She's still trying to win a mate, and I think she sees this as her best opportunity to find one."

Melissa was over in the corner talking to Andrew. She was as beautiful as she was vapid; long legs, long blond hair, and a long list of male conquests. One of our cousins from Montana, she usually confined her interests to big burly men that she brought to the summer picnics so they could drool over her in a bathing suit. I had been unaware of the fact that she might have come into season this early in the year. Shit. One more thing to add to the discussion list.

"Be sure to let me know if you see her trying to pull something, okay?" I said.

"No problem," said Bobby. "You had better watch your boy, though. He's staring."

I glanced over to where John was ogling Melissa with the same rapt attention he'd given the car. I felt a wave of annoyance come over me. It's not like she wasn't gorgeous, but I knew that she was the same kind of girl that hadn't given him the right time of day in high school. She was the type who would have wrapped him around her finger, used him for everything he had, then thrown him away when he was broke and broken. And she would discard him, just like her picnic pals, if it would serve her interests.

I watched as she studied him, giving him a long, slow once over. He was not at all used to that kind of attention, and I left my amused brothers to go over and intervene.

"Hey, John? Why don't you come meet my Aunt Theresa? She's another lab tech, and I think you have a lot in common."

"Oh...yeah, sure," said John, tearing his eyes away from Melissa and following me. My aunt's work dealt with tRNA and mRNA, and John was soon lost in technological conversation again.

My mother finally stood up and rang one of the large meditation brass bells that she kept for just this sort of occasion. The sound stopped all conversation, and everyone turned to where my mother waited.

"Welcome! Most everyone is here, so I just wanted to make sure to acknowledge that we have a new-found wolf among us tonight. My daughter's friend John came with her after he discovered his gift only yesterday. Please be sure to go easy on him this weekend and make him feel welcome."

A susurrus of whispers went through the twenty or so people in the room, and John turned to me, startled to be called out.

"The rest of the family is due to arrive tomorrow by noon," continued my mother, "so we will do gifts and challenges then. There are plenty of snacks in the game room, and the bar is freshly stocked. Lunch will be served in the dining room at one o'clock. Please enjoy yourselves until then!"

Everyone began to talk once again as Mother walked over and motioned for me and John to follow her. We trailed her out of the living room, across the foyer, and down to her study. It was bigger than Kathy's by about four times, but there was a carafe of hot coffee waiting for us on a tray and a plate of scones that smelled divine. It had been hours since breakfast with the corbies, and I was ravenous.

"Please, sit down and help yourselves," said my mother, taking one of the floral antique chintz-upholstered chairs. "I wanted to have a chance to go over some things with you before everything gets too chaotic. Have you given any thought to what you are going to do?"

There were layers to that question. What I was going to do about Rich. What I was going to do about John. What I was going to do about school. Those questions. I think I knew where she was going with this, but I was going to make her spell it out.

"About?"

"You know what I mean," she said, giving me *that* look. "The cities are getting too dangerous. Your boyfriend is obviously not trustworthy. And now your best friend has become one of us."

I waited. My mother gave an exasperated sigh and continued.

"Fine," she said. "I want you to take John under your wing. Train him. Teach him how to stay safe. Keep him from harm. I want you to be his Mentor."

That mentor had a capital M that even I could hear. Coming from Mother, it was not just a request, it was a decree. I had been charged with John's instruction, even if it went against my own self-interests. Until he was trained, he was my job and my duty. I groaned as the weight of it set in. Her word was Law.

John looked at me, confused.

"Sash," he said, "if you don't want to help me, I'll figure it out on my own."

"It's not that. It's pack policy," I said shortly. "You're stuck with me. I would have helped you anyway, but now I kind of don't have a choice. The pack follows the decree of the wolves in charge so long as it is not detrimental."

"Do I get commanded too?" asked John sharply to my mother.

"No," she smiled. "You are not bound to us, so I can't command you. And I don't usually need to command anyone. Sasha tends to be a bit more headstrong than most."

John continued to stare belligerently at my mother, and again, she stared him down.

"I'll see you both at lunch," she said and left the room.

John watched her go before turning to me.

"And you're okay with that?" he asked.

"It isn't usually like this," I said, pouring myself a cup of coffee and liberally dosing it with cream and sugar. "The news reports have everyone on edge. She wants you trained so you won't get caught and be a danger to the family. That's all. I already promised you that I'd see you through this, didn't I? She's just being protective. It's her job as the pack leader."

He didn't say anything, but made his own cup of coffee and took one of the scones. He sat back in his chair, sighed, then looked at me expectantly.

"Okay, I'll admit, I'm out of my depth here. What do I need to know?"

"Well," I said, picking up my coffee. "First thing first. Don't bait my mother by locking eyes with her. It's considered not only rude, but a challenge to her authority. She won't back down, and she is cutting you some slack by not taking you to task for it. You don't have to be submissive...I mean, we still live by human rules too in this pack...but don't push her. It just adds tension which none of us needs right now."

"Okay," he said, relaxing a little. "I really just did it the second time because she was bugging you so much."

"It's fine," I said, waving it off. "She's one of the most supportive mothers I know, but she also has the entire pack to take care of. It takes a strong will to be in that position."

"I would guess," he said.

"There's a lot that I am going to tell you that is situational, but I need to address one other sticky issue right now," I said. "Do not let my cousin Melissa get her claws into you, literally or figuratively. My brother told me that she is not allowed to become a wolf this weekend. She will cause serious harm if she does, and you don't want to get involved."

John looked at me puzzled. I sighed, resigned to having to explain Wolf Sex Ed to my best friend.

"*Our* pack lives most of the time as humans," I began. "Not all packs do that, but we do. As humans, we follow the natural cycles humans do, and females are fertile once a month. Follow so far? Good. Our wolf side also follows a natural cycle, and some packs and family groups live more as a wolf than as a human. Their fertility cycle more follows that of the wolf. Melissa's family tends to be more of the latter. Do you see where I am going?"

"So, her wolf side is in heat? That's all kinds of messed up."

"Well, it's not messed up so much as not appropriate to bring to the family Holiday party," I said. "It is always important to keep in mind that shapeshifters are not human, no matter how much we might pretend to be. Melissa has promised not to shift this weekend, but...well, watch yourself around her. She chews men up and spits them out like bubble gum that has lost its flavor."

"Good simile," said John, approvingly.

"Thanks," I grinned. "Now. We have something else we need to settle. After lunch, I guarantee you there will be a free-for-all romp in the woods. If you are going to join us, you need to get your wolf-self settled. I am going to need you to transform."

"Here?"

"I was thinking the conservatory," I said. "It's relatively private; no one should be out there with the feast of snacks now underway. Hungry wolves and spinach puffs, you know. We can go there, and I will give you a few minutes of privacy to undress and figure out the furry part. Then we are going to get you used to being on all fours."

John wiggled his eyebrows at that, so I punched his arm lightly.

"Get your mind out of the gutter," I said with a mock growl. "Come on."

Leaving the study, I led the way down through the east wing of the House. The smell of chlorine and warm, moist air intensified as we passed the corridor that led to the large atrium where the pool lay. I thought dreamily of the warm waters I had swam in extensively as a child and promised myself a good swim later that evening. I might even be able to cajole John into joining me. Oddly, I didn't even know if he *could* swim.

We reached the conservatory and went inside. There was, as predicted, no one there, and I closed the door, feeling slightly apprehensive for my friend. Figuring out the best place for him to change, I pointed to a stand of potted plants near the wall, away from the huge windows all around us.

"Go over there and change. I'll step outside for a couple of minutes."

"How will I let you know when I'm ready?" he asked. "Bark three times?"

"I'll just check in. If you answer in English, I'll know to give you more time."

John nodded, and I left to go stand in the hallway. I fidgeted impatiently for about five minutes before going back into the room, looking around for John. It took me a moment to realize that he was peering at me from behind the potted plants, his long black nose twitching furiously as he took in my scent.

"Why are you still behind there?" I asked, raising an eyebrow.

He whined, and I continued to stare at him uncomprehendingly for a moment before going over to see him. He ducked back behind the pots and dodged around them as I approached, his tail tucked firmly down under his legs.

"What the heck is the matter with you?" I asked, laughing at his antics.

He whined again and kept his body out of my line of sight for several circuits. Then it dawned on me, and I sat down on the floor, literally quite stunned.

"Oh my god," I said, laughing. "You are absolutely right."

John was still thinking in human terms, and in human terms, he was completely naked, fur or no fur. Poor John felt horribly exposed.

I sighed. This was not something I had anticipated. All the male wolves I knew were as happy being naked as humans as they were when they were wolves. Wolves didn't wear clothes because wolves weren't human. John didn't see it that way; he still thought of himself as a human being. I sat, feeling somewhat an idiot at that moment. John peered at me from behind the pot, his expression apprehensive, ears back, eyes sorrowful.

"Okay," I said. "You can't hide behind a plant forever, and I promise you, as a wolf, no one is going to be gawking at your naughty bits. I know this is going against all of the training of being human, but this is something you are just going to have to get over. Think of all of the male dogs you've seen. They don't think of themselves as naked. They don't even notice. People notice because they have hang-ups about sex. Wolves do not."

John closed his eyes for a moment, then opened them and resolutely stepped out from behind the pot to stand in front of me, tail down, golden crescent eyes anxious. I got my first real view of him. He was a tall, rangy male, definitely higher in the shoulder than I was in my wolf form, and stunningly beautiful. His black coat appeared soft and thick and was the color of midnight on a moonless night.

"Wow," I said, grinning up at him from where I sat. "I'm jealous. My coat is nowhere near that thick. It looks really soft too. Can I touch it?"

John seemed a little startled, but took a step or two nearer so I could reach him. I got to my knees so I could reach his back, running my fingers through the deep ruff around his neck. I reached up to scratch behind his ears, and he closed his eyes in pleasure. His fur was very soft, for a wolf. I listened to him breathe as I continued to scratch his head but, eventually, not wanting to overdo it, I stopped and got to my feet.

"Well, fair is fair," I said. "Wait here."

I walked over behind the plants, stripped quickly, and shifted into my own wolf form. When I stepped out, he took several clumsy steps backward. He had not expected me to change so quickly, and I think a small part of him didn't really believe that I was actually a wolf. Seeing me for the first time clearly startled him, but I knew he needed to understand who and what we both were.

I approached him with a raised tail and a calm attitude, something he should instinctively read as friendly. He responded by raising his own tail a little and stepping a foot or two nearer. Wolves don't really wag their tails, and I resisted the desire to sniff him which would have been a more appropriate greeting, but...well...baby steps. He walked around me, taking in my wolf form, and gave a rather doggy grin. Yea, score one for me.

I pointed my nose at him and then at the bushes. He thought for a second, then trotted back around them, and I heard him getting dressed. I sat down and waited for him to come out. He did so a couple of minutes later, still barefoot, and sat down on the ground near me.

"Holy shit," he said, staring at me and trying to take it all in. "I am not sure what to think about everything, but I was not expecting this."

He reached out, and I leaned towards him so he could touch my fur. Fair is fair, after all, and I loved having my ears rubbed as much as the next canine. I leaned into his fingers as they dug into my coat and made appropriate, appreciative sounds.

Finally, feeling like we might have a better conversation if we could both fully communicate, I went back behind the plants, changed, dressed, and returned to sit next to him. John shook his head as I sat down.

"I have no words," he said. "I absolutely do not know how to feel right now."

"It's a bit overwhelming," I said. "This is weird for both of us."

He nodded and sat contemplating his hands, turning them over and over.

"What do I do now?" he said, sounding a bit lost.

"Now?" I asked. "You don't have to do anything right now. We could sit here and talk if you prefer, or I can get a lunch made up for us picnic-style so we can just hang out if that is what you'd like."

"The latter sounds good, actually," he said. "Can we just go to some quiet room and eat there?"

"Sure," I said. "We'll go to my secret hideout. It's got a comfy couch. Come on. Get your shoes on, and we'll go to the kitchen."

It was only noon, but I knew that Marseille, chef extraordinaire throughout my entire life, was always prepared for strange requests. Lord knows, I'd made my fair share during my time living in the House. Marseille was one of the few humans who worked for my family without any direct ties to shapeshifters. He had applied for the job on the recommendation of a corbie friend of my father's and had moved into the House without batting an eye at the strangeness of the situation. The rumor was he might have been involved with a shapeshifter at some point, but I believed he was just a kind man who didn't care if we weren't always human. After thirty years working for my family, Marseille was a fixture I knew I could depend on.

I led the way once more through the House, feeling like I was leading a lost soul through the underworld. On reflection, John seemed more like a lost lamb than a vagrant spirit, but no less out of place and unsure of what the future would bring.

Once more back at the foyer, I made my way behind the stairs and down a short passage to the kitchen. It was a grand affair, and Marseille and his two assistants, wolves who loved to cook, were busily creating some gourmet dishes for lunch. The food smelled wonderful and John's stomach growled loud enough to hear. I also knew that his dinner would make this seem like a pittance. Marseille glanced up as we entered, his curly black hair frosted now with grey, and when he saw me, he grinned like a maniac.

"Sasha, girl, it is so good to see you!" he cried, his Creole accent no less pronounced than when he first came to the House. "Is this the new wolf the walls have been whispering about?"

"Yes, Marseille," I said, giving him a kiss on the dark skin of his cheek. "This is our new wolf, John."

"Brand new, if what I am hearing is true," said Marseille. "These two brought me the tale earlier, but I was looking forward to hearing it from you. All of this a little overwhelming, son?"

"Yes, sir," replied John.

"Well, you just stay with Sasha here, and she'll set you to rights. And knowing her, this isn't just a social visit."

"It's that," I said, smiling, "but it's also a mission of mercy. John's needing a bit of a break from the insanity of the last twenty-four hours. I was hoping you could pack us a picnic so we could go hide for a bit."

"Can't say I blame you," said Marseille. "It's a lot to have dropped on you all at once. I'll set you up with all the fixings if you'll give me a moment or two. Bill, can you remember to tell Eloise that these two are hiding out and not to worry about them?"

Bill, one of the assistants working at the stove, gave a quick thumbs up before going back to sautéing onions. Marseille snorted and pulled a picnic basket down from a shelf, then filled it with a bewildering variety of items.

"There," he said, handing the basket to John. "You two go and eat. Bring the basket down later. You know the drill."

"Yes, Marseille," I said, mock-rolling my eyes. "I should hope so after all of the picnics over the years."

"Exactly, my girl. Now scoot! I've got to prepare to feed the horde up there."

I smiled at him again and grabbed John by the hand not holding the basket, dragging him out of the kitchen. His eyes were beginning to glaze over. It was time to go to ground.

5
NIGHT SWIM

I stopped in my room to grab my computer, but instead of staying, led John with me through the maze of the second floor, and to the servant's stair leading to the third. He didn't do more than raise an eyebrow as we went, but when we ducked into the little sewing room, and I shut the door, he looked at me in surprise.

"No matter what message I send them, my family will come to check on us," I said. "All of them. One at a time. This is one of my favorite hiding places. It will take them a while to come up here."

John nodded and set the basket down, absorbing the atmosphere of the room. Most of the furniture was covered, but I pulled a sheet off my favorite chaise lounge, which was an old moth-eaten velvet monstrosity with peeling gilt work and splintering wooden legs. It was still somehow the most comfortable seat around and was big enough for two. Leaving John to open the basket, I pulled over one of the little antique sewing cabinets, set my computer on top of it, and found the episode of *Gun Gale Online* we had not finished watching the previous afternoon.

John stopped poking around in the basket to notice what I had done, raising an eyebrow at the anime on the screen.

"Hey, it was a good episode," I said. "I don't know about you, but I'd like to finish it."

John gave a strained smile, and when I sat down on the chaise and pressed play, he joined me. The bright colors and cheerful theme song soon swelled around us, and we ate in silence for a while before John tentatively pointed out how weird it was for Llenn to name her gun P-chan. I responded that I agreed with him, but thought it was weirder how hung up she was with her height in the real world. After another episode, he and I were chatting back and forth as if nothing had happened, and the food had all but disappeared. After the third episode, I turned off the video player and glanced at John.

"You look better," I observed.

"I feel better," he said. "Thanks. I needed some normal."

"Yeah," I said, peering at him. "The little "tilt" light was going off in your eyes."

He chuckled a bit at that, and then turned to give me his full attention.

"Seriously," he said. "How do you manage it? Everything seems like so overwhelming."

I took a deep breath, letting it out before speaking.

"You have to remember, I have lived with this all my life. I was raised around shapeshifters, taught what everything meant from the time I could reason, and was running around the woods as a gangly pup at ten. It will take time, but you can do this. I'll guide you through everything, I promise. You just have to give yourself a little time."

He studied my face for a moment, then nodded his acceptance of my words.

"This all scares me," he said. "It's almost too big."

"One step at a time," I said, trying to reassure him. "Take things at your pace."

My cellphone suddenly buzzed in my pocket, and I pulled it out to read the text message my mother had sent me.

Pack run in twenty minutes. Please come join us.

I showed John the text.

"It's up to you," I said. "If you want to go hibernate in your room for a little while, I can go and give you some space."

He thought about it and shook his head.

"I might as well try it," he said.

"Okay, if you want to. Grab the basket, will you? We'll drop it off on the way."

I re-draped the chaise lounge and put the sewing cabinet back. Stopping in my room, I left both my phone and the laptop there. After dropping off the basket to Marseille, John and I went into the living room where my mother and brother Mark stood.

"The others already gone?" I asked.

"Yes," said Mark. "I'm staying here, obviously, so I was talking to Mom about watching Melissa. She's edgy. Bored. I'm a little concerned about her doing something reckless."

"I've warned John," I said, and John nodded.

"She's a canny one," said my mother. "We'll have to assign someone to her this weekend besides you, Mark. I know you miss out on some of the fun already, but you shouldn't be the only babysitter."

"I can take a turn," I said. "It'll give John a chance to do his own thing a bit."

"Yes," said Mark. "She can't corrupt the Incorruptible."

John looked at me curiously.

"I seem to be immune to most of the little magics shapeshifters have," I explained. "For the most part, this ability is innate and unconscious, but there are some things that are done with a purpose. Those I seem to be able to thwart."

"Except commands," smiled my mother, "but I couldn't fight them either when I was younger. You have my gifts, Sasha. Maybe you will take over from me eventually."

"Mother," I said, rolling my eyes. "I'm really not sure I want that. Too much responsibility."

Her eyes filled with something akin to pity, but she said nothing.

"Right," I said and turned to John. "We'll be going downstairs to change, and then going out into the woods. Mother, are you coming too?"

"I will be down in a few minutes," she said. "Mark and I just need to go over a few details, and I'll be along."

"Right. Come on, John."

We walked back into the foyer and through another, less obvious door that led down a curving set of stairs to a warm room with a wood stove. There were two little rooms off of it, and I waved John towards one while I went to the other one. I had put my clothing in one of the little wall cubbies, taken my wolf form, and was sitting by the stove well before John made his appearance. He also was in wolf form and still seemed a little bit shy, but he tried to move less self-consciously as he came out. I rose and led the way to what amounted to an automated door. A button a foot or so up the wall triggered the door to open; I pushed it with my nose and let us outside.

The air was still somewhat chill, but it had warmed up a little since we had arrived. The snow crunched underfoot, and I stepped onto it, feeling it press between my toes and into the soft webbing. It was good snow for running. No hard ice crust to cut my feet and make me bleed. Great for gripping and traction. I snuck a peek at John as he stood like an ebony statue, smelling the air and, without warning, I launched across the lawn, heading for the woods. My wolf side had been denied this for too long, and the urge to run and run and *run* just tore through all of my normal hesitations. Behind me, I heard John clumsily try to keep up.

With wild joy, I flung myself forward, leaping over fallen logs and dodging larger tangles of brush. The snow sprayed from under my paws, and I jumped one of the small streams that crossed the property with ease. As I always did, I lost myself in the sensation of being a wolf, of living through smell and sight and sound, and I wondered anew at the glory and economy of running on all fours. After that, for a time, all human thoughts were left behind.

Two wolves now ran in from my left, and I found myself shoved by my brother Bobby. This was a familiar game. Big, grey brute that he was, I had to throw all my weight back at him as he tried to push me off the track. The other wolf was his mate, Angie, and she joined in buffeting me from the other side. She was more of a lightweight, though, so I was able to push her away easily. With a quick dodge, I left her behind and only had Bobby to contend with. Being slightly smaller and more agile, I could double back quicker, and I gained some ground on my brother by doing so; his bulk slowed him down. He eventually caught up, though, and began to push me once again.

A large, black form slammed into him from the other side, and Bobby stumbled to his knees. I looked over as I ran to see that John had caught up and was running with me, his long legs allowing him greater strides than my own. I glanced back to see that Bobby had stopped, and I came to a halt myself, panting hard. John slowed down and followed me when I walked back to check on Bobby. Angie was licking a cut on his leg and growled at John when he came near. Bobby raised a lip at her, and she dropped her gaze, not wanting to challenge him, and resumed her ministrations.

I walked up to Bobby and head-butted his face. He snorted, managing to appear aloof and amused at the same time – not easy for a wolf. He then turned his gaze on John and nodded once. It was his equivalent of saying "Good play." I'm not sure how John interpreted it, though. He mainly appeared confused. I walked back to him and bumped him in the shoulder, and he let himself grin as he got the message.

Bobby heaved himself to his feet, licked Angie on the nose, and trotted off into the woods. Angie glanced at me, snorted, and followed her husband. John made an inquisitive sound, and when he started back toward the trail, I fell in next to him, letting him choose the way we went.

For the rest of the afternoon, John picked our trail, exploring all the winter-muted smells of the woods. At one point, we flushed a rabbit, and there was a brief all-out chase before it flipped its fluffy tail and dove into the cover of a dead fall. John briefly searched for it, but the rabbit was firmly entrenched and not budging from the shelter.

Finally, as the afternoon shadows began to lengthen, I led the way back to the House where we changed once again and went in to dinner.

Two huge roast turkeys met our eyes as we approached the table, and John sat in tired happiness while listening to Bobby and me take turns claiming the victor of the chase. The others laughed and poked fun at Bobby for having lost to a newbie.

"Hey!" said Bobby. "I would have had you dead to rights if your boyfriend hadn't knocked me over!"

"He is not my boyfriend, idiot, and your wife was trying to do the same thing to me!"

I saw Melissa go still out of the corner of my eye and realized that she had not known up to that point that John and I were not an item. Shit. That would be all he'd need. John was nothing if not honorable, and if she ever put him in the position of paternity, he'd be bound to follow through.

My mother caught my glance, and after dessert, asked me to excuse myself to John for a few minutes. I joined her, curious to see what her thoughts were. We walked down to her study again, and she stood silent a moment before speaking.

"Melissa seems to be actively thinking about making a move on John," she said finally. "Should she decide to go in that direction, and your friend gets ensnared in it, I wanted to tell you something that you can do to stop her."

I waited patiently for her to gather her thoughts. She seemed to be struggling a little with how to present what she was thinking, and I could only guess that it was very serious.

"I said earlier that you might be the one to take over for me. You have the qualities needed for it, although not the desire. That may come in time. If not you, David has them as well, so either of you will do. He's more inclined to it, truthfully. However, there is one ability that you both share with me. It's a pack leader quality called Claiming."

She appeared to be uncomfortable as she spoke and seemed to be struggling to tell me.

"It is not something that should ever be done lightly," she said. "I never have. Historically, it was used in battles when one pack was trying to take over another. It basically binds one wolf to the other's will."

"If Melissa manages to trick your poor boy into a bad position, I would not hesitate to recommend for you to use this skill. Call him by name and make a claim on him. Put all your will behind your words, Sasha, and believe them. He'll be bound to you. It will keep him from harm."

"Can I release him later?" I asked. "It sounds kind of horrifying."

"Yes, though it is difficult. He would have to hate you passionately for something you did." She sighed. "There is a reason we have not used it often," she said. "Don't ever speak of this to anyone. David is the only other one who knows how much the cost is for using this. Taking away someone's will without good cause is a serious crime among our people. I can compel you, but I am already your leader...and your mother. But that boy doesn't deserve the hurt she would inflict on him. She'd destroy all goodness in him."

She started to leave the room, then turned back to me.

"One other thing you should know," she said. "When you told Bobby that John wasn't your boyfriend, John looked very, very hurt. He likes you very much. Did you not see that?"

I stared at her, my mouth falling open. John? *John?* He *liked* me? He liked *me?* I was dumbfounded.

My mother smiled at me.

"You had no idea, did you?" she said. "Didn't it seem odd to you that he just dropped everything to come with you this weekend? That he trusted you enough to let his wolf side take over for the first time last night? He trusts you completely because he has such deep feelings for you. How could you have missed that?"

"But, we're friends!" I exclaimed. "Best friends. That's what friends do. We trust each other. I mean, I trust Nevermore because we're friends."

"Honey, from what you have said and left unsaid over the years,

John doesn't have a solid family, no siblings, and few friends. You are his best friend. He trusts you. From there, it's a natural extension. He might just have been waiting to see if you and Rich were going to make it before asking you."

"Oh," I said.

I had always put John in the "no dating" category because of having been his teacher, sort of, his senior year of school, and I had been fairly certain that he'd put me there too. He'd never shown any overt interest, but then again, I'd been with Rich for a number of years, and John was too much a gentleman to try to come between us. I really had never thought of him that way, though the idea of Melissa going after him had put my teeth on edge earlier that afternoon. Until now, I had chalked that up to my dislike of Melissa, but now I wondered if that was the only reason.

"Thanks," I said. "I'll have to think about all of this."

"You're welcome," she said and left the room.

I went back to the dining room and found that most of the family had cleared out. Some probably were going to go for a run in the moonlit woods. Some had been making plans over dinner for a game of killer Monopoly, while others decided to retire early. John was still there talking with David about technical stuff. He glanced up when I came in, and I watched his reactions as I poked fun and called David a "nerd" when he made a joke about RNA that only he and I would have gotten. If there was some deeply burning unrequited love in John's psyche, I thought, he hid it well. Knowing my mother, though, if she said it was there, it was.

"Well, gentlemen, I am going for a postprandial swim. You are welcome to hang out here or you can join me if you like. Unless you guys are too tired from running this afternoon."

"Cramps," said David, stuffing a huge forkful of pie into his mouth. "Sorry."

"Jerk," I said as he winked.

"I'll come," said John, rising. "I could use a swim to stretch out after today."

"Sounds good," I said. "Let's go."

Once back in my room, I slipped into my one piece bathing suit, pulled the tunic coverall over my head, then donned my flip flops. The House was never cold per se, but the marble floors could get a mite chilly in the winter; I had enough years of cold feet in my youth to not really relish the idea anymore. When I opened the door, John was already waiting for me, clad in swim trunks and tee shirt. I smiled at him, then pointed at his bare feet.

"You might want to grab slippers or something," I said. "The floor downstairs is not for the faint of heart."

"I'm out of luck there," he shrugged as we began to walk down the hall. "I didn't bring any, and I'm too lazy to go back for my shoes."

"Your funeral."

The pool room greeted us with a blast of humidity and warmth that had been only hinted at when we had gone to the conservatory earlier. The atrium was closed off from the rest of the House by a pair of glass doors, but once inside, the room was warm and as humid as a tropical jungle. The pool was a decent size, but not overwhelming, and provided a good workout for its length. I snagged a towel from a stack by the door, carrying it over to the Adirondack chair near the wall. Kicking off my flip flops, I pulled the tunic over my head, tossing it on the chair, and turning, I found John shedding his tee shirt. When he looked over at me, he stopped. And stared.

"What?" I said, though I already knew what.

In all the years I'd known him, there had never been occasion for us to go swimming together. He was too different from the rest of my friend group to have been invited to summer gatherings with the people Rich and I hung out with. Not that he cared; they weren't his cup of tea either. He had never seen me in a bathing suit before, however, and that gave him pause.

Well, again, fair was fair. I gave John a good once over. He was still too thin, tall and gangly like his wolf form, although his shoulders had broadened a bit over the years. He always stood awkwardly, was a bit clumsy, and seemed uncomfortable in his skin the majority of the time.

I still didn't find him any more physically attractive than I had before – not that he was unattractive, mind. He was a known quantity to me, being one of my first real friends in the city, and one of only three in Boulder I could trust, if you counted Kathy and Paul. Rich and his friends were fun, but not safe. That had become painfully evident as of late.

"Um..." John said, and looked away, flushed.

"Oh for god's sake, John. It's me. Sasha? Nerdy girl, remember? We ran in the forest as wolves earlier. Don't get weird on me now."

"Sorry," he said and smiled a little. "It's just that even though we've known each other for years, I've never gone swimming with you. And you do tend to always wear jeans and tee shirts. This is...different."

"Yeah, yeah," I said, grinning at him. "I had the same thought. Strange knowing someone for ten years and getting hit with everything new about them at once."

"Pretty much," he said, echoing my grin.

"Okay, weirdness is over?" I asked. At his nod, I said, "Good. Come on; come swimming."

I took two strides and dove into the water. The temperature was always too warm for most people, but I loved it. I found the heat soothing, and I never felt chilled after being in it for a while the way I did in some pools. I swam under for a few lengths, then came upon the far side near the wall. Brushing water out of my eyes, I was just in time to see John do a cannonball at the deep end of the pool, sending up a huge wave.

John may have been awkward on land, but in the water, he was astoundingly graceful. If he hadn't already proven himself to be a wolf, I would have bet that he was a seal or an otter the way he moved. I was a good swimmer and completely at home in the water; John seemed like he was made for it. I found myself completely enchanted.

He finally paused in his antics to come over near where I was clinging to the wall. He was barely out of breath, and he laughed to see the dumbstruck expression on my face.

"Well, now you know how I feel!" he said, trying to catch his breath between laughs. "You're seriously surprised? I know I mentioned at least once in the last ten years how much I loved to swim."

"Why didn't you ever go out for the team?"

"With those jerks?" he snorted. "They made fun of me from when we were in first grade through most of high school. Why would I want to join that team of entitled assholes?"

"Point," I said. "You're pretty amazing, though. Where did you learn to move like that?"

"My aunt ran a co-ed summer camp, and my folks sent me there pretty much every summer until my sophomore year. The coach saw that I had some natural talent and gave me private lessons. She was an amazing swimmer, too. Her camp name was Otter."

"I wonder if she was," I said thoughtfully.

"What, an otter?" he asked. "Is it possible?"

"Were there any real otters in or around the lake?" I asked.

"As a matter of fact, yes," he said. "There were some on the other side, near the springs. I saw them a few times when I was out on the lake in a canoe."

"Hmmmm," I said slyly. "And were any of these private lessons ever...other?"

John turned beet red and would not meet my eyes. I laughed.

"Otters tend to be a bit...promiscuous. They are also very fond of humans. I suspect your aunt discovered your little tryst somehow, and your parents found you something else for the summer of your junior year, hmm?"

"Oh my god," said John, his skin turning from beet red to ashen. He looked as though had the earth opened up under his feet, he would have gladly dropped in without a fuss. I found all of this incredibly amusing.

"You never mentioned any of this during our "how to date a girl" chats," I said.

"Well, no," he admitted, not making eye contact. "I was kind of mortified that she had seduced me. I mean, she said she was only twenty-one. I was sixteen at the time, and it didn't seem like that much of a difference to me. It's only five years."

I almost reminded him that I was only a year older than that, but I refrained.

"You should go there sometime," I said half-jokingly. "See what has happened to them."

"I mean, now I'm really curious," he said, splashing at the water with the hand not clutching the side of the pool and blinking up at me. "Maybe we should."

I was inordinately pleased with that comment. It told me two things: one, that he was coming to terms with the fact that life as he had known it would go on, and two, that he was accepting the sudden appearance of the paranormal in his life. Three things, I amended: he was including me in his plans. That part warmed me to the core for some reason and also confused me totally. I dove under the water to cover my sudden panic and proceeded to swim to the shallow end of the pool. He beat me there.

"You waste too much energy," he said. "You have to work with the water, not flail through it. Watch."

He stood and dove back under the water, swimming with breathless speed to the other side. I couldn't quite tell what he did, but his version of the crawl was almost silent, and his breaths were quick and efficient. He turned at the far end and swam back to me. The whole lap had taken less than a minute. He stood up again when he reached me and grinned triumphantly.

"Okay," I said. "I'm not quite up for lessons today, but if you think you can teach me to swim even a quarter that well, I'm willing to try tomorrow."

"Excellent!" he beamed, seeming really happy for the first time in a long while. When had the last time been that he'd been visibly happy? I couldn't recall.

"Okay, so I am going to go swim poorly for a while. You go be impressive if you feel like it, but I need to actually unwind."

With that, I proceeded to backstroke out into the middle of the pool, and John did laps for a while until I finally felt relaxed enough to call it a day. Swimming to the shallow end of the pool, I climbed out of the water and grabbed the towel from the chair. John heaved himself out of the pool at the side he was closest to and went to get a towel of his own. He also seemed more relaxed, not quite so awkward, as he concentrated on drying himself enough to throw his shirt on.

"The room across the hall from yours is one of the upstairs bathrooms," I said, pulling my tunic back over my head and continuing to fluff my hair with the towel. "Why don't you go take a shower there, and I'll hit the one in the other wing. We can watch anime after if you want, or whatever."

"Okay," he said. "I'm not sleepy yet, but I probably will be after a few episodes."

"It's been a long day," I said.

"Yes it has," he agreed. "Ready?"

6
UNEXPECTED TWIST OF FATE

The morning light crept in through my window as it had every dawn during my childhood, scrawling familiar patterns up the walls as it slipped through the folds of the sheer curtains. I lay on the soft bed for a long while, luxuriating in the feeling of indolence that only happened a few times during the year. Like most teachers, I worked during the summer in some education-related job, so Christmas vacation was one of my few down times. For me, it was usually summer school and helping the kiddos who had struggled and failed during the year. Rich never really knew why I wanted to work so much when he made enough for both of us. I told him I would die of boredom if I didn't do something. He had just smiled, and that had been the end of it.

I had thought long and hard about Rich last night. Innately, there was nothing wrong with Rich except his feelings about shapeshifters. He was great to me. He had never given me a hassle about hanging out with John, he had tolerated both my houseplant fixation and love for animals. He even got a cat who we named Cecil who ignored me completely to dote on Rich, a fact we both laughed over.

Maybe, given enough time, I could have won him over to accepting who I really was, but his friends all felt so negatively about shapeshifters I seriously doubted it. I had listened with revulsion to their derogatory comments when Sam revealed our existence. For good or ill, shapeshifters were now in the spotlight, and the court of public opinion was not totally in our favor. It annoyed me that so many humans knew us, were friends with us...were dating us, even, and yet had such a horrible opinion of us. Sam was our spokesman, and even he was hidden so far away that no one could find him. Of course, there were shifters who were not happy with what he had done as well, but the shapeshifter community, by and large, agreed it had to happen.

I had come to the unhappy conclusion during the night that I was going to have to break it off with Rich. I hated it, but I knew my mother was right. Finding a place to live wouldn't be that hard; Andrew had his hands in real estate all over the Boulder area. Chances were, he could find us a place to live within a day or two, and we...

There were those words again. *Us. We.* I sat up in bed and wrapped my arms around my knees. When had I subconsciously decided that John was going to live with me? Was it when he had refused to go home the other night and stayed at Nevermore's? Was it when Mother had decreed he was my responsibility? Was it last night as we sat watching anime, throwing Marseille's infamous kettle corn at each other, and I suddenly found myself wondering what it would be like to kiss him? Damn my mother for telling me John liked me and planting that seed in my head! Damnit, damnit, damnit! I had shut that thought down almost before it had entered my mind, but it was too late. I realized in that moment that while I might not be overly physically attracted to John, mentally and emotionally, I had found him very appealing for a long time.

Fuck.
I did not want this.
But I did.
But I didn't.
But I did.
Fuck fuckity fuck fuck fuck.

All of a sudden, I needed to go for a long, long run. I went to step on the floor, only to kick something soft that growled slightly when my foot made contact. I closed my eyes for a moment, counted to ten, and then looked down to see a large, black shape sleeping on the floor next to my bed. I took a deep breath, pulling my foot back up in case he sleep startled, before raising my gaze to the ceiling and exclaiming, "What the actual fuck?"

John came instantly awake, jumped to his feet, and turned to see me glowering at him from the bed. He curled his tail between his legs and cowered. Still scowling, I tossed my pink bathrobe onto him and turned away while he changed back and arranged the garment to cover himself.

"I can explain," he said, his voice tinged with panic.

"Oh, I hope so," I said, my annoyance clear in my tone. "There had better be a really good reason I almost used you as a fuzzy footstool this morning."

And yet, as I saw him sitting on the floor, stammering, I couldn't help feeling oddly pleased to see him, too. I knew John had gone to his own room last night; I had seen him out the door. And yet, here he was this morning, in my room, somewhat chivalrously sleeping on the floor next to my bed. He had come back, and instead of waking me, had shifted and slept near me at a respectful distance.

"There was someone else in my room last night," he said.

I stopped glowering at him and went very still.

"Was it Melissa?" I asked.

"Yes," he said. "She crept in sometime after I'd gone to sleep. I woke to find someone nibbling on my neck. At first I..."

"Go on," I said.

"Well, I thought it...might be you," he said, not meeting my eyes and blushing, "But the smell was wrong, which just sounds very weird to say out loud. So I sat up and flicked on the light. She was naked on the bed behind me, and when I told her to go, she refused. So I decided to leave instead. I'm sorry I didn't even knock; I was afraid that if I hesitated, she'd find me. You were sleeping, and I did not know what else to do. I figured you would *not* be happy if I got on the bed, so I went wolf. I slept pretty well on the floor, all things considered."

He was upset over the whole issue and who could blame him? It wasn't John's fault, though, so I tried to keep my outward reaction in check.

Inside, though, I was royally pissed. I was going to kill her. Not literally, albeit tempting, but we were going to have some strong words as soon as I caught up with her today.

"Okay," I said, trying to wake up enough to make everything make sense. "First of all, why would you think it was me?"

"Well, you've kind of been acting weird lately," he said, "and kind of possessive? So I thought that maybe you were interested..."

He sighed and shook his head.

"I am being dumb," he said, staring at the floor.

"John," I began, then stopped as words refused to flow; I really wasn't awake enough for this conversation.

I tried again, clearing my throat. He glanced up at me.

"You are not being dumb, John."

"I'm not?" he said, sounding confused and a little hopeful.

I sighed and shook my head, utterly defeated now.

"No," I said, "you're not. Things are a little complicated, though. I have to deal with Rich first. I really have no choice but to break up with him. He's a threat to you, me, Nevermore, and my entire family. Regardless, it has to be done tactfully AND without getting you involved. He deserves better than to just be left cold. Then I need to find a place to live. Someplace you can stay, too, if you want. I know going home is not a good option for you, especially now, so I am pretty sure Uncle Andrew can find us an apartment or house or something. After all of that gets settled...we can talk about it. We actually can probably discuss it before then, but let's take one thing at a time. Okay?"

He looked like he'd been poleaxed. Stunned. Then the smile he gave me was the sweetest I'd ever seen.

"Okay," he said. "Very much okay."

I took a deep breath to clear my head.

"Right. Go get dressed and meet me downstairs in like ten minutes," I said. "I just woke up and need to get my brain refocused before I see my family. I also want to go for a run, so I may abandon you for a little while after breakfast if that's okay with you. I need a clear head to deal with Melissa, and right now, I'm beyond angry with her. If you see her, avoid her. She doesn't give up easily."

"Got it. Hey, so, um, my clothes are in my room, so are you okay with me borrowing this?" he said, indicating the bathrobe.

"Take it," I said. "Pink really isn't your color, though."

He made a face at me, and then stood up with as much dignity as he could while holding a baby pink bathrobe around his waist and left the room. As soon as he was gone, I flung aside the covers and jumped out of bed, dressing as fast as I was able. Moments later, I raced out of the room, storming downstairs to the dining room.

Even though it was after eight o' clock, only my brothers and my uncle were having breakfast in the dining room. My mother had left early to pick dad up at the airport, and most of the rest of the clan were notorious late sleepers. Especially Melissa, I thought grimly.

"Morning, Sis," said Bobby, grinning at me. "Yelling this early, are we?"

"I nearly stepped on John this morning," I said. "Get that smirk off your face, Bobby. He came to hide in my room last night after being woken by a certain someone who freaked him out completely. He spent the night on my floor in wolf form."

"That would be funny if not for who it was," said David, folding the newspaper he had been reading and setting it on the table.

My brothers frowned at each other, and Andrew finally spoke.

"I assume you will be speaking to her about this?"

"Oh yes," I said, grinning with teeth bared. "As soon as I catch her, we're having words."

"Excellent," said Andrew. "Is John handling all of this well?"

"As best as can be expected," I said. "Andrew, I need to ask a favor. I know things with Rich have to end. I get that. And John is going to need a place away from his parents. Can you see if there is an apartment or a house we can move into in or around Boulder?"

"Moving in already?" teased Mark, grinning.

"His parents suck, Mark. They never supported him."

"Yeah," he said, sobering. "We talked a little about that yesterday while Mom was lecturing you."

Andrew smiled at me kindly and took out his cellphone.

"Hi Michelle," he said. "Yes, I am on vacation, but I need to find someone a place to live. Is that house in Gunbarrel near Twin Lakes still available? The blue one on Idylwild Court? It is? Pull the listing. Yes. I'm going to. In full. No, it's empty. Have Nancy go over and clean it Monday morning. Yes. Michelle, you're a wonder. Have a great New Year's Eve yourself! Great. Bye!"

Andrew hung up the phone and looked smug.

"Well, my dear, you will have yourself a house," said Andrew. "The estate bought it last month with an idea to lease it, but it has a pretty high rent, so there have been no takers. If I sell it to you, it will take a week or two for the paperwork to go through, but you can move in next weekend. In the meantime, you can stay at my condo in the city center if you need to. The other question is do you want to be the official owner and take out the loan under your name or do you just want to pay me a monthly amount?"

"How much is the house?" I asked.

"A little over $650K," he said. "You certainly have enough of a share to buy it outright as I don't think you've even touched your money since college. There is at least half the price in interest alone."

"Three-quarters, I think," came a familiar voice from the hall. I jumped up and walked quickly out of the dining room to see my father setting down his suitcases as my mother closed the front door.

"Hi Dad!" I said, running over to give him a huge hug.

"Hi, Kitten," he said, calling me by the childhood nickname I earned after getting stuck in a tree when I was six. "I hear we have a new wolf?"

I pointed to John who was dressed and now descending hesitantly from the second floor. My father turned and greeted him with a warm smile.

"I've heard a lot about you the last few days. All good, I assure you," he said, reaching to shake John's hand when he came down to the bottom of the staircase. "Welcome."

"Thank you, sir," said John, shaking my father's hand.

"Call me Dennis," he said, and turned to me. "I overheard Andrew talking about what you have saved up in interest. I think you can get the house without any problems. The estate will set you up with a loan to cover the rest and some extra to get some furniture. You should be able to handle that, I assume, between the two of you? A low interest loan of about 2% will do the trick. I can get that set up by the time Andrew sorts out the rest."

"That...yes!" I said, doing the math. "As long as John helps..."

"What's going on?" asked John. "Remember, I just got down here."

"It's a bit complicated, but we can have a place to move into by next weekend," I said. "If you still want to, that is."

"Oh!" said John, utterly surprised. "That soon?"

"We'll leave you two to work things out," said my father. "Come to breakfast when you are done."

He and my mother exited the foyer, leaving the suitcases by the stairs. John watched them go, then turned back to me.

"Your uncle found us an apartment?" he asked.

"A house, actually. Right near Twin Lakes."

"A house," he said, surprised. "A house? We are going to rent a house?"

"Own, actually," I said, laughing. "Well, I am, mostly. But if you would be staying there too, you could help out with bills?"

"Of course I would!" he beamed. "The only reason I've been living at my parents' this long is so I can save up to buy my own place, so I can definitely afford it. I have quite a bit saved, actually."

The two of us stood in the hallway for a moment, grinning like idiots, until John's stomach rumbled. I led the way back into the dining room where the others were talking to my parents. I caught Andrew's eye and gave him a thumbs up.

"Oh good; you'll love it," he said, passing me the French toast. "It's a great neighborhood. The house is backed right up to the park. I'd had my eye on it when the listing went up a month ago, and we bought it as an investment right away. It wouldn't have lasted for long in today's housing market."

That settled it. Food was passed around, magically reappearing from the kitchen just as we ran out of something; Marseille had fed wolves long enough to know how much we all tended to eat. Other family members began to trickle down from the bedrooms or arrive at the House, and soon enough, the whole mansion became chaotic. I kept a weather eye on John, but he seemed to be fitting into the group really well. Well enough, in fact, that when I spied Melissa gliding down the stairs into the hallway, I was able to slip away from the conversation without John noticing.

I intercepted her at the bottom of the stairs.

"Hey, Coz," she said indolently, "I guess you had better luck with John than I did last night. I thought he wasn't your boyfriend."

I grabbed her upper arm hard enough to hurt and hauled her, complaining, down the hallway to the conservatory. Once there, I thrust her at the wall and got right up in her face.

"John is my friend, and you are going to keep your hands off him! He isn't one of your boy toys you can just use and dispose of. Stay away from him."

"You can't claim what isn't yours," she smirked. "You have a boyfriend, remember? John isn't tied to anyone, so you can't tell me what to do."

"No," said a voice from behind us, "but I can."

I turned around. My mother stood with her arms crossed, glaring daggers at Melissa.

"This is my home, Melissa, and my territory. You are an invited guest of this pack, by way of my tolerance and your mother. I don't think you would risk the ire of the whole pack by disobeying me, and I know that my sister would not approve of it either, would she? Leave the boy alone."

Melissa's face contorted like she was going to spit nails, but she stood up straight and glared at me.

"Fine," she said. "I'll leave him alone. But if he decides not to leave me alone, that's another matter."

She shrugged away from me and stalked down the hall.

"You would think that my sister could have done a better job with her," my mother sighed. "Twenty-years-old, and spoiled for having everything she ever wanted. I keep hoping she'll grow up. I'll have a chat with Cassandra when she gets here. That child needs to be compelled to behave."

We walked back to the foyer, stopping by the bottom of the stairs.

"Thanks for intervening," I said. "That should hold her for now, until she figures something else out. I'll continue to keep an eye on her."

"Remember what I told you," said my mother, soberly. "You may need it."

We parted, and I headed downstairs to change. A run was definitely in order to get my mind settled.

Once in the woods, I felt better. Breakfast still weighed a bit heavily in my stomach, so my run was more of a trot through the underbrush for a while. No one else seemed to be out, and I reveled in having the freedom of solitude, something that was missing in my life too often.

Being a wolf was like suddenly gaining the ability to see scents; everything left a trace that painted a complex picture of what it was doing in the world. Deer leapt gracefully among the ferns, rabbits scampered from brush to brush, foxes trotted their straight lines on their daily errands. It was like seeing the world in an echo that also held hours and minutes. I was in bliss.

The state forest backed right up to our property, and the line was clearly marked with "Do Not Trespass" signs all along the boundary. I never paid them much attention, and sometimes, like today, felt the need to wander further afield than our forty acres of land. The park was usually not busy during the winter, although there were often cross-country skiers who used the trails for practice. This far out, there was no one.

Twice, I chased deer for the fun of it, letting my instincts take over and running behind them, snapping at their heels. I always let them get away, however, feeling a little guilty for using up some of the energy reserves they needed to survive. The second time I let the deer go, I found myself at the edge of a meadow, and on the far side, two hikers in bright winter parkas stood with binoculars trained first on the fleeing deer, and then on me. I stood motionless watching them watch me for a long moment. The still air carried their words to me.

"Oh, look at her! What a beauty! Get the camera, Mary! Quick!"

A little vain, I pretended not to see them and waited as I heard the sound of the camera shutter click in rapid succession. I even stared right at them for a moment before turning and trotting back into the forest. I heard them make appreciative comments as I moved away and chuckled to myself at how fast those photos would probably make it to Facebook or Instagram. Silly of me to preen, maybe, but I needed something to feel good about as I made my way home.

The trek back was long, and I finally broke into a lope in order to get there sooner. I was worried about John; he seemed to be all right at breakfast, but I hadn't left him alone so long before with the family and felt a little anxious about him fitting in. I shouldn't have been concerned.

As I approached the House, a group of wolves dashed out of the front yard, racing into the woods. I recognized my brothers, a couple of cousins who must have just arrived, and John as they bolted past, not even seeing me as they raced by. Chuckling to myself, I went into the House, changed, and went up to spend some time with the rest of the new arrivals.

The remainder of Friday and most of Saturday were spent relaxing, swimming, eating, and just generally hanging out with family. There were madcap chases in the woods both day and night. Saturday evening was the New Year's Eve family serenade, and all members were there, even Mark and the human members of the family who wanted to go. Melissa had announced that she was going to stay in the House since she wasn't allowed to fully participate; none of us really missed her sulky presence. When Cassandra had arrived, Melissa had gotten an earful and had not been seen for most of Saturday.

The serenade was a chorus of howls started by the oldest wolves – this year Uncle Andrew and my father, then my mother and her sister, and from there, the rest of the family joined in descending order to the youngest. David's daughter was the last to join the howl, her high pitched cries bringing joy to our hearts as the newest generation gave voice. John had joined the chorus right after I did, and his howl grew more confident as the song continued. The pack serenade was about family and togetherness, and I doubted if John had felt a sense of belonging like this any time before in his life; he sang with every fiber of his soul.

The serenade eventually gave way to an impromptu game of chase, and David's daughter raced away with many of the younger wolves in pursuit, myself included. She led us a merry dance through the woods; being smaller, she could dash between the branches better than we could. Before long, half of the pack was scattered trying to find her.

I had lost track of John several brooks ago, and I turned, intending to seek him out, when my nose caught a scent, and my hackles rose at once. How dare she? How *dare* she? I knew then without a doubt what had caused John to become lost so easily.

Following the scent, I bolted through the woods, racing now in a panic. Tired as I was from the chase of my niece, my paws found wings, and I ran into the clearing just as John was about to do the unthinkable. Without stopping, I plowed into him, ramming him aside from where he stood with his forepaws on Melissa's back. He yelped and fell to the ground, and I turned, snarling, on the cream-colored wolf who had disobeyed all orders from everyone.

Melissa snarled back at me, ferocious in her wanton need, and lunged at me. I met her charge and slashed my fangs at her throat, feeling her get a mouthful of my ruff. She spat it aside, glaring. I had missed, but wheeled and leapt at her, going for the soft spot under the jaw where I could catch her and immobilize her without having to do worse. She dodged aside and growled her defiance.

I glimpsed John out of the corner of my eye climbing to his feet and saw that he was still entranced by her condition, though wolf instincts were no longer clouding his mind as much as they had been. Then I was back into the fray, with Melissa slashing at my ear, and me gouging her left foreleg with an errant claw. There was a flurry of snapping jaws, and I scored the top of her muzzle with my fangs. She yelped and retreated, momentarily at bay.

I wheeled to face her and watched as John turned to her woozily once again. I made the decision then, regretting it as I did, that I would have to take my mother's advice. With all of my being, with all of my soul, I snarled out my fury at this corruption of the sacred and focused on the one overwhelming thought that I pushed out towards John.

MINE! I CLAIM YOU, JOHN VINCENT ARNDT!! GET. DOWN. NOW.

John dropped to the ground under the weight of both the claiming and the command, and Melissa stopped in her confusion, glancing first at John and then over to me. I shifted back to my human form then, ignoring the cold, ignoring John's eyes on me.

"You DARE?" I screamed at her. "You heartless slut! Have you lost your mind? Are you so desperate for a mate that you have to go after someone who just three days ago learned that he was a wolf and has no idea what this could mean?"

Some of the other wolves were gathering around us now, growling, and Melissa stood still in the center of the family members. She looked wildly around from one to the other, then bolted for the trees as fast as she could. The unmated males hung back, but the rest of the pack chased her, snapping at her and snarling in their fury.

I glowered at John.

"Get up," I said in disgust, putting just enough command into it to release him from my earlier edict. Then I turned on my heel and stalked back towards the House, not caring if he followed me or not. I knew, KNEW, it wasn't his fault entirely, but I was still pissed about the fact that he hadn't even tried to break away.

I shifted back into wolf form and ran the rest of the way, wanting to just hide in my room. I made it back before the others and bolted upstairs, not even bothering to retrieve my clothes. I shifted back when I reached my sanctuary, twisted the lock once inside, and then buried myself under the covers.

John knocked a little later, asking, pleading to be let in, but I ignored him; eventually, I heard him go away. A bit later, my mother came to the door, and this time, I opened it.

"Melissa has been taken home and is banned from all further family gatherings," said my mother, handing me my abandoned clothing after I had closed and relocked the door. "Your young man came down to talk to me. He's very upset about all this and terrified he's ruined your friendship. I told him what you did to save him, and he says he doesn't care, that you could 'turn him into a mindless brain-eating zombie, and he'd still want to be friends with you.' His words, not mine, by the way. He's down with your brothers, uncle, and father right now. They like him a great deal, you know, as do I. He fits with us in a way that Rich never could. You could do a lot worse for a mate.

"He meant no harm," she continued when I didn't say anything. "And your reaction to this situation should tell you something about your feelings for him. Don't torture yourself or him needlessly."

She was right, of course, but I was still hurt and told her so.

"When I saw him mounting her...my heart fell. All I could think of doing was getting him away from her, not only for his own sake but for mine. I couldn't stand to see him with her especially, but now that I think about it, I'm not sure I could bear to see him with anyone else. Why does it have to take this to make me see something so obvious? Why didn't I notice it sooner?"

"You," said my mother firmly, "wrap yourself up so tightly in the role of being a teacher that you don't leave room for anything else. You forget that you have to be a real person first, then an educator. You forget that the students want to see your humanity, not just your mantle of responsibility. You wear it like a shield and then wonder why people have a hard time getting close to you.

"You met John at the beginning of your career, but already that veneer of "teacher" was forming a bubble that cut you off from others. Rich allows you to hold up that shield. He expects it because he sees you first as a professional and then as a person. John sees you mostly as a person and then as a professional. He did not get a full dose of you in that role. He saw you as a friend first. It's you who have kept him at a distance. He cared enough about you to ignore that and stick with you, even after you moved in with Rich. John loves you. You know that, right?"

I nodded, tears coming into my eyes. I knew, and I obviously felt some of that towards him too, judging by my reaction tonight.

"Mom," I said, using the appellation I only used when I was upset, "how do I tell Rich that it's over?"

"Be honest," she said. "As much as you can be, that is. You are never going to be able to be totally honest with him about a huge part of your life. When you are ready, the boys have volunteered to help you move your possessions out of his apartment, so just let them know. I'd keep John away, though."

"I plan on it," I said, putting my clothes on. "I suppose I ought to go down and talk to him, huh?"

"I think that would be wise," said my mother with a slight smile. "Be gentle with him. He's beaten himself up quite enough over the situation as it is."

I nodded, and together we went downstairs. I heard my brothers' voices coming from the living room, and from the sounds of it, they were regaling John with tales of their own high school experiences. They broke into laughter just as we came through the door, and when

John saw me, he turned pale, all signs of humor leaving his face, and he stood up from where he'd been sitting on the couch.

"We'll let the two of you talk," my father said, giving my brothers and my uncle a meaningful glance. "We'll be in the small ballroom. It's movie night, so come join us if you feel like it later."

They made a tactical withdrawal from the room, leaving us alone.

"Sash, I am so sorry," John blurted out as soon as they had left. "I know what you said, and I tried, *I tried,* but something came over me, and I...stopped resisting. Which was wrong of me, I know. And then it was like something else was controlling my actions. It was like being lost in the thrill of running through the woods the other day."

I walked over to where he stood and just embraced him without saying anything. He hesitated for a moment and then hugged me back. We stood there for a long time, not speaking.

"I forget sometimes what it is like being a wolf for the first time," I said, still holding him. "For me, it was a long time ago, and I had all the guidance I could want from the people in my family. You are so new to it that all those instincts I learned to control years ago are still going to be a challenge for you until you understand them. This is one of those times.

"Mating is such a basic, primal urge that you didn't know how to fight it. Melissa planned her assault on you with precision, and if I had been more aware of how desperate she was, I might have seen that she was just waiting for the opportunity. I just thought that she had better manners than to go after you after I specifically warned her off, and her own mother had told her to stop playing games with people."

"Aight," he said in reply. He pulled back a little so he could see my face. "Are we okay then?"

"Yes," I said, and hugged him, tighter. "Are you okay with what I did?"

"Well," he said, returning the embrace, "I don't think I have much choice. Your mother said you'd have to do something pretty egregious to make me hate you enough to break it, so I think you're stuck with me."

"I won't use it unless it's a life or death situation," I promised.

I released him, but neither of us stepped away. I looked up at him, wondering again what it would be like to kiss him. He studied my face and appeared to be thinking along the same lines but was unsure how I'd react. I made up my mind for the both of us and kissed him lightly on the lips.

Surprise crossed his face, and then he returned the kiss with interest, reaching up to cup my face in his hands and pausing finally to gaze at me with an expression of dumbfounded wonderment. I knew how he felt; I had not expected his reaction to be so intense, nor my response so deep.

I stepped away a little and motioned to the couch.

"Sit, before you fall down," I said.

He sat, and I did also, as close to him as I dared.

"When we head back tomorrow, things are going to be different," I said. "We have to get our lives in order, school is starting back up for me on Monday, and you have to work. I am going to have to break up with Rich, which is going to be painful and messy. There is going to be a crazy week ahead of us. You need to start packing, too."

John's eyes lit up when he realized what that meant, and his smile was heart-breaking.

"I'd almost forgotten," he said. "A house..."

"Yeah," I said. "I could have gotten one years ago, but there didn't seem to be a point. It was cheaper just to move in with Rich, so I never bothered because he really had no desire to take on the "trauma of home ownership" as he put it."

He snorted, an odd expression crossing his face.

"What?" I asked.

"This is just all so weird," he said. "I mean, you kissed me."

"Yeah, well you kissed me back!"

"Do you have any idea how long I've wanted to? I pretty much told myself that it was a pipe dream and to forget about it ever happening."

"I honestly had no idea you were interested," I said. "I never had any indication from you that you even saw me that way, so you weren't even on my radar."

He seemed a little crushed by this admittance but gamely tried to hide it. Now that I recognized his poker face, however, I wasn't fooled.

"Sorry," I said. "You know I'll always be honest with you. I'm not going to lie and say that I had a secret crush on you when I didn't."

"So what changed?" he asked.

"Well, a lot of things, I guess," I said, scratching my head. "This whole weekend has been kind of a giant boot to the head for me. You and I have similar interests, and those have definitely brought us closer over the years. Your trust in me from the start of this little adventure was a big factor. My mother pointing out that you liked me was another. She can see through lead walls, I swear.

"Once I really started thinking about it, I realized there was something there that I had never noticed. Like how the word *we* keeps creeping into our conversations lately. What happened tonight really gelled the whole situation for me, though," I paused for a moment and then looked him in the eye. "I mean, I don't think I'm quite at the same place you are, but I could see myself getting there, you know?"

I sighed and remembering my mother's words about walls, tried to be as open and honest as I could.

"The thought of Melissa getting her hands on you or sneaking into your room disturbed me a lot. I mean *a lot* a lot," I said. "At that time, I just thought I was defending you from the evil succubus, you know? But seeing her about to induce you into what almost surely would have ended up in a shotgun wedding sort of situation was the defining moment for me. I didn't just not want her to have you; I realized I didn't want anyone to be with you unless it was me."

John stared at me with surprise, but I held up a hand to forestall his reply.

"That revelation, John, was what caused me to crash into you and fight her," I said. "I've never fought another wolf like that in my life. When I stormed off after, I wasn't just mad at you, though that was part of it. What really frightened me was how strong those feelings towards you are. I told you that the wolf side of us runs on instinct. That side of me already saw you as my partner, my...mate. I've never felt that before, and it freaked the hell out of me. There were a lot of emotions attached to it, and they were complicated. They still are."

"You see me as your mate?" he asked quietly.

"The wolf side of me does," I admitted, feeling my face grow hot. "It can get confusing sometimes, getting everything lined up so that it makes sense. The wolf side didn't even acknowledge Rich, but he never saw it obviously. I, the human side, am a jumbled mess. Being a wolf simplifies things a lot, and everything is pretty cut and dry. Humans don't have that option. There are always new plans, always new problems."

We sat in silence for a few long moments, neither of us knowing what to say. What was between us was huge, and I didn't completely know how to deal with it.

"I don't know what my wolf side thinks," said John. "I think it's a little fried from today's events. I know that I am seriously hoping that I won't go to sleep tonight and wake to find that our conversation was a dream."

"You won't," I said. "We are going to watch anime all night and pass out at some obscene hour wherever we are. Right now, I am going to go get a bottle or two of wine from Marseille, and we are going to talk about how stupid we both are."

"Do we have to just talk?" he asked shyly.

I sighed.

"Until I get everything sorted out with Rich, I think it would be best if we just keep it to that, yes," I said, and grinned slyly. "And possibly kiss since that bridge has already been crossed."

"Burned," he said, grinning. "That bridge has been burned."

I rose, pulling John to his feet. Together, we went to procure the wine from Marseille.

7
RETURNING TO REALITY

The next morning dawned just as bright and clear as the one before, though this time, I knew that I was not alone in my room when I awoke. After an amazingly short number of episodes, the wine and the sheer exhaustion of the day found John snoring where he lay on one side of the bed. I also caught myself dozing off and shut down the computer, placing it on the bedside table. Because John was laying on top of the covers, I couldn't turn down the blanket to get under it, so I finally gave up, went to the bathroom, and came back as a wolf, carrying my clothing. I had hopped onto the bed and soon was curled up fast asleep next to John.

When I rose the next morning and blinked over at where John had lain the night before, I discovered that he had woken up in the middle of the night, found me changed, and decided to stay. The black wolf snored slightly as I watched, and his forepaws twitched. It was adorable. Part of me wished we could stay at the House longer just so as to avoid the issues that were going to arise during the course of the next week. I also knew that hiding here was not the answer, and all problems were better faced head on.

As loathe as I was to move from the comfort of the bed just yet, other, more urgent needs were calling. I grumbled my way to the floor, grabbed the fresh clothes I had laid out before the animefest, and went to prepare myself for the morning. After I was dressed, I checked on John, who was still snoring softly, and headed downstairs to grab some coffee and real food. Marseille's popcorn aside, I hadn't eaten since supper the night before and was ravenous. When I arrived downstairs, a number of my relatives were still at breakfast.

"Ah, there you are!" exclaimed Andrew. "John?"

"Still sound asleep," I said, yawning. "Pass the coffee, please Stephen? Thanks. We stayed up watching anime until we both passed out. And no," here I shot Bobby a look as he started to open his mouth, "nothing else happened."

Bobby made an exaggerated snapping motion with his fingers, grinning as he handed me the sugar bowl. Mark rolled his eyes as he gave his oldest daughter a plate of eggs. Her mother, a shapeshifter named Helen, had arrived with the kids on Friday and was managing the plates for the younger two. It was all very Norman Rockwell.

I sat and talked with them for a long while over breakfast and was still there when a sleepy John finally joined us almost an hour later. I wordlessly handed him a cup of coffee, and he added cream and sugar. He filled a plate with sausages and eggs, some sourdough toast, and a couple of grilled tomato halves, then sat back to enjoy the chatter.

Andrew surprised me (and probably everyone else) by offering John a chance to drive the Mustang, and John inhaled his food as fast as he could. Everyone was making plans for their last day, and when I checked the time on my phone, I found a voicemail from Rich letting me know that a bunch of our friends would be coming over tonight and did I have a preference for pizza flavor in case I ran late? He ended with a message that he missed me and wished he had been able to be at the family party this year. The "I love you" at the end was like a knife to my heart, and as soon as John went out with Andrew, I made for the woods.

As I ran, I tried to straighten out everything that had happened this weekend. In an unbelievably short amount of time, my best friend had become the central focus of my world, and everything I thought I understood had changed. My normal life which included going out to bars with friends on the weekends was about to take a steep nose dive. Most of those friends had started out as Rich's, and I was pretty sure most of them would side with him if – when – I abruptly got up and left him.

The other problem was that I would have to teach Monday, and an emotional night of upheaval tonight was likely to cause me to have a very bad time. If it were at all possible to wait a day or two, it might be better, but then again, the longer I waited, the harder it would be to tell him goodbye. That would not help either of us. And I did care about him; that was the kicker. But since he persisted in his viewpoint, I had to let him go.

And then there was John, who had always been there waiting, not saying anything, on the sidelines, hoping against hope this time would come. John who, despite being somewhat antisocial, was a better match for me than anyone I had ever met. As I ran, the wolf part of me had some very clear thoughts about John. She knew his scent, his heartbeat, his form. Not to mention the fact that his fur was so soft it was almost criminal. She would defend him to the death, and there was no one else on this planet who she desired to be with. The wolf and I were one and the same, but when I was the wolf, my thoughts were clearer, less clouded by anything but pack bonds. John was mine by claiming, too, and that was another side of things that couldn't be ignored. That connection would overshadow anything else for us forever, as I could not imagine doing anything that could ever drive him away. That alone would have doomed any other relationship.

As I trotted back into the yard a little while later, I found my black wolf waiting for me. He saw me, and he seemed to grow in stature as he stood, head high. Once he had my eye, he trotted to the wood's edge and glanced over his shoulder for a second before leaping gracefully into the brush. I followed.

Running with John was a joy that morning. We both knew that this would be the last time we could run as wolves this freely for a while, and we made the best of it. Bounding side by side, chasing each other, racing, we spent the morning exhausting ourselves and ended our run at the hot tub before lunch. We had gone inside just long enough to don bathing suits and grab towels, and when another couple came to soak following their morning run, we made room for them to join us. They had also taken the time to change out of deference to John. The woman was another cousin from my dad's side, and her boyfriend was from Western Massachusetts. They had met at the University in Boulder and were both bio majors. We traded lab horror stories and had John equally laughing and confused by our comments.

Lunch was the big farewell affair, and anyone who had not left yet was there. Aunt Cassandra had returned early that morning, tight lipped and apologetic to John, my mother, and myself. No more was said about her daughter's behavior.

"It has, as always, been a wonderful time having everyone here, and although a bit of an adventure, it has been a weekend for the books," said my mother to those gathered. "Please remember to stay in touch and keep an ear out for anything that might affect us with the news. We will do the same and relay out what we find."

John and I made our farewells, and when it came time to say goodbye to my mother, I found it hard to get the words out.

"Have a great New Year and a safe drive home. You and John will be fine," she said. "Trust each other, and everything will turn out for the best."

Andrew hugged me and promised to call the next day, and my dad winked at both of us.

"The money is all arranged," he said. "I transferred your interest plus the loan to your account. When Andrew has everything ready, just get him a cashier's check, and everything will be set. You will have enough to go furniture shopping with too, provided you don't spend more than $20,000 on what you choose."

I thanked him, and we took our bags out to the car. I glanced back at the familiar House and almost felt as if it looked different to me now. More stately, I guessed. Or maybe it was just my weird perception of how much things had changed.

As I started the car, John took a last glance at the Mustang.

"How'd it drive?" I asked.

"It was amazing," he said. "You do know that your uncle had really wanted to get me out to have a little chat, right?"

"I had my suspicions," I said. "Was it the usual 'take care not to hurt my niece' discussion?"

"A little. It was more a 'Here's a spare house key to my condo if you need a place to stay.' He said you have one."

"I do," I said. "You might be better staying at Nevermore's house tonight, though. He tends not to stock his fridge, and the décor is pretty basic."

"Is she okay with that?" he said. "I don't want to impose."

"She said she's fine with it. I texted her earlier."

"Okay then," he said. "Since we are going there anyway, I might as well. What about you?"

"I have to go home tonight," I said. "All of my school bags are there, along with all of my clothes for work. Tonight might not be the best night to talk to Rich as he is inviting a bunch of friends over, and we may not get a real chance to until tomorrow. I won't put it off later than tomorrow, though."

"Okay," said John. "I just wish that you didn't have to go back."

He didn't sound happy, and I couldn't blame him.

"A little too Moulin Rouge for you?" I asked, referencing one of his favorite non-anime films.

"Yeah, just a bit."

"I'm sorry," I said. "Nothing will happen, don't worry."

"I think my wolf side also claims you, just so you know. I felt it this morning, in the woods," said John. "Like all is right when you're with me."

"Yea," I said. "That's what it feels like."

We drove down the long driveway to the main thoroughfare, turned on to it, and headed for the highway.

"What are you going to tell your parents?" I asked.

"That I found a roommate," he said, "and she invited me to share a house with her that her uncle owns. No need to get more complicated than that. They'll get upset, I'm sure, but what can I do? I can't be there to carry groceries or move furniture forever. They'll have to figure that out themselves."

"Speaking of furniture, if you want to, we can go shopping later this week," I suggested. "I have nothing to bring with me other than clothes, books, and some small treasures. Andrew tells me there are three bedrooms, and 2.5 baths. He is willing to meet us Wednesday after you get off work to walk through the house, and then we could go to Furniture Row or one of the other local stores. Maybe Arhaus?"

"Arhaus? Aren't they pretty pricey?"

"Yeah, that's why I mentioned Furniture Row. We do have a whole house to decorate."

He was silent for a moment, and I looked over to see him chewing on his bottom lip.

"What?" I asked.

"Well, I was trying to figure out how to bring up the sleeping arrangement in a tactful way," he said.

"Huh, I hadn't thought of that," I said. "Do you want your own room? We have three bedrooms. I figured one would be an office, but I didn't want to make a choice for you as to where to stay."

"Do *you* want your own room?" he asked.

I sighed, reminding myself that he had never lived with anyone before. Everything was completely new to him, and I would have to take the lead on a number of things.

"I think what you are really asking is if we are going to share a bed," I said. "I mean, we did last night and no one died, right?"

He blinked at that, and a little of the discomfort left his face.

"John, just because we are sleeping in the same bed does not mean that we have to have sex until and if both of us want to," I said. "I would be fine getting a king-sized bed and sharing it. Wolves tend to be pretty gregarious. I can almost guarantee that if we had gone to movie night, some of the younger people there would have been in a cuddle puddle on the floor. However, I know that sometimes you might want your own space. You have been raised with human mores and human values. Those are pretty hard to overcome after twenty-seven years."

"Oh," he said. "I hadn't thought of it that way."

"Yea, ever-practical me, right?"

He snorted.

"You're always more practical," he said. "Was it hard to move out of the House and try to learn to live with humans all the time?"

"A bit," I said. "I went to the local schools growing up, so it wasn't like I wasn't used to humans in general. But learning to live with roommates in college, and Rich after...that was hard. There was no simple solution; I just watched what others did and emulated them. Being adaptable has helped us to survive."

"So you are saying that I can overcome my natural reserved tendencies to move in with someone I know pretty well if you were able to overcome all of the problems you did?"

"You got it," I said, grinning. "He can be taught!"

"Oh, shut up," he grumbled good-naturedly. "So, could we share the master bedroom, and use the other two bedrooms as an office and a guest room?"

"Sure," I said. "If that is what you would be comfortable with, I'm good with it."

"I would like that," he said quietly. "I'm sorry I'm so hesitant. Things have been going so fast since last Wednesday that I haven't had time to wrap my head around them."

"I know what you mean," I said. "I had been planning on a nice family visit with the usual drama, but nothing earth-shattering. Don't forget, my life all changed last Wednesday too, just not quite as much as yours. Once we get into the house, though, things should slow down a little. Until then, we'll do our best to muddle through."

The rest of the drive to Nevermore's house was uneventful. The discussion turned to more mundane matters such as address changes at work and for car insurance, as well as a myriad of minutiae that John hadn't even thought about. I found myself getting excited about the prospect of furnishing an entire house that would be our own. This also distracted me from thinking too much about Rich. Eventually the conversation drifted on to a discussion of the anime we had been watching, and we arrived at Nevermore's by about four in the afternoon.

After a brief recap of the weekend in the kitchen over tea, Kathy sat looking at us skeptically.

"Wolves never think of the more human issues," she said, shaking her head. "Your break up with Rich will be the talk of the school for weeks. You can't bring John up in connection with this for a bit. While I whole-heartedly approve of your budding relationship, most of them don't know how long you two have been friends. Be discreet for a while."

"I plan on it," I said, then grinned. "How much do you want to bet that Frank will ask me to dinner within a week?"

Frank was the head of the science department and had harbored a not-so-secret thing for me since I started at the school ten years ago. He was a forty-year-old balding man who thought his sense of humor was a riot. Most of the kids disliked him, and he'd managed to alienate me in a record time of two days. When I started dating Rich three years into working at the school, he'd retired to sulking in my peripheral vision, but once word got out, he'd be an annoyance that I'd have to dodge. Nevermore had made a game of running interference in the past, and I can tell by the twinkle in her eye that she was ready to take up the challenge yet again.

"Game on, partner?" I said.

"It's *on*," she said enthusiastically, and we high-fived. John snorted with amusement.

Around five, I stood and stretched.

"Sad as I am to do this, I have to go," I said. "Kathy, thank you for taking in John for a few days."

"My pleasure," she smiled.

"Walk me to the car?" I said to John.

He rose, and we went out the front door. I hollered a Happy New Year to Paul who yelled back to us from the office. John closed the door behind us, and we stepped outside under the bright silver of the waxing moon. When we reached my car, I turned to him, and he bent to kiss me gently, then stood back a pace.

"I'll text later and let you know the lay of the land," I said.

"Sure," he said, looking a bit lost.

"Hey, it's only a few days and then, boom, house, right?" I said quietly. "We have to get through the hard stuff first. Then it will be okay. I promise."

He nodded as I got into my car, started the ignition, and drove away. I glanced in the rearview mirror and saw him standing by the porch, watching me go. Leaving him behind was the hardest thing I'd ever done.

8

THE BURNING OF THE BRIDGE

I arrived at the apartment I had shared with Rich for the past six years, feeling nervous and out of sorts. Everything felt alien now; even unlocking the front door and stepping into the chaos of our friends shouting at a football game on TV felt like something from another life.

My arrival was greeted enthusiastically by the houseful of people, and Rich met me with a lengthy kiss that I returned somewhat perfunctorily. He didn't seem to notice, though, and led me into the fray of beer cans and pizza boxes. He had gotten my favorite, mushrooms and sausage, and it lay untouched amid the wreckage. He grinned when he showed it to me, and I mustered a smile back, then went to put my duffle bag in our room.

I sat on the bed for a few minutes looking around at the life that had been mine for so long and would not be existing very much longer, at the curtains we had argued over, at the landscape painting that he found at a yard sale that I had hated until he painted a reasonably good Godzilla in the middle of it and was now my favorite picture in the world, at the trophy we'd won during the three-legged race two years ago at the high school fair, all the little reminders of my time with him. It had been a good life.

I left my duffle bag packed and threw a few extra clothes into it, along with two changes for work and other necessities, like my favorite stuffed animal from when I was really young and pieces of jewelry I would want in the next few days. I put the bag in the entrance to the closet and slipped back out to join our friends.

The halftime show was just getting underway when I went into the living room, so I fielded questions about my family visit, vaguebooking over most of the specific details. I managed to make Melissa's egregious behavior seem more like a bratty cousin episode and had them laughing at the image of us all playing tag in the woods. Rich asked me about my brothers, and I gave him a quick rundown of what was going on in their mundane lives. It felt weird to leave out the part about Mark's daughter's recent shifting, and this reinforced how big a gap lay between their reality and mine. Then the game was back on, and I went to have a slice of my favorite pizza. It tasted like ashes.

When the game ended at 9:30, talk turned to recent events. A few people had to go home and relieve teenage babysitters of their charges, but six of the core group stayed to chat for a little while longer. I told Rich privately that 11:00 would have to be the cut off time for me, a subtle reminder of school the next day. He nodded absently, and we lounged around drinking beer and listening to the post-game chatter, arguing good-naturedly over some of the highlighted plays. I wasn't a huge football fan, but I could hold my own in a pinch, and sided with one of our friends, Jennifer, as to the ability of the refs to keep score. Juxtaposed against it all was the mental sight of John in his wolf form, his black fur shining in the morning light. My John, whom I now wished desperately to get back to.

Post-game analysis gave way to the news around 10:00, and a few stories into the broadcast came news about Sam and the other shapeshifters. It was mostly about the progress of negotiations with the government, and several of the people in the room booed the reporter who was trying to take a balanced view of the proceedings.

"I think they need to round them all up and ship them to an island somewhere," said a big guy named Todd. "Like in that old movie about the scientist who tried to make animals human...what was that again?"

"*The Island of Dr. Moreau*," said Jennifer, who was a fourth grade teacher at the Thistlewood Elementary School, which was not too far from the new house.

"My cousin at the Bureau of Indian Affairs said he's been told that they were here even before the Native Americans," said Tanya, one of the people in the group I considered to be a friend. "You saw how well just shipping *them* to crappy locations worked."

"These shapeshifters aren't even human," retorted Todd, swigging his beer.

"Human enough to pass for one of us," said Rich, chuckling. "Though I'm sure eventually they'd do something to give themselves away."

"I'm not so sure," said Tanya, glancing at me oddly. "Apparently the tribes coexist with them peacefully."

I shrugged and took a sip of my own beer, which was way too warm now for it to be truly enjoyable. If she had ever had any suspicions, she had never mentioned them to me. I didn't think I had ever said anything to her that might have given that impression, but Tanya did claim to be half Cherokee on her mother's side, something that might have gifted her with a certain awareness.

"Well, I am," said Gary, another of Rich's college friends, walking to get another beer. "I say find out who they are and dispose of the lot of them. Someone on Twitter claimed that they were actually demons, sent from hell to take over our country, and I think they could be right. They'll be taking our jobs next, like the Mexicans, only worse."

I had heard it all before, of course, and more, but for Rich's sake, I hadn't said anything. Now, with everything else that had boiled up this weekend, I found that my tolerance for stupid had just about run out.

"Gary, you're drunk; get someone to take you home. You too, Todd.

I have had about enough from both of you," I said angrily. "I have put up with your overt racism for the last time. I am done. Get out!"

"What? What'd I say that was racist?" said Gary, turning to me in surprise.

"I think it was the Mexican comment," said Jennifer, looking at me for confirmation.

"I think it was all of it," muttered Tanya under her breath.

She got up and went to get her coat.

"I'm gonna go," she said to me. "Call you tomorrow?"

I nodded, still glaring at Gary as she closed the door behind her. Gary put the fresh beer can on the counter and went to pull his coat off the rack. Todd followed, somewhat hesitantly, and Jennifer joined him. They all left, Gary giving me a furious glare over his shoulder.

I turned to Rich, my anger unabated. He was staring at me as if I had lost my mind.

"What the hell, Sash?!" he said angrily. "Why'd you kick them out? So his comment was a little off-color. You know Gary! He even describes himself as an equal opportunity racist. He hates everyone!"

"Rich, you know how I feel about that. I have put up with him for your sake, Todd too. What they say is unkind and untrue almost one hundred percent of the time. And you do nothing to stop them!"

"Sasha, what he said about the Mexicans was wrong, okay. I'll admit that, but his comments about the shapeshifters are true. They are monsters, Sash. They have infiltrated our society and...okay, I don't think they are demons, but they aren't human. There is nothing natural about them."

"How is being able to turn into an animal not natural?" I countered. "Remember, biology teacher? If it exists in nature, then it must by definition be natural. The problem is people don't know all that much about them. If the Native Americans aren't worried about them, though, we shouldn't be either."

"The Native Americans are steeped in all kinds of foolish superstitions. They believe in skinwalkers too, don't they? Don't tell me those are real. They're made up for TV."

The skinwalkers were, in fact, very real, and we had all been warned against them because you don't mess with crazy. Several members of a coyote pack who lived on a reservation in Navajo country had been taken out by skinwalker witches last year. I couldn't tell Rich that, of course, but if any group could be called demons, they'd be my first choice.

"Regardless, the racism of your friends and your support of it has gotten out of hand," I said. "I don't understand your completely negative reaction to the revelation that they live among us. Anyone could be a shapeshifter. Your boss could be! The guy at the checkout counter at Walmart...anyone. How would you know?"

"Like I said, they'd give themselves away. Maybe that was what was wrong with John the other night. He's weird enough to be one."

This hit far too close to comfort and just made me even angrier.

"What was wrong with John was bad sushi," I said. "Ptomaine poisoning. Not some crazy shapeshifter plot. Seriously."

"Hey, I don't know. He still lives at home, doesn't have a girlfriend; who the fuck knows?" snorted Rich. "Regardless, you had no right to kick our friends out of the house!"

"Are you telling me that I don't have a say as to who can be in the place I have called home for the last six years? That I just pay rent to stay here, and I have no other say in what goes on?"

Rich shook his head. "No, that isn't what I'm saying, but you come home from your folks' house and act all high and mighty because you've been pampered all weekend in the lap of luxury. I've been working to pay the bills, don't forget. Then you pull this! The whole group agrees that those creatures are a menace. Why can't you see that?"

"You included, I assume," I said.

"Yes, me included. You haven't said anything about this before," he said, "so why now? Why did it matter enough tonight to ruin a fun evening with our friends?"

"Rich," I said, "I have said things several times before, just not this loudly. Most of your friends are racist assholes whose attitudes need a severe adjustment. Are you going to stand there and tell me that I can't kick them out when they say things that are morally and ethically wrong?"

"Look, I don't know what you're so upset about in the first place," Rich sighed. "I mean, I get that the Mexican thing was wrong for Gary to say, and he should totally not have said it."

"What about Todd and his comment about shipping all the shapeshifters off to an island, like in a concentration camp?" I said. "That's some Nazi level bullshit right there."

"Sasha, I don't know what you are so upset about. Shapeshifters aren't even human. Come on! They are animals. They don't have morals; you know, 'nature red in tooth and claw!' What would they care if they were moved to some game preserve somewhere. They wouldn't know the difference. They could live all together and wouldn't be a danger to the normal folks."

"And then what? You'd sell tickets, like in a zoo?" I exclaimed. "Or take safari tours through it? These are people, Rich! They have lives and homes and jobs, just like you and me. They have children! How can you think that way?"

"Can't you see that these people, these things, are dangerous," he said, his face beet red. "They could lose control and kill people at any provocation. They're animals!"

"If that was the case, don't you think it would have happened by now? They've been with us the whole time we've been on this continent!"

"I don't know why you can't see it," he shouted. "Todd and Gary and everyone else can see it! They are monsters! They'll always be monsters! Why are you so willfully blind?"

I looked at him, slack-jawed.

"I can't believe you! I can't fucking believe you! I thought you were better than this, Rich. I really did. That's it. I'm done. I'm leaving. If your friends and their opinions are more important than me, and you can't even try to see my points, then I'm not staying around to be insulted and belittled!"

I spun around and stormed into the bedroom, making a show of grabbing my duffle bag and shoving a few extra items in it. Rich tried to reason with me, but I wasn't having any of it. I was overreacting a bit to make my point, and I knew it, but it wasn't like I didn't feel this way anyway.

"You have work tomorrow," he said. "Don't be ridiculous! Where are you going to go at this late hour?"

"I have a key to my uncle's condo," I said, pushing past him to get my school bags and computer. "I'll stay there."

"Oh, and then what? You just going to move out?"

I stopped and faced him, putting my bags down to slip my coat on and take my purse from where it lay on the counter.

"I don't know, Rich," I said. "Your comments tonight make me think that I don't know you anymore. If you can't agree to even consider my point of view, why am I living with you?"

With that, I snatched up my bags, stalked to the door, pulled it open, and stormed out, giving the door an emphatic slam. I made it down the stairs, threw my bags into the back seat, put my computer in the front, and was pulling away by the time had Rich run out the door, calling after me. I drove for two blocks, pulled over in an empty parking lot behind a drugstore, and cried my eyes out.

It hurt. It hurt so freaking much. I hated the fact that he had proved my family right and hated the fact that I was relieved that he'd given me such an easy excuse to leave. It should have been harder for me to walk out that door, but the anger I felt towards him was as real as the pain. Rich and I had been happy up to three months ago, then Sam and the others had shown the world that we were here. As much as the break up was bound to happen eventually, the timing really, truly sucked.

I texted Nevermore and let her know what had happened. She called me right back, asking where I was, and then insisted that I come back to her house, call out of work the next day, and get my head in order. I almost told her no, that I would go to my uncle's condo, but she wouldn't have it. I could hear John asking questions anxiously in the background, and that decided me more than anything. I got myself settled and drove over. On the way, I called the district subline to tell them I would not be in. The number of times I had taken time off from school was almost zero in ten years. I felt they could cut me a little slack this time. I was in no mental state to teach.

My phone buzzed several times as I drove, and each time, it was Rich. He left multiple voicemails that I erased without even playing. I called my brothers and asked for their help moving out from Rich's apartment the next day. They all instantly agreed to help me. I really loved my brothers. I thanked them and told them I'd meet them at Andrew's condo around ten a.m.

It started snowing about the time I pulled into Nevermore's driveway. I have never been more relieved to arrive somewhere. Even before my headlights were off, John had run to the side of the car and was opening my door. He let me get out, then pulled me into a huge hug. The snow swirled down around us, and I noticed almost randomly that John wasn't wearing a coat. Or shoes.

"Come on," I said wearily. "Before you catch your death."

"Ha!" he said. "Do you think a little cold could kill me?"

He was buoyant, but as much as I wanted to, I couldn't share his mood. I was very relieved to see him, however, and the pain of the previous hour receded minutely. I grabbed my computer and purse as John pulled the duffle bag from the back seat.

"Leave the school bag," I said. "I called out tomorrow. I just can't even."

Nodding, John went back to the porch while I locked the car. One good thing was that while Rich knew where my uncle's condo was, he had no idea where Nevermore lived. That was one of the deciding factors for me to go to Kathy's house. I didn't think I could handle another confrontation tonight.

I followed John inside and was ushered into the kitchen where Paul was brewing a large pot of coffee. Kathy got me settled with a cup of coffee while John brought my bags up to the guest room. I wrapped my shaking hands around the mug, and then filled everyone in as to what had happened. Paul was enraged when he heard what Todd and Gary had been saying, and when I repeated what Rich had said, John curled his hands into fists. He looked as if he wanted to break something. Nevermore shook her head.

"You are going to stay here until your uncle gets that house in order. No buts. The guest room is big enough for both of you, and we can carpool Tuesday morning in case he gets the idea to wait by your car to talk to you."

"No, I'll drive myself," I said. "I don't want him to know where you live, and I can probably spot him before you do. But yes, I would rather stay someplace where he can't find me until we figure out the house. Kathy, he was serious. He really believes that shapeshifters are not real people."

Her face clouded, and Paul took her hand.

"We knew that we would face this kind of prejudice," he said. "No matter how careful we were, people in groups like the Mystery Seekers were going to eventually find us the way they did Sam."

"At least *they've* settled down now," I said. "Nothing for them to prove anymore."

"Hon, it's almost midnight...no, it's past midnight," said Kathy, rising to take the cups to the kitchen. "We all need some sleep, you most of all. I'll tell the right people the right things tomorrow, don't worry. You get some rest. We'll sort this out more in the next few days. Your brothers will be a big help, too. Off you go now."

I rose and followed John up to the guest room, feeling totally drained. After retrieving my oversized tee shirt and my toiletries, I went to the bathroom to brush my teeth and get ready to sleep. When I got back, John had drawn back the covers for me, and I climbed under them gratefully. He stood awkwardly by the bed, seeming undecided as to whether to join me.

"Oh, just get in," I said, grinning. "If you're planning to share a room with me, you should at least get used to sleeping next to me. Unless you're going to curl up on the floor as a wolf for some undetermined period of time."

"I don't really have pajamas," he said. "I usually sleep nude."

"You could sleep in your underwear and a tee shirt if you are too weirded out," I said, yawning. "Nothing else is going to happen tonight other than sleep, unless you count me falling apart sometime during the night, which is possible given how shitty I feel right now."

John hesitated a moment longer, then he unbuttoned his jeans, gingerly stepping out of them. I flipped back the covers on his side of the bed, and he got in, quickly pulling the blankets back up.

"There," I said, turning out the light by my side. "Sleep."

I could tell from the tension in his posture how carefully he was holding himself away from me. After a few minutes of listening to him barely breathe, I rolled over, peering through the darkness.

"John," I said. "You have two choices. You can either relax, or I'M going to become a wolf, and sleep on the floor so you can rest. You still have to work tomorrow."

"It's just," he began, then paused. "I'm afraid to do the wrong thing, you know? I don't want you to wake up and find that I've moved too close or something. Being in wolf form is one thing. Being human is another."

"Okay," I said, purposefully moving closer to him. "Let's fix that. Move your arm out of the way...there."

I cuddled up next to him before he registered what I had done. My head was nestled against his shoulder, and my right arm was resting lightly on his chest.

"Now hold me, silly," I said, closing my eyes and relaxing into his warmth.

I felt him hesitantly place his arm around my shoulders as if afraid I would break, and his other hand stole up to hold mine. Gradually, I heard the frantic hammering of his heart begin to slow, and he held me a little tighter until he drifted off. I fell asleep soon after he did; surprisingly, or maybe not, I didn't wake the rest of the night.

9
MOVING DAY

Morning dawned, pale and grim, and I woke to the sound of people moving around downstairs and the smell of coffee. John and I had moved apart over the course of the night, and I peered at him as he slept. It was the first morning we had woken up together as human beings, and as I stared down at him, I smiled at how peaceful he seemed. I checked the time on my phone – 6:00 am – and found there were at least five more messages from Rich. I got up, put on my pants and slippers, and walked downstairs to talk to Paul and Kathy.

Both of my friends seemed a little tired from the night before. Kathy smiled reassuringly, and I took a proffered cup of fresh-brewed coffee from Paul just as John wandered downstairs. He was dressed in sweats and sat down at the table to have coffee with the rest of us.

"I'll be leaving soon," said Kathy, "but Paul will be here for a little while more. John, the morning commute is a bit rough from here to the university, so you'll also need to set out in the near future."

"I know," he said, yawning and grabbing a bagel. "I wish I could take the day off, too, but I already pulled the cough-hack-sick card last week. I'll be back right after work, though, and you can text me if things get hairy. Pun intended."

"Ha ha. Don't worry. My brothers will be with me," I said, "and I can guarantee that Rich will be at the office today. That huge presentation that he had to finish last weekend has to be shown to the company bosses this morning."

Kathy got up and put her dishes on the side of the sink.

"I'm going to go get dressed," she said. "There is a spare key under the toad statue in the garden if we're not here when you get back."

"I have a fairly easy schedule, so I can be around later in case you need me," said Paul, also rising. "I'll hold the fort for you all."

Kathy and Paul left the room, and I took my own bagel, spreading it liberally with cream cheese. I chewed thoughtfully for a time, trying to kick my brain into gear and feeling pretty numb from the fight. I was not ready to listen to the voice messages that had been still appearing on my phone.

John finished his food a few minutes later and rose, clearing his dishes and trotting upstairs. I heard the shower running, and in a short amount of time, he came down looking a lot more awake.

"I'm going to stop at home tonight before I come here," he said. "I need a few changes of clothes and to let my parents know that I've found a place to live. Who knows? Maybe they'll actually be happy about it."

He fetched his coat and came over to me.

"Are you okay with a kiss?" he said.

I held up one finger so I could chew and swallow the last bite of the bagel.

"Timing," I said, standing to kiss him goodbye. His smile when I pulled back was radiant.

"Text me if you need me," he said and left.

Alone for the first time in days, I went back upstairs, showered, and got dressed. Both Kathy and Paul were gone when I came down, and I drove to a grocery store near my uncle's to get as many boxes as I could. Not as good as a liquor store, I mused, but at 7:30 in the morning, it was the best I could do.

After dropping off the boxes in the garage, I puttered around Andrew's rather bland condo for a while, then went to my bank when it opened at 9 a.m. to arrange the cashier's check. I made it back by quarter to ten. Andrew wasn't there often, and while he had a housekeeper to make the place tidy and stock it if he needed to stay in town, the place felt barren. It was warm, though, and I sat down on the couch to wait.

I must have fallen asleep because the next thing I knew, my brothers had arrived, making enough of a racket to wake the dead. David and Stephen had brought their vans, which I assured them would have plenty enough space for my things. Mark, bless him, had pillaged another grocery store for a bunch more boxes. Bobby had ridden over with Mark and was full of questions. I told them I'd treat them to lunch when we were done, and with my car in the lead, we drove to Rich's apartment. I was still tense as we entered, but it was unoccupied. We set to work.

Moving my beloved plants was the most time consuming by far. Everything else could be thrown into trash bags or placed in boxes, but the plants required a warm car and some, like the *Ficus lyrata*, had reached pretty epic proportions. Stephen's van was designated the plant transport. There was no organized plan of attack, and I went through every room, pulling my stuff out and handing it to one of the boys to pack. Finally, I was certain I had found everything, even some items in the downstairs storage unit I had forgotten about. My eyes fell on the hideous landscape of my beloved Godzilla painting. *Screw it*, I thought, taking it from the wall and handing it to Bobby. He peered at it with a raised eyebrow, but otherwise did not comment.

I glanced around the apartment that had been my home for the last six years, feeling empty and hurt. I had been happy here, and my life had felt pretty much complete - until last week, when everything changed. With a giant sigh, I gave Cecil a farewell pat, which he ignored completely, and put the keys to both storage and apartment on the kitchen counter. I twisted the lock and shut the door behind me for the last time. It was shortly after 1:00.

I texted John that everything was all right before we drove back to my uncle's to stash the boxes in his garage and the plants in the living room. On our way, I called Andrew to let him know my plan, and he told me he'd meet me back at the condo. My brothers had filled him in, but he wanted to get the whole story. He also advised me to call my mother, which I did.

"John is safe?" she asked.

"Yes, he went to work this morning. There is no reason for Rich to actually believe he is a shapeshifter; he was just being an ass."

"All right," she said. "These comments of his are concerning, though. I am going to contact a few other clan leaders and let them know what happened and what was said. In particular, I think I might call Susan Winston."

"Sam Winston's mother?" I asked. "You know her?"

"By reputation, yes. I have her number for emergencies, but you know how reclusive some of the clans tend to be. I think it's time we connect."

She let me go, bidding me to say hi to John, and I hung up feeling relieved. The fact that my mother knew some of the other important people in our world made me feel just a little bit better. It was no longer just our clan and our issue. This was bigger than only one family.

The rest of the way, I listened to the voice messages Rich had left me. He was apologetic but still completely puzzled as to why the comments about shapeshifters had upset me so much. There were a few more along the same vein, then the last one was from Tanya. It had come in while I was listening to the others, and she simply said that she had heard and would I call her? It was still a few minutes until we arrived at the condo, so I did.

"Oh my god, Sasha! What did you do? Rich called all of us and told us that you walked out! Are you back? Are you going back? What happened?"

"It's a long story," I began. "I'm going to be busy for a little while yet. Will you be free later?"

"I'm off work at four," she said. "I can meet you somewhere near the school."

"I called out today," I said. "Why don't we go to the little coffee place near your apartment. What's it called?"

"Ampersand?"

"Yes, there, and then we'll talk for a bit."

"Sounds good," said Tanya. "I'll see you around 4:30?"

"Sure," I said. "See you then."

When I arrived at Andrew's, he was already there, along with his office assistant, Dan. While my brothers moved my boxes and bags into the garage, Andrew led me up to the kitchen and pulled a sheaf of papers from his briefcase.

"You can thank this young man for diligently working on New Year's Day and making sure that all of the papers for the house are in order. You have to sign a few things, including the deed and the house insurance binder, all of which I have here, and by Friday, the house will be in your name. Lawyers," he said, rolling his eyes, "are the slowest people on the planet."

I signed everything in triplicate, then filled out the paperwork my father had sent along for the loan. When I was done, I handed Andrew the cashier's check I had procured at my bank; it was the cost of the house, minus the $20,000 my father had built in for furniture, and Andrew agreed that we'd still meet Wednesday night as planned to go view the house.

As the plants began to proliferate in the living room, he chuckled under his breath.

"You brought a whole jungle with you," he said, shaking his head. "Just make sure not to bring in anything that might eat the housekeeper."

He hugged me goodbye, and when he and Dan left, I went to help the boys finish the greenery assault on my uncle's bay window. If nothing else, if Rich drove by, he would assume I was here. I left the living room light on and took my brothers out to lunch. They had earned it.

Over beer and pizza, the guys cheered themselves at the awesome ease of the move. In reality, it had been the fastest I had ever relocated anywhere, and I decided that when the boxes and bags needed to make their way over to the new house, I might hire a moving company to make it in one trip. The plants I would take myself.

"You said you were staying with your teacher friend, right?" asked David. "Is John staying there too?"

"Yes," I said. "Kathy took us both in. I think she figures we are safer with them."

"Probably right," said Stephen. "Staying at the condo is not the wisest move, though I think if you threw the barrel cactus that almost impaled me at Rich, he'd be out of your hair for some time. Possibly for good. Those thorns are sharp!"

We all laughed and, between us, we managed to consume four large pizzas and three pitchers of beer before the boys declared themselves full. Then we sat around and chatted for a while before finally settling up the check to call it a day.

"Hey," said Bobby, giving me a hug, "call us if you need anything, okay? Or if you need "manly men" help to move things."

"Okay, tell me if you find some, and I'll let you know!" I said, as I opened the door to my car.

All of them groaned, and Mark gave me a high five for getting a good dig in on Bobby. Bobby stuck his tongue out at me, I punched him in the shoulder, and we went our separate ways.

10
ANCIENT HISTORY

I made it to Ampersand with ten minutes to spare and ordered a double latte, paid for it, and took myself to find a suitably secluded booth. Tanya came in a few minutes later, spied me, and waved as she ordered her drink. She walked over, cradling her coffee in her hands to warm them. I couldn't blame her. The air felt like snow again, but the forecast claimed that we were not likely to get any for a few days at least. With my luck, we'd get three feet all at once, and I'd have to dig a tunnel to move into the new house.

"So what happened?" she gushed. "I heard his side; tell me yours!"

I did, with as much detail as I could recall, and Tanya's eyes got wider as I described in what terms he defined the shapeshifters. She cheered me for leaving when I did and applauded my swift decision to move out.

"Bravo!" she said. "You never did seem to fit with him anyway. So what now? Where will you go?"

"I have a line on a place," I said. "I'm staying with a colleague until things get finalized. Rich knows where my uncle lives, and I want to avoid him for now until things settle down."

"I don't blame you," she said. "I guess when he called Todd the other night, he was kind of crazed. Jennifer texted to tell me about it. She said she could hear Rich freaking out on the other side of the phone. I'm sure I'll get a call from her as soon as he finds out you're gone."

"Probably," I said, sipping my latte. "In any event, it's done."

"Yeah," said Tanya. She paused for a few moments, then whispered, "Look, I know what you are. I'm totally okay with it, and I won't tell. Your people and my people coexisted for thousands of years, way better than my people and the Europeans. We've been friends for years now. Please trust me."

I gave her a quizzical glance, neither admitting or denying what she said. She sighed.

"Remember when you met my grandmama last year, the one from the Rez? Our family follows the old ways, and she knew you for what you were. She said that you were an ally to her tribe. My grandmama is very gifted in the ways of Spirit, and they told her what you are. You can deny it, and I won't push. But I want you to know I'm pretty well done with that crew after yesterday's debacle, so you can be sure I won't go running to them with anything you tell me."

"If I was," I said slowly, "what then?"

"Aside from a million questions?" asked Tanya. "Probably just keep going out shopping the way we have been, getting coffee together, and beating you at *Mario Kart*."

"Hey, lady! I beat you!" I retorted.

"Occasionally," she laughed. "Very occasionally."

My gut, which was very wise, said to be cautious even though I generally trusted Tanya. It wasn't that I thought she would betray me on purpose. She was just prone to talking too much when she was nervous. I was going to have to test the waters before taking the full plunge. But I wanted to. I liked Tanya and desired to keep her as a friend.

"So what exactly did your grandmother's spirits say I was?" I asked casually.

"She said that the spirits called you 'the wolf that walks on two legs.' It's kind of a long name for a werewolf, though."

I almost snorted my coffee, I laughed so hard. Setting the cup down, I had to take myself in hand before I could answer her.

"Did she use the word werewolf?" I finally managed.

"No, no," she smiled. "That's more my translation."

With a sigh, I picked my cup up again and said, "Ask."

"Ask...you?"

"Yes," I said, staring her straight in the eyes. "Ask."

"Oh," she said and went completely silent for a long minute, dropping her gaze to her coffee.

I had seen this before, of course, when one of the family members brought a human friend or spouse to the House for the first time. When suddenly confronted with the unknown, even when anticipated, there was too much jumbled in the mind to sort it all out. Often, and I could bet that this was the case with Tanya, there was a fear of offending the other person or people by saying the wrong thing.

"I'm still me, Tanya," I said softly. "Still the same person you've known for six years. I'll do my best to answer you straight."

A sudden noise distracted us as a pack of boisterous teenagers rushed through the door, all elbows and shouting. Five of them piled their coats and bags at the table right next to us, then ran over to order coffee. Tanya and I gave each other a knowing look. There would be no way to talk privately with that crew right next to us, though they would probably make so much noise, they'd likely never hear us. Still...

"Do you want to go and sit in my car?" I said. "It'll be quieter."

"I think that's an excellent idea," said Tanya.

We gathered our things and went out to where I'd parked. There were still a few items in it from the apartment, but I was able to make enough room in the front seat for Tanya to get in. I turned on the car and cranked the heat up, letting the engine do its thing. The motor was still pretty warm, so heat began to spill out of the vents almost immediately.

"Okay," I said. "You may fire when you are ready, Gridley."

"What?"

"I don't actually know," I admitted. "It's one of my dad's sayings. Something from the Spanish-American War in the late 1800s, I think. He is always quoting random things he's read about or seen in movies."

"Parents are weird," she said, wrinkling her nose and taking a sip of her coffee.

"You have no idea," I said half to myself. "Basically, I meant just ask your questions when you are ready."

"Promise you won't take offense?"

"I will do my best not to," I said.

"So what exactly are shapeshifters?"

I sighed.

"That's a complicated question that I have never gotten the best answer to because no one kept records back then. We have oral traditions, but much like those of the Greeks and Norse, a lot of the stories tend to take on fantastical properties and become jumbled. Volcanic eruptions with lightning in the clouds from the friction of particles became Zeus and Hephaestus having an all-out battle. Some things were just lost in the mists of time.

"To the best of our knowledge, there was a council of the animals who came together from all over the world to discuss a new type of creature - humans - that was worrying them a lot. This animal was a tool user, which was fine, but then they discovered how to make and use fire. Fire is what the animals feared more than anything else. And these creatures were breeding pretty quickly! No one said "like rabbits" because that would have been unfair to the rabbits, and the humans didn't breed *that* fast, but it was definitely enough to warrant concern."

I closed my eyes as I warmed to the tale.

"The other problem was that these creatures didn't hear the complaints of the rest of the animals. They had their own language and refused to listen to the words of the birds whose nests were threatened or the fish whose rivers could be clogged with ash, or the bears whose cubs might smother in their dens. They pretended that they couldn't hear the animals at all, and this had become a problem. Some clans stated that if they were just confined to this one area in what we now call Africa, they would not likely spread too much further. One of the oldest animals, an elephant I think, laughed bitterly and said that they had just moved into his valley and were already letting their fires get out of control. He said, 'They are not going to stop there either. They are resourceful and will someday be all over the earth, you wait and see!'

"The other animals who had witnessed the kinds of human expansion that the elephant had nodded in agreement. They, too, had seen the destruction left in the wake of untended fires. Killing all the humans was wrong because the humans were animals, too, and had as much a right to live as the next creature. But there needed to be a check and a balance of some sort, some way to mitigate the effects of an invasive species who just would not listen.

"The wisest of the animals was a sun bear, or so it is said. He was very old, and he had an idea that he felt might work. If the council appealed to the Spirit of All to give them the power to talk to the humans about their pitiful fire management skills, then they might be able to slow or stop some of the destruction. The council agreed, and they and their families went to a great valley in which the sun bear made his appeal to a tiny blade of grass, for all blades of grass are connected directly to the All and therefore all grass has the ear of the All.

"The Spirit listened, for it was compassionate and understood that the animals had valid fears. It spoke back to the sun bear, offering to give the members of the council the same form and the same language as the humans. The animals stated that they still wanted to be animals and not just become another type of human because they were concerned they would lose their connection to the land as well. Then the Spirit of All suggested a compromise and gave those animals, and the members of their families who wanted to, the power to be both. Animals from all corners of the earth – mammal, bird, reptile, amphibian, and even a few fish – were granted the ability to take the form of human beings in order to interact with them and teach them how to live responsibly.

"There was one condition, though. These animals must live in peace with the humans and try to teach them their ways. No matter what, the transformed animals must never go into all-out war with the humans. There could be disagreements and animosity, there might even be deaths from time to time, but never could those families who made the pact with the Spirit of All come together as one to attack humans, else they would lose their gifts for all time.

"Gradually, many of the Changed Ones, as they came to be known among the rest of the animals, merged within the societies of men, and they did their best to mitigate major problems that arose. They had some of their best successes with the Native American populations as well as other tribes around the world who connected deeply with the earth. Over the course of many generations, the animals who could become people continued the work of their ancestors who once sought to curtail the irresponsible use of fire."

I stopped, opened my eyes, and looked at Tanya's open-mouthed expression. The story was probably more mythology than reality, but Nevermore had often told me how the kernels of truth were always there. She had done extensive research on our origins and, other than the old myth, one which *every shapeshifter clan all over the world shared*, our origins were still pretty mysterious.

"Wow," Tanya finally said. "That is an amazing story. How true is it?"

"Every shapeshifter clan knows it," I said. "My friend Nevermore has looked into it and, aside from that myth, we don't have any deeply-rooted histories. The fact that the disparate clans all tell the same story, however, gives it a bit more validity in our minds."

"My peoples..." she said. "Then it is true? Your being a shapeshifter?"

"Yes," I said. "And before you ask, there are other humans who know, people we trust. Some are our spouses, some are our friends and allies. Rich was completely wrong; there is nothing different between you and me physically when I am human."

"That sounds so weird."

"I know," I said. "Trust me. So...outside of my extended family, you are the only human that knows what I am. That means that you have to promise that none of this will pass your lips."

"I swear!" she said, earnestly. "Only..."

"What?"

"Can we still hang out?" she asked in a rush. "I mean, I can't really hang out with the others anymore. I mean, I can, but I don't want to. They have really been so negative lately and given what my cousin told me and now you...I just can't stomach them."

"What about Jennifer?" I asked.

"Well, yeah, Jenn is fine when she's not with Todd, but when she is...phew! She's just as bad. It's like she has to impress him or something with how cool she is."

"Yeah, I've seen that," I said, thoughtfully. "Of course we can still hang out. And when I get settled, maybe you can come over and see my new place."

"One other thing? Can I tell my grandmama she was right?" said Tanya. "She's visiting my cousin right now, and she doesn't have a phone at her home."

I glanced at my watch. It was getting on towards 5:15, and almost as if I were prescient, John called.

I nodded to Tanya and answered the call.

"Hey," I said. "What's up?"

"Hi," he said, tersely. "It's been a day. I caught hell for calling out twice, but I promised I'd make up the work next week. I did get your text, though, and I'm glad you're out of there. I'm on my way over to my parents' house to talk to them. Do you want to meet for dinner around 7:00 somewhere? I don't want to inconvenience Kathy tonight by being late. I already texted her."

"Sure," I said, as Tanya watched me. "How about The Mountain Sun Pub?"

"Sounds great," he said. "I'll want a beer by then."

"Okay, I'll see you there," I said. "Take care and best of luck."

"Thanks," he said. "I'll need it."

I hung up and turned to Tanya.

"Friend of mine," I said, putting the phone away. "Had a rough day."

"Oh," she said. She paused a second, then asked, "Another shapeshifter?"

"Yeah," I said. "I do have a few friends who are shapeshifters. We're looking into finding a place together."

"Well, that will make it cheaper," she said. "My roommate and I split things pretty evenly, and it's a lot easier to survive that way."

"Hmm," I said. "Tanya, is it possible for you to call your grandmother where she is now?"

"I can tell her in person when I...wait! Do you want to see her? Oh, she'd be thrilled! My cousin's apartment is only twenty minutes from here."

"I would like that," I said, "and I have time. You want to go get in your car, and I'll follow you?"

"Yes!" exclaimed Tanya, opening the door and almost bouncing out of the seat. "Come on!"

I waited for her to pull out of her parking spot, and then followed her car onto the main road. On the way, I called Nevermore and told her where I was going. She was cautiously in favor of the idea and agreed that if the grandmother was connected to the spirits that way, speaking to her might not be a bad thing.

"John let me know you wouldn't be home for dinner, which was nice. Tomorrow, you two need to be here, though. Paul is planning a feast!"

I agreed and told her we'd be back later. I called John and also let him know where I was going. He told me to text him the address when I got there, just in case.

A short drive through the city later, we pulled up in front of a very modern apartment building, and after texting John, I followed Tanya inside. The building was fancy enough to have an elevator, and we rode up in silence to the top floor. Walking a few steps down the hall, Tanya stopped at the first door on the right and knocked.

A young man about my age opened the door and greeted Tanya with a hug and a kiss to the cheek. I got a handshake and a cursory once over that made me wonder if Tanya had let something slip about me.

"Chuckie, this is Sasha, my friend that I told you about," said Tanya.

"Tans, how often do I need to ask you not to call me Chuckie? Seriously," he said, addressing me now, "she's called me that since we were kids. Come on in. Grandmama is in the living room."

I nodded to him as he led the way into one of the rooms right off the hall. An elderly woman with long white braids sat in a chair facing us across from a couch that otherwise dominated the room. She must have been about eighty years old, and her face was a roadmap of sepia-toned wrinkles. She was stocky in build, wore a faded blue dress, and had the most grandmotherly feel I had ever encountered. When we entered, she turned off the TV, stood, and walked slowly over to me.

"It has been a long time," she said, looking at me. "Your people have hidden themselves so well within the cities and faraway places that we never see you anymore. When I was a child, I remember meeting an old coyote-man. At first, I thought he was the trickster himself come down for a visit and a jaw, but my grandpa also talked to the spirits. He introduced me to the existence of shapeshifters. My own spirits have kept watch for your tribes for many a year, but you are the first I have met for decades. Charles, do not stare at the young lady. It is rude to do so."

Charles, not Chuckie I noted, was absolutely dumbfounded. This was the cousin who had told Tanya the story about us being allies to the tribes, but it appeared like he hadn't really believed that we existed all that much either. Make that three humans who knew, I amended mentally. They might be the good guys, but it was still a little unsettling.

"I'm sorry," he said. "It's just not every day you see a figure from myth walk through your door. You are...?"

"A wolf," I confirmed. "Yes. Your grandmother was correct, Tanya."

"Can we see?" asked Tanya, now even more enthusiastic than before in her excitement of the confirmation. She was almost bouncing.

"Tanya!" exclaimed her grandmother and cousin together. Tanya blushed to cover her embarrassment, and her cousin put his hands over his eyes in utter disbelief.

"I'm sorry," Tanya said, her voice wavering. "I didn't mean to be rude or disrespectful, honest! I just...I mean, I know what you told me and what grandmama told me and what Chuck...Charles told me, but I just really want to..."

"Grok it?" I said, using a science fiction term from Heinlein I knew she'd get.

"Yeah," she said, nodding, a tear rolling down her cheek.

I sighed and addressed her grandmother.

"For you, if you would like, I will change. So you can see again what you saw so long ago."

"I would like that very much," she said, smiling, her eyes all but disappearing into the wrinkles.

"Bathroom?" I said, turning to the cousin.

He pointed further down the hall, and I walked out of the living room, conscious of their eyes on me. In for a dime, I thought, and went into the small white-tiled room, quickly undressed, and folded my clothes in a pile on the edge of the tub. I changed, then nosed the door open enough to get through, walking as calmly as I could back to where they waited, my heart beating like a triphammer.

Tanya was talking to her cousin, her back to me when I came in. Charles saw me, though; he froze, and his reaction caused Tanya to turn. She gasped when she saw me but moved aside a little when I walked over to her grandmother.

"You honor me," said the old woman, tears forming in her eyes. She reached out a gnarled hand, and I let her stroke the fur on my neck, running her fingers through the coarse guard hairs to the soft undercoat beneath. She was speaking in a language I did not know, but something in the rhythm told me it was a blessing or a prayer that she must have learned from an elder long ago. I stood still and let her have her moment, ignoring the quiet discussion going on behind my back.

When her grandmother had finished and removed her hand, Tanya came over closer to where I stood. Her cousin joined her, and they both knelt down on the floor, presumably to be close to my level. Tanya looked at her grandmother, who said, "Ask her."

"May I?" asked Tanya.

At my nod to her and Charles, I allowed myself to be touched. Tanya sat almost entranced as she stroked my ears, and her cousin was patting my back very gingerly. I sneezed and startled both of them but made an effort to wag my tail in the most dog-like manner possible to set them at ease. Body language, man. No wonder we couldn't communicate with primitive humans. They were not great at reading simple shifts of ears or nose even now with centuries of dogs living with them; we had to go all out.

Finally, I'd had my fill. I inclined my head to Tanya's grandmother and trotted out of the room. Once clothed, I made my entrance again and sat down on one side of the couch. Charles stood by the door, a bit stunned, and Tanya sat on the complete opposite end of the couch. She wasn't afraid; I could instinctively tell that much. Rather, she seemed to feel as if she was in the presence of some foreign dignitary who she had just recognized for the first time. Her giddiness from earlier was totally subdued. Her grandmother bowed to me.

"Thank you," she said. "You have given me a gift. You have made a life-long wish come true. I saw the coyote-man become his true self only as he left, never to return. My grandchildren will repay you for me at some point. The kind of help you may need in the struggle to come is not such as I can repay any longer."

Tanya nodded, and Charles said softly, "We've got your back. We'll let the tribe know that their help may be needed as well. They are very traditional and will listen to Grandmama. We will help where we can."

"Thank you," I said.

He smiled. "It isn't every day that a being from legend walks through your door."

"You have my word," said Tanya. "My absolute word. I mean, I believed you, but well, seeing you as a wolf kind of nailed it for me. No wonder people are so shaken about you all existing. It's awe-inspiring, but kind of terrifying at the same time, you know?"

"Great," I said, rolling my eyes. "Now I'm terrifying."

"I mean, not really terrifying-terrifying, just..."

"Can you dig your grave any deeper?" chuckled Charles. "She gets what you meant."

I looked at my watch. Six-thirty already. Shit. I was going to be late.

"Respectfully, I have to go," I said. "Tanya, we can talk tomorrow if you like. I'm free after work, but I do have plans with another friend for some sort of home-made dinner. Grandmama, it was a pleasure to see you."

"My pleasure as well," she said, smiling wrinkles once more. "Be safe. We will not meet in this life again, but this one," she nodded to Tanya, "will be your guide, and this one," she pointed to Charles, "will be your shield."

Charles gave me a friendly smile, and Tanya walked me to the door.

"She's going to want me to stay," she said. "Grandmama has been telling me that I would be the next spirit-talker, but I never believed her. I guess I do now."

"Faith goes a long way for success," I said, winking.

"Thank you for today," said Tanya. "For everything. This made my grandmama happier than she has been in years. This meant the world to her...and to me too."

I gave her a hug goodbye and went back down the elevator, wondering what I had just unleashed in my friend's life. It felt stupidly good to have allies, I thought, and hurried out to my car to go meet John.

11
FUTURE DAYS

When I got to the restaurant, John was already there and had claimed a table for us towards the back. He waved me over and greeted me with a hug, then we sat down and figured out food. Both of us were starving.

Once the waiter had taken the order and the menus, John sighed.

"Were they awful?" I asked.

"No," he said. "They weren't awful. I was right; they are okay I'm moving out. They did ask me if I was moving in with a guy or a girl. I said a girl, which seemed to make things better and worse. I didn't tell them who. They obviously think I'm making a bad decision, but at least they don't think I'm gay. Great trade off, right?"

"I'm sorry," I said. "How long will it take you to get everything moved out?"

"I don't know," said John. "A week or so maybe? I don't want to get you involved just yet. They already think our friendship is strange enough."

"Yeah, I know. Me, the evil teacher trying to seduce my student. Bwa ha ha!"

"Something like that," he said. "How did your day go? How was Tanya's grandmother?"

"Oh, that was all kinds of weird," I said. "She knew what I was right off, and I did something I've never done before; I brought my wolf to her. Tanya and her cousin saw, of course, but it was almost a religious experience for all of them. It was uncomfortable and humbling at the same time."

"Tanya saw you? As you?" he asked incredulously.

Our drinks arrived then, and I made a production of putting my cream into my coffee to cover my confusion.

"Yes. It was only because her grandmother's greatest wish was to see one of us again before she died. Tanya and her cousin were surprised when I did. Her grandmother sang a prayer of some sort, and the three of them were suddenly adamant that they help me as much as they could. It was very strange. I need to ask Tanya more about it when I talk to her tomorrow."

"What does all of it mean?" asked John, picking up his own coffee to sip at it. "I mean, you told me that Tanya's grandmother already knew what you were, why now?"

"Given the state of things, perhaps there is something they will be able to do that we can't," I said.

"Maybe," said John.

Our food arrived, and we tucked in without hesitation. After a few minutes of concentrated munching, John glanced over at me, a slightly perplexed expression on his face.

"You know," he said. "We need to figure out a few things too. When you came in, I didn't know if I could kiss you. I mean, can I just kiss you? I am so out of my league with everything going on right now. Just our relationship alone seems complicated. Toss everything else on top of it, and there is so much confusion."

"Yeah," I said. "Why don't we go for a drive before we head back to Nevermore's house? We can take my car and leave yours here. Maybe go peek at the house; it's not too far from here and talk on the way there and back?"

"That sounds good," he agreed.

I paid the check in cash, and the two of us got into my car, heading for Idylwild Court. The streets were still plenty busy at eight o' clock at night, and we made our way along at a rather sedate pace.

"So what are we?" asked John after we'd gotten onto the major road. "I know what our wolf sides have decided, but how does that translate? Are we dating? Lovers? What?"

I sighed.

"You know how you told me on the ride to my folks' how so much had happened recently that you couldn't figure out which side is up? That's how I feel too. I just ended a six year relationship yesterday. I mean, it had to be ended, but it still stings. I want to make a clean break, though, and I haven't even looked at my phone this evening to see if he called when he came home to find all traces of me gone.

"So, yeah, I'm dealing with that. But there's also you, and this weekend brought it sharply home that you and I work so well together that our wolf sides have already bonded. Wolves mate for life, you know. There's nothing magic about that, and even though you had no idea what you were until last week, your wolf side knows all of these things instinctively."

We turned down Idylwild Court and pulled up in front of 6809, our soon-to-be home. Like the other houses on the street, it was fairly modern but had some old-fashioned touches to it like the white picket fence and the pillared porch with an entrance at the front right corner. Gingerbread trim scrawled along the porches, and a light burned somewhere deep in the house, giving it a welcoming feel. I put the car in park and turned to John.

"Beyond that, I want to be with you. Me, the people me. I want you, John. I want to live in this house, maybe have children, and grow old together. So when you ask if you can kiss me without asking, the answer is yes. Even your being nervous about sleeping in the bed together is amazingly sweet and endearing to me. All I ask is that we take this slowly. I'm just going to need a little time for this all to make sense. In answer to your question, yes, we are together, and it will become whatever it becomes."

His sweet smile blossomed in the late light, and his eyes spoke volumes. I smiled shyly back, and then we turned to look at the house.

"So," I said, "what do you think?"

"I can't believe that we're going to live here," he said, peering up at the peaked roof. "I've never lived anywhere like this."

"Well, it will be ours in a matter of days," I said. "I mean, some of the paperwork will take a week or so to clear, but we can start to move in on Thursday. We'll do the walk through with Andrew on Wednesday."

He smiled at me then and leaned over to kiss me.

"The house is wonderful," he said, "but honestly, I'd live in a shack if I could just be with you. I'll give you whatever time you need, and I'll be happy to grow old with you. I've never thought about having kids, but I'm not opposed to it. I just never thought I would find someone to have them with."

That thought made me sad. How many people had overlooked John because he wasn't the handsomest or because he was into anime? How many women never saw past the awkward exterior. I was so stupidly glad that I had talked to him his senior year, and that we'd had years to build our friendship based on interests rather than superficial things. I blinked back tears.

John peered at me in the fading light, concerned.

"Are you alright?" he said.

"Yeah, it's been an emotional day, and I'm just overwhelmed by everything that has happened." I said, driving around the end of the cul-de-sac and heading back to Mountain Sun to get John's car.

"I was thinking," said John as we drove onto the main thoroughfare. "We are both wolves, so this all worked out pretty well. What happens if two different shapeshifters fall in love? It must happen from time to time."

"It does. Sometimes, they don't even know each other is a shapeshifter at first. They usually figure it out pretty quickly, though. I had a great aunt who was a Stellar's Jay, and my great uncle, a wolf obviously, loved her to pieces. They had a few children together too. The children are either one or the other – no winged wolves flying about, I'm afraid, though the jokes about it on that side of the family are still thrown around when the cousins get together. They are a rowdy bunch, but really fun."

"I'd like to meet them," he said.

"It's inevitable that you will," I said. "They usually come to the family parties, but this year, the weather in New England was awful, so they had to bow out. They got hit with all our snow, apparently."

"That reminds me. There's a big storm coming in at the end of next weekend," said John. "I heard on the news earlier that the pattern is finally breaking. We're going to get slammed."

"Fun," I snorted. "Well, I guess we'll have to get as moved in as we can before then. I like the idea of being snowed in together for the first time. That should be fun. Add shovels to the list."

The rest of the drive back to the restaurant and then to Kathy's was uneventful. I called my mother to update her as to how the day had gone; she sounded relieved that I was out of Rich's apartment, but the incident with Tanya's grandmother made her pause.

"I'll have to do some more research into the family's connections to the tribes in the area," she said. "It might well be that we have standing agreements with some of the tribal holy men. Hmmm."

We finished our conversation and I hung up, then checked my voicemail. There were more than ten voice messages, all from Rich, ranging from somewhat normal around noontime to all out panic and then fury by dinnertime. His last one, from about ten minutes before, was somewhat calmer and asked if we could at least meet at the Dunkin' Donuts near my work the next afternoon. I replied to none of the messages and erased them all.

Somehow, I beat John to Nevermore's house, and she let me in with a grin.

"Frank was so startled when I told him why you'd called out that he nearly dropped his coffee cup this morning. He was genuinely concerned, though, bless him, and said that if you wanted more time off, he'd make sure that there were no problems with the head office."

"No," I said, taking off my coat. "I need to get back on the horse, so to speak."

I was telling her about the move when a knock came at the door. Kathy went to open it, and John walked in carrying a bag with what looked like subs in it.

"I figured that neither of us thought about lunch tomorrow, so I stopped on the way over and got us each one. Italian or turkey, your choice. They both have pickles and tomatoes on them."

"You hate tomatoes," I said, accepting the bag so he could take his coat off.

"Yeah, but you don't. I can just pick them off."

"How sweet of you, John!" said Kathy, taking the bag from me and putting it in the fridge. "I hate to be an old lady, but it's been a long day. I need to get some rest. You do too, Sasha. You seem completely wiped."

"It has been a day," I acknowledged.

Kathy bade us goodnight as we trooped upstairs. John and I made our evening toiletries and climbed into the bed, John somewhat more at ease with the situation than the previous night. He still wore underwear and a tee shirt, but at least he wasn't pretending he was a stone statue anymore. We lay awake talking for a long while, and when we did turn out the lights, I fell asleep nestled in the crook of his arm once again.

12

SHOWDOWN

In some ways, going back to school was a blessing. I got in early and was ready when the first period students arrived. They were glad to see me and somehow, in that mysterious way that kids have, they all knew about the breakup. They were sleepy at that hour, but gave me condolences. My Honors Bio class was next, and they rushed in, surrounding me with sympathy and reassurances that I was wonderful and would find a much better boyfriend soon. They regaled me with their Christmas break stories and, by the time their class was over, I was on a much, much more even keel for the first time in days.

Third block was my prep period, and once in the science staff room, I found myself being handed chocolate by the chemistry teacher, Darlene, who reminded me that the molecules in chocolate were similar to serotonin and would help my emotions if not my waistline. We all chuckled at that. Mike, one of the physical science teachers, related a story of his class trying to make ice cream with the ice and salt shaking method which ended with a bag explosion and a student covered with half-formed ice cream and chocolate syrup. Each of my colleagues had something sympathetic to say, which was one reason I loved my department.

Fourth block was my lower level biology students, and they could be difficult. On this occasion, however, they were angels. They had also heard the news, and even the tough kids were nodding saying things like, "Yeah, man, we've been there." We accomplished a fairly substantial discussion on DNA, and I could tell that they were really trying to get into the information for my sake. I told them they rocked as they left for the afternoon and then quietly sank into my chair for a few long moments after the last of them had left.

Kathy came up to find me a few minutes later.

"Why don't you come home," she said. "We can grade some small things and just relax for a while. It's actually nice having you at the house. Were you and John going to go furniture shopping tonight after dinner?"

"Tomorrow," I said. "We wanted to see the layout of the house first, although from the pictures Andrew sent, we can at least buy a few things like the bed and a table, some pots and pans, dishes...I guess we might go out tonight to get a few things. I dunno. I haven't talked to John yet other than a quick lunch text."

"Or you could just rest tonight," laughed Kathy. "You're going in circles. When was the last time you unwound?"

"I suppose we could do some online browsing so we have a better idea when we get there tomorrow," I said. "Depends on how we feel. Tonight won't be a late night in any event."

Kathy walked over to my window and peered through the cacti lining the sill. She froze and motioned me over. "Is that Rich out by your car?"

I joined her. Sure enough, Rich was standing by the hood, looking from the building to his watch with undisguised impatience. Damn it. He had hinted in his texts about meeting me today, and I hadn't responded. Apparently, he'd decided to take matters into his own hands. Kathy and I moved away from the window, and I grabbed my coat and bags from the chair.

"I don't want him to see you with me," I said. "He only knows about you, not what you look like."

"What are you going to do?" she asked.

I grinned the most evil grin I could.

"I am going to go talk to Ahnold."

Kathy literally cawed in laughter.

"I've got to witness this first hand," she said. "I'll come out after the fireworks start. Let me gather my things and some other supporters. This is going to be priceless!"

Rickard Jones was one of the gym teachers and wrestling coach, and he had made no bones about the fact that if we ladies ever needed him to discourage someone from bothering us, he would be more than happy to intervene on our behalf. Ahnold, as we affectionately called him, was a well-educated and completely wonderful Southern gentleman. He had won multiple weightlifting competitions, for which he still trained, and his girlfriend, the school nurse, Zoe Hill, was the tiniest little slip of a thing. We all adored him for his intelligence and his dedication to making even the least athletic kid try their best. John had loved him, I recalled with a smile.

We walked down to the English wing, and along the way, Kathy poked her head into her friend Rachel's room. Rachel's Southern Alabama accent echoed along the hallway as she laughed.

"Whoo, boy," she cried. "This I gotta see!"

Rachel came out of her room with her own coat and bags in hand. She was a tall, stately black woman with a piercing gaze and no end of compassion for her students – and no patience for excuses, either. I knew that Nevermore had told her all about the breakup with Rich, leaving out none of the scathing commentaries, and I had been informed of Rachel's rather dark comments about her family's forty acre farm where a body would never be found.

Rachel's yell had caught the attention of the rest of the department, and in no time, the entire English coterie had prepared to make their exit from the building a few minutes after I sent Ahnold out. They were all chuckling at the idea, so I assumed they knew the break-up story as well. Reinforcements in hand, I headed for the gym.

Like everyone else, Ahnold had heard of my woes, and when we told him that Rich was outside, he blew the whistle, calling the wrestling practice to a halt.

"Guys, I have to go deal with a minor inconvenience for Ms. Wellington here. I'll be back in a moment or two."

Some of the kids were either past or current students of mine, and they got what Ahnold meant immediately. As we left the gym, they followed at a discrete distance, and if Ahnold noticed, he didn't say anything.

"You go out first, Ms. Wellington," he said. "I'll be out presently."

I saw Kathy leading the bevy of English teachers down the hall to the other front door at the opposite end of the building. This was going to be hysterical.

Leaving the school, I noticed one of the front desk secretaries, Sally, glance at Ahnold, then out into the parking lot. She seemed amused, and I heard her yell to the principal's secretary Tina to inform the principal as the door swung shut behind me. Oh, now the fun really *would* begin.

Rich looked up as he heard the door close and straightened as I came across the parking lot. He was dressed in his business suit, and he must have taken an extended lunch to be there when I came out. I didn't see Ahnold exit and walk over to his truck near where I was parked, but I did hear the door to the building close behind me.

As I approached, I noticed that Rich seemed like he'd seen better days. His eyes were sunken, and his hair was a bit unkempt.

"I called you," he exclaimed. "I called you Sunday night and all day yesterday, and I came home to find everything of yours taken. And the Godzilla painting? You took the Godzilla painting?"

"Yes, Rich, I took the Godzilla painting," I said, never expecting that he'd actually care about that, of all things.

"For god's sake, why?" he asked. "Why wouldn't you call me back? Why not give me a chance?"

"Rich, this has been coming for a long time," I said. "Gary's overt racism reached a point where I couldn't tolerate it. You didn't back me, and then told me I had no right to kick them out. That was the deciding factor, right there."

"Jesus, Sasha, you're leaving me over some lame-ass thing Gary said? Give me a break!"

His voice had been rising steadily, and his face started turning beet red as he took a step forward. I heard the other front door close, followed by approaching footsteps. Rich heard neither of these, and when Ahnold stepped up next to me a second later, he was taken totally by surprise.

"Ms. Wellington, is this man bothering you?"

"No, I'm..."

"Yes," I said firmly. Behind me, I heard the door by the office open again and a stream of hushed voices. "Yes, Mr. Jones, he is bothering me."

Rich stared at me incredulously.

"Sasha," he said, "we had a fight, that's all. It wasn't something to move out over. It was just a stupid fight over nothing."

"Sir," interrupted Ahnold. "I think the lady is asking you to go."

"This doesn't concern you," Rich said to him. "Go back to your weight room and leave me to talk to my girlfriend."

"Ex-girlfriend," I said to Rich. "I am your ex-girlfriend and intend to remain that way."

"Sir," said Ahnold with a tone I had heard him use with a bully once or twice when a much smaller kid had been the target. "You need to leave now. This is school property, and the lady has clearly stated that she has no desire to speak with you."

"Look, you," said Rich, trying to sound stern. "She hasn't asked me to go, so you..."

"Yes, Rich, I have. I have clearly stated that I want nothing more to do with you by moving out of your apartment. How hard is it for you to understand?"

Rich took another step in my direction, and Ahnold stood up very straight, shoulders back, and stared him down. Rich retreated the step.

"Is there a problem here?" asked a voice from behind us, and we all turned to see Principal Turner, a tall, slender, ebony-skinned man, coming towards us calm and neat in his suit jacket and tie.

Ahnold gave Mr. Turner a wink before turning back to Rich. Thomas Turner hadn't been principal as long as he had without knowing how to deal with irate ex-boyfriends, girlfriends, wives, and husbands. He had likely already called the police and was about to make Rich's life miserable. Behind him in front of the building stood the entire wrestling team in their tanks and shorts – the kids never seemed to feel the cold – the office staff, the English department, and a growing number of students and faculty who had caught word of the incident and had come to see. Ahnold would be a hero for weeks, and I would be the tragic heroine. It was priceless.

Rich paled when he saw the array of witnesses to his testimony, but doubled down.

"I just came to talk to my...Sasha...about her suddenly moving out without telling me, and this guy started harassing me."

"Is that so?" Mr. Turner said, directing his calm eyes on me, then back to Rich. "Yes, I heard something about your fight. There were some rather racist remarks, I understand."

"Oh, not you too," said Rich with disgust.

"Sir, this is city property. At this point, I must ask that you leave the premises and please do not return. I have already called the police," he went on as a siren sounded in the distance, "and if you do not leave now, I will have you forcibly removed."

Swearing under his breath, Rich turned and stormed off, followed by a few cheers from the students. Ahnold smiled at me and made to go back to the building, pretending not to notice his wrestling team racing in ahead of him. The members of the English department headed over to me, and Mr. Turner smiled wryly in my direction.

"Perhaps you would be so kind as to park in a visitor's spot near the building for the rest of the month?" he said. "Right next to my car, in fact. It would be best if we keep a closer eye on your vehicle, don't you think?"

He turned and walked away as Nevermore and the rest surrounded me, all of them talking at once. Several of the science teachers also joined in, and it was decided on the spot that I needed a drink, and they all would go along to "better protect me." Everyone headed to their cars, and we drove to Murphy's Tap House.

Occasional jaunts to get sushi or have a beer are some of the things that keep teachers sane. Usually, we do this on a Friday after a long week, but today was an exception. I was delighted when Ahnold came to join us after wrestling practice, driving up in his gleaming pick-up truck with Zoe sitting proudly in the passenger seat.

I had exchanged texts with John and told him about the experience with Rich. When he heard that Ahnold had helped get rid of Rich, John asked me to say hi. Ahnold seemed surprised when I told him.

"I had wondered what happened to John," he said, smiling at the unexpected hello. "You've been in touch with him this whole time?"

I nodded, taking a sip from my beer.

"He didn't have anything to do with your break up, did he?"

"Not really, no," I said. "Rich brought him into the conversation to be an asshole, and that ticked me off more because there was no reason to do so."

"I can see why it might have annoyed you at that," said Ahnold. "John's a smart kid and worth about ten of that Rich character."

I blinked back tears and smiled.

"Yeah," I said. "He's been really supportive."

Ahnold gave me a questioning look, but said nothing, though the corners of his mouth quirked up an infinitesimal amount before he turned back to the ongoing conversation. Nevermore caught my eye and winked.

John texted me again a little while later and asked me where I was. When I told him that I was still at the pub, he didn't answer right away, and it didn't surprise me when he suddenly appeared at my elbow. Nevermore's eyebrows went straight up into her hairline when she saw him, but it was Ahnold who rose from his seat, shook John's hand, and made space for him to join us. About half of the older teachers remembered him and welcomed him enthusiastically when they found out he had "been there when I had fallen apart at Nevermore's table" as the old bird spun it.

A few of the teachers who knew him looked at me curiously, but as I was not showing him anything other than friendship, I was pretty sure no one really gave his appearance much more than a passing thought. One of the older science teachers overheard me make an anime reference, looked at John, and snorted, returning to the conversation with the other science teachers. Nothing like a good anime reference to quench all fears of anything romantic.

Eventually, around six o' clock, we said our goodbyes, and John and I headed home to Kathy's house. Paul was just pulling a huge chicken out of the oven as we came in. Dinner was a chatty affair, and Kathy regaled Paul with the story of Rich's epic defeat by the chivalrous Ahnold and the iron fist of Thomas Turner. Paul laughed heartily throughout the whole story which Kathy, a born storyteller, recited with abundant embellishments.

"I don't think you've seen the end of him," said Paul. "You might want to carpool with Kathy tomorrow so he doesn't see your car."

"Or we can trade," said John. "I don't think he's ever seen mine."

"I think the huge anime stickers might be a giveaway," I said, chuckling. "I might ask Andrew if he has something – not a Mustang, John, don't get your hopes up! He sometimes keeps a spare vehicle for winter driving. He's already done so much for me, though. I can ask him tomorrow."

"What are your plans for this evening?" asked Kathy, rising to clear the table. "I know I'm going to grade and then watch some Netflix."

"I think we need an evening off," I said, taking my plates to the sink. "If it's all the same to you, I might just drag John off to watch anime upstairs."

"I completely understand that," said Kathy. "It sounds like exactly what you need."

13
HOUSE CONCERNS

I had completely forgotten to get in touch with Tanya that afternoon, but she texted me as I was settling in to go to sleep. We met at a bar near my uncle's office Wednesday while I waited for John to get out of work, and over the sound of the bar's television, she filled me in about what she'd heard from Rich's side of things.

According to Jennifer, who was the only one Tanya was still talking with, Rich claimed that some "gorilla" had come up to him in the school yard when he was having a civil conversation with me and attempted to intimidate him. Rich had "chosen to leave" instead of creating a scene in the parking lot. He had neglected to say anything about Thom Turner or the fact that the cops were on their way, something I told Tanya, much to her amusement. I commented that if Ahnold had really wanted to fight him, Rich would be in traction.

The other thing that got me was that Rich had told the others that he would absolutely be able to win me back, something I laughed out loud at.

"No," I said. "Absolutely not. That ship has sailed. Completely."

"He seems convinced," she said. "He also seems to believe your friend John is a shapeshifter and that you are covering for him."

"Are you kidding me?" I said. "He actually latched on to that? I thought he was just using John to get me angrier."

"Nope," she said. "He thinks that John getting sick last week had something to do with him becoming a shapeshifter, and that you know and are protecting him. He also is under the impression that John has some sort of 'magic shapeshifter hoodoo' power that he used on you to make you break up with him."

"I told him that was ptomaine poisoning," I grumbled, rolling my eyes. "John has no more 'magic hoodoo powers' than I do."

Tanya had met John and, like the rest of Rich's friends, had dismissed him as juvenile and harmless for his anime fixation. That I shared this interest never came up, apparently, because I would watch football with them. It was somewhat maddening the way they dismissed him, but I compartmentalized my life so much anyway that one more section wasn't all that hard.

"It's because John's antisocial, and Rich seems to think that's a sign," said Tanya, shaking her head and sighing.

"Huh," I said, then smiled at what I saw over her shoulder. "Well, you can ask John yourself. Here he comes."

Tanya twisted around in her seat and stared open-mouthed at John as he approached the door to the restaurant.

"He seems different somehow," Tanya remarked. "More confident maybe?"

I hadn't noticed because we had been together so much, but she was right. John stood straighter, and he did seem to be more sure of himself. His black hair was less scraggly, and he moved with a grace he had never before possessed prior to a week ago. He no longer appeared cowed by everything in the world around him. Tanya wasn't the only one who noticed this; several of the waitresses eyed him speculatively as he came in.

Once inside, he looked around for us; I waved to him, and he strode over. I scooted across the seat so he could sit next to me, and he joined us, his expression amused as Tanya continued to stare at him.

"Hey, John," she said as if she wasn't trying to dissect him with her eyes.

"Hi, Tanya," he replied a little stiffly. "How are you?"

Our waitress came over and smiled at John.

"What'll it be, hon?"

"A sixteen ounce Blue Moon," he said.

"You got it," she said. "Anything else right now, ladies?"

"Can you maybe get them to turn down the volume on the TV?" I asked.

She nodded, rolled her eyes at the bartender, and went over to speak to him. Once she left, John and I glanced at each other, and as the volume on the television dropped a few decibels, I dove in.

"Tanya was just telling me about all the insanity that Rich has been spouting. He's apparently convinced you are using 'magical powers' to lure me away from him."

John snorted. "Oh, that's funny! And it makes so much sense! Why would I possibly have been able to win you over when he's done such a great job making an ass of himself?"

"Good point!" I laughed. "I couldn't possibly like you for you! Must be magic! Give me a break!"

Tanya looked at us as we laughed, and her eyes narrowed.

"Waaaaaaiiiit," she said, slowly putting two and two together. "Is there something I should know?"

I grinned at her.

"No!" she said in astonishment. "Really? When?"

I grinned at John who shrugged at me.

"You might as well tell her," he said, taking the beer from the waitress and thanking her.

Once the waitress was gone, I told Tanya a slightly edited version of the events over the past week. It was still hard for me to wrap my mind around that one week ago, I'd found John cowering in a cardboard box next to a dumpster, terrified that he was going to turn into a ravenous monster and devour me. Things had changed so much; as I told the tale, leaving out Nevermore's real name, huge chunks of the wolf politics, and Melissa's nearly devastating machinations, I got a sense of the enormity of the last seven days.

"So wait," said Tanya. "Man, I thought our chat at my cousin's apartment was weird. Rich was right in some very wrong ways, and you two are now together?"

"Yes," I said, smiling at John. "Right now, we're trying to get a place to live straightened out so we aren't staying at my friend's house. We're meeting with my uncle at six o'clock...in fifteen minutes, wow... to go see the place."

"Well!" said Tanya, smiling at us, then sobering. "You have had a week of it. Congrats, John. You should be aware that Rich is going to do his best to find you. He's already trying to track you down on the internet, and he has friends who are good at finding where people live. Gary has connections in the city records department as well as on the police force, and they might trace you back to your parents' house. Keep an eye out for him and warn your folks not to talk to strangers showing up at their door."

"Thanks, I will do that," said John. "They don't need to get dragged into this."

"So now what do we do?" asked Tanya, drinking the last of her beer. "Do I just pretend to be dumb, or do I drop breadcrumbs leading the opposite way?"

"I think it will depend," I said. "Breadcrumbs could be beneficial, but denial might get more information. We'll have to play that by ear. Silence for now might be the best choice."

"Gotcha," said Tanya.

A crash of breaking glass caused us all to turn to where the sound had come from, and we watched as the bartender bent to pick up something behind the bar. Above, the television set was playing the 5:30 news report, and I was startled to see Sam and some of the other shapeshifters giving an interview in an official-looking room. Tanya glanced at me askance, but the volume was now too low to hear.

"It figures," I said. "I'm not sure what's going on."

"Damned monsters," grumbled a man sitting at the bar to the guy next to him. "I can't believe they want to give them the same rights as people."

The man next to him ignored him and took another sip of his beer, but the bartender, a burly man who had just stood up holding a dustpan full of glass, glared at the speaker in disgust.

"They are people, lads, for the most part just like you and me," he said, his voice an odd mixture of Scottish brogue and French sibilants. "Where I come from, there is a little village where most of the families are shapeshifters and their descendants. They are hardworking, honest folks, fishermen mostly, and they are no different in their ways than you and me. They're not one of them monsters. Try thinking of them as people and learn a thing or two. Stop listening to the rubbish on the internet."

The first man made a harrumphing sound and stared into his beer, but the other appeared thoughtful.

"Did you know any of them?" he asked the bartender.

"I did," said the bartender, "though it's been a long time since I was home. Still exchange Christmas cards with a few of them."

"They celebrate Christmas?" the man asked.

"Those that have a mind to, yes," said the bartender. "We are all God's creatures, and they know that as well as you do."

"I don't believe a bit of it," snorted the first man. "It would be like giving a dog voting rights to allow these beasts to be recognized as a race with privileges like humans have."

"They already have them," said the bartender, turning to serve another customer. "They just want to make sure that your kind doesn't take them away."

The first man stood up, slammed cash down on the bar, and stalked from the room. I watched him storm out, relieved to see him gone. Next to me, John let out a breath I was fairly sure he was unaware of holding.

"I heard that in England, they have already been recognized as a legitimate group with full protection under the law," said the second man once the door had firmly closed. "What's keeping us from doing the same?"

"People like your friend there," said the bartender, drawing a beer from the tap. "What else?"

"He's not my friend," said the other, taking a drink from his beer. "Nor would I want to be friends with someone like that."

Those in the bar that had all been drawn to the confrontation slowly drifted back to refocus on their own conversations again, though I heard a lot of them privately discussing the issues surrounding shapeshifters. On the television, the news had moved on, but obviously, the customers had not yet done the same. Tanya put a ten on the table and got up.

"I'm going home, but I'll call you later. John, good to see you. Take care of her."

"I aim to," he said. "Let us know if Rich does anything crazy."

"Will do," said Tanya. "Bye, guys."

We settled up the bill with the waitress, then drove over to Andrew's office. My uncle was just finishing up some paperwork when we went in, and he beamed at the sight of us. We quickly caught him up to date.

"Sounds like you have been having an adventure," he said. "Meeting a tribal shaman, fighting off an evil ex, almost involved in an altercation...exciting times! Well, everything is in order. I deposited your funds from the estate, and you have the money for shopping, yes? Good. The house has a new fridge, stove, and dishwasher, but you'll need a washer and dryer, plus any other appliances. It has central air and heating, so no window units for AC. It also has a central vacuum system, so aside from a dust buster, you won't need a vac. Are you ready to go see the house?"

I grinned at him and bounced up and down a little. John just seemed overwhelmed. Andrew laughed and ushered us to his Mustang.

"You have to arrive in style after all," he said.

We chatted on the drive, and he brought up the episode with Rich and Ahnold. I told him what Rich had been saying, and Andrew became increasingly concerned.

"It's always wonderful when a bully gets his comeuppance, but it sounds like he isn't giving up. I'd be very cautious. John, did you call your folks?"

"On the way over," said John. "I told them that Sasha had broken up with her boyfriend and was hiding from him. I warned them that he was hunting down all of her friends in hopes of finding her. My parents were surprisingly supportive of you, Sash. They like our friendship more than I thought they did and feel you've been helpful to me over the years. They promised to be clueless as to your whereabouts and tell him I'm moving out with college friends, which I'm not sure they totally believe anymore. Either way, they are not going to help him."

"Good," Andrew said. "Rich may not give up, but this way, no one is going to make things easier for him."

A short drive later, we arrived at our new house on Idylwild, and Andrew led us inside the little entryway and into the rest of the house.

"It has a fairly open concept in the living and dining room, but there is a little space through there where a home office had apparently been installed," Andrew said, pointing. "The kitchen has its own area."

He continued to lead us through the house. There was a front terrace nook on the other side of the garage and little closets in odd, out-of-the-way places. Downstairs, the cellar was finished with a section set up as a game area, and there was a little bar complete with a tiny glass-front mini-fridge.

From the cellar, we then trooped upstairs to see the bedrooms, and I was instantly smitten with the master suite. It had a walk out balcony and a walk-in closet, along with a bathroom complete with jacuzzi tub and separate shower. Two other smaller bedrooms led off the landing, and another, less expansive bathroom was set between them. I watched John become more and more enthusiastic with every find and felt a surge of happiness.

Even though I had grown up in the House, this was an awesome place to call my own. And John's, I amended. It was John's house too, and I had quietly told Andrew to put him on the paperwork as co-owner. I would tell him as a surprise when Andrew brought over the deed next week for us to sign. I wanted him to feel he was going to be a permanent part of my life, and it seemed that giving him that security might help him believe it. He had enough to adjust to without worrying about having a stable place to live.

"What do you think?" asked Andrew, beaming. "Isn't it marvelous?"

"I can't believe I am going to live here," said John. "I figured I might get some sort of tiny postage stamp house, not something like this!"

"Well, as of tomorrow, you are welcome to start bringing things over. We can take some time in the afternoon, Sasha, to transfer services to your name. I'll help you with that. Are you two going shopping tonight?"

"Yes," said John, looking at me. "That was the plan."

"Well, then, I'll drive you back to the office. You can leave one of your cars there until you're done if it's easier. Up to you."

He led us out of the house and drove us back to the office. John and I left from there, taking both our cars to Kathy's, then headed to Furniture Row in mine. A dizzying tour of the show rooms commenced and, two hours later, we made our first purchases - bedroom sets, a living room set, kitchen and dining room tables and chairs, and some office furnishings. It was enough to get us started, and the sales people directed us to an appliance store for the washer and dryer. Once those were purchased and the delivery arranged for Saturday morning, we made plans to shop for plates and other essentials the next night. Done, mentally and physically, we went back to Nevermore's, where I graded with Kathy at the kitchen table, and John played on his computer alone upstairs for an hour.

That night in bed, however, we didn't fall right asleep, but instead talked excitedly about the sleigh bed we had found for the bedroom – our room – as well as the other furniture we had bought for our house. For the first time in days, I found myself with enough ardor to really enjoy John's company and feel like we were going to be okay. The kissing started gently, but then became more passionate, more sure. John hung back for a moment and searched my face, but I just pulled him back into our embrace.

We restrained ourselves from going much further than that out of respect for Kathy and Paul, though I doubt either would have cared. We did, and that was what mattered. Neither of us were comfortable with taking advantage of their hospitality that way. Admittedly, there was some exploration of each other's bodies through touch that did occur, but we both agreed, a little reluctantly, that we should wait until we had our own bed in our own house. A few more days really wouldn't matter. If anything, it heightened our desire, and sleep was a little slower coming as we whispered to each other, holding hands in the dark.

The next two days were stressful, but all the little details, all the little pieces, began to come together. We bought pots and pans and dishes, sheets and blankets, and table cloths. We had to furnish an entire house, and John added his savings as my funds began to run low. Literally we were starting from scratch. How did neither of us own a spatula? How had we never had a coffee maker? A microwave? A soap dish? All the appurtenances of life; we were starting with nothing. A trip to Target prompted laughter as we realized we didn't know what kind of soap our washing machine used. We agonized over cotton or flannel sheets and bought both.

It was wild and heady, and I realized much to my surprise that I was really falling for John. I hadn't expected it. I really hadn't. But all of those parts of what had made our friendship work so well for ten years fell into place as we spent time building our life together from the ground up. And what I came to realize was this. John knew me. Like, really knew me. And I knew him too. He was the one all my defenses went down around. He was the one I knew would have my back. He was the one who had trusted me to make the right decision regarding letting Tanya in on his secret. He knew I would never lie to him. The 72" TV for the home theater area? Totally bought for John to game on. The popcorn maker? How else could we watch anime? We worked as a couple in ways I never knew people even could.

Thursday and Friday evenings had been filled with shopping, dropping off packages to the house, retrieving my boxes and bags from Andrew's condo – though the plants would stay until Sunday – and getting everything ready for the furniture to arrive on Saturday morning. We made it back Thursday night exhausted but exuberant, and on Friday, Paul cooked enough for a small army, wrapping up the leftovers to send with us the next morning to the house. He and Kathy planned to come over to help us organize chaos Saturday morning, and my brothers had stated that they would come over as well to help with any arranging of furniture that we couldn't manage. The house would be full of life.

One ominous presence was the storm that had been rumored to be moving in. It was now bearing down on us across the upper western states as warmer, moist air that wasn't traveling in any particular hurry. The weather calculations predicted us getting slammed, though, sometime Sunday evening, and Kathy and I agreed, with the amazing intuition that teachers develop in their first two years of teaching, that there would likely be no school Monday and possibly Tuesday given how much the system looked to drop on us. If nothing else, though, the prospect of getting snowed into our brand new house was somewhat exhilarating and romantic. It was a perfect way to begin our lives together.

14
MOVING DAY

Early Saturday morning, John and I went grocery shopping for staples and items we felt we might want to have in case of a prolonged storm. The frenzy had already begun at the market, and the layers of milk jugs had been decimated. We managed to snag some of the essentials and escaped as fast as we could. There was a generator at the house, full courtesy of Andrew, so we would have some power if the main lines went down, but where our local power lines were buried, we were less likely to have that happen than in other parts of Boulder.

We had just finished putting the supplies away when my brothers arrived, followed shortly by Kathy and Paul. We gave our guests a tour, and "oohs" and 'ahhhs" told us that they were suitably impressed. Then the truck arrived from Furniture Row, and the madness began. My brothers were actually pretty coordinated and with the burly men from the store, they were able to get everything in and placed without too much trouble. The sleigh bed was one of the biggest pieces that had to go upstairs, and it fortunately came disassembled. The mattresses did not, however, and they were hauled up the stairs with much effort. The bureaus and the smaller bed for the guest room were much easier to manage.

The appliance store truck also showed up at this time, so I moved upstairs with Kathy to make the beds and stay out of the way. Though I was pretty strong, the two men, one carrying the washer, and the other the dryer, put any effort I could do to shame. Paul likewise did not do any heavy lifting, but he offered his advice to John on how to hook up the washer and dryer in the small laundry area in the bathroom near the cellar stairs. The appliance guys left as silently and as quickly as they had come, finished with the job in less than ten minutes.

Finally, about 11:00 a.m., the Furniture Row truck pulled out, and we all took a few minutes to walk around the house, marveling at what a difference furniture made. It wasn't quite home yet, but it was a start. Kathy and I made notes of what John and I might want to pick up, while my brothers drove out to get pizza at one of the local shops they found on Google. Paul and John were busy puttering around down in the basement with Andrew. It was a weird feeling, walking around the house and knowing it was mine.

"It will take a while to sink in," said Kathy, winking at me. "When Paul and I bought our house, it took a whole five years before we truly felt it was ours. You'll get used to it in time."

Armed with pizza and beer from a place called Proto's Pizza, the boys came back a short time later. We all dug in, famished, and sat round our new kitchen table, eating greasy, delicious pizza off paper plates and imbibing ice-cold beer. It was then that we realized we had forgotten to buy a trash can, of all things, and Kathy added that to her list of items we should pick up.

After lunch, my brothers gave us all a farewell hug, promising to visit and annoy us regularly. I stuck my tongue out at them as they left, and then Andrew took his leave as well.

"I'll have papers for the deed next week," he said, putting on his coat. "I can come over here to make it easier on you when they are ready."

"Thanks for everything, Andrew," I said.

"Yes, thanks a lot," said John.

"You're welcome, the both of you. It was my pleasure," Andrew said, smiling. "I'll see myself out."

Kathy and Paul also were preparing to go, and Kathy handed me the list as they were leaving.

"We'll leave you to get adjusted to your new place," she said, winking at me. "You also need curtains for the bedroom."

And she and Paul left for home.

John and I stood looking at the door for a long moment, and then at each other.

"So, shopping?" I said with some amusement.

"Might as well," John said. "We probably need curtains for other rooms, too."

"And trash cans," I laughed. "How did we forget that?"

John peered at the list Kathy had provided us.

"Apparently we also missed a bath mat and bedside lamps," he said. "Might as well take one more hit to the bank card and get a few things."

I grabbed my coat, and we locked the door to our house. Our house. I reveled in the idea that we would be coming back to stay tonight for the first time, and I felt a sudden anticipation at being alone in our own room in our own bed. I glanced at John as we got into his car and headed off for the nearest Target fifteen minutes away.

"Have you stopped to think," I said, "about the insanity of this week?"

John glanced at me as he drove and grinned.

"Every damned day," he said. "I keep expecting to find it's all a dream, but then I wake up to all of this. Even then, I have to pinch myself. It's unreal. Is this sort of sudden house acquisition normal in your family?"

"Sometimes," I said, laughing. "People get houses as wedding presents. Ten to one, our loan would be paid off if…"

I stopped myself, not wanting to overstep, and John looked at me oddly.

"If we got married?" he said, softly.

"Yeah," I said.

"Would you want to?" he asked. "I mean, not right now, but sometime?"

"Possibly," I said. "Let's see how we survive living together for a while first."

"Right," grinned John. "No point worrying about marriage when the house could be the death of one or both of us."

"See? Exactly!"

The trip to Target yielded curtains and curtain rods, some basic power tools we felt we might need, trash cans for several of the rooms, and the rest of the things on Kathy's list. Corbies were pretty observant, and her list was revealing in what we had missed on our other trips. I also found a few throw pillows and blankets for the couches. We agreed that we didn't have to finish shopping all in one day, but when we found a framed photo of a black wolf standing majestically in the snow, we both felt that we had to have it for the living room. We bought our purchases and headed home.

The garage was full of our boxes and bags, so the cars were currently parked in the driveway. As we carried our loot inside, we decided that everything from the garage should be moved into the house by tomorrow so the cars could be put in before the storm. We would need both of the vehicles to get the plants from Andrew's anyway, so we could just drive the cars in and unload them.

After we put up the curtains, we spent the rest of the afternoon bringing our possessions from the garage, taking the clothing either to the laundry room to be washed or upstairs to the bedroom to be put away. My boxes contained a lot of books, jewelry, and the rest of the bric-a-brac I had accumulated over the last six years. I would sort it more over the next few days. Anything that I didn't want could go to the Salvation Army store in town.

John's boxes held anime and manga, his game systems, a lot of novels, computer parts, and a small army of painted figurines that I recognized as Warhammer Fantasy. He had a few friends that he played with, and he had talked about setting up a painting studio in the basement. There was certainly enough space in the finished area to have a permanent Warhammer battle table, and I told him so. The grin he gave me was answer enough.

I was astounded that we had managed to get everything inside the house by dinner time. We still had a few things to buy, but the bedrooms and the theater room now had blackout curtains for each window. Neither of us felt like cooking, so we pulled John's car into the garage and drove mine to the closest restaurant we could find. We were both beyond exhausted and having a nice, relaxing dinner out felt wonderful.

"It's weird," said John, as he took a break from devouring his steak. "We can say 'go home' and not mean Nevermore's house. Or my parents' house. Or even Rich's. We have a *house*. This is going to take a while to get used to."

"Kathy said that it took her five years. Hopefully, we can make the house home sooner than that."

"You know what else?" he said, dropping his voice. "I know we've shared the same bed for the last few nights at Kathy's, but we're going to be in our own bed tonight. I have to admit, it's kind of making me nervous."

"Performance anxiety?" I joked.

"Kinda," he said, coloring.

"Hey, I'm nervous, too," I said. "We can wait. There's no hurry. Just 'cause we got our own bed now doesn't mean we have to christen it tonight. Let's play it by ear, okay?"

He looked at me and smiled that ineffably sweet smile of his.

"Okay," he said. He paused a moment, then continued, "It's funny, but I can handle your family, my 'epic' evolution, getting the house, telling my parents I'm moving out, and the likely eventuality of some sort of confrontation with Rich better than I can having sex. With you."

"Sex is scary," I said, taking his hand. "Sex is being vulnerable, more vulnerable with a person than at any other time in your life. It can mean committing to another person for a long time, maybe even forever. Sex binds people together spiritually and emotionally. It may be the most honest expression people can have with each other. I get it. It can mean risking everything you have with that other person.

"We have ten years between us," I continued. "Ten years of friendship and anime and bad jokes. Ten years of life together already as best friends. Risking that is terrifying. I get it."

"Yeah," he said, "it is. I don't want to lose you in any fashion."

"Well, don't forget, our wolf sides, which are instinctive, have already decided," I said, chuckling. "Don't think for one second that they will let us off the hook"

"Have you ever dated one of your...our...own?" he asked.

"Once," I said. "In high school. And you can better be damn well sure that he and I came nowhere near each other the one time my wolf side came into season. I pretty much locked myself in my room for a week. It was overpowering, and I was terrified that I would slip up. It was easier to just not leave the house."

"That can happen?" asked John, picking up steak fry with his free hand. "I thought just clans that didn't stay human most of the time had that problem."

"Nope," I said. "It happens to all of us, just not as often. We don't let it rule us the way they do, though. I knew what was happening and what the result could be. Stef stayed away, and we just talked on the phone that week. My mother told the teachers I had a bad case of pneumonia and was staying home to recuperate. My brothers brought my homework to me. It was just safer. I never had to worry about it with anyone else I ever dated, so it's never come up."

"Oh," said John. "So it could with us?"

"It could," I said. "It would be different, though. We're already connected."

John gently drew his hand away so he could cut his steak and ate thoughtfully for a few minutes. I wondered what his thoughts must be. He knew, from his own experience, that wolf instincts could be pretty strong. It was all so new to him, and he hadn't, to my knowledge, even transformed since last weekend. I wasn't really sure if he'd given himself time to really think anything through completely. Honestly, I was dead tired and actually looking forward to the incoming snow storm because it would give me the opportunity to stay in one place for at least a day. Making sense out of everything would take longer than that, but it would be a start.

"I wouldn't mind that," he said, finally. "And I have a million questions. Now is probably not the time, though."

"Nor the place," I said with a slight smile, gesturing at the noisy pub around us. "There'll be better times for those discussions."

He nodded, and we concentrated on finishing our meals. Once the check was paid, we drove home and sat down in what we had decided to dub "The Theater" to watch something stupid on John's Xbox. The internet company had not yet come out to hook us up, though they were supposed to show tomorrow afternoon between twelve and two, so we had resorted to a video from John's anime collection. *Vampire Hunter D* was one I hadn't seen before, and for an early 80s anime, it was pretty gory. We settled down to cuddle on the couch with popcorn and watch Doris almost get turned into a vampire bride only to be saved by the hero, D, at the last minute. It was awesome; almost as good as *Akira*, which was my personal favorite for standalone films from the same era.

When the movie ended, we both found ourselves dozing. The events of the day had begun to catch up with us, and it was time to go to our new room and our own bed. Neither of us tried to make a big deal of it when we turned out the lights, leaving the popcorn bowl by the sink for the morning. I headed upstairs while John checked the locks and set the security system. I stuck my head into each of the rooms, studying them. They seemed so barren. The desks in the office were brand new, and while John's computer components were scattered across his desk and my school bags were sitting on mine, they felt rather sterile. We hadn't put up any pictures yet, though some were leaning up against walls in various rooms, along with small shelves and other places for knickknacks. I knew it would eventually become home, but it was not there yet. That and I was just too tired to think clearly that night.

I shuffled into the bedroom, turned on one of the bedside lamps, and went into the bathroom. A shower could wait, I decided. I was too tired to do anything else but brush my teeth and climb into the big sleigh bed. We had opted for king-sized, and as I settled down into it, John entered the room. He glanced at me and went into the bathroom, closing the double frosted glass doors. I heard the shower run and grumbled mentally to myself. Of course John would decide to get all clean before bed. Now I felt grubby.

I toyed for a moment with going in and joining him, but after deciding he'd probably have a heart attack, I went across the hall to the other bathroom instead, mentally thanking myself for stocking it earlier. I hopped in the shower, and by the time I got out and was dressed again, John had dried off and climbed into bed.

"I had wondered where you went," he said.

"Yeah, well you shamed me into it," I said, still toweling my wet hair. "New bed, clean sheets. I felt I should at least do the same."

I folded the towel and put it on my pillow, not wanting to totally soak it. Climbing into bed, I snuggled back down under the covers, letting the warmth from the shower radiate.

"Want to get the light?" John said, sounding a bit wooden as if afraid to be taken the wrong way.

I wiggled my eyebrows suggestively, sending him into sputtering laughter. I joined in. Laughter always settled nerves, I knew, and I had used it to defuse student tensions for years. Mad skills of the teacher, I.

"I needed that," said John, his tone warmer now. "It's so stupid, but I needed that."

"Yeah," I said. "I'm nervous too."

We lay looking at each other for a long moment. It was awkward, having our own bed. We'd shared space together, but it wasn't ours. This was.

"Executive decision," said John. "We're both exhausted, and I firmly believe that we both really want to be awake for our first time. Zombie sex just isn't my style."

"Braiiinnnzzzz," I said, leaning over to pretend to chew on his head.

He laughed, playfully pushing me away, and I lay back down, letting the weight of everything that had happened drag on me. I reached for the light and lay in the dark, listening to John breathe. It really wasn't long before the events of the day finally lulled me to sleep.

In the still of the early morning, I awoke and turned to watch John where he lay sleeping. Not wanting to disturb him, I slid from the bed and went to the bathroom. When I returned, I found him wide awake.

"I was hoping to let you sleep," I said softly.

"I keep waking up," he said. "It's the new bed, the house smells funny...I mean, yeah, we're fine, but it's been a lot to take in, you know?"

"I hear you," I said. "How often does life throw this many curveballs at you all at once? You have a right to be weirded out."

He nodded, then looked at me for a long moment before hesitantly leaning over to give me a kiss. It was gentle, like the touch of a butterfly's wing, but his touch set me aflame. He started to pull away, but I moved forward and kissed him back. I could feel the tremble in his lips as he leaned in, and it was like the barriers finally broke down for both of us. I barely was conscious of taking off my nightshirt, and John stripping beside me in the dark; suddenly he was kissing his way down the side of my throat, and my hands reached around his neck to pull him closer.

John breathing was ragged as he lowered his head, kissing the hollow of my collarbone, then working his way back to my neck and then my lips, with slow but eager anticipation.

"Is this okay?" he whispered, and I knew he meant more than just his kisses.

"Yes," I said and pulled him to me.

I caressed him while he expressed his love in a manner better suited than words ever could. I felt the fear and worry in my chest loosen, and I joined him, letting go of my inhibitions. In that moment as we became one, I discovered that I loved him completely. Why hadn't I seen this before? Loving John was effortless, like breathing.

Afterwards, John lay with his head on my shoulder. Sleep didn't come for a long time, and we talked into the early morning hours, words we had not been able to say to that point flowing freely. Around three o'clock, we began again, slower this time, still in the dark, and spent time getting to know each other through touch and taste. Our joining this time was slow and more like a dance than a race. John was inexperienced, but he made up for it by being attentive. When we finished, it felt to me like the final chord of a grand symphony, and we lay tumbled together in the darkness.

I climbed into the circle of his arms, pressing myself into him. He yawned and settled deeper into the mattress. Turning to look at me, silhouetted against the dim grey light, he stared at me hesitantly for a long moment, then said,

"Is it okay to say...I mean, after that...it is okay to tell you I love you? I mean, I know you sort of knew after last weekend, but is it okay to tell you that now?"

"Yes," I said, leaning up to kiss him.

"I love you," he said. "I have loved you for years, Sash."

"I love you, too," I said, looking up at his face in the dark.

"Really?" he said, his voice breaking.

"Really," I said. "It's been creeping up on me all week, popping out of odd corners when I least expected it. I almost feel guilty; I mean it hasn't even been a week since I left Rich, but the truth is, I think my feelings towards you have been building for a long time, and I've only just allowed myself to acknowledge them."

"I'm glad I could finally tell you," said John. "I was afraid I'd never get the chance."

We lay back down together, holding each other in the fading dark.

Sleep stole upon us shortly after that, and we fell into it without dreaming.

15
THE RESCUE

The alarm I had set for the arrival of the internet company went off a little before noon. John lifted his head, glanced at the time, and swore.

"I totally did not mean to sleep this late," he grumbled, jumping out of bed.

He seemed somewhat alarmed to find himself naked in the curtain-filtered light of day. I got a solid eyeful as he grabbed his clothes and fled to the bathroom to shower again. I didn't really think about it this time and joined him. His reaction was in all respects hysterical, and we laughed hard enough that we had to stop and remember how to breathe.

We did manage to get clean somehow, and while he dressed in the bathroom, I made my way out into the bedroom, scrunching my toes into the soft carpet as I walked. A few minutes later, fully clothed, we had made our way downstairs. I started coffee brewing in the new coffee maker while John cooked some eggs in a new pan, and we ate at the new kitchen table off new dishes with new silverware. It felt great to be doing those small, mundane things together in our own place. As we were loading the dishwasher after breakfast, the doorbell rang, and I finished up while John answered the door.

Two routers later, we were hooked to the internet and had basic cable for the local news. Our computers were online again, and John's Xbox hummed to life as it merged to the web. Being reconnected to the world was one more small contribution to my sense of normalcy.

Around two o'clock, we drove both cars to Andrew's condo to fetch my plants. The sky had begun to darken, and the clouds were becoming ominous to the west. Loading the cars took us about a half an hour, and once I had cleaned up a few fallen leaves, we drove home, the *Ficus lyrata*'s pot nestled in the floorboards of my passenger seat.

By the time we had wrestled the plants in from the garage, the sky outside was growing positively leaden. We stepped out onto the back deck; I could feel the air pressure shift and smell the snow in the air, even as a wind began to stir the empty branches of the oaks in our backyard.

"It's coming," said John. "It's going to be a big one."

My cellphone rang, and it was the message from the superintendent Nevermore had predicted; school was closed for Monday as the projected amounts had risen from at least a foot to over eighteen inches. I grinned at John, and as my phone chimed again – this time it was Nevermore – John got a text from the college. He showed me that his campus, too, would be closed.

"You heard?" Nevermore said, sounding smug.

"I did indeed," I said, as we retreated inside to escape the rising wind. "Called it!"

"It's about time," she said. "It's been a dud of a winter. How was the first night in the house? Sleep much?"

"Some," I said. "Not really, though."

"Well, you can get plenty of sleep tomorrow," chuckled Nevermore. "Have a good day settling in. I predict we'll have at least a delay on Tuesday as well. This one is going to be big."

"Yeah, I think so too. I'll call you tomorrow."

By 4:00, the snow had begun to fall, lightly at first, then with more urgency. John and I checked all the doors, made sure the garage was secure, and while he went to set up his computer, I shuffled the plants to various windows around the house. I fussed with which had the most light and watered each of my collection thoroughly. I put the *lyrata* with its big leaves in our bedroom as it had long been my favorite, and it made me feel happy to have it there. I tucked the giant spider plant with its trailing babies in the office and several small varieties of vining *monstera* in the guest bedroom. The greenery made the rooms feel more homey, and I went downstairs to reheat some of Paul's leftovers for dinner as the snow began to pile up on the ground outside.

It was midnight, and the snow had fallen for over six hours unabated. I lay in bed, half asleep, listening to the snow hissing against the house. John was sleeping next to me, a hand resting on my shoulder, dreaming deeply. Our lovemaking that evening had been slower, but with no less passion. We'd explored each other, leaving the lights on this time. Even after so short a time, John remembered things I liked and things I didn't. I had to learn him as well and found out pretty fast what the limits of his experience really were. We took our time that long evening and had fallen asleep only an hour ago after sating ourselves.

It was midnight, and it was snowing.

I woke John, put on my bathrobe, and went downstairs. Disabling the security alarms, I put my robe regretfully on one of the hooks by the back door. The cold on my naked body was one of my least favorite parts.

"There's no better time than a storm to run in the city. We won't get lost, and the snow will fill in our tracks," I said. "I'm going to leave this door unlocked. There is a fence that runs between us and the Twin

Lakes park behind us. It's about six feet high, and we can jump it with a running start. Change now; I'll follow."

I went out and instantly shivered, but I closed the door firmly against the wind and changed. Fur cut the chill to my bones, but did nothing for the snow lashing at my eyes. I turned my nose away from the force of the storm and sniffed deeply, the cold, clean air filling my lungs. I led the way, jumping the fence with ease. John also cleared it with little effort, which made him turn and grin at me as if to say, "Ha! Did it!" Snorting, I darted to my right, and we engaged in a game of tag as we raced through the snow, John dodging, me darting, and the spray flying up behind us.

We eventually turned to make our way back home and were still intent on our game when a sound caught my ears. Nodding to John, I bounded towards our neighborhood and looked at the street from behind a screen of brush. Several police cars were parked across from our house, and the wind carried the distraught wails of a woman standing in the snow, pleading with the officers to find something. The man standing next to her was dressed for the weather and sounded desperate as he spoke to the policemen. It took me only a minute or so to understand what had happened. They had been watching TV and had thought their child was safe in bed. When they went upstairs to check on her, they found their little girl was not there. A frantic search of the house led to the discovery of the unlocked kitchen door and the parents had gone hunting for her after calling the police. Their hunt had turned up nothing, and we were almost overpowered by the scent of their fear coupled with the fumes from the cars.

I changed back to human, hunkering my body down against the trunk of a tree.

"We need to find her," I said.

John changed back as well and crouched next to me.

"Shit," he muttered. "What can we do? Can we stay out here to search?"

"If the child was going anywhere, my guess would be the park.

According to Google Earth, there is a path at the end of the cul-de-sac. She could've cut into the woods from there. That's where we'll head. Be careful not to be seen."

Shifting back, my nose was assaulted by the smell of exhaust once more. I focused in on the parent's scent, registered it, then turned and raced towards the woods, John at my heels. I thought I caught a faint whiff of something in the air that was similar to the parents, though not exactly the same, but it was gone before I could pinpoint a direction. I whined at John, and we trotted through the hock-deep snow, peering through the wind-lashed curtains of swirling white.

In the darkness ahead, we could see the officers' bright searchlights, and we swung out away from the voices of the police. I smelled a hint of the scent again, and cast about, trying to follow it. John had angled further to the north than I, swerving toward the lake. I caught up to him just as he put a foot into the water, breaking the fragile ice. We looked at each other with alarm, hoping that the much lighter child hadn't stumbled onto it and fallen through.

We paced along the shore, peering through the snow to see if the edge of the water was broken anywhere, but nothing appeared to be amiss. I was getting more concerned, however; the girl had been out here for who knows how long at this point. It was cold, well below freezing, and she wouldn't last much longer. I worried that we would find a little frozen corpse instead of a child if we didn't find her soon. John picked up on my worry, and he cast about, nose to the wind, searching.

As we made our way along, I suddenly caught a faint sound, almost like a bird song, high and tremulous. There was fear in that cry. John's ears pricked up; he'd heard it too, and as we followed along the lake shore to the right, the sound came again, louder. The wind changed directions, and in the gust, we caught the child's scent much more strongly than before. John altered his course abruptly, and I followed him into the brush along the shoreline.

We found her huddled under some sort of evergreen, half frozen and terrified. It was the little girl, and when she saw us coming, she began to cry even louder. With unspoken accord, we huddled around her, sheltering her with our bodies. The snow on top of the bush and the two of us blocking the wind made the air in the little hollow warmer, and the child's crying was reduced to hitches and sobs as she curled up against my fur, shaking. John and I looked at each other. We had to get her home, fast.

John moved behind me, hiding as best as he could, and shifted back into human form.

"What's your name, honey," he said, peeking over at her.

Her eyes went round as he spoke to her, and she whispered "Sara."

"Okay, Sara, we're going to take you home now," said John. "Climb on my back when I'm a wolf again, okay? We'll get you safe to mommy and daddy"

She nodded and clung to me harder with her cold little hands.

He changed back into his wolf form and crawled outside, staying crouched so she could climb aboard. I nosed her to leave the shelter and get on his back. Once she was on and had a firm grip of his ruff, John stood, and I steadied her as we walked through the storm back to the house. There was no help for it; we'd have to risk being seen. John moved as quickly as he could, and I tried to buffet the wind for them both as much as I was able. She huddled against John, making no sound and hiding her face in his warm fur. We reached the trail again and headed for the break in the fence that led to our cul-de-sac, turning down the path toward the neighborhood.

There was only one police car there now with its lights on, and the child's mother could be seen through the window of the house. John gritted his teeth and paced up the walkway to the porch steps. The little girl glanced up and, seeing her house, slid from John's back to run up the stairs. John backed up a few paces to where I waited, and we stood watch as she stretched up to ring the bell. The door opened, and with a cry of happiness, the woman came out and swept her daughter up in her arms, hugging her and crying her name. Then she looked out and saw us, her breath catching in her throat.

I nodded to her, and John cocked his head to one side. The child turned and said, "Mommy, mommy! The doggies brought me back! The big black one told me to ride on his back, and they brought me home!"

Her mother glanced down at her daughter, then back at us. John bowed his head to her, and we turned to leave.

"Wait," said the woman. She put the girl down, shooing her inside, and came back to the edge of the porch, staring at us where we'd paused on the walkway.

"Thank you. Thank you for finding my baby. I'll let people know what you did for us. That you are good. Thank you so very much!"

John grinned a really goofy grin at that and wagged his tail, after which I head-butted him gently, and we raced off into the snow as we heard the police returning from their searches down the trails. John and I headed towards the lakes, ran a good mile to the right down the paths, then turned and made our way back to our own yard. We leapt the fence again and raced up to the porch where I changed back long enough to let us in and lock the door. John trotted upstairs; I reverted to wolf form and curled up on the couch in the living room to watch the action across the street.

Moments later, John joined me, dressed in his sweatpants and sweatshirt. Not long after, an ambulance arrived. The little girl was probably okay – she'd had the presence of mind to put on shoes at least – and when the ambulance left, no one went with it, so I guessed I was right. Finally, I had warmed up enough to become human and fetch my bathrobe. I put on the kettle, making a mental note to thank Kathy for adding it to the list, and found the box of cocoa that John had snuck into the carriage while we were shopping. While the water heated, I ran upstairs to find something warmer than just my bathrobe to wear.

The kettle was whistling when I came back downstairs, and I made a cup of cocoa for myself and John before joining him. We stood looking out the window at the neighbor's house as the police finally left. The lights went out one by one in the houses along the street, but across from us, one little light still burned softly in an upstairs room. I would bet it was Sara's room, and her parents were going to sit with her throughout the night. I know I would have if she were mine.

It was three o'clock and still snowing when John and I finally returned to bed. We curled up together for comfort and slept, not caring when we woke the next morning.

16
AFTERMATH

The snow had still not stopped by Monday evening, which prompted another call from the district canceling all of Tuesday's classes. John's boss instructed him to work from home as well.

Nevermore had called earlier that afternoon, and I filled her in on our adventure the night before.

"And it didn't cross your mind that they might put two and two together with their new neighbors?" asked Kathy. Her tone was light, but I could tell she was concerned by the turn of events.

"We left quite a trail out towards the lake before we took the long way back to the house," I said. "The snow was falling so fast, our tracks wouldn't have lasted long anyway."

"Just be careful," she replied. "That legislation Sam Winston is involved with creating isn't even written yet. You know how slow the government moves. Who knows how long it will be before that happens?"

After the announcement for the second day of no school, Kathy called me again. Her tone was a little more serious than it had been during our earlier conversation.

"Word is among the corbies that reporters have contacted the family across the street for a statement," she said. "I'm sure your mother will hear about this as soon as the news vans fight their way over to your neighbor's house. Have you called her?"

"I will," I said. "Have you heard it mentioned yet?"

"No, just that there was the rescue of a child in the snow last night under unusual circumstances," said Kathy. "Nothing more specific than that."

Tuesday morning arrived, and we woke close to our usual time. John and I had stayed up until almost midnight the night before, and there had thankfully been no crises. Neither of us were inclined to get out of bed, and we lazed about for a while before finally getting dressed and wandering downstairs to make breakfast. The snow was still coming down at an impressive rate, though the weatherman on the kitchen radio stated that it should be slowing down by midday and likely stop before the evening commute. There was a brief mention of the lost child on the radio, and a hint that she had been brought back by something more than dogs, but that was it.

I called my mother a few minutes later, and told her the story of our night rescue.

"You did the right thing, of course," she said. "I'll call Susan Winston this morning to pass the word along. She will be most interested to hear about this. This incident might be a good thing for Sam's group to bring up to the committee."

"I'm sure the reporters will be here as soon as they allow travel," I said. "It's still pretty nasty out there right now."

"Here, too," said Mother, "though there are not many reasons on our road to plow before the storm ends. Our team has been down to the end of the drive several times, and the main road has barely been touched. It may be a while before we are clear from this storm."

I got off the phone and sat down with John in the Theater to eat. The weather was on, and I cuddled up to him, holding my coffee like a talisman. Almost two feet had fallen in the last thirty-six hours, and it looked like we might easily top that by evening. Going out to shovel the driveway, we finished just as the first plow rumbled down the street and dumped snow right into our freshly-shoveled driveway. The driver waved apologetically and kept going around the cul-de-sac. We cleared out the end again with me muttering under my breath about the stupidity of plow drivers.

Less than an hour later, while John and I were working in the office, the circus arrived across the street. We watched from the window as they descended; five news vans had pulled up in front of the house, and as the snow finally stopped, a number of the neighbors made excuses to walk their dogs right by the house, peering in curiously. We went out to shovel a third time – another half an inch had fallen – and listened to the newscasters and cameramen gossiping together.

The basic story was correct. The child had been lost, police had been out searching, and the child had been found and returned by two large wolf-like dogs. There was hot debate as to whether they were shapeshifters, though the fact that the little girl claimed that one had become human briefly and spoken to her before carrying her back home led most of them to believe that was the case. The mother's statement about the wolves nodding and acknowledging her thanks lent credence to this belief. The reporters talked to some of the dog walkers as they passed, and we finished shoveling and went inside before they could think to come ask us any questions.

On the news that night, we watched the interview and were delighted as the reporter asked the little girl about the experience. Her mother encouraged her to thank "the doggies," and the little girl shyly thanked us, her face pressed into her mother's leg.

"Did you have any concerns for your child's safety with these alleged shapeshifters?" one reporter asked.

Sara's mother stared straight at the camera and shook her head. "If this is the way shapeshifters really are," she said, "then people really need to rethink about calling them monsters. I really hope I can meet them again someday, and express how grateful we really are."

"Well," said John as the reporter returned the attention back to the newsroom, "there's at least two people who don't hate us, right?"

"I suspect there's a few more than two," I said, "though it's going to take more than that to win over the general public."

Later that evening, my mother called to let me know that her conversation with Susan Winston had gone very well, and that Susan would pass word along to her son so that government allies could use it in their efforts. There had been recent reports of ravens guiding lost hikers out of the woods, and any positive stories would help our cause.

"Susan also wanted to know if you might be willing to speak to some of the shapeshifters working with the government," my mother said.

"What do you think?" I said, looking over at John.

"I'm all for it," he said. "If anything in my own experience could be helpful to them, I'll be happy to. The opportunity to talk with Sam and the others? That would be awesome."

"They are like the rockstars of our world right now," I agreed and turned my full attention back to the phone. "Please let Susan know we'll do it."

The next morning, we got up for the first time to our normal schedules. I had a slightly longer drive than John's, so we both were up early so we could spend a few minutes together. It was already Wednesday, and I was relieved to have had the extra time to get my grading done. John was looking forward to returning to the college, even though, he said, he would be more than happy to spend another day with me.

"Separation makes the heart grow fonder," I said, though I could have cheerfully done the same.

After spending so much time in the house, we had become very comfortable with each other. This would be the first time we would be arriving home from work to our own place. Mine and John's, I thought, smiling. It still seemed odd but also very right.

I had never felt that way with Rich, belonging together, I mean. Sure, at the beginning of that relationship, dating a human was exciting, and as there had been no real world knowledge that shapeshifters existed, I had felt pretty secure. Only the crackpots who belonged to groups like Mystery Seekers believed that we existed. They were considered to be like the rest of the cryptid hunters – whacked attention seekers bubbling with conspiracy theories. Things were so very different now.

When I arrived at school – early, as it turned out because all of the heavy traffic was flowing through the city, and my route took me south of it – I walked into the staff room and into an augment between two social studies teachers who were yelling about whether or not the incident with the child had been an overall good thing. Some of the other later arrivals had joined the fray, and as I hung up my coat, the principal himself arrived to break it up.

"That is enough!" he said. "A child was rescued. Her life was saved. Anyone going to disagree with that?"

Everyone shook their heads, and the ones who were arguing had the grace to seem embarrassed.

"Those wolves, be they regular wolves, though I doubt it, or shapeshifters, saved a child's life. Anyone here who is an educator and does not see this as a positive thing might consider that they are in the wrong line of work.

"We know that they are living among us now," he continued. "For all we know, some teachers in this very room might be shapeshifters – did you all think about that? The government branch that works with them is lobbying, and lobbying hard, to gain them the same protections that any of you have for their jobs, their homes, and even their lives. Now you can agree or disagree with my statements and their avowed humanity, but know this, especially you history teachers. Anyone who can't see the parallels between the way these people are being treated and the way any minority has been viewed over the centuries should take a good long look.

"On top of that, there are probably children in your classrooms who are from one or more of these families. Their parents love them and care for them as much as any human parent does. They are just different. We have a responsibility to teach them and treat them the same as we do any other child in this school. I will never stand to see any of you treat them any differently if they ever become known, and if you do, you will no longer be working here. Am I clear?"

There was a moment's pause, then someone in the back of the staffroom began to applaud. I joined in and saw Nevermore clapping her hands vigorously and nodding in approval. The teachers who had been arguing apologized and shook hands as they went their separate ways.

Turner spied me and walked over, which in light of the recent conversation, made me very uncomfortable.

"Just a word, Ms. Wellington. Your ex was seen near here again last Friday before classes let out. I alerted the police, but you know the saying…forewarned is forearmed."

"Thank you, Mr. Turner," I said, relieved it wasn't related to the previous topic. "I'll keep an eye out for him. I know his car from a mile away, and I hope he'll get the hint soon."

"I hope so," said the principal, smiling at me. "In my experience, however, people like this rarely get the hint."

17
LINES DRAWN

Although I checked near and around my car every day, there was no sign of Rich lurking nearby, but I continued to park next to Mr. Turner out of expediency. Friday after school, Kathy and I met up with Tanya for coffee. She had called me Wednesday afternoon, but neither of us had been free. Kathy had not been able to contain her curiosity any longer and had accompanied me after a hasty text to Tanya confirmed that it was fine with her.

When we sat down at the coffee shop, Tanya looked at Kathy, almost as if trying to place her.

"You're different than Sasha, aren't you?" she said.

I grinned at Kathy and nodded to Tanya encouragingly. Tanya tried to focus for a moment, but then shook her head.

"Grandmama says I'm getting better, but I'm still not hearing spirits clearly. I get glimpses, though, and you don't seem like John and Sasha."

"Right," said Kathy. "I'm different. I'll give you a hint. Sasha calls me Nevermore."

"Oh!" said Tanya, her face lighting up with recognition. "Okay, that makes sense. The image I kept getting was of a dark, feather-rimmed eye. That makes sense now."

"So," I said, "You said you have news?"

"Boy, do I!" said Tanya, a look of glee on her face. "Rich and company got the smackdown for going to John's parents' house. His folks clammed up right away and told them nothing other than the fact that John was not there. When Rich asked if John had been sick with Ptomaine poisoning, they stood up for their son, and when he tried to find out where John had moved, John's father shut the door in Rich's face. Let me tell you, I know John had a rough time with them, but they had his back hardcore."

"Yeah," I said. "They seemed appalled when John told them Rich was after me. I think they would have done anything to get rid of him. I apparently fall under 'good influence'"

"Not only that, Rich was totally bullshit about you 'lying' about going to your uncle's. He told Todd, who told Jennifer, that the condo was empty. No one had been in or out when he's been by, and there are no lights on in the windows either," Tanya chuckled. "He's convinced that you and John are shacked up in some sleazy location."

"Ha!" said Kathy. "If only he knew!"

"Yeah," I said. "I'll check with John about a good time to invite you over. The house is pretty cool."

"I believe it!" said Tanya. "Okay, more serious, though. The guys found out where John works. Tell him to watch out for Rich's car too, okay? He hasn't given up. He's bound and determined to prove his asinine theories. The news story? That just fed the fire. He and Todd and Gary apparently got drunk at Todd and Jenn's the other night, and Gary was saying all sorts of things, like how all shapeshifters ought to be shot for attacking small children, that the news was lying, all that BS about Fake News. Total garbage. I knew that their opinions were out there, but man!"

"Yeah," I agreed, shaking my head. "The crazy is strong with those guys. We should watch out for Todd too. When he's drunk, he's mean and stupid. But when I've seen him try to figure something out when he's sober, he's downright tenacious. He's not going to let it go."

"Jenn said he's been going onto shapeshifter hate groups on social media more and more, hunting for local groups. I guess a lot of the former Mystery Seeker people have jumped on there, too. Jenn's already thinking about leaving and moving home to her parents' if he gets any more obsessed with it."

"Those Mystery Seekers are the dangerous ones," said Kathy, sipping her tea. "They wanted to be able to expose and manipulate the shapeshifters, so when Sam Winston and the others came out, there was a huge amount of pushback from them about treating shapeshifters the same as human beings. They have just gotten more diverse with their methods."

"Shoot," said Tanya, glancing at her phone. "I've got to get going!"

We quickly made plans to meet later in the weekend and headed for our respective homes. I texted John to let him know about Rich discovering where he worked and drove completely out of my way into downtown Gunbarrel just to spot anyone tailing me. There was no one.

It was ten to five when the doorbell rang, and I froze in the middle of grading a report about biomes in Africa. Cautiously, I peeked out of the office window and saw our neighbor from across the street, little girl by the hand, carrying what looked to be a brick wrapped in tinfoil.

Grinning at the thought of it being an actual brick and not, which I supposed, a loaf of banana or zucchini bread, I trotted down the stairs to open the door.

"Hi!" said the mother. "I'm Ellen, your neighbor across the street. And this is my daughter Sara. You folks just moved in last weekend, didn't you? I was baking this afternoon and thought you might like some. It's chocolate chip banana bread to say welcome!"

"Oh, thank you! That's wonderful! Won't you come in?" I asked, smiling down at Sara. "Did you help your mom make the bread?"

"Uh-huh," said Sara, hiding behind her mother.

Ellen laughed and tugged her daughter inside. I shut the door, then led the way to the kitchen.

"Coffee?" I asked.

"I'd love some," said Ellen, taking off her coat and removing Sara's as well. "This house is lovely! It's such a different design from ours. I thought some investors bought it, though."

"Oh," I said, smiling as I filled the coffee pot, "that was my uncle's real estate firm. They were going to rent it, but my boyfriend and I needed a place to live, so we bought it from them."

"Ah," said Ellen. "That explains it. We'd seen people in and out a few times, but it had been empty for almost a month. Anyway, welcome to the neighborhood!"

"Thanks," I said. "Sara can have some milk to go with the bread if you'd like. Does that sound good, Sara?"

The little girl nodded, and while the coffee brewed, I showed them around. When we got to the living room, Ellen saw Sara looking at the picture of the black wolf and then over at me.

"Where did you get that?" she asked, pointing to the picture.

"Um, Target, I think," I said, glancing at Sara who was staring at it as well. "Why?"

"Oh, I thought you might have heard, given all the media presence," said Ellen.

"Right! Your daughter was the one rescued in the snowstorm!" I said, trying to cover up my sudden discomfort. "She was brought back by wolves, wasn't she?"

"Shapeshifters," said Ellen. "I think they were shapeshifters. They were way too aware to be regular wolves or dogs. They knew when I thanked them. Real wolves wouldn't have brought her back to us. They wouldn't have known where we lived. Besides, there are no real wolves in Boulder."

"Yeah, that would make sense," I said. "Well, they do say that the shapeshifters are just like you and me, so I'm not surprised they helped her. In any event, I'm glad she's home safe."

"Oh, yes! I was so scared for her," said Ellen as I led the way back into the kitchen. "Did Target have another copy of that picture? I know Sara'd love a copy."

"I think so, yes," I said. "You could probably order it online if not. We can look it up if you like."

We fixed our coffee, and I got a glass of milk for Sara. Retiring to the dining area, we continued to chat. Ellen was a stay-at-home mother for the time being. Her husband, Bob, was in the tech field, working for an up-and-coming business in Silicon Valley. He telecommuted one week, and the next, he'd fly out to California. I mentioned my job at Viceroy High School, and she was excited to find out that I was a teacher. I told her John worked at the university and was due to be home soon if she wanted to meet him.

"Sure, we can stay till then," she said, smiling as she watched Sara exploring the room. "How long have you been together?"

"A while," I said, not wanting to get into the insanity of the last few weeks. "We've known each other for over ten years. We *are* pretty new as a couple, though."

I heard a vehicle come up the drive then and John's car pull into the garage.

"Let me just go warn him we have guests," I said. "If it's been a bad day at the lab, there might be some language Sara ought not to hear."

Ellen chuckled, and I walked out of the room and through the short passage to the garage. John was just getting out of his car, and he smiled as I came to greet him with a kiss.

"We've got company," I said. "Our neighbor from across the street brought us chocolate chip banana bread to welcome us. Her daughter Sara is with her. Figured I'd warn you to watch your 'language.'"

The last was said with air quotes, and John smiled as he caught the double meaning.

"Right, thanks for the heads up," he said. "Does she know?"

"No, but she expects us to know about the incident, so acknowledge it and move on gracefully. There's coffee in the kitchen if you want some."

"Sounds good," he said, and we headed into the house.

We walked into the dining room, and I introduced John to Ellen and Sara. He greeted them, but we both saw the dawning recognition in Sara's eyes when she heard John speak. While I guided Ellen out to the kitchen, I saw John put a finger to his lips and wink at Sara. She nodded and giggled, then followed John to the kitchen, grabbing his hand and holding it tightly.

Ellen looked over at the two of them when they came in and smiled.

"Well, she's certainly taken a shine to you," said Ellen. "Normally she's shy around strange men."

"She can peg someone who likes kids," said John as Sara ran over to take a piece of the bread from her mother. "Especially brave ones."

"She is that," smiled Ellen. "Sometimes too reckless, though. She scared me to death going out in that storm."

"Snow is magical," said John, stirring sugar into his coffee. "I can't say I blame her for wanting to go run out in the first big snowstorm, though I would have waited for the next day when I could see better, myself."

"I suppose, yes," said Ellen. "I was saying to Sasha how grateful I am that those shapeshifters returned her to me. Do you suppose they live near here? I mean, you just moved in and all, but... Sasha, you teach biology. Do they have territories like regular wolves?"

"They might," I said, surprised at the depth of her question. "My biology training never covered shapeshifters, Ellen, but there are probably some similarities between them and their wild kin. So maybe, yeah."

"Oh, I do hope so," said Ellen. "I hope they eventually feel safe enough that I can thank them in person. I wasn't sure what to think about them before this, but I believe they must be good, don't you?"

I sighed, needing to explain, and struggling to find the words.

"I think they are people, Ellen. And like all people, some are good, others not so much. As a whole, they will not be the monsters everyone believes them to be. But like any people, I think you will find the lazy ones, the smart ones, the ones that are good with money, and those who are not. I believe you will find ones who work in all walks of life, and some who stay reclusive. Most will be like people you meet every day, but there will be some who, just like normal people, you can't trust.

"That outlook, Ellen, is what I think we should bring to our understanding of them. They've been among us for a long, long time. It is not unreasonable to believe that they are different from us only in that they can become animals, which, for some people, is already too great a difference to overcome."

She looked at me, surprised, and nodded.

"So if we view them as people, that's the best way to approach them," she said. "I guess that's a good way to see anyone."

"I think you will have a chance to thank them at some point," I said smiling. "If the legislation comes through to add them to anti-discrimination laws, maybe some of them will feel safe enough to be open about their presence."

"Oh, I hope so!" said Ellen. "Both Bob and I would love the chance to meet them."

A few minutes later, we bid them goodbye, telling Ellen she was welcome anytime Bob was away and needed company. Sara shyly shook John's hand as they left, and he stood there watching them cross the street with an odd expression on his face.

"I know you want one of those," I chuckled, "but let's establish ourselves a bit more firmly before we have that discussion."

"Yeah, I do," said John, wistfully. "I want to have a child who grows up knowing his or her parents."

I looked at him, I mean really looked at him, for the first time since we'd gotten back from Wyoming. He'd changed a good deal in the last few weeks. He really did come across as more sure of himself, more "grown up" in how he carried himself. He'd never really expressed a great interest in children before other than as an abstract concept. Today, I'd seen a different side of him.

"Okay," I said. "Let's go sit down and talk about it."

We went into the living room and sat on the love seat, angling ourselves to face each other. I waited expectantly, and after a moment, he sighed.

"I know what you mean by waiting a little bit before we go down that particular path," he said. "We just got together, we just got this house, we both have had some huge, life-altering events already. I get waiting for a few months or even a year, but I'd rather not wait longer than that to start trying. If you want to get married first, we could do that too. I do want to have children, though. With you."

I looked at him and sighed

"All right," I said. "I'll admit, I'm thirty-four now and waiting too much longer isn't the best idea. Not to mention, our wolf sides have already made up their minds. I do want to get married first if we can because I feel it's important. I just don't want to rush into anything more until we both get our heads wrapped around what has already happened to us. I also believe that until we deal with Rich, a child will be a liability. So we'll have to figure him out first."

"Agreed," said John.

"Good. Are you okay with getting together with Tanya and Kathy sometime this weekend?"

"Sure," he said. "Tomorrow?"

"Okay," I nodded. "If they're available, we'll come up with a plan then. For tonight, however, let's go grab some dinner in celebration of our decision to make future plans."

John smiled a huge grin at that, and we left to find some place to ponder our possibilities.

18

STALKING

Midway through Saturday afternoon, John, Tanya, Kathy, and I met at what was fast becoming our favorite coffee shop. Over lattes, we talked about the visit from the neighbor and tried to figure out what to do about Rich and the others. Tanya had heard nothing new, but she agreed that they were a major problem.

"So," smiled Kathy, trying to lighten the conversation, "is there any good news?"

"Well," I said, looking over at John. "We were discussing the possibility of getting married in the not too distant future."

"Married?" asked Tanya in surprise. "But you just got together!"

"When some types of shapeshifters find their partners, they are already bound together by those ties," said Kathy. "Ravens also pair bond, so marriage becomes merely a symbol of what they already know. An important symbol, to be sure, but it doesn't change what the couple already feels intrinsically. Paul and I were married within a year of meeting because our raven natures knew each other so well."

I nodded, glancing at John and smiling.

"Well, then I guess congratulations are in order," Tanya said.

"Hey, hey!" laughed John. "We're not even engaged yet! I mean, where am I going to find a ring pop in this city anyway!"

I pretended to hit him, then talk turned to other things. As well as we knew Rich, we didn't know what he was likely to do next, but Kathy commented that the local corbies would probably have no problems keeping an eye out for Rich if we asked them politely.

"I do know that Rich and the others are searching for you, John," said Tanya. "They may have already been tailing you. Watch your back."

"What can they really do, though?" asked John. "It's not like I'm going to make a spectacle of myself. They can't make me angry, like the Hulk or something, and trick me into changing. I mean, that can't happen, right?"

"No," I said, "but they could hurt you. They're not thinking rationally. On top of that, Rich is angry and looking for someone to blame."

"I'll keep that in mind," John said. "I don't want any trouble with those guys. Gary and Todd always scared me in a thuggy sort of way."

"Good," I said. "They scare me too. I can't believe I never saw what they were really like."

"They hide it well," said Tanya.

Talk soon turned to other things, and eventually, we bade each other goodbye and went home. On the way, John and I chatted about trivial things, normal things. Neither of us brought it up, but I was sure both of us were thinking hard about what Tanya had said. I couldn't believe how obsessed Rich had become over the idea of John being a shapeshifter. I mean, yeah, it was true, but nothing had happened that would have made him come up with it on his own, was there? Was there?

Sunday morning, I woke at dawn with the undeniable urge to run. John was still asleep, so I didn't wake him, but instead threw on sweats, left him a note, and took out my car. The last few days had been warmer, and a lot of the snow piles by the road had melted down to mere nubs. What I needed was a place to run without being seen. The snow was too slushy to run in the woods without leaving deep, easy-to-follow tracks, so I drove out of the city and into the foothills of the mountains to the west. It was not a bad drive this early in the morning; I cut over to 119 and followed it towards the mountains. A little drive to the north, and I was soon headed down one of the main roads into the canyons. I had driven out here frequently over the years, and found it to feel very much like home.

Once out of the city, however, I noticed that there was a car on the road a little ways behind me that seemed to be keeping pace with me, and I got a creeping sensation of unease. I tested the theory by speeding up, and it kept the same distance. It wasn't a car I recognized; the car was tagged as being from Ohio and was pretty nondescript; the perfect car to tail someone.

The earlier parts of Lee Hill Road were residential, scattered with neighborhoods and coffee shops, but once past all of that, the area was pretty barren. I knew how to loop around from where I was, though, and I made no attempt to speed up or slow down as the car followed me the whole way through the scenic forest drive, and back towards the city

I finally got back into the busy part of Lee Hill and found an open coffee shop. Pulling into the parking lot, I watched to see what the car would do. It drove in after me and came alongside. It was Rich.

I got out of the driver's side and stormed over to where he was coming out of his car.

"What the hell do you mean, following me like this?" I asked as he shut the door. "How did you even find me?"

"You used to tell me when you would disappear Saturday mornings that you would drive up into the canyons around here," he said, closing his door and walking around to lean against the left front fender. "I took a shot that you'd do the same no matter where you were."

"In a rental car?" I said. "So I wouldn't recognize you?"

"Oh, this was just for convenience," said Rich. "I've been following your friend John around. Apparently he's taken up residence in the Gunbarrel area near the Twin Lakes Park. You had coffee with him yesterday...him and Tanya and another woman. I think she might be the other wolf."

"No, Rich. I can tell you with absolute certainty that she is not a wolf," I said, exasperated. "Why are you so determined to believe that my friends are shapeshifters?"

"Sash, you heard the reports that a child was rescued from two shapeshifters? I think one is John and the other must be that friend you were hanging with. I told you John was a freak. The guys and I are working on a plan to expose him for what he is as soon as we catch him howling at the full moon, or whatever it is that shapeshifters do. Stay away from him. He's dangerous."

My anger had been rising this entire time.

"Oh, yeah, they were so dangerous that they rescued a little girl from freezing in a snowstorm," I snapped. "Give me a break."

"Sasha, the people who live near there need to be warned!"

"Rich, I didn't want you to have to find out this way, but that's *my* house you're stalking. *I* bought that house in Gunbarrel through my uncle. John moved in with me. As for John, he's no monster, and he's less dangerous than you and your drunk friends are."

Rich seemed momentarily at a loss for words.

"John moved in with you?" he asked incredulously. "As a roommate? You bought a house, and he lives with you?"

"Yes, Rich, he lives with me," I said.

"Please tell me you're not sleeping with that creep," said Rich, shaking his head.

"And if I am?" I said, glaring at him. "You and I broke up! You don't get a say in what I do anymore."

"We didn't break up; you left," said Rich, his anger clear. "Come on, Sasha, he's just a low-life kid. He's not worth you! Your family will kick you out of your inheritance before they let you stay with him."

"Was my family's money all you cared about, Rich?" I snarled. "We are through! You don't get to choose who I see, who I hang out with, or who I sleep with, got it?"

"Sash, he's a shapeshifter!"

"Rich," I said, staring him in the eyes. "You're insane."

"Sasha, I know he is, and I'm going to prove it to you," said Rich, his hands balling into fists.

"Rich, you have absolutely no proof that he is anything other than a normal man," I said. "I'm done with this. Do *not* bother me or John again, or else I'll take out a restraining order on you and your band of merry men, got it? That wouldn't do any of your reputations any good, especially since I have witnesses to your antics at the school. Just go away."

"I can't do that, Sash!" said Rich. "Damn it, I love you. I was going to ask you to marry me. I was going to plan a family with you. We can still do that; it's not too late!"

"Yes, it is," I said. "It's way too late."

I walked back over to the driver's side of my car and took out my phone. I made a show of dialing the police, and I told them that my ex was following me in a rental car and had just threatened me and my new boyfriend. The officer asked for the license number, which I gladly gave him as Rich got into the car and sped off. Once Rich was well out of sight, I drove to the nearest station to file a report.

After a stress-filled hour at the police station, I still had the urge to run, so I drove over to Jimmy Forebear's place in the Boulder Creek area. He was an older badger, and he and his wife had a working farm out there. Jimmy wasn't the most friendly man to deal with, but he was relatively understanding about the needs of wolves. As long as I didn't bother his chickens, he didn't care if I ran the land. He and his wife were fairly solitary, hired farm help when they needed it, and generally did okay for themselves. The land wasn't as secluded as I liked, but after this morning, I was thankful that at least it was private.

After watching carefully behind me, I made it to the Forebear's farm. Jimmy was out in the farmyard when I pulled in, tinkering with a tractor. His wife Sally came out of the house when she saw me. She was much more social and had softened Jimmy towards me when I'd brought them a homemade apple pie last Thanksgiving.

I half-skated across the icy driveway, and Sally greeted me with a hug when I went over to see her. Jimmy stood up, walking over to stand with his wife.

"Was that you and one of your kin who rescued that little girl the other day?" Sally asked, smiling at me.

"My mate," I said. "He's a friend of mine who's a late bloomer. We've known each other for years. Yes, we found her and got her home safely."

"Been better if you hadn't been seen, maybe," said Jimmy. "But I guess it will all help those folks in Washington convince the ones too stupid to listen to sense."

"I hope so," I said.

"You come for a run?" asked Sally, her eyes twinkling.

"Yeah," I said, sighing. "I was going to go up into the canyons this morning, but my ex followed me out there, and we had a bit of a confrontation."

"Did you win?" grinned Jimmy.

"James Ulysses Forebear!" said Sally, then turned to me. "Sasha, go for your run, and *then* come back and tell us what happened."

I nodded, texted John that I'd be home in a bit, and jogged up into the orchard. There was still snow on the ground, but the air was warmer – almost in the fifties – and stripping wasn't nearly as traumatic as I'd anticipated. I rolled my clothes up, stuck them in the fork of an apple tree, and changed. Loping across the orchard moments later, I gave tongue to some of my pent-up frustration, and then bolted top-speed towards the woods by the creek. The land on this side of it belonged to Jimmy, and I didn't have to worry much about anyone being around with all the snow still on the ground.

I ran something like five miles before turning and heading back to the farmhouse, finally tired out. Clothed once again, I went to the car, retrieved my phone, and returned to the house to have a cup of Sally's coffee and a slice of her huckleberry pie while I told her of my morning confrontation with Rich.

"Your ex sounds like he is going to be more of a problem than you bargained for," said Jimmy, shaking his head. "I'd like to meet your new wolf, though. Sounds like a decent fellow."

"Tell you what," said Sally, glancing at Jimmy for confirmation. "You two come up here for runs. The weather pattern is supposed to hold, so if you come visit next Sunday, we can meet him. Not as exciting as the wilderness out west, but safer for now."

"Maybe deal with some of those rabbits," said Jimmy, nodding. "Or run the deer out of the orchards."

"James Forebear!" said Sally.

"What? Easy way to pay us back!"

"Actually, that would be fine," I said. "John needs practice being a wolf. I could train him on your farm with rabbits and deer just as easily as I could with antelope and bobcats. And it's safer too."

"See," said Jimmy, glancing at his wife. "Works for everyone."

Sally just gave him a look.

"It's fine," I said, smiling and standing to go. "I'll see you next Sunday morning, then."

"See you," said Sally, walking me to the door. "Be careful on the ice."

"Thanks," I said, and half-skated to the car, my thoughts already in a more centered place. The Forebears were definitely right about one thing, though. Rich was going to be much more trouble than any of us had bargained for.

19
UNEXPECTED SUPPORT

Sitting with John during a speakerphone call with Nevermore and Tanya that afternoon, I filled them in about my run-in with Rich and the trip to the Forebear's farm. The news made everyone uneasy, and John was livid when I repeated Rich's words.

"A lot he knows," said Kathy, her tone darkening. "Where does Rich get off saying that your relatives would not conscience John as your mate?"

"Considering they practically threw him at me?" I said, rolling my eyes at John. "I mean, his idea that my family wouldn't welcome John is not based on anything but his own ego."

"Of course, it is," snorted Kathy. "Rich just doesn't understand. His world is based on the idea that money marries money. He doesn't understand pack structure or how the hierarchy works within it."

"Naturally," I countered. "Honestly, Tanya, he doesn't know anything about my relatives other than what they've shown him. John, on the other hand, is a member of the pack through me. Even if we weren't in a relationship, by extension, he is already connected."

"Which is totally weird," said John, running his hand through his hair, "but I'm glad it's that way. How often do you get accepted into any family that fast?"

"Well, they never really liked Rich," I said, smiling. "They liked you right off."

"So, who are these people you were talking about?" asked Tanya. "Are they shapeshifters too?"

"Yes," I said, "though you likely won't meet them anytime soon. They're badgers and are pretty solitary people. Good folks, though."

"How many shapeshifters are there in the Boulder area?" asked John.

"Rough guess, around 20,000 in Boulder County," said Kathy. "That includes the whole area around us. I've heard more are coming here because it's such a good area for families."

"Twenty thousand shapeshifters?" asked Tanya. "There's that many?"

"Just about," said Kathy. "And that's just in the Boulder area. You forget, we have been part of your society for centuries. We simply are within it. There are bears and deer and otters and even moose that I know living in this city, which is probably more than the rest of you did. Viceroy High has had quite a few shapeshifter students through it, but they are hard to pinpoint. Corbies hear more than other clans because, as crows, ravens and, jays, we can fly around the city unnoticed. It's a little hard for a moose to wander through downtown Boulder!"

"So you have seen more than we have," I said. "And just who have I had in class?"

"A few of the AP and honors kids you have now are shapeshifters," said Kathy, grinning. "You should come to our after school reading club. You might get a surprise. I'll check with the parents of the ones who might be receptive to the idea and arrange a specific meeting just for those members sometime next week."

"You're on."

"I hate to interrupt, but none of this helps us figure out how to get Rich off your cases," said Tanya. "Jenn said that they're planning something soon, but she's not going to stick around to find out what. Todd slapped her the other day for asking why they are so obsessed. She's packing her bags to go home as we speak. We need a plan."

"Running away is not an option for us," said Kathy. "Can your mother get us through to Sam Winston's mother, Sasha? She might have an idea."

"I think Rich's going to try to expose us," I said. "To the community and to our workplaces."

"It also sounds like he still thinks you are human, Sasha, although why he can't put two and two together is beyond me," Kathy said. "There were two wolves, after all."

"Maybe he doesn't want to admit to himself that he was dating you for six years and didn't know would be my guess," said John, snorting. "He can't admit that his ex-girlfriend might have been one of those 'abominations.'"

"He wouldn't be able to handle that," I said. "I'll call my mother. Let's see what she can come up with."

I added my mother to the group call and repeated this morning's incident. Her stony silence was palpable through the line. I could hear her calling to my father and listened as dad came onto the extension. Mother filled my father, and he grew still as well.

"If they out you and it goes badly, we'll support you, both you and John," said my father.

"And I spoke to Susan earlier," said my mother. "She wants you to call at your earliest convenience – today, that is. If you are all together there, we can simply add her. Hold on."

I heard my mother make the call through on another line, and a young child picked up on the other end.

"Hello?"

"Hi, sweetie," said my mother. "Could you get Grandma Susan to come on the line? Tell her it's Eloise Wellington."

"Kay. Grandma!!! Ms. Wellington for you!"

We heard the sound of boot heels walking over to the phone, and someone picked up the line.

"Hello?"

"Hi, Susan," said Mother. "It's Eloise. We're both here, along with my daughter, her mate John, her friend Kathy, who is a corbie, and one of the local native tribe members who is an ally to us. We figured it might be better to all talk to you together."

"That's quite a crew," said Susan, sounding a little surprised. "Did something happen?"

"You heard about the little child rescued by wolves. That was my two here. Her ex-boyfriend, who is very anti-shapeshifter, is trying to gain proof of John being one of us. He thinks he can win Sasha back, but apparently does not believe or will not believe she could be one of us. We think they will try to out them to their workplaces, and we are trying to figure out what progress has been made at the legal level."

"Well," said Susan, thoughtfully. "This is a bit of a pickle, isn't it? Sam told us two days ago that they are very close to crafting an amendment that will include shapeshifters in the anti-discrimination legislature. He said that he had testified along with the other delegates, and most of the Democrats seemed convinced, mainly because they think it will go over well with their voters. The Republicans seem to be mostly fine with it too as long as it wouldn't mean any extra money added to it. The few that are dragging their heels are those who claim that we are against their religious beliefs. That argument is being countered by the fact that there is nothing in the Bible that speaks about us one way or the other. Then some groups switched over to us being like demons. Most people started to scoff at them then.

"The long and the short of it is that it might not even be that big a deal, especially for John and Sasha. They rescued a child. Your ex is clearly unhinged and has had the police called on him once..."

"Twice," I said with satisfaction.

"Not to mention that the principal gave the other staff members hell for arguing about it the other day," piped in Kathy.

"Yes, that may be to your benefit, though not everyone is likely to simply toe the line," said Susan, her voice thoughtful. "I can relay a message to Sam, though I am not sure what impact it will have. We think that they will vote on including shapeshifters in the laws sometime in the next few months. Hang in a little longer. If he does try to out you to your jobs, call me, and I'll see what Sam and the others can do to help you."

"Thank you, Susan," said my mother.

"Oh, and Sasha?" said Susan.

"Yes?"

"Why don't you, John, Eloise, and Dennis come up to the ranch during Sasha's next break from school? That would be the end of March, right? After the incident with the little girl, I'm sure Sam would love to meet you. The family is planning a small wedding ceremony for him and Laura the first weekend of your break. You folks being here could be seen as a gesture of good will between clans."

"I would love that!" I exclaimed.

"That would be lovely," said my mother, and my father agreed with enthusiasm.

"Excellent," said Susan. "We'll be in touch with more details closer to the day."

She left the call, and we returned to making our plans.

"Now," said my mother, "I think your best course of action is just to lay low for the time being. If he tries to out you, we'll sue him. I don't care if he is the purest blood human in the country. When our lawyers get done with him, he'll wish he had never spoken a word."

My parents bade us goodbye and left the conversation. I turned my attention back to my friends.

"Kathy, I'll be at the meeting after school Monday. Get in touch with any of our previous students who are shapeshifters and ask them to come too, if they can. Let's have a discussion about how to stick up for ourselves. We're going to need to."

"Will do," she said. "I can open a Google Meet for them to hop onto if they can't get there physically."

"Send me the link to that, too," said John.

"I'll be at work," said Tanya. "You'll have to catch me up later."

"And I will brace my principal, Mr. Turner, and let him know about

Rich coming in to stir up trouble," I said. "I think he would be amenable."

"Good, then we're agreed. The Corbies will start telling other shapeshifters about what may be coming, and alert them that we may have to take a stand," said Kathy. "The corbies will spread the news, don't worry. By the way, have you decided where to register for wedding presents?"

Talk turned, blessedly, to other things and, soon enough, the others left, and John and I had time to be with just each other again.

The rest of that night was as it should be.

Monday, back at school, was fairly uneventful, and during my prep period, I went to meet with Principal Turner. He received me warmly, bidding me close the door.

"What can I do for you, Ms. Wellington?" he asked, settling behind his desk.

"My new boyfriend and I are still having problems with my ex. I had to file a police report because he followed me in a rental car all the way up into the canyons. I'm worried he's going to try to do something to try to get me fired. He's already threatened my boyfriend."

"Ms. Wellington," Thom Turner said, peering over the top of his glasses, "What on earth could he have on you?"

"Well, he is convinced that my boyfriend is a shapeshifter," I said. "He promised to out him to his employer. He may do the same to me."

Thom Turner eyed me speculatively for a long moment before speaking.

"Ms. Wellington...Sasha...I know that there are shapeshifters among my staff and students. I have been here a long time, long enough to witness a few very strange events. I am not going to ask you whether you are or not...that is none of my business...but you are one of my finest teachers, and I would no more let this immature man-child threaten one of my best teachers than I would fly."

My eyes brimmed over with tears then, and I reached for a tissue in the box on Mr. Turner's desk. I got myself under control as fast as I could and looked back up at the man across from me.

"I grew up in this town," he said gently. "One of the best people I ever got to meet was a young teacher in the first grade named Mrs. Woodhaven. On more than one occasion, she protected the children when necessary, even from their own parents. I remember biking back to one evening when I was ten to get the brand new catcher's mitt that I had left in the outfield; the office had called my parents to let me know they'd found it. There was some PTA event going on, so one of the office staff was there late.

"I came out of the building and peered through the twilight out across the field. There was Mrs. Woodhaven, out behind the big wooden castle-like fort near the woods at the edge of the playground. She was standing mostly hidden, so I certainly didn't see anything a child shouldn't, but then suddenly, out walked a bear from where she had been. I must have yelled in surprise because she suddenly stood up and saw me. And then she waved, just like a person, dropped back to all fours, picked up a gym bag in her teeth, and lumbered off into the woods behind the school.

"I really thought I was seeing things, but the next day, she saw me in the hall and motioned me to come to her room. She asked me to never say anything about what I saw, or she might lose her job. I swore to her I wouldn't, and I never did. Do you know, after all these years, I'm still in touch with her? Nicest woman I've ever known. Retired now. When the official word came out that there were shapeshifters, I called her immediately, and she confirmed what I'd always known. She told me that she hoped that there can finally be the understanding that they are as much a part of the world as the humans are and just want to continue to cohabitate in peace."

He smiled at me, obviously lost in thought, then refocused his eyes, seeing only me.

"I love that old woman," he said. "When I lost my own mother, she was the first one after my family that I called. She was a mama bear to the lot of us. Never had kids of her own that I know of, but then again, I didn't know a lot about her life outside of school. If all shapeshifters are like her, the world will be blessed to have them."

"They're not all like that, but many are," I said at his unspoken question. "They're people. We love, argue, and struggle just as much as any human being. Mostly, we try to make the world better."

"You do that," agreed Mr. Turner, kindly. "So don't you worry about that ex-boyfriend of yours. And Ms. Wellington? If he does come after you, know I will defend you and any other of the teachers here who share your unique gifts. Thank you for your trust."

"Thank you for yours," I said, standing to leave the office.

I looked back, but he had turned to gaze out the window, obviously lost in thought. I let myself out and shut the door.

I went through the rest of the day in a daze, and when the final bell rang, I pretty much sprinted to get to Nevermore's room, curiosity almost eating me alive. Several of my honors students were already there, and they greeted me enthusiastically as soon as I entered. As a few more trickled through the door, Kathy checked her text messages, nodding to herself.

"They'll be here soon," she said.

"Who?" asked a girl named Marci impatiently. "You said that earlier. Who are our special guests?"

Kathy just smiled and shook her head.

"You'll see," she said.

The students started chatting about the book they had been reading, and Kathy occasionally glanced at her phone. Finally she grinned, and seconds later, we heard people coming down the hall from the entrance. I knew those voices, and when the group of people walked through the door, I bounced over to them and embraced them one at a time. They all were laughing at something. Some of them had graduated last year, but there were a couple I hadn't seen since my first year of teaching. As Kathy closed the door, I wondered how she had managed to stay in touch with all of them as she wasn't into social media. We turned to grin at our bewildered current students.

"Kids, some of these folks you know, but all of them have graduated from here in the last ten years or so. All of you have something in common. Can you guess?"

Sammi Juniper, a sophomore, hesitantly raised her hand, and said, "They all like books?"

One of the newcomers, Garrett Young, chuckled.

"I do love books," he said, "But that isn't it."

"Well, I know that a couple of them were in AP classes," said Leonie, a junior. "But I'm betting it's not that either."

"No," said Kathy, her eyes twinkling with mischief. "Anyone else?"

"They're like us," said Paulo, another junior, shyly. "They're shapeshifters."

All of the current students looked around at each other, alarmed at the sudden turn of events. Obviously, Paulo knew that a couple of his classmates had to be shapeshifters, but he'd put connections together with the same speed he intuitively leapt to ideas in my class.

"Yes," said Kathy. "We are all shapeshifters here. There are others I'm in touch with, but they can't make it today. I do have some of them coming to the Google Meet I am going to set up, however. Hang on, let me start it."

Sammi stared at me in surprise.

"You, Ms. Wellington?" she asked. "I never would have guessed."

"We all hide it well, don't we?" I said, grinning.

Garrett snorted and poked one of the other graduates, "Some of us do. Ovaltine over here is pretty obvious."

"That's Olivia to you, Gravel-brain," said the woman he had spoken about, poking him back affectionately.

Kathy opened up the Meet window where people were already in the waiting room. She let them in, and I was pleased to see John waving at me through his camera.

"Hey!" said Garrett, seeing John on the screen. "John Arndt, what are you doing here? You're one of us?"

"Yeah, Garrett. I'm surprised to see you too," said John, his tone barely concealing his old dislike for the football player who he'd known when he was a junior. "Small world."

"Very," said Garrett, laughing. "Look, man, it's been ten years. Bygones and all. We don't need the animosity between us. There's enough of that to go around in the rest of the world."

Marci glanced at the screen and then around at everyone else.

"I don't know if I should be here," she said. "I mean, I haven't changed yet, so we don't even know if I count."

"Marci, you're only fourteen," said Kathy. "You have plenty of time, don't worry."

"Hey, I'm twenty-seven and just changed," said John. "You've got time, believe me."

Marci smiled, and Kathy winked at John.

"So," said Maryann Wright, a current senior, "Why did you call us all here today?"

I gave them a slightly edited version of what had been happening to us, starting with John's transformation a few weeks ago and ending with Rich's recent stalking attempt. Garrett's eyes went wide when I mentioned that John and I were living together, but he held his tongue, a definite change from his student days. I didn't feel it was my place to share Mr. Turner's personal story, though, and only said that he was sympathetic to our plight. When I was done, they all looked at each other, current and former, and then over at Kathy and me.

"What do we do?" asked Kim, one of the visitors. "Some of us knew each other before, it's true, but if we have to make a stand..."

"It's scary," said Will, another of the former students. "Our parents have cautioned us since we were little never to talk about it...which, by the way, makes this super awkward."

"I think it's great," said Leonie, enthusiastically. "I mean, I never knew about the rest of you either."

"Which is why I never told you about each other before," said

Kathy, "It's your parents' decision. Do you think that your parents didn't know some of the other shapeshifters? They do. But the decision was made long ago, right or wrong, to be as discreet as possible, and that meant no special schools and no shapeshifters-only clubs, though you all gravitated here on your own without anyone's help. They wanted you to live as normal a life as possible, to make your own friends, your own choices.

"It also has to do with how powers manifest," she continued. "Marci is a good example. I'm sure she already compares herself to her own family members, some of whom have gone through our school, but it's hard if your friends change before you too. There is no rhyme or reason for when you will change. John is not the oldest I've known, but he's close. There are also still a lot of issues between the clans. Better to spare the children that problem till they're older."

"Too true," said Olivia. "My clan has been at odds with several others for generations. The kids don't need to see that."

"But what if," said Paulo, "we became friends? Wouldn't it make more sense to rid ourselves of those prejudices now?"

"Parents do have the choice for their children," said Kathy, "But you all need to know what's coming. When things change in our society, we can be more open about who we are. We'll still have to be careful, though. Change happens slowly."

"A lot of us fear the government," said James, another graduate on the Meet. "What if they insist on creating lists of us or registries, tagging us like wild beasts?"

"I don't think that will happen," I said. "Sam's mother seems pretty confident we will be covered under existing anti-discrimination laws."

"You spoke to Susan Winston?" asked Will, his eyes wide.

"We both did," said Kathy, "And John too."

On the screen, John nodded.

"I think that the more we know each other now, the safer we'll be," he said. "We need a sense of solidarity rather than isolation."

Everyone was silent for a long moment, looking around the room. I got it; I had been raised that way too. I didn't know my classmates as anything other than people, and I was pretty happy just being treated like a human child. But, I reflected, there were definitely times I had wished to know if any of my other classmates were shapeshifters. There was a certain type of loneliness within the groups I played with, mostly because I'd had to hide that aspect of myself. What if I had been able to share my first transformation with friends who could understand it? Even having one friend at school who knew might have been a game-changer for me. Studying the members of the AP group, I saw that potential open to them now.

"Look at them," said Kathy to me, her voice happy. "This was a good idea."

I glanced around the room. Shy Paulo was talking with Leonie. Maryann was joking about her first transformation with Marci. Even John and Garrett were exchanging awkward pleasantries. It was awesome to watch them really see each other as they really were.

Kathy sidled up to me, saying, "Now we just have to convince the rest of the parents."

"I think they'll come around too," I said. "I mean, Garrett and John? Never thought I'd see the day those two would be friendly with each other."

Kim and Will came over to us, nodding at the others in the room.

"So the question is, what do we do?" asked Will.

The other conversations in the room faltered as everyone listened.

"Get the word out to the clans," said Kathy. "Let them know we may need to stand together if the group Rich is with takes some drastic action. People are going to need to be ready for anything."

"So what are you all?" asked Olivia. "I mean, if you're willing to say."

"For the record," I said. "I come from a wolf clan."

"I as well," said John quickly, "though I don't know what one."

"Orphaned?" said Garrett. "Me too, though I was brought up by a relative. Puma clan."

"Snow goose," said Kim.

"Big Horn sheep," said Will.

"Lynx," said Leonie.

"Fox clan." This came from Marci.

"Pronghorn," said Paulo.

"Swan," said Casey, a junior.

Watching the kids name their clans made my heart soar. They seemed happy to be doing it as well, and all of them looked around at the others with a new sense of self-knowledge. Olivia hesitated the longest, then fist-bumped Garrett and said, "Grizzly" in a tone that defied any to challenge her badder-than-thou attitude. Maryann hugged Garrett when she announced that they shared a clan, and Sammi, blue jay, seemed overjoyed to find out that Kathy was another corbie. Abbey and Ted, two of the other graduates who were also siblings and both weasel clan, were talking to one of the other seniors, Brock, who was from the skunk clan.

John and I smiled at each other through the camera and listened to the kids talking excitedly with the past graduates. James quietly announced that he was from another of the wolf-clans further to the west, and he and John fell to chatting.

"Hey, guys," I said to the younger students. "I know it's cool to find out about each other, and I don't think you should stop doing that. Just remember not to ignore your human friends. They're still important to you, and if they are real friends, they will stick with you through everything that is to come."

Leonie nodded her head fiercely.

"I won't," she said. "But I hope that our new friendships are important to them as well."

"We'll have to work on that," said Marci. "Make sure they know they are still our friends no matter what. Someone is bound to get jealous or hurt. It won't be easy."

"But it's totally worth it," said Leonie decisively, drawing sounds of agreement from the others around her.

After a few more minutes, we decided to call it a day. Phone numbers and Instagram accounts were exchanged between the previous and current students, and Olivia quietly invited Kathy and me to join the graduates at the local Applebee's in Broomfield. We agreed to go for a short visit and found that the upperclassmen had followed us, dragging both Sammi and Marci along with them. I sighed and rolled my eyes before being reassured by the younger girls that they had texted their parents to let them know. Blue jays and foxes tended to be a bit more chill than some of the other clans, but they would still be worried about their children if they didn't let them know.

Of course, being in public, we couldn't talk about anything related to our previous conversation, so we caught up on safer topics, like where everyone was living now, what they were doing for work, and what their future plans were. Olivia and Garrett gasped when I mentioned Melissa's foiled plan, and Garrett shook his head over John and me living together.

"It figures," Garrett said, sighing. "John gets one of the hottest teachers we've ever had. Only he could've that kind of luck."

"If I recall, you ranked him to the dogs and back," said Kathy, giving Garrett the evil eye. "Don't tell me you don't think the universe might have owed him one?"

"Well, back then he was just weird, strange John," said Garrett. "He seems to have settled a bit since then."

"He's changed a lot since high school," I smiled. "I think discovering he's a shapeshifter has made a marked difference in him too."

"Or you have," said Olivia. "You steadied him and stood by him. I heard the undertone of what you didn't tell the kids. Rescuing him from your cousin has a lot more significance to us older, more worldly folk."

She said the last with a slight twist of sarcasm, but smiled afterwards to soften it.

"I'd like to see him again in person," she said.

"Me too," said Garrett.

"We'll arrange something. Maybe dinner? Are you two still dating?"

"Yes," grinned Garrett. "And before you ask, we told each other everything a few years ago, so we knew. Granted, our families were a little weirded out, but it's been good. We actually have both sets of parents over from time to time for dinner. I think they're trying to out-polite each other. Bears and pumas are both too political for their own good sometimes."

Shrieks of laughter erupted from the table where the AP students were eating. Leonie had apparently just told them something funny, which had set them laughing hysterically.

"You know," said Kathy, "I think that is the happiest I have ever seen Paulo. Or Casey, for that matter."

"It's good for them to meet other shapeshifters," I said. "You know how it made a difference for us. They need to have people their own age around who know what they're going through."

After a short while, we left the restaurant and headed home. It had been a day of surprises for me, and although Kathy hadn't said it, I knew she too was well-pleased.

20

THE CAVALRY

It was around six on Wednesday that my stomach, which had its own internal clock, had apparently guessed the lateness of the hour. I glanced up from grading papers to notice that it was dark, and John had not yet come home. I checked my phone: no call, no text. Something was not right. I called his cell, and it rang and rang before finally going to voicemail. Two seconds after I hung up, my phone chimed with an unfortunately familiar tune. The caller ID confirmed it was Rich. A chill came over me.

"Hello?" I said hesitantly.

"Hi Sasha." It wasn't Rich; it was Gary, sounding very pleased with himself. "I guess you were expecting your little wolf buddy, huh? Well, he's here with us right now, but he's too tied up to talk to you."

"What do you want, Gary?" I said, feeling my gut twist with anger and fear.

"We want you to come down and join the party. Rich is here, and Todd, and a few of our other friends who are looking forward to seeing the expression on your face when John turns into a wolf. He will, you know. At some point, he'll change. And then the whole world will know."

"Gary, I don't know why you all think John is a wolf, but what you are doing now is kidnapping, you know that, right?"

"It's not kidnapping if the person isn't human," said Gary, smugly. "Here, let me give you to Rich."

Gary handed the phone off, and I heard muttering off to the side.

"Hi, Sash," came Rich's voice, sounding way too calm. "You know, John's starting to seem a little worse for wear. Why don't you come down, and you can see what he really is. He'll have to transform eventually. These beasts can only keep control for so long. We're at Gary's dojo. You know where it is. Come alone. No police."

He hung up, and I felt a cold frisson of fear run down my spine followed by a burst of fury.

"Alone, hell," I said and called Kathy.

Her response was exactly what I had expected.

"Call Garrett and the others," she said. "Have you called the police?"

"Too risky," I said. "Gary has friends on the police force. They might tip him off."

"All right," Kathy said grimly. "Text Paul the address, and we'll meet you there. We're leaving now."

A call to Garrett was greeted with the same reaction I had gotten from Kathy, and several minutes and a few other numbers later, I was out the door and on my way to the dojo. I drove fast but not recklessly. Making the calls had kept my panic at bay, but now my terror was growing as to what John must be going through. I was trying not to panic, and the only thing keeping me from doing eighty down the road was the knowledge that getting stopped while wearing only my pink bathrobe would not help him.

I pulled up in front of the dark building and looked to see a pair of ravens perched on a fence nearby. Down the street, a van idled, and Kim stepped out, walking to the back and opening it. A grizzled wolf, James I assumed, hopped down, followed by Olivia and Garrett, both wearing dark robes. Seconds later, Will, fully dressed, followed. They headed for the shadows of the alley beside the dojo.

I nodded to the ravens and carefully approached the door of the studio, leaving my keys in the visor of my unlocked car. The asphalt was cold under my bare feet, but I ignored it, focusing on getting inside as fast as I could. The anger at what they had done to John was beginning to overwhelm my fears, and my imagination was conjuring up images best left in the dark, full of flashing teeth and blood. I made my way to the entrance. It was ajar, and I slipped inside.

Although the front area of the dojo had seemed empty, a man appeared from the alcove to my left as soon as I came in, blocking my exit. He glanced outside suspiciously, and then motioned me further into the dojo. I could hear laughter coming from the back room as I followed him into a scene right out of some old thirties mob film.

A single fluorescent bulb, flickering the way they do right before they die, illuminated the center of the room, but left the edges in shadow. Rich, Todd, Gary and about a dozen people I didn't know were standing in a circle around a bloodied figure tied to a chair. It took me a moment to recognize John, and I looked at him, horrified at what they had done. His face was puffy and bruised with one eye swollen completely shut. He sat slumped in the chair, and I had no way of telling what other damage they had inflicted on him. Gary struck him across the face again as I came into the room. Dazed, John rolled his one good eye at me, and then went limp, sagging against the ropes that held him.

"Oh, come on!" yelled Gary. "He's unconscious? Really?"

"He must be faking," said Todd from where he stood filming John, then glanced up to see me come in. Noticing my bathrobe, he sneered. "Hey, Sasha. In such a hurry to get to lover boy here you didn't even get dressed?"

"Sasha," said Rich, coming over to me and trying to put his hands on my shoulders. I backed up a step and he stopped, seeming hurt. "Aren't you glad to see me?"

"Are you deranged?" I yelled. "You kidnapped my best friend and beat the hell out of him. Why would I be glad to see you?"

"Sash, he's an animal. Any minute, he'll become a giant wolf, you'll see."

"Rich, he's unconscious. Seriously. He's not going to become a giant anything."

"He's just shamming," said Gary, grabbing John by the hair, using it raise his slack face. He let John's head drop, then kicked the chair over, sending it crashing to the ground. I started forward, but Rich blocked my way.

"Sash," said Rich. "He's a loser. Why would you be with someone like that, huh? He works at the college in a lab; he makes like no money. Plus, he's a monster. You know I can do better for you than he can."

"I don't think so," said Garrett from behind me. I looked over to see him leaning insouciantly on the doorframe with his arms crossed. He winked at me.

"Who the hell are you?" asked Rich.

"An old friend of John's," smiled Garrett coolly, and then threw his robe off in one agile movement, blurring into a puma at the same time. He crouched, ears lowered to his head and screamed a challenge to the men around the room. Seconds later, another roar joined his, and a grizzly stalked in, rose to her full height, and roared again. A swipe of her paw batted the camera out of Todd's hand, smashing it to the floor. James followed her into the room, snarling at anyone who moved.

Several of the men gaped; expressions of horror crawling across faces which had gone pale as milk. The sharp smell of urine filled the air as one of the unknown men lost control of his bladder. With a shout, Gary pulled a gun out from inside his jacket and pointed it at the puma. His hand shook so hard, I didn't think he could even aim it right, but that didn't mean it was any less dangerous. I felt a cold crawl of fear in my stomach.

When Olivia roared again, distracting Gary, James leapt at him and snapped at the hand holding the weapon. Gary dropped the gun, screaming as he fled to the far corner of the room, and the wolf snatched the weapon from the ground, retreating back to the doorway.

I ran over to where John lay and began to untie him while Olivia and Garrett kept the men at bay. James left the gun by Olivia and came over to bite at the ropes tying John's legs to the chair. Together, we freed him.

"Here, let me help you," said Will from behind his ski mask. He picked up John, carrying him out of the room while the rest of the rescue party kept the kidnappers occupied. Rich reached out to grab me and when two ravens swooped in and dove at him, he fell back with a cry of terror. Supporting John between us, Will and I got him into the van, and while Will peeled out, heading for Nevermore's house, I ran back inside to where Garrett, James, and Olivia were keeping the men from leaving. Picking up the shattered camera, I glared at Rich as he stared at me with a mixture of disbelief and anger.

"You are *working* with them?" he demanded. "You knew?"

"What you did tonight to John was insane!" I yelled at him. "What did it accomplish, Rich? Your intolerance is what drove me away in the first place. How was kidnapping John going to win me back? That beating the man I live with and deeply care about was going to change things in the slightest? You are absolutely out of your goddamn mind!"

"Sash, you are siding with these...these things. They came to John's aid. Don't you care if he is one of them?"

I sighed deeply, dropped the camera into my pocket, and smiled a humorless smile.

"Rich...*I* am one of them."

I unbelted my robe, letting it drop to the floor. As I took my wolf form, I saw the dawn of sudden understanding break across Rich's face. All the color drained from it, and he stepped back from me as if I were on fire. I snarled, showing him all of my fangs and venting the depths of my fury. As a wolf, everything was clearer. Rich and his friends had injured my mate, and all of my anger and fear for John rippled out as a growl from deep in my chest. At that moment, I saw that Rich was devastated, but I could not feel any sympathy. Not a bit. He had denied to himself even the possibility; there was no room in his thoughts that the woman he loved might be a shapeshifter.

Regaining my human form, I snatched the robe and put it back on.

"Leave us alone," I said to Rich angrily, holding up the camera. "Don't think I won't turn this over to the police."

"It doesn't matter," sneered Todd. "I pushed the erase button. You have nothing."

"I have John," I said, turning my glare on him. "He will certainly be able to let them know who did this to him."

James took the gun in his mouth again and followed me to the front door as Garrett and Olivia backed out of the room, snarling. Once outside, I booked it to the car and sped to the rendezvous point two blocks away to meet them. When they got there, Garrett and Olivia were in their robes and along with James, who had stayed in his wolf form, they jumped inside, pulling blankets over themselves as the heater began to warm the car.

I drove as fast as I could to Kathy's, pulling in next to the van and hopping out to run inside with my backpack full of clothes. The kids wrapped the blankets around themselves and likewise darted in on my heels, though James took the time to nose the gun under the back seat before he joined us. Kathy met us at the door and sent everyone in different directions to get dressed. I handed the broken camera to Paul, who took it wordlessly and went to his study to see what he could do.

"How is he?" I asked as I followed Kathy upstairs.

"He regained consciousness in the van, but they beat him pretty badly. No broken teeth, but he might have a fractured cheekbone, and his nose will need to be seen to. He's going to have one hell of a shiner, and I think he has a broken rib. He's lucky they hadn't done worse to him by the time you got there. This was as much to punish you for leaving Rich as it was to hurt John."

We went into the spare bedroom where John lay, appearing even worse than he had under the fluorescent lights. The bruises were really beginning to color, and he glanced over at me and attempted a smile.

"Hey," he said hoarsely, "you made it."

"We need to get you to a doctor," I said.

"Actually, Dr. McGee is on his way," said Kathy. "Old friend of the family. Makes house calls."

"Shapeshifter?"

"Jackdaw," said Kathy.

At my look of surprise, she smiled. "He's British."

The doctor arrived, and I went to get changed, then made my way downstairs. The others were still there, milling around the kitchen and living room, waiting.

"He'll live," I said. "You lot were magnificent."

"Those guys really were cowards," said James, standing awkwardly with his hands in his pockets.

Paul came out from his study, shaking his head.

"They erased it, and when the camera fell, it broke the chip. There is no record of the event."

"They don't know that, do they?" said Olivia smiling. "John needs to go to the police and report the beating as soon as possible. Give them the camera and the gun; let them deal with the situation."

"As soon as he's feeling up to it," I said. "Let the doctor have a look at him first."

A few minutes later, Dr. McGee came back downstairs.

"He'll be okay," he said. "I set his nose. The cracked rib will heal on its own; I taped it, but he should rest as much as possible. He's not going to look pretty for a little while, but there was no permanent damage done. Try to discourage him from changing for a few days as well. He doesn't need to be running around right now."

"We're going to file a police report," I said. "Can we give your name to them for verification?"

"I will be more than happy to report on the damages done by those cretins," said the doctor. "Beastly men, beating up that poor boy. What did they think to accomplish? He couldn't have shifted with his arms tied behind him! He'd have broken his shoulders. Canines don't bend that way! He'll be down in a few minutes, I think. I gave him some painkillers for his nose and rib, but it's only enough to take the edge off. I also wrote a script for something stronger he can take tomorrow – only if the pain gets too bad, mind – and a note for his work. He should rest the remainder of this week and through the weekend. Good evening to you all."

We thanked Dr. McGee as he left, and I went back upstairs to where John sat on the edge of the bed, wincing as he got dressed in the clean clothes I'd brought him. Kathy handed me the note and the prescription, then went downstairs to talk to the kids. I looked at John and breathed out a huge sigh. My fear for him had only started to abate, and I sat on the bed next to him, reaching over to gently touch him on the shoulder.

"Are you all right?" I asked.

"I think so," said John, his voice still shaky. "I texted my boss and told him what happened. He said that the college security cameras caught them grabbing me and throwing me into a car, but they were wearing masks. They did notify the police, and he feels terrible that they couldn't catch the license plate. He also told me not to worry about the rest of the week. They'll pay my salary until I'm ready to come back."

"Well, that's something at least," I said. "Do you think you can make it downstairs?"

He nodded and took my arm as we made our way slowly down. Paul had called the police, and while Kathy organized the others in the living room to order Chinese food, the officer, one D. J. Barber, took our statements. Kathy and Paul stayed out of it, but the rest of us told our parts of the story, leaving out the fact of being shapeshifters.

"Why didn't you call us?" he asked. "That would have been the smart thing to do."

"Gary knows people on the force," I said. "I was afraid they'd tell him, and he'd kill John."

Officer Barber's face clouded, but he motioned us to continue.

"They'd called me to come down and watch them beat John up because they were convinced he was a shapeshifter," I said. "Todd was videotaping them in hopes he'd become a wolf. Gary broke John's nose just as I got there."

Officer Barber raised an eyebrow and he looked over at John.

"Do you want to press charges?" he asked us.

"Absolutely," I said. "We don't know who the other men are, but I bet Gary or Todd would know."

The officer took down Dr. McGee's number and promised to follow up with him as soon as he could. He then asked us to come down to the station the next day to sign the report, and he and his unit would take it from there. James went out to my car with Officer Barber to retrieve the gun, and as soon as it was stored safely in an evidence bag, he turned and addressed John and me.

"Just so you know," he said. "Even if you are shapeshifters, what they did is still assault and battery. Given that it was because of who you are, it's also a hate crime. When, not if, that legislature goes through, you can also add racism to the list of your complaints. I know a few shapeshifters. They are good people; some are good cops. I'll be in the office tomorrow. Ask for me. We'll get this sorted out and the right people behind bars."

We bade him good night and went into Kathy's crowded living room to join the others. Everyone made a fuss over finding John a place to sit down, and the entire group was speaking at once. Garrett and John exchanged a few awkward comments, then Garrett lightly punched John in the shoulder, and John flinched but did the same right back. Kathy and I gave each other amused glances, and then the Chinese food showed up.

We made sure John was given a plate before the rest of the ravening horde gathered around the food and dug in, then Kathy, Paul, and I sneaked out to the kitchen to give the kids some room. A few minutes later, I was dragged back into their midst when they discovered from John that he and I were practically engaged. Kathy commented from the kitchen doorway that there was going to be a lot of preparation for it, and then all of the clamoring began again as our young friends planned out our entire wedding for us.

After dinner, the painkillers really began to take effect, and at Kathy's whispered suggestion, John and I left for home. The others insisted on going with us as a "security force" back to the house.

"Are you going to be okay?" I asked as we drove down the highway, the occasional headlights of late night drivers giving me only glimpses of John's battered face.

"I think so," he said slowly. "But I don't mind telling you, I was terrified, Sash. Being picked on in high school was nothing compared to what those guys put me through."

"I am so sorry," I said, tears coming to my eyes. I blinked them back and tried to hold it together while I was driving, but all I wanted to do was crawl into bed and cry for days.

"It's not your fault," said John, taking my hand. "Neither of us could have predicted they'd go that far."

"Sometimes I just wish that Sam and the others had never come forward," I said, sighing. "I just hope that something good actually comes from it. Otherwise, this sort of thing will happen to more shapeshifters, and there will be nothing to stop it."

We traveled the rest of the way in silence, and by the time we arrived at the house, I had pulled myself together again. Our impromptu security force pulled into the driveway behind us and got out, exclaiming in muted voices over how cool the house was. We went inside, where John insisted on showing them the Theater first. After everyone was done exclaiming over it, we took them on a tour of the rest of the house.

"How did you get this on a teacher's salary?" asked Kim, who was an education major.

"My family is helping me," I said. "They set up a loan."

"That makes sense," Olivia said. "My family has been helping me through law school, and when I graduate this spring, they will be expecting me to pay them back in pro-bono services for their businesses."

"At least yours deal with ski resorts and other adventurous pursuits," said Kim. "You know what mine own? Car dealerships!"

She rolled her eyes, and we dissolved into a fit of giggles. Somehow the idea of shapeshifters owning car dealerships was completely hysterical, but then geese were wont to travel, and many of them never gave up their migration in some form or another. Kim shook her head and sighed.

"I hope they arrest Rich and his friends and put them away where they won't harm anyone again."

"I think we broke Rich tonight," I said, and I sobered, a wave of exhaustion washing over me. "At least I don't have to worry about him chasing me anymore, trying to win me back."

"There is that," said Olivia, "though I would not discount him doing something else. We made a fool out of him and his friends tonight. They aren't going to let that go. I'll help you any way I can from a legal standpoint. John didn't have a chance tonight. Twelve to one? What kinds of odds were those?"

"No kinds of odds," I said. "I am so glad you were all there. Thank you so much for saving John. I couldn't have done it alone."

We went back down, and although he seemed to be enjoying himself, I could tell that John was peopled out. I quietly shooed our friends out with promises of having a hangout session on Saturday, then bade them all good night. Turning out the lights downstairs, I called out of work the next day and guided my wounded one to bed.

John did not protest going up to bed at 9:00 at night. In fact, once he had showered and was under the covers, he fell asleep almost at once muttering only a sleepy "I love you" before drifting off. I looked at his poor, bruised face and slipped out of bed to creep into the office where I broke down into muffled sobs, letting the emotions I had bottled up for the last few hours finally have their release. As I cried, I wondered how John could still feel such love for me when all I had brought him was woe. After a long while, the storm of tears finally slowed, leaving me cleansed and exhausted. I went quietly downstairs to check the alarm system, then slipped back upstairs and into bed with him.

I gazed at his face in the dim light, reflecting with a sense of clarity that I had also brought joy into John's life too by being there for him when he changed and bringing him into a place where he was loved and accepted for who he was. I felt a smile tugging at my lips as I lay watching him breathe in the stillness of our room, and finally closed my own eyes, falling asleep almost at once.

21
A NEW TWIST

The next morning, after submitting my lesson plans for my sub to carry out, John and I went down to the police station. The officers had wasted no time and had already arrested Rich, Todd, and Gary. We dealt with all the necessary paperwork to press charges, and afterwards, Officer Barber sat back with a heavy sigh.

"We're going to try to get them to tell us who the rest of the assailants are, though I'm not holding out hope that they will, so be careful," he said. "The video was ruined, but the gun has Gary Miller's prints all over it. If nothing else, we have the three of them. We're set here for now if you want to go. I hope this will put an end to it. If not, you have my number."

As we lay in bed that night, John finally broke down about what had happened, processing the terror and the guilt he felt at not being stronger. Kathy had warned me this would likely happen, and I simply held him, letting him cry himself out. His sobs abated slowly, but his sense of security was gone. For the first time, he had experienced the feeling I had known all of my life - that low-key sense of fear that what he was might bring him bodily harm. It was an aura of "otherness" that he, as someone from a white American family, had never before experienced. His involvement in anime and gaming had given him a taste of it, but this was totally different.

"I just don't know," he said. "I'm worried I'll never feel safe again going to work when I barely convince myself that I can leave the house and not get attacked."

"You will," I said. "They, the three "they," are locked away for the time being. The rest will most likely lay low. Regardless, Rich and his friends will be made an example of, never fear."

"I wish I was braver," he said. "You were so calm when you came in."

"You have no idea how scared I was," I said. "I was terrified of what they'd do to you. I just let my anger take over and tried to ignore how I really felt. But underneath? John, if I had let myself give into that fear, I would have been utterly incapable of acting. I had to focus on how angry I was with myself for dragging you into my messy life."

"I was not dragged into it," he said indignantly, then softened. "Well, okay, after I transformed, I was kinda dragged into it, but you couldn't have done anything else, really."

"Sadly, I doubt Rich and friends are just going to give up so easily," I said. "Being arrested will make them think twice about acting overtly, but I suspect they won't give up. I'm as much a target now as you are."

"I'm sorry I made you all risk yourselves that way," he said. "Now he knows what you are."

"And maybe that *will* make him think twice," I said. "But nothing more is going to happen tonight. Sleep now, love. You've been through enough."

Settling down again, neither of us took long to drift off. Sleep would be good as I would be returning to work the next day. Hopefully, the nightmare of Rich and his friends would soon be over.

After school, Kathy came to find me as I was getting ready to go home.

"There has been an email to the district about teachers being shapeshifters. The email contains some BS about shapeshifter teachers who are a danger to the children of the district and urges parents to come together to stand up to the superintendent and insists that the menace is dealt with accordingly," she said, fury written across her face. "You know where this is coming from, right?"

"Oh, I have no doubts," I said grimly. "Rich and his friends are now determined that they're going to get me some other way."

"He hasn't given up," said Kathy. "They'll call an emergency school board meeting for early next week, mark my words. We have to have a strategy."

"We'll figure it out," I said, though I didn't feel that way. "I think I'm going to stop by to see Mr. Turner before I leave."

"Mind if I pop over to see John on my way home?"

"Kathy, my house isn't on your way home."

"It is by the scenic route," she said innocently.

"I'm sure he'll be happy to see you," I said, sighing and shaking my head. "Incorrigible corbie."

"Stubborn canidae," she shot back affectionately. "I'll see you at your house."

I left my room a few minutes after she did and headed to the office. The secretaries ushered me right in, and Mr. Turner glanced up as I closed the door.

"I assume you've heard," he said.

"Yes," I said. "You know they'll call a meeting."

"Yes," he replied, "and you and I will be there. How is John doing?"

I paused, wondering how much he really knew.

"He's better," I said. "Recovering, thank you. He's pretty shaken up about it, though."

"He was a fine youngster while he was here," he said. "Quiet, but smart. A bit wounded. If I recall, you befriended him while you were a student teacher. Have you been friends all this time?"

"Yes," I said. "Being something more is a very recent event."

"So I gather," said Mr. Turner. "I'm not recriminating you, if that is your worry, Ms. Wellington. There was nothing wrong with your friendship then, and there is nothing wrong with your relationship now. Are we clear?"

"Yes," I said, looking at him.

"Good. Bring him with you to the meeting, whenever it occurs. I shall bring an old friend as well."

"Oh?" I said, studying his face. As usual, he was incredibly hard to read.

"Yes," he said, and he smiled at me with a twinkle in his eye. "She may have some bearing on the matter."

It took me a second, then I groaned loudly. A smile crept across his face.

"In any event, we will give them a showing they will not soon forget. Have a good weekend, Ms. Wellington. Kindly give my regards to that young man of yours."

My mother called that evening.

"Put on the news," she said. "You should see this."

With a feeling of trepidation, I went into the Theater and asked John to pause his game to change over to the news. He did so, an expression of worry crossing his face. A reporter stood with the district building behind him. On one side stood a crowd of angry people carrying signs and chanting. I couldn't quite hear all of what they were saying, but the words "beasts must go" were repeated several times. Across from them stood another group bearing pro-shapeshifter signs waved them fiercely in the air and shouted back at them.

"...an email to our station just earlier today that some of the personnel are rumored to be shapeshifters. Officials have no comment at this time. Parents frightened by what this might mean to their children's safety have been outside protesting since the announcement was made. Earlier, we spoke with the parents. Here's what some of them have to say."

The camera changed scenes to focus on a woman who looked scared and was holding a sign demanding "Schools, not Zoos."

"I don't know why they have to be in the cities anyway, let alone teaching our children. They should all go home to the forests and leave cities to the real people."

The image changed to a blonde man holding a sign that said, "Not human, not welcome."

"Let them teach their own kind, if they feel the need to be educated," he sneered. "I don't want them around my kids. Animals are unpredictable. Someone's going to get hurt."

The picture changed, and an older woman with silver hair stared at the camera.

"It's unnatural," she said. "I don't feel safe anymore."

The news reporter came back on again. With him stood a man in a gray jacket wearing oversized glasses.

"With us now is Professor Burke from the Hayden Institute for Anthropological Studies. Professor, can you give us your impression as to why these shapeshifters have decided to come out in the open now and what it means for the country and the world?"

The professor chuckled, gently pushing the glasses back up on his nose.

"I can't speak to the whole world, but I can speak to the country at some level. These beings have been around us for thousands of years, and it was only recently, when we began to mistreat, hunt, and pursue them, that they came forth to tell us they were here. Governments will have to figure out a whole new layer of anti-discrimination legislation and workplace protections. They have been among us for generations. You may never know who is a shapechanger in your workplace unless they tell you, but I imagine that it will become a protected group a lot like those of religious or cultural persuasions."

"And you believe that they have every right to continue working with children?"

"Of course," said the professor. "They are as American as we are. They've been here even longer than our earliest European ancestors.

There are no stories of them ever attacking people that haven't caused them grief. They should be allowed to continue to coexist alongside us."

It was a relief hearing someone with knowledge of history making so strong a statement. It didn't completely negate the shock I felt from the other comments, but it did help to soothe my nerves a little. If other, more reasonable people could be convinced to speak up on our behalf, maybe there was a chance for us to be accepted after all. It was a strange feeling, this stirring of hope, and I held onto it as tightly as I could, praying that it would be enough to see us through.

The APkids, as I had taken to jokingly calling them, descended on our house around ten o'clock Saturday morning. John was still asleep when the doorbell rang, and I answered it to find a full complement of all eight graduate students from the meeting the previous Monday, plus the four upperclassmen. Before I knew what hit me, they invaded with donuts and bagels and orange juice and boxes of Joe from Dunkins.

"Guys!" I said as my kitchen island became a food station for an astounding manner of baked goods. "Graduates are fine, but students still in school can get me fired!"

"We won't tell," called Leonie cheerfully. "Besides, our parents know. They heard all about what happened, so we're here to support you and John."

"Once," I sighed. "Just this once. I'll go get the walking wounded. Be right back."

I went upstairs and found John slowly getting dressed.

"You heard?" I said.

"The rampaging wild elephants?" he said wryly. "Yes. How could I not?"

I snorted my amusement, and we went downstairs. Everyone had grabbed something to eat and drink and were sitting around the living room chatting. They all sobered a bit when John entered the room. His bruises were starting to yellow but were still pretty livid, and his cracked rib made him move very stiffly.

"Oh, wow," said Paulo, eyeing John's face.

"Yeah" said Maryann. "It looks much worse than I imagined."

"Thanks," groaned John, sounding aggrieved.

"Oh, I didn't mean…"

"I know," said John. "It's okay."

"So we came over to see you and to talk about the meeting. They're arranging it for Monday or Tuesday," said James. "We wanted you to know we'll all be there."

"All of us," confirmed Casey. "My parents too."

"And mine," said Garrett.

The others all nodded.

"This is big and is not just about us," said Olivia. "Legally, so close to Congress making its ruling, this is going to have a huge impact on the proceedings."

"My parents think so too. They won't be there, but they support us," I said.

"Oh, mine will," laughed Leonie. "My dad's a lawyer, and if you don't think he has some strong words to say about all of these events and the attack on John, you've got another think coming! He's going to offer his services to John pro bono to deal with those clowns."

"*I* think that we shall have to wait to see what happens," I said. "In any event, it should be well worth attending the meeting."

Garrett looked at me suspiciously. "Wait, you know something, don't you?"

"Maaybee," I drawled, "but I don't know if my suspicions are correct. We'll have to wait and see."

With that, John and I were hounded with more questions. The one thing that we could tell them was that Rich, Gary, and Todd had made bail but had all been suspended from their respective jobs because of the assault charges. If they even so much as breathed in our direction, I had been told, they would be arrested again and held without bail.

Officer Barber had also helped arrange frequent drive-bys in our neighborhood, just in case they decided to do something else.

By the time the kids finally left around 4:00 in the afternoon, they had played multiple rounds of video games with John, ordered pizza, watched a movie, talked us into chaperoning at prom, and done everything in their power to try to weasel the information out of me about what might happen at the meeting.

With that, they left us to our own devices, and those devices, though rather cautious, were very sweet indeed. We eventually shut down the house, set the alarm, and went upstairs to the bedroom. Lighting a candle, I turned off the rest of the lights, and led John to the bed, gently pushing him to sit on the edge.

"Marry me," he said as I sat next to him. "I know we discussed this a little - about doing it sooner or later, but I am calling this a full-on proposal. I'll get a ring pop somewhere, I swear. Just...marry me."

He searched my face nervously for any hint of an answer, and in response, I leaned over and kissed him.

"I will absolutely marry you," I said. "I love you, John, more than I ever imagined possible. I will marry you and have children with you and grow old together with you. And you don't even have to find a ring pop. I accept your proposal."

"Say that again," he said with tired happiness.

"What?"

"That you love me and will marry me."

"I love you," I said, meeting his eyes as I ran a finger gently across his chest. "And I will marry you, and we will have babies who will run with the clan and know their true natures as you should have known yours a long time ago."

"That just sounds so weird..."

"You'll get used to it."

We cuddled in the warmth of our promise, and I was just dropping off into a nap when he suddenly groaned.

"What's the matter?" I asked, the sound jolting me awake.

"My parents," he said. "How am I going to explain this to them?"

"What, your black eye?"

"No, idiot," he said affectionately. "Our marriage."

"Sudden, unexpected pregnancy?" I joked. "I mean, we haven't exactly been careful."

"Couldn't we just elope?" he asked. "Just say nothing and run away to Las Vegas for a weekend?"

"Not with my family, we can't," I said. "They are going to create some elaborate to-do, and there's no escaping it. Not to mention the grads will have it all planned out. Nope, your parents are just going to have to deal with a fast wedding. I think they'll be too overwhelmed by my parents' soiree to complain over much, don't you think?"

"Quite possibly," said John. "Given what I've seen so far, they would have no idea how to handle it."

"Good," I said with a quiet chuckle. "Then we won't worry about it just yet."

He kissed me again, and we spent long hours into the night planning and talking about our future. Eventually, John's couldn't keep his eyes open for more than a few seconds, and we finally fell asleep.

22

THE SCHOOL BOARD MEETING

The next day was Sunday, and John and I drove over to the Forebear's farm. I had almost forgotten my plans with the badgers, but the calendar on my phone hadn't. As we drove over, I found myself relishing a good run to shake off some of the stress from the last week. John was looking forward to a run as well and was curious to meet the odd badger couple.

We arrived at about ten A.M., and Sally came out to greet us, inviting us in for donuts and coffee. Jimmy had been up for hours already and appeared from the back room when he heard us come in. Over coffee, I told them about what had happened to John, and the outcome of the rescue, plus our subsequent visit to the police station. Sally disappeared into the back room and came out with a small container.

"Calendula and comfrey salve," she said, handing it to me. "It will help with the swelling and bruising. Apply it twice daily, but be sure to wash your hands after. Neither of those will be good for you if you are trying to start a family."

"Thanks," I said, pocketing the little container.

"You were lucky," said Jimmy. "Those people meant business.

Having a law won't stop them, but it might make them think twice. They will have to be made an example to the others."

"True," I said. "I just wish they hadn't been so stupidly determined. I mean, they got what they deserved, and I'll bet it isn't the end result they expected."

Jimmy snorted. "What, did they expect they were going to be seen as heroes?"

"Go for your run," said Sally kindly. "You need to get this out of your head. Then come back here, and we can chat a bit more."

John and I left our clothes in the barn and ran out into the orchard under the bright morning sun. Being able to run together for the first time since the snowstorm was magical, and we leapt the brook at the back of the property several times, chasing and being chased for miles through the snow. John's long legs might have made him faster than me, but my agility once again won out as I was mostly able to dodge his feints. As we played, I reveled in the freedom of running, lost in the wolf's senses and the absence of clocks.

John appeared a lot less battered in this form, though one eye would not completely open. My handsome mate, I thought, and when we stopped in the orchards to catch our breath, I nuzzled his ears, and he nibbled the back of my neck in a gentle caress. I watched him trotting off across the field toward the farm house and followed, grateful to have him safe and alive. In this form, the protectiveness I felt towards him was powerful indeed.

Once changed and dressed, we went back inside to visit with the Forebears a little while longer. Sally made us some more coffee, and we talked about the message that had been sent out at the end of the school day on Friday. She shook her head.

"This is not going to end the way they think it will," she said. "There's too many people on our side now, especially after the incident with the child. Don't you worry. It will all work out right in the end."

A little while later, we headed home. As we drove back into the city, I thought about what Sally said about people being on our side. Was it just wishful thinking or did people genuinely care enough about us to help? Only time would tell.

True to form, the school department planned an emergency meeting for the following Tuesday, and Paul, Kathy, John, and I were among the gathered staff and parents. The auditorium was packed, and I was certain that no few of the attendees were shapeshifters anxious to hear what would be said. I know I was.

Outside, the news media was having a field day. There was a large crowd that had not been able to get inside before the doors closed, and many of them were very vocal about their opinions. There were people chanting slogans like "Monsters go home!" and other, cruder phrases. There were also some people there in support of the clans, but their voices were drowned out by the anger and the fear of the restless antagonists.

Inside, it was clear that some people were there in opposition, and shrill voices carried over the crowd before the meeting had even gotten underway. The lack of real information about shapeshifters led to some people repeating lies that had been spread on social media for months. It was disheartening.

The meeting was soon called to order, something that took quite a few minutes to achieve. Once quiet had been established and the meeting finally started, the head of the school board made the opening statement.

"We just want to start by saying that the rights of any shapeshifter employees will be upheld as strongly as those of any employee, the same way we view gender, race, or creed."

There were some boos from people in the audience, but when he held up his hands for silence, the noise of the crowd died down to a murmur.

"We're going to open the floor to public comment," said the superintendent, "but let me remind you that this is to be a civil discourse.

You may certainly make your statements, but you will be held to a strict time limit of two minutes and anyone who cannot follow these rules will be removed from the meeting."

He stepped back and let people approach the podium.

Some of the comments made were simple, honest concerns, and I could forgive those people their misunderstandings. It was the speakers who were malicious towards us that made my blood run cold. To stand there and accuse people - teachers - dedicated individuals, of eating children or of having "killer instincts" was infuriating. Their willful ignorance appalled me.

The superintendent let people talk for a long while before finally thanking everyone and ending the public commentary. When everyone had settled down again, he returned to the podium.

"As we stated before," he said, "if there are any shapeshifters among the teaching staff, they are unknown to us. If we become aware of any shapeshifters in the district..."

"You'd do what?" came a commanding voice from the audience.

Everyone looked to see an elderly black woman walking down the aisle. She must have been about seventy years old and used a cane to make her way slowly to the microphone. Several people greeted her as she passed and a whisper of recognition ran through the crowd. When she got to the podium, she turned and smiled out at the audience.

"My name," she said, "is Mrs. Barbara Woodhaven, and I see quite a few people here tonight who I have had as students over the years. Including you, Mr. Baxton."

Bill Baxton looked somewhat poleaxed.

"That's the woman Mr. Turner told me about," I whispered to John.

He shot me a wide-eyed glance, then we turned back to watch.

"I taught in this district for over fifty years," she said, peering around the room, "and I just want to say that what I am hearing tonight is shameful. No teacher has ever mauled or eaten a student! I am not going to bandy fine words with you, because I am too old and too tired of these arguments to play these games.

"I am a shapeshifter, a member of the bear clan. I loved children and loved teaching. I was unable to have my own, much to my sorrow, so I loved yours. I can't stomach the fact that there are people here, good people, people I cared for, who I have heard arguing about how vicious and predatory my people are. Shame on the lot of you. I taught you better than that, and your parents did too."

The undertones in Mrs. Woodhaven's voice expressed the deep sadness that she felt, and the murmuring of the crowd made evident the cognitive dissonance that so many of them were experiencing. People stared at the woman by the podium, and no few of them looked discomfited by her criticism. She lifted her head proudly, and then turned to face the superintendent.

"I don't understand you, Bill Baxton, being able to claim that there are no shapeshifters in the schools. Of course there are. There always have been. Would you fire them all? Would you tell them that they are not allowed to do the jobs they love? Teach the children of whom they have grown fond? They are people, Bill, and they love and fear for their families as much as anyone does."

Kathy stood up, and I heard her mutter under her breath, "In for a dime."

She walked down to join Mrs. Woodhaven at the podium.

"I am Katherine Corbeau, one of the English teachers at Viceroy High. Many of you know me as well. I am not a bear. But," and here she looked at the school board and faced down Bill Baxton firmly, "I am a corbie. One of the raven clans, in fact. I have been teaching here for over thirty-five years. I've been here long enough to have some of my first year students' children, and I've done nothing more subversive than teach *Taming of the Shrew*, dirty jokes and all."

She turned to Bill and smiled.

"Gonna fire me, Bill?" she asked. "Cause the union might have something to say about that, and there's some anti-discrimination legislation coming right around the corner. If Sam Winston and his crew hadn't gone public, you'd never even know we existed. But he had to, Bill, because of people like the men who attacked one of our former students last week. People with more misinformation than actual facts. People with an agenda or a bias or something as stupid as being jealous of an ex-girlfriend liking someone else. You can get ahead of this or you can bury your head in the sand. But we have just as much a right to live and work in this community as anyone else."

A smattering of applause broke out in the auditorium, and for the first time in his tenure as superintendent, Bill Baxton looked completely at a loss. He glanced around him at the school board members, and then at Kathy and Mrs. Woodhaven.

"Well," I said to John. "We can't let them do this alone."

John nodded, and we stood up and walked down to the front to where Kathy stood. I stepped up to the podium and addressed the packed auditorium.

"My name is Sasha Wellington," I said, "and this is John Arndt. My ex Rich and his friends had been stalking us for weeks to try to find out where we worked and lived with the intent to discredit John. They caught him after work last week, and Rich and a dozen of his friends did this to John because Rich was jealous and because they were afraid. We are both of the wolf clan. Some of you know me as a teacher in this district. Mr. Arndt here was a senior when I did my student teaching, and we've been friends ever since. I was raised in a family clan not too far from here, went to school with non-shapeshifter students, and then went on to college, just like many of you have done or your kids will do.

"None of us are 'ravening beasts' as some have called us. Most of us grow up, raise our families, and live our lives, just like you. Aside from being able to become animals, we are no different. Some clan members even marry humans, and they live wonderful lives together. Some, like John, get adopted into human families and never know what they are, until they change as he did relatively recently."

"She and John are also the ones who found the little girl and returned her to her parents during the storm," called out Kathy, much to my surprise, and she chuckled to see my stunned expression.

A huge furor broke out in the auditorium, and John and I glanced at each other, embarrassed. Mrs. Woodhaven smiled at us and winked.

Bill Baxton called for the room to settle down, which took a considerable while. After a few minutes, Paul joined Kathy at the front of the room and was peering up at the superintendent, obviously amused.

By the time people had finally quieted down again, Bill had developed a strained expression.

"We will not be firing anyone," said Bill Baxton. "However, I will be asking the shapeshifters in the buildings to identify themselves to their administrators."

"Why?" came a voice from the crowd.

We spotted Garrett and the rest of the graduates as they stood and walked down from where they had been sitting in the far back. I noticed with some satisfaction that they were dressed neatly and presented themselves like the former top students that they were.

"Why do they have to out themselves for your satisfaction?" asked Garrett.

"Who are you, sir?" asked Bill.

"Former graduates of Viceroy High School," said Olivia. "And all shapeshifters from local families. As a law student at Colorado Law, I can tell you that legally you can't ask them to state who they are. You can ask them to volunteer, but you can't mandate it. Even though they may not be covered by anti-discrimination laws yet, they are covered by their employee rights. So no, you cannot ask them."

More people began to stand up around the room, and I could tell by their attitudes that they were with us in solidarity. I spotted Peter Young, the student rep recording the meeting, talking quietly to Garrett. John went over and said something to Peter, who grinned and fist-bumped John in return.

Returning to my side, John whispered "He'll send you a copy, never fear. He's owl clan."

Bill once again wrangled the meeting back to order, focusing his gaze on where we stood, then around at all of the people in the audience. I saw a number of my students, some I knew were shapeshifters, some that I never would have guessed, standing with their parents, watching us. Several teachers I knew from other schools came down to join us, grimly determined. And finally from the back came a voice I had been hoping to hear.

"Mr. Baxton," said Sam Winston, "We would like a word if we may."

Down from the back of the auditorium came the ambassadors from the clans who had been working so closely with Congress. With them came the mayor of Boulder. Bill seemed suddenly very pale and glanced at the rest of the school board members, who were also appearing somewhat overwhelmed.

Sam Winston made his way over to me and said very softly so only I could hear, "Your mother and my mother should *never* run for office."

"I hear you there," I said, swallowing hard.

"Gentlemen," said the mayor, taking the podium. "Having conferred with my colleagues as to the state of the bill soon to pass through Congress, it is my recommendation that Boulder serve as a model for the country as the first city to embrace the shapeshifter clans as equal citizens. Colorado as a whole will soon follow suit, according to the governor, but we will set Boulder as an example in the eyes of the nation. No shapeshifter shall be fired due to their race, and if there is any hint of biased judgment against them, this board and its superintendent shall be held liable along with the administrators who act against them.

"These are uncharted waters for the whole world. We have lived with shapeshifters among us this whole time without even being aware of their presence. Given as they have never offered us harm, it behooves us to extend the same courtesy to them. Gentlemen, ladies, Mr. Baxton. You have your charge."

The mayor turned his gaze on us and nodded.

"You tell me if they don't," he said and walked away with the rest following.

"Don't forget! March!" smiled Sam and went to join the delegation.

We regarded each other with undisguised joy, and then I turned to the superintendent.

"We'll help you understand, Bill," I said. "Nothing has really changed all that much. Just be the voice of reason is all we would ask."

Bill Baxton took a deep breath.

"I suppose a task force to help with adjustments making this work correctly would be in order," he said. "And I can't think of any people I'd rather have on it, Ms. Wellington, Mrs. Corbeau. I'll ask for some volunteers from the other schools as well so that we have a range of representation. We have our marching orders, it seems. I trust you will help to make it seamless?"

Kathy and I grinned and, of course, agreed.

The meeting began to break up then, and Barbara Woodhaven came over to say goodbye.

"You're a brave person, Sasha Wellington, and you too, John Arndt. Don't forget it."

"Thank you, Ma'am," said John. "We won't."

"Unless I miss my guess, John is using some of Sally Forebear's bruising salve, correct?"

"Yes?" I said.

"Tell Sally I say hi," smiled Mrs. Woodhaven. "Been a while since I've seen those two."

Mr. Turner joined our group, and Mrs. Woodhaven nodded to him as he looked at her fondly. He then turned to us and shook first my hand, then John's.

"Congratulations to the two of you," he said. "I think you will do well together."

"You have been so helpful to all of us," I said. "Bringing Mrs. Woodhaven here tonight was one of the most pivotal things you could have done."

"My pleasure," he said. "I figure this is my way of repaying Julia for her kindness to me and all of those who were adrift over the years."

Mrs. Woodhaven smiled, and after promising to visit with us again, bid us all farewell. She let Thom Turner take her arm and escort her up the aisle.

Kathy and Paul took their leave then; the kids and some of their relatives walked out with us. It was clear that not all of the people leaving the auditorium were happy, but most seemed as if they at least willing to watch where the turn of events would lead. With the mayor backing us, there was a positive precedent for them to follow.

"Be ready for just about anything," said Olivia's mother, who had been introduced to me as Irene. "There are going to be protests and demonstrations, so don't be surprised at what will follow. We have a long road ahead of us."

"I can only hope that common sense will win out," I said. "With any luck, everything will settle down now that the mayor has had his say."

23
TEST DAY

Irene wasn't wrong. By the time I got to school the next morning, there was a group of protestors holding signs on the property's edge. I parked in my normal spot, but as I started to walk into the building, Janet, one of the secretaries, ran out and told me to park in the front row where they could keep an eye on it. Nevermore's was there too, and after I moved my car, I heard someone shout an obscenity at me from the people gathered by the street. I went inside quickly.

Janet waved me into the office, and I entered. Tina and Sally had also come over.

"We," said Janet, "wanted you to know that you have our whole support. We've known you and Kathy for years, and if you need anything, just come down here or call us. Mr. Turner told us about the meeting last night…"

"I was there!" interrupted Tina.

"…And he told us how brave you all were for coming forward," finished Janet, nodding at Tina.

"So we felt you deserved to hear that from us," said Sally.

"Thank you," I said, smiling at them. I felt a wash of relief at their words.

I could tell, though, that they were bursting with questions they were all too polite to ask. This was going to be the weirdest day I'd ever had at school.

"Mr. Turner is going to call an assembly during A block this morning," said Tina. "Apparently he wants to address the elephant in the room head on."

"Oh," I said, feeling my stomach twist.

"He's going to discuss the meeting and the mayor's decree," said Janet. "Parents have been calling us. He wants to reassure the students and clear up any misconceptions right away."

"Go get settled in," said Sally kindly. "It's going to be a rough one."

I nodded and left the office, walking out into the main hall. Some of the kids waved hi to me like always, but no few of them stared as I passed. Unnerved, I headed for Kathy's room. I could hear the rest of her department, especially Rachel, talking with her loudly through the closed door. Taking a deep breath, I went inside.

"Hi Kathy!" I said, grinning from ear to ear in what must have been more of a grimace. "How is your morning going?"

"Oh, you know," said Kathy, grinning back. "The same as yours, I'd imagine. Had to move my parking space, everyone is staring in the halls, my whole department is mad at me for not telling them..."

"Damn straight!" said Rachel. "You could have trusted us!"

"Rachel," said Kathy, sighing fondly, "old habits die hard. I wanted to, but I have kept this secret for so many years. It's rather hard to share."

"Well, we've got your back, Kath," said Mickey, the department chair. "And yours too, Sasha."

"Thanks," I said. "I'm going to head upstairs. Thanks for your support."

"Anytime," smiled Michelle, another member of the department.

Leaving the relative safety of Nevermore's room, I steeled myself and went upstairs to mine. I opened the door to find Frank and the rest of the department waiting for me. Darlene looked a little frightened but was trying to hide it, while Mike just solemnly nodded. The others, Tim, Bill, Natasha, and Shri smiled in greeting.

"Of course, we heard about the meeting," said Frank, never one to take his time and be tactful about leading into a subject. "Mr. Turner spoke to me this morning about you. We are to give you our full support, which, of course, we would have anyway. I do have a few questions, however."

"Tons of questions," said Natasha, who taught biology. "I have tons of questions."

"My main one," said Frank, ignoring Natasha's enthusiastic outburst, "is if you are going to stay. We, all of us, want you to, but we are understandably curious. Nothing is known about shapeshifters, really..."

"Which is why we have questions," finished Natasha. "The more we know, the better we can help."

I ignored her momentarily and turned to Darlene, who shrank back a little.

"I would never hurt you," I said to her. "You've known me for years, Darlene. Trust me. I am no different now than I was before."

She nodded but still hung back. I mentally sighed and turned my attention back to the rest of my department

"Okay, nosy," I said to Natasha, smiling. "Tell you all what. How about, after school, I sit down with you guys and you can ask me whatever you like – keep it clean, Mike, I know you! Will that help?"

The group broke out into laughter, and the impromptu meeting adjourned with everyone but Darlene leaving the room.

"What's up?" I asked, noting that we had about three minutes before the bell rang for first class.

Darlene stepped a little closer to me and looked up to meet my gaze.

"How do we know you aren't all demons, sent to take over the world?" she asked. "My pastor said that you are really evil creatures from the underworld. I don't want to believe that of you, but this is sorcery. Isn't it?"

I gave a huge sigh.

"No," I said. "We were born this way, Darlene. Nobody does spells, no one makes deals with evil forces to learn to shape shift. I was born in Wyoming to loving parents who also happened to be shapeshifters. Originally, we were animals trying to save our families from a reckless species who seemed bent on everyone's destruction. Now we are just people with an extraordinary gift granted to us by a creator god long ago, at least according to our mythology. There is no greater motive than that. We don't want to 'take over the world'; we just want to survive."

"It's just so unreal," she said, sagging into a chair near one of the student desks. "How is one supposed to react to this kind of news?"

"One would hope as sanely as possible," I said. "My people have been among yours for generations. It's just become too hard to hide anymore, so it was decided we should stop. You aren't the only ones who feel afraid. It's been terrifying for all of us to go through this as well. You remember John from that day we all went out for a drink after my ex confronted Ahnold? He's brand new to this. He was brought up human, and he got a wake up call about a month ago when he first changed. Because he was orphaned, he never had anyone to teach him, so it's been a double whammy for him. It almost got him killed."

"Yeah, you were telling us he got attacked last week," she said, softening. "I never thought of it that way."

The bell rang then, and Darlene stood, smiling at me tentatively.

"I'll be here after school," she said and left as the first of the kids came into the room.

My usually chatty first block class was absolutely silent as I took attendance. They had filed in, glancing at me with hesitant eyes before looking away and not saying anything. I noticed that there were a few of them missing that morning, and I felt for certain that some parents had decided that their children would be safer at home. Only one of the students, Brad Cuomo, would meet my eyes for longer than a second, and I had had a feeling for a long time that he was from one of the clans. He nodded at me, and I smiled slightly in return.

After submitting attendance, I read my email, noting the announcement for a meeting at 8:00 that morning. Fifteen minutes.

"Okay," I said, taking a deep breath. "We are going to be called down to the auditorium in a few minutes to have an assembly. Let's quickly go over the work from yesterday and make sure no one has any questions. Please take it out."

A couple of them blinked at me, then pulled out their Chromebooks. The banality of going over the schoolwork had the desired effect, and within a few minutes, they began to relax into the routine of the day.

"Ovoviviparous," I corrected when one of the students guessed wrong about what a platypus would be counted as. "Remember, they and the echidna are the only mammals to lay eggs. If it looks like a duck..."

Several students groaned in unison and made correction marks on their assignments. A couple were laughing by the time the announcement was made to go down to the auditorium. The humor had dissipated the tension from the room, and as we walked through the halls, a number of them spoke to me about upcoming projects. Although there were a lot of eyes on me, the ease that my students had with me was contagious, and many other kids took their cues from them. Some of the students from my later classes also greeted me, and I felt a little bit better.

As we entered the theater, Paulo and Leonie caught up to me and peppered me with questions as to how John was feeling. As we chatted, Casey and Maryann also fought their way over to where we stood, and Sammi and Marci weren't far behind. I felt better with them around me, and before shooing them off to their seats, I promised I would catch up with them later for an update. Kathy came to stand with me, studying the students as they filed in.

"Thom asked me to speak to the kids. I've been here the longest, so he feels they will react the best to me. He said you're welcome to join me, but only if you're comfortable."

"We *are* the reps for the task force," I reminded her, "though if I'm honest, I've felt pretty queasy all morning. It's been rather like living in a fishbowl. And Darlene had a religious moment."

"Oh lord," groaned Kathy. "I hope you disabused her of any demonic notions?"

"So far," I said. "I'm talking to the department after school."

"Me too," said Kathy. "I think my department is a tiny bit crazier about it than yours. They are absolutely thrilled."

"Well, I think you said that half of them are into fantasy novels," I chuckled. "Small wonder!"

Motion at the front of the auditorium caught our attention as Mr. Turner and our vice-principal, Shelly Brunelle, walked to the center of the stage. Mr. Turner took the microphone from its stand.

"Take your seats quickly, ladies and gentlemen," he said over the speakers. "Settle in, settle in."

Shelly left the stage to go deal with a group of boys who were arguing over their choice of seats, and Mr. Turner stood waiting for the crowd of teens to quiet. They did, faster than I would have given them credit for, and no few of them snuck peeks over at Kathy and myself where we stood in the side aisle halfway to the stage. When the noise had died to a few whispers, Principal Turner spoke.

"You have been called here today in the wake of last night's meeting to discuss the topic of shapeshifters in the schools. As you may know, there is truth to this, and several of our staff members are shapeshifters. Most of them did not know the others existed, but we have two here who are going to be working with the school board. The mayor of Boulder was also there at the meeting last night, and it is his wish, as well as the governor's, that all shapeshifters be treated equally within our city. Boulder has long been a leader for free speech and equal rights. I believe it is important that we embrace that as well.

"Bearing that in mind, I am going to turn the floor over to one of our most respected teachers, Mrs. Kathy Corbeau, who will share with you some of the realities of what shapeshifters really are."

Kathy winked at me, and the two of us walked up to the stage where Mr. Turner eyed me approvingly and handed Kathy the microphone. Mr. Turner stepped back, and nodded encouragingly, signaling his support.

"Good morning," said Kathy brightly, holding the microphone close to her chin. "Most of you know me, but until this morning, you probably didn't know that I am one of several shapeshifters who teach here. My friend Ms. Wellington and I will be working with the school board to try and make sure that you young folk and your parents know what shapeshifters are and what we're not.

"I've worked at Viceroy for almost thirty-five years, and I have been a shapeshifter all my life. I first changed when I was very young, a teenager like you, and I had a lot to deal with being both a teen and a new shapeshifter. I have been to college, raised three children, and have lived as a normal member of Boulder society for that whole time. Never has anyone even noticed anything different about me – other than my love for cartoons, that is!"

A few of the kids chuckled at that, and Kathy's natural ability to win people over with her honest charm began to have the intended effect. The people in the theater were listening.

"When Sam Winston and his group first went public, it was the scariest thing that had happened to our family in a very long time," continued Kathy. "Admitting that we existed to the world was risky, and it wasn't really our choice. We all were worried. What would happen to our children if we were discovered? What would others think of us? We have some close family members who are humans; would they still accept us? Would we lose our jobs? This was seriously frightening for us.

"Then there are the people who want to hurt us just because we are different. Sasha's friend John was beaten and most certainly would have been killed if we hadn't rescued him. These men, including Sasha's ex-boyfriend, had beaten John savagely trying to make him transform into an animal. In the end, *we* had to resort to our animal forms to save John, and I am proud to say that we did it without leaving so much as a scratch on any of his assailants. Even in our animal forms, we retain our human minds, and we were able to scare the attackers enough to rescue John and get him to safety.

"So keep this in mind: shapeshifters are among you. They have always been among you, but because they stay human most of the time, you may never know who they are. All we want to do is go on with our lives. We love teaching, books, television – Sasha here loves anime – and pretty much everything most people do. They are students, staff, teachers, store clerks, CEOs, car salesmen...you name it; shapeshifters are in every part of society. We have no special powers, other than the ability to become a type of animal at will. We are not tied to the moon or the tides or anything else because it is not a curse and it is not magic. It is part of who we are.

"That is all I have to say. We can field questions now if you like."

A number of hands shot up in the air, and we took turns answering them as best we could. Most of them were pretty general. We could tell that the kids were starting to relax and even think that it couldn't be all that bad if two of their teachers were being so open about it. When the bell rang to go to block two classes, and everyone began to make their way out, the atmosphere was much calmer.

"Thank you," said Principal Turner, turning off the microphone and placing it on the stand. "I hope that will go a long way to making things much more acceptable. Now if only we can get some of the parents to see it that way. Several of them called fearing you'd eat their children now that 'your cover was blown' as they put it. The ladies in the front office have come up with some ingenious comments, throwing it right back at them and asking how they'd feel about worrying if their children would end up as fur coats. Oddly enough, it seems to be working."

Both Kathy and I broke out laughing as we left the stage and headed to our second block classes. Walking the halls felt a lot better now, and more students were saying hello to us and smiling. When I got to my room, I was assaulted by Casey, Paulo, and Leonie who jumped up and down around me, cheering, much to the confusion of the other AP students who were similarly trying to speak to me all at once. I finally got them settled down, took attendance, and spent the rest of the class talking with the kids about my life growing up. Leonie couldn't contain herself anymore by about halfway through and admitted to her own shapeshifter heritage, which of course made Paulo and Casey follow suit. A few minutes later, a quiet boy named Martin admitted to being a fisher cat, and we all sat chatting with the human students until the bell rang. They all left together, still chatting, then I fled to the staff room to spend my prep in peace and quiet... which I didn't get.

My prep period was full of teachers from other departments popping in and asking questions to the point where I considered putting together an FAQ sheet so that I wouldn't have to answer the same questions fifty times over. Darlene came in very contritely, and we spent a good twenty minutes eating some of her horde of Taza stone-ground chocolates and picking apart conspiracy theories that her minister had been tossing at the congregation for months. Mike and Shri also came to sit with us, and I gave up on doing any prep for my fourth block class as I probably would be educating them about shapeshifters instead of preparing them for the upcoming quiz on DNA.

Fourth block went as predicted, and I was impressed once more by my tough kids when they were genuinely curious. They asked some honest questions that I answered to the best of my ability. Although no one came out and admitted to it, I had a pretty good notion that there were three other shapeshifters in the room, and when the bell rang, they hung back to talk to me about their own families. Tyler, Kaylee, and Brent – hawk, falcon, and Canada goose respectively – already knew each other as shapeshifters, but had been unaware of any of their teachers also sharing their gifts. They didn't stay long as they all had to get to their respective rides home, but they assured me their parents were very grateful that we were willing to stand up for them. They ducked out when Frank and Natasha entered the room, saying a hasty goodbye. I had a feeling I'd be chatting with them again.

"I bet you had an exciting day," laughed Natasha as she watched the students hurry off. "Sorry to bring even more inquiries to your doorstep."

"It's fine. The kids were great. They were genuinely curious, and there were only one or two weird questions that I was not about to respond to," I said, grinning.

"I can only guess!" laughed Natasha. "They are probably ones that I would have asked too. I just know better!"

"I am far more willing to answer certain questions to adults only," I said, shaking my head. "And truthfully, I can only tell you about my clan and how we do things."

The rest of the department filtered in, and we all moved desks into a circle to better see each other. Bill, the physical science teacher, had brought chocolate kisses and tossed them around to each of us. I missed my catch and had to go chase under one of the lab tables. Shri had to do the same.

"Bill," Shri said, shaking her head. "Throw the kisses to people, not over people. You would think you'd be better at using parabolas!"

I sat back down as Bill apologized, then studied my department. No one spoke for a few minutes as they ate the chocolates, then Natasha sighed.

"Okay, I'll go first. When you change, what's it like?"

"You mean what does it feel like?" I asked, and she nodded. "Well, it's really nothing. The change is pretty much instantaneous. There's no real feeling to it."

"Does your clothing change?" asked Tim.

"Nope," I said. "Total drawback time. You have to strip unless you want to find yourself tangled in clothes that don't fit any more."

"Bummer," said Tim.

"Tell me about it," I said, rolling my eyes. "Winters around here are cold!"

"So are you and John..." began Bill.

"We're together," I said. "Our wolf sides more or less decided we were good for each other. The wolf and I aren't separate entities, but that part of me understands things differently, more instinctively. The first time John and I ran together in the woods kind of cemented it."

"It sounds horribly romantic," said Natasha, jotting down notes.

"Well, if you recall, I had a boyfriend at the time. I mean, I was already in the planning stages to break things off with him due to his comments about shapeshifters, but it was definitely not the way I had planned."

The department chuckled together, remembering the incident with Ahnold.

"Do shapeshifters have relations in animal form?" asked Tim, tapping his pen against his front teeth.

"I haven't," I admitted. "Some couples do. Most of us are raised to avoid the more primal parts of our natures, other than hunting. I'd still rather have my steak cooked, though."

"And there are human and shapeshifter couples?" asked Frank.

"Frequently," I said. "There is actually a lot of intermarrying. Sam Winston and his fiancée Laura are a good example. She's completely human, but Sam obviously isn't. They fell in love even after he told her. Their children, if they have them, may or may not get the gene to shape shift. It doesn't always manifest. My brother Mark can't change, but my other three brothers do. Mark's oldest just changed last year."

"So, in reality, some people might never know?" asked Shri.

"We try to make sure that doesn't happen," I said. "We keep a pretty close eye on clan members, but even then, some slip by us. Take John, for instance. His mother gave him up at birth, and he had no idea what he was until about a month ago. I'm just glad I found him when I did; he was completely confused and had no idea how to even become human again. We try to prevent orphans from being raised away from a clan if at all possible. John's real mother probably was a loner who got pregnant. It happens occasionally."

"So there are lone wolf-type shapeshifters?" asked Natasha.

"That is where the form does sometimes follow. Not so much for us urban types, but those up in the outer reaches of Montana or Canada? Yes. Form follows type a lot. Some of them prefer animal shape to human. They still interact with people occasionally, but they tend to own small cabins up in the woods somewhere. They don't own a lot of human "stuff," and they can be pretty reclusive. The rest of us like our double espressos too much to live that far away from coffee shops."

"The urban wolf," laughed Mike. "Tamed by coffee shops."

"And Netflix," I added with a grin. "John and I are suckers for good shows on Netflix."

"Oh my!" exclaimed Darlene. "*Bridgerton?*"

"The Duke?" said Natasha.

"The Duke!" Bill, Shri, and I intoned and broke into giggles.

Frank and Tim looked at each other, then at Mike, who shrugged.

"I haven't seen it," said Tim.

"Maybe we should," said Mike.

Frank shook his head, and the three of them watched as the rest of us gushed about the handsome characters in the show, particularly the Duke of Hastings. A few minutes later, we decided to call it a day and went our separate ways to pack up our bags. Natasha and Darlene met up with me outside my room, and we chatted all the way to our cars before bidding each other goodbye. The police had dispersed the protestors, and I left feeling lighter than I had in months. And more tired too. I called Nevermore, who was likewise headed home, and promised to catch her up when next we met.

24

PLAYING WITH MATCHES

John arrived home around six-thirty that evening, having called me to let me know he'd be late and was fine. He came in through the door, appearing as exhausted as I felt, and fell onto the loveseat in the living room with a loud sigh. I had started a roast for dinner and brewed some coffee. I brought us both out mugs heavily doctored with cream and sugar.

"Work was lousy today," he said, accepting the mug. "Thanks. Of course, they heard what happened last night, and they had a lot of questions. Nobody is thinking of firing me, though, after what Rich and his pals put me through. Thankfully, engineers are practical people. Once they were satisfied I wouldn't "be eating the neighborhood poodles" as one of them jokingly put it, they pretty much just left me be, and we slogged through the usual lab mess. The biggest problem was that the laser lenses wouldn't line up properly. Once we got that sorted out, it was already quarter to six."

"I'm glad you called me," I said. "I was starting to get nervous."

"Yeah, well, we have something else to add to our list of interesting problems," he said. "My folks saw the school board meeting last night. On top of now knowing I'm a shapeshifter, they've figured out that I'm living with you. I also had not told them about was the kidnapping incident. Thankfully my bruises have faded some, but they still noticed them on camera. We've been invited for dinner. Friday night. Six-thirty sharp. We're going to get grilled, figuratively speaking."

"Been there, done that," I said and filled him in on what had happened at school.

When I was finished, he groaned.

"Do you think it will ever settle down?" he said.

"Once we are no longer the newest thing?" I said with a hint of sarcasm. "Sure. I think we have a ways to go before that, though. Two or three years down the road, maybe?"

"Don't even joke," he grumbled.

The doorbell rang.

"Oh, lord," said John. "Now what?"

I went to the peephole in the door and saw Ellen and her husband Bob, who I recognized from the night of the storm. They appeared anxious, and Ellen spoke to someone out of my line of vision. Of course. Sara would be with them. John came up behind me and peeked out.

"You should probably open the door," he whispered.

I shot him a death glare but unbolted the door, opening it wide.

"Hey, Ellen, Sara," I said. "This must be Bob?"

"Yes," said Ellen, clearly ill at ease. "Can we come in?"

"Sure," I said, backing up a pace.

Ellen studied John's bruises and winced.

"What happened?"

"I had a run in with someone who didn't like my face," said John dryly.

"Oh," said Ellen, wincing. "It looks painful."

"I just made some coffee," I said. "Please come have some."

"Sure," said Bob a little stiffly. "Thanks."

I led the way to the kitchen and poured mugs of coffee for Ellen and Bob, then got a glass of juice for Sara, who was talking in whispers to John. He nodded very seriously at whatever she was saying, and I noticed that both Bob and Ellen watched the interaction tensely.

I handed them their mugs, then regarded them.

"I'm glad to see you, but I get the feeling this isn't just a random social call," I said. "Would I be wrong in guessing you saw the school board meeting last night?"

The two of them abruptly relaxed like all of the air had been let out of them.

"Oh, I'm so glad you brought it up!" said Ellen "We were really pretty sure, but I didn't want to jump to any conclusions. So it was you two the night of the storm? You brought Sara back?"

I smiled at her, then nodded to where John had crouched down to be at eye level with Sara.

"She knew him right away the last time you were here," I said. "We had gone out for a run that night in the snow because it's the best time to avoid being seen. We heard you talking with the police, then went hunting for her. She heard John's voice when he changed back briefly to human form. He was hidden behind me, but she saw his face and heard enough to remember him."

"We can't thank you enough," said Bob. "I have never been so terrified as I was when I found the back door open. The police tried to help, but with the snow and the wind, we were all just running in circles. I am so glad that you were there that night. It's kismet that you moved in when you did."

"Yes," said Ellen. "If there is anything we can ever do…"

"Just please don't tell anyone," I said. "We're trying to live a quiet life. Neither of us want news crews around. I just want to do my job and teach my high schoolers."

"The news crews already came back earlier today," said Ellen. "We told them that we didn't know who you were."

"Thank you," I said.

I looked over at John, who noticed my glance and rose, coming to stand with the rest of us. Sara walked over to her mother and hugged her leg tightly.

"Sara was telling me that she hoped to get her own doggie sometime," said John, smiling. "She's really adorable."

"She is that," said Bob, ruffling Sara's hair affectionately. "Now we'll just have to convince her not to run out into the next snowstorm in hopes of finding "her doggie" again. She seems to think that it's the only time she will see him."

John and I exchanged a glance. I shrugged.

"Up to you," I said.

"Would it help if she saw me here, now?" asked John, turning to Ellen and Bob. "So she doesn't only associate me with the storms?"

"Is it safe?" asked Bob.

"I mean, the hardwood floor might suffer some if John loses his balance," I said lightly, "but yes, seriously, it is safe. We always maintain our sense of who we are, Bob."

"I'll be right back," said John, ducking out of the room.

"I didn't mean to imply that he'd do anything to hurt Sara," said Bob, sounding worried.

"We know that," I said. "There is a lot of misinformation out there. I can't speak for all the clans, but ours is not the most forthcoming with letting people know about us. Humans have a lot of misconceptions about wolves to begin with. Add to that the idea that we must be some secret invasion force infiltrating communities to take them over? It's ridiculous."

My back was to the hallway, but I heard the click of claws on the floor and turned to see John step into the room. Ellen and Bob froze where they were at the sight of the large black wolf. John also stopped moving, unsure of how to not alarm them further. With a cry of joy, Sara immediately detached herself from her mother and ran over to John. Ellen grabbed at her belatedly, but by then, Sara had already thrown her arms around John's neck and was hugging him tightly. Bob looked askance at me, a little alarmed.

"He won't hurt her," I said, "though she might squish *him* to death."

John gave one of his goofy, doglike grins and sat down, allowing himself to be hugged and patted. Ellen had grabbed one of Bob's hands and seemed to be holding her breath.

"He's so big!" she breathed. "I didn't really get a sense for how large he was that night."

"He is on the larger side, yes," I said. "I would guess his clan is one of those farther north than my own. He was adopted as a baby, so we don't really know anything about his parentage. Up until recently, he didn't even know he *was* one of us. John is probably on of the most unwolf-like wolves I've met. He's been raised as any human would be. You can imagine his surprise!"

"So wait," said Bob, moving to stop Sara when she tried to climb on John's back. "I got back last weekend from a trip and as I got out of the Uber, a whole herd of kids was descending on your house. Were all of them shapeshifters too?"

"My former students," I said grimacing. "And yeah, they came over to check on John after he was assaulted by my ex. They recently all found out about each other, so they're all hanging out together."

"And they're all wolves?"

"Only one," I said. "The rest are from different clans."

Ellen smiled tentatively.

"So is the invite still open to come over when Bob is away?" she asked. "I mean, if this doesn't change your opinion of us? We kind of barged in here."

"Why would it?" I asked. "Does it change yours?"

"No, no! Absolutely not!" said Ellen emphatically. "If anything, I trust you more since you are willing to help Sara to see that she doesn't have to go out in a blizzard to find you. You'd be welcome to join us for dinner anytime."

John gently detangled himself from Sara and left the room. Sara ran back to her mother, grinning from ear to ear.

"Did you see the doggie?" she exclaimed. "He lives here! Can we see him again? Pleeeeaaaseee? Please, Mommy?"

"Only if you promise not to run out into any more storms," said Ellen.

"Right," I said, squatting down next to Sara. "You can peek out the window, and maybe you'll see him, but you can't go out 'cause we might not always be there. You stay in where it's warm and dry, okay?"

"'Kay!" said Sara.

"Promise?" said John, walking into the room tugging his shirt to straighten it.

"I promise!" said Sara, running over to hug him again.

He picked her up and walked back to us, handing off Sara to Bob.

"You're really great with kids," Bob said, hugging his daughter. "Are you two planning to have your own at some point?"

"We've talked about it," I said, winking at John. "We'd like to get married first, though."

"Don't wait too long," laughed Bob. "They take a lot of your energy. They're totally worth every last erg, though."

"We'll see," John said, smiling that enigmatic sweet smile of his.

"We should get going," said Ellen. "Thank you so much for being willing to be open with us. And for making sure Sara understands she doesn't have to go wandering in the snow to find you."

We walked them to the door and bade them a good evening. The roast was beginning to fill the room with a wonderful aroma, so I set John to work cutting up salad greens while I started the little rice cooker, one of the few appliances that I had brought from the apartment. I spared a thought for Rich then and wondered what he was up to. There had been no sign of him, but that didn't mean he'd given up. Outing us to the public had backfired, so it was more than likely that the other people at the dojo that night would start trouble for us now. Not knowing who they were put us at a distinct disadvantage.

Dinner was a quiet affair. We had decided there was no point in having a dining table if we didn't actually eat at it, so we had made a point of sitting down together each night without electronic distractions. Both of us seemed to be feeling reflective, however, and conversation kept grinding to a standstill.

"So if we're going to get married..." said John, breaking the silence and trailing off, hesitantly.

"We should just do it?" I finished.

John nodded.

"Still thinking about what Bob said?" I asked. "About having kids?"

"Yeah," said John. "I know it seems like we are going awfully fast, but I don't want to wait. We've talked about this, and we both agree…"

"So let's set a date," I said. "Let's pick one in late June when school is over. That will give us time to plan. My parents will put up everyone at the House or at the hotel in Laramie. They will hold the wedding at the House, of that I am sure, unless we pick somewhere else."

"I can't think of anywhere grander than the House," said John, "though it will be difficult for some people to get there."

"We can charter a bus," I said, laughing. "It's been done before."

"That's not a bad idea," John mused. He pulled out his phone, opening the calendar app. "How does June twenty-sixth sound?"

"It sounds perfect," I said. "No finals to worry about, no snow. I think that will work."

He beamed at me, then wiggled his eyebrows.

"Make the call." he said, trying not to laugh.

Giggling, I picked up my phone and dialed my mother's number. Placing the phone between us on the table, I hit the speaker button and waited for her to pick up.

"Hi, honey, is everything all right there?" she asked. "How was school?"

"Better than I'd hoped," I said, grabbing John's hand. "We need to ask you something. Can you host a wedding in June?"

"Oh my, yes!" exclaimed my mother. "Absolutely, yes! Denny! They've set a date!"

I heard my dad cheer from a more distant location, and then the sounds of footsteps coming into the same room.

"That's great news, Kitten," he said. "When?"

"We were thinking June twenty-sixth," I said, "if that will work."

"It definitely will," said my father. "In fact, it is right between conferences. Absolutely perfect. Wait till I tell Marseille!"

"Ungodly pink confectionaries, here we come," I muttered to John. "Marseille has some very set ideas about petit fours being pepto pink."

The conversation wound on through basic plans, and it was decided that we would fly to and from Montana in March via the Laramie airport so that we could solidify plans. My mother also insisted that they come into town the next weekend to go shopping. Had I chosen Bridesmaids? How about John's groomsmen? My head was spinning when we hung up the phone with my mother, promising her we'd arrange a dinner with John's parents.

"They won't know what hit them," I said of my soon-to-be inlaws.

"Friday night's dinner is going to be soooo much fun," he sighed. "I'm bringing wine. Lots of it."

"Sounds like a plan," I said, rising to take my plates out to rinse and put in the dishwasher. "Life hasn't been boring lately, that's for sure."

"Feel up to making a few lists tonight?" he asked, following me to the kitchen with his own plates.

"Sure, but the calls can wait until tomorrow night," I said. "I need to spend a while grading."

"Sounds good," he said.

He turned and kissed me with a suddenness and a hunger that I could feel. I kissed him back with the same intensity.

"Maybe we could take a *few* minutes before we start making some lists?" I said, feigning reluctance.

"Maybe we could indeed," he replied, glancing at the stairs. "Race you?"

25
AN UNEXPECTED TURN OF EVENTS

Thursday was better. There were still a few protesters early in the morning, but my classes were full again and, aside from a few tentative questions in my first block, the students seemed to have basically accepted our presence. Two of the shapeshifter kids stayed after for a few moments to thank me before the AP Bio group descended, and we also had a good class.

Prep was a bit more crazy. Darlene had a few questions for me, but Natasha had an actual list that she had apparently compiled the night before. She was fascinated by the idea of how natural wolf instincts worked within a human framework. When I explained right as the bell rang that some of the more northern groups spent more time in wolf form than in human, she made me promise to chat with her after class.

D block was fine, and the kids who had spoken to me before stayed even longer to chat, not leaving until right before Natasha came back in from bus duty. They felt very much alone as they didn't know too many others, and I suggested that they come to the literary club on Monday to talk to a few of the other students there. The three of them, none of whom had ever picked up a book outside of school in their lives, hesitantly agreed but when I promised there would be brownies, their attendance became more assured. They left wishing me a good rest of my day, and a few minutes later, both Natasha and Nevermore breezed in, chatting animatedly.

"Hey guys?" I said, getting their attention. "How would you feel about starting something like the Gay/Straight Alliance, but for shapeshifters and their human friends?"

"I think that would be fantastic," said Kathy. "The humans in the lit club were a little annoyed they weren't included that one Monday, you know. Some of them are great friends with the shapeshifter kids."

"Good, let's plan on putting that together in the near future," I said. "They need solidarity and not all of the shapeshifter kids are bibliophiles. We should probably ask Mr. Turner about setting this up."

"I'll join you, if you like," said Natasha. "It might help to have a human advisor there too."

"Excellent idea," said Kathy. "Paul can't accuse me of spreading myself too thin if you two are running the show, and I just pop in occasionally."

"Meaning every week," I laughed.

"Depends on when it is," said Kathy. "It could happen, it could."

"Kathy came up with me to see if she can help answer questions too," said Natasha, checking her cell phone, "but my daughter apparently had a rotten day and is not feeling like being alone when she gets home. I'm going to have to take a rain check."

"That's fine," I said. "We can talk later."

"Great," said Natasha. "I'll see you both tomorrow."

She left the room, and I went to gather my coat.

"How have things been going?" asked Kathy. "I know it's been nuts for me since Tuesday."

"The same," I said. "Last night, John and I set an official date for the wedding."

"How wonderful!" said Kathy. "After school lets out?"

"End of June," I said as I grabbed my coat. "Can I count on you to be my maid of honor?"

"Matron of honor, and yes! I'd be thrilled!" said Kathy, hugging me. "Who else will you have?"

"Well, Tanya, of course. Olivia and Kim, if they'll agree. That's about it. There aren't that many women in my life, but I owe those two big time. John is asking Garrett, James, and Will. He'd like to ask Paul as well if he'd be willing."

"I'm sure he would," said Kathy, smiling. "Have you asked the others?"

"I'm going to call them this evening. Not something you text about, really."

We walked out of the building together, noting that there were still some protesters from this morning. One of them seemed familiar, a big guy who held his sign in a matter-of-fact way and peered directly at me with narrowed eyes.

Kathy saw him at the same time I did, but she didn't react. Instead, she made a big production about having left her keys on her desk, and she walked back in with a muttered "call you later." I got into my car and left the school, keeping a close eye on the man in the little group. He was one of the men who'd been at the dojo, of that I was sure. As I drove away, he was talking to someone on his phone, and I left, heading to my uncle's office instead of home. I didn't spot a tail, but the roads were packed that afternoon, and I couldn't be sure.

When I got to Andrew's, my uncle was in a meeting, so I chatted with his receptionist, Martha. As we talked, I kept looking out of the front window, watching the cars to see if I recognized anyone. My phone buzzed; it was a message from Nevermore.

GUY LEFT RIGHT AFTER YOU. ARE YOU SAFE?

YES, I AM AT ANDREW'S.

OKAY, AS LONG AS YOU'RE OK. CALL YOU LATER.

Andrew strode out as I was putting my phone back in my pocket, took one look at my face, and waved me back towards his office.

"Your color is awful," he said. "Coffee?"

"Please."

"Martha," he called. "Could you bring us two coffees please?"

I heard a small chuckle from behind us as Andrew led me towards the small kitchen with its Keurig and stash of flavored coffee pods.

As we waited for it to brew, I filled him in on what had transpired over the past few days. My mother had already contacted him about the wedding, and he was thrilled to hear about it. The strange man among the protestors was a bit more disconcerting. When the coffee was done, we went into his office where we sat in two overstuffed chairs. Andrew stirred his coffee thoughtfully and studied me.

"I think I might take tomorrow afternoon off, maybe just do a little drive around the school for a look-see. You might want to give that nice officer a ring, Barber wasn't it? I know your mother told me his name."

"I'll call him," I said. "Right now, I just want to go home."

"All right. Stay for a few more minutes, and then I'll walk you out. Call him on the way, though."

"I will," I said, relieved by the thought.

"I am going to see you this weekend, I expect?" he said, trying to change the mood in the room.

"With mom and dad down, absolutely," I said. "That reminds me, mind if I make a few calls before I forget? I need to actually talk to the bridesmaids and ask them to be bridesmaids."

"Certainly," said Andrew. "There's an empty office next to this one. I'll walk you out when you are done."

"Thanks," I said and went next door.

All of the calls had the desired effects. The three younger bridesmaids agreed with happy cheers, and we set plans to meet for breakfast at the Motherlode Café and Tavern. Nevermore confirmed the plans on her end, and she readily agreed she'd be there.

As I hung up with Kathy, I heard a voice in the front asking for

Andrew, and Martha calling down the hall to my uncle. Andrew himself answered and stepped out into the hall. There was a shot, then a second. I heard the bullet ricochet down the hall. Panicked, I dropped to the floor and dialed 911, creeping over as quietly as I could to lock the door.

"911, what's your emergency?"

I heard Martha cry out, and there was a thump as something landed heavily on the carpet.

"I'm at Culger and Wellington Associates," I whispered. "It's on 33rd Street. There's been a gun fired, I think at my uncle, and the receptionist might have been hurt. Please send someone, quickly!"

"I'm sending the call ahead now. The nearest car should be there in less than three minutes. Stay on the line."

There was another shot, closer this time. I crawled under the desk and hid as best I could, peering out from beneath it.

A shadow moved beyond the door, and the door knob rattled. An eternity passed, then it rattled again, harder this time. As I sat frozen, I heard a gun being primed, then something else moved behind the shadow. There was a loud *crack,* and the first figure dropped to the floor with a thud.

"Sasha!" called my uncle. "Are you all right?"

"Andrew!" I cried and threw myself at the door. Andrew stood there, bleeding heavily from his right shoulder, holding a baseball bat loosely in his left hand. On the ground was the man who had been at the school earlier. He was out cold.

"Ma'am!" came the woman on the phone. "Ma'am, can you hear me?"

I lifted the phone back to my ear.

"Yes," I said, my voice sounding a little shrill. "Yes, my uncle had a baseball bat and knocked out the shooter. Please let the police know that the attacker is down, and my uncle needs a doctor. He's been shot in the shoulder and is bleeding pretty badly."

"I'll let them know. They should be there momentarily. An ambulance is on its way."

Andrew swayed a bit on his feet and glanced out towards reception.

"Poor Martha is going to have an awful headache come morning from the blow he gave her," said Andrew faintly. "Better let them know she's injured too."

"Let's get you sitting down. Come on," I said, leading him towards the reception area.

As I assisted Andrew to the front of the building, I relayed the information to the dispatcher and held the line until the police arrived a few seconds later. They took one look at Andrew, who seemed as if he was about to fall, and while one went back to deal with the unconscious shooter, the other helped me lay Andrew down in the waiting area, gently taking the bat from his hand. He then went to check on Martha, speaking rapidly into his mike. The dispatcher told me over the phone that the police would handle it from there, and we disconnected.

The officer who had gone to cuff the shooter came back carrying the rifle in one gloved hand, heading out the door. Seconds later, the ambulance pulled into the parking lot, and the EMTs came in, assisted Andrew gently onto a stretcher and then rolled him out to the waiting vehicle. I followed them outside as two others went in with a stretcher for Martha.

The first police officer came out to speak to me.

"What's your name, please?" he said, pulling out a little notebook and a pen.

"Sasha Wellington," I said, and he peered at me with new interest.

"Should I call Officer Barber?" he asked. "He's supposed to be notified if your name comes up."

"He is?" I said, feeling relieved. "Yes, please. We know him, and he's talked to us before."

"D. J. is one of the best," smiled the officer. "Let me alert dispatch."

He stepped aside for a moment to speak into his shoulder mike, then came back over to where I sat.

"He's on his way," he said. "I'm Officer Cloverly. Deej is my cousin. You're one of his shapeshifters, aren't you?"

I blinked at the abruptness of the statement, and he shook his head.

"That came out all wrong," grimaced Cloverly. "I mean, he helped you and your boyfriend, correct?"

"Yes," I said.

"Okay," he smiled. "Is the shooter one of the men who assaulted your boyfriend?"

"Yes," I said. "I saw him near my school today. He was with the little group of protestors, and he got on the phone when I was leaving. I watched to see if I was followed, but I didn't notice anyone."

"We should check your car over," he said. "They could have used something to track you, like a GPS locator. Then they could pace you one street over and you'd never know. When D. J. gets here, I'll go have a look."

"How would they have put it on?" I said. "My car was right out front."

"It wouldn't have taken but a minute," said Officer Cloverly, "and some of these guys are pretty clever, pretending to drop their keys or tie their shoes. This one is not going to be feeling all that well when he wakes up. Your uncle wields a mean baseball bat. Not that I blame him in this case."

Another police cruiser turned into the parking lot, stopped, and then D. J. Barber stepped out of the car. He saw me and came right over.

"Are you all right?" he asked.

"I'm okay, but it appears that another of that group has made himself known. He's still inside," I added.

"I'll go check your car" said Officer Cloverly and walked away.

"How's John feeling?" Officer Barber asked, moving towards the ambulance where Andrew was being fussed over by two EMTs.

"He's better," I said. "Thanks for asking."

"You're welcome," said Barber. "Let's get you and your uncle to the hospital. I'll stay with you, and I'll talk to you more when we get there, okay?"

"Okay," I said.

I stepped into the ambulance and found Andrew sitting on the gurney. He was very pale, and the EMTs putting pressure on the wound were speaking to him calmly. I sat beside him, not saying anything. Outside, another ambulance was arriving for Martha. I could see that she was awake now but seemed dazed. The EMT with her waved over the men from the second vehicle, and I caught the words "concussion" and "shock" as they loaded her into the ambulance and drove away.

A minute later, a third ambulance pulled in, and there was a brief flurry of activity as the EMTs took that gurney and rolled it into the building.

"Well, at least I gave as good as I got," said Andrew, smiling wanly.

"Mr. Wellington," said the EMT. "We need to go straight to the hospital. Are you related to him, miss?"

"He's my uncle," I said.

"There is tissue damage here I can't do anything with," she said. "He's going to have to have stitches and possibly surgery. We need to go now."

"Andrew, listen to her," I said. "You were shot. Like with a gun. It's not a weakness to get fixed up. You're still bleeding pretty badly."

Andrew tried to focus on me, his eyes slightly glazed.

"Fine," he said. "You stay with me and make sure they don't do anything untoward."

"Absolutely," I said, and added. "You look like crap."

"Thanks," he said sarcastically and turned to the EMT who was in the process of inserting an I.V. needle and attaching a bag of saline solution. "This is the thanks I get from my niece."

The EMT winked at me, and Andrew turned away, staring at the ceiling of the ambulance until she had finished.

"I'm also going to give you a shot of pain killer," she said. "The adrenaline will be wearing off soon, and you're going to want it."

Andrew grumbled under his breath, but said nothing. I took that as a sign he was already feeling considerable pain and just didn't want to show it.

Officer Barber came over to where we sat as the man who'd assaulted us was rolled out. I could see that he was handcuffed to the side rail, and Officer Cloverly, along with the other officer, escorted him as he was wheeled inside. Cloverly climbed into the back of the ambulance with the EMT, and they drove away.

"His name is Millis Walker," said Officer Barber. "He has a pretty long rap sheet and apparently runs with an offshoot of the old Mystery Seekers crew. My cousin found what appears to be a GPS device on your car; we're taking it down to the station to have it examined. I'll drive my car to the hospital and meet you there. If you need it, I can give you a lift back here for your car later."

"Sure," I said. "We'll see you there."

He left the ambulance, and the EMT stepped out for a moment to talk to the driver. She came back in, the doors were closed, and we began to move. Andrew was very quiet, for him, and I took this as a sign that he was worse off than he'd let on.

"Andrew," I said, "I am so sorry to bring this down on you. I had no idea."

"Not your fault," said my uncle, making an attempt to pull himself together a bit more. "Hopefully, the police will find the rest of them and that will be the end of it."

"I hope so," I said.

We pulled up to the hospital a few minutes later, and they rolled Andrew straight into the emergency room. There was a flurry of activity, and they put us in a bay. A nurse bustled right in and began taking Andrew's information.

During the short wait for the doctor, I texted John and let him know what had happened.

Hey, I'm at the hospital with Andrew. There was an attack, but I'm okay. Andrew was shot, and they are prepping him for surgery. You don't have to rush right over. DJ is here.

WTF???

The phone rang; it was John, sounding panicked. I pointed out that we were probably in the safest place we could be, and he promised he would be right over. I hung up just as Officer Barber came in.

"Your assailant got quite a good rap on the head, but he'll probably recover in a few days' time. He'll be under guard here until he is well enough to go to jail for assaulting your uncle with a deadly weapon and giving Ms. Sanders a nasty concussion. You said that he was one of the ones who assaulted John?"

I nodded as the doctor arrived and asked myself and Officer Barber to step outside of the bay for a few minutes while he examined Andrew. I gladly did so; all the blood was making me queasy. I texted my mother to let her know the news, promising to call later on.

When we had repositioned ourselves by the nurse's station, I took the opportunity to ask D. J. the question that had been nagging me since he had been called to the scene.

"Your cousin told me you had to be notified if anything came up regarding John or me," I said. "What is that all about?"

Officer Barber looked at me in surprise for a moment, then colored.

"Of all the stupid...He knows he isn't supposed to tell you," he said angrily.

"Why?" I said. "What's the big secret?"

He took a deep breath.

"The mayor's office assigned me to be your liaison and to keep an eye on you, something that I more or less messed up today," he said. "Your school seemed safe, so I took the chance to follow a lead rather than your car. It was a poor choice. It would have led me to Mr. Walker eventually anyway, and I was nearby when Clover called me."

"So, normally, you've been following me around?" I asked.

"Well, myself or one of the other men who have been assigned to the newly created Shapeshifter Liaison Office, yes," he said. "After Sam and his group made their announcement, our captain thought we ought to create a team to deal with cases like John's. We never made a big deal about it, just held it in reserve until it was needed. Our task is to deal with any hate crimes and to protect shapeshifters. Since you, John, and the rest who came forward at the meeting have so kindly painted targets on your backs, we have our hands full keeping tabs on you.

"We've also been keeping an eye on Rich, Todd, and Gary. They seem to be behaving themselves for the most part, but we are certain they have been in contact with the rest of their merry band, including Mr. Walker. Hopefully, we can get him to give someone else away."

"And here I am just teaching classes and making wedding plans," I chuckled.

"Well!" he said, surprised. "Congratulations! I thought the two of you just got together?"

"We've actually known each other for ten years," I said, "and we have been through a lot in a short amount of time. At this point, we are considering our friendship a *very* long courtship, I think, and just skipping the lengthy engagement."

"I can't say I blame you," he said. "If you've been friends that long, then you definitely don't have to get to know him in a lot of little ways."

"Oh, there's other things to learn," I said, smiling. "He snores like a bear, and he likes ketchup on his eggs. Imagine knowing someone for ten years and just now learning about that!"

"A total travesty," smiled Officer Barber. "My girlfriend also likes ketchup on random foods and has a weird penchant for maple syrup on French fries."

"Is that a thing?" I asked, making a face.

"Apparently in her family, yes."

"How long have you been together?"

"About eight years," Officer Barber said. "She'd love to meet you. And I saw that look! Before you ask, she isn't some super secret

Mystery Seeker spy. No, she just is fascinated by the idea of shapeshifters and wants to understand you all better."

I was laughing by that point, and it made me realize how infrequently I had seen the humor in anything as of late.

"Okay, she can pick my brain some time," I said. "In return, I have one question."

"What's that?"

"D. J. stands for...?"

"Douglas James," he said. "It's a mouthful, but I hate being called Doug, so D. J. it is."

We chatted about interests, found we liked some of the same Netflix shows, and were getting into a serious argument as to whether *Riverdale* was actually good or not when the doctor called us back into the room.

"He's very lucky nothing struck the bone," said the doctor, scowling at my uncle. "However, there are several major arteries that have been damaged, and he will need to go in for surgery immediately to repair them. They won't stop bleeding by themselves. He wants you to be with him, so I would ask that you can confirm that you have had no recent illnesses?"

"No, I've been fine," I said. "Andrew, are you sure you want me to be there?"

"Sasha, you can dissect a pig's heart in front of a class, but you can't handle a little blood?"

"Not when it's yours," I said, "but I'll do my best."

"We can prep him for surgery and be done in around an hour at best guess," said the doctor. "The reconstruction won't take too long once we are in there. Then it is just a matter of recovery for a couple of days."

"Couple of days, hell," said Andrew, his voice slurring slightly. "I am going to leave tomorrow morning if I have to wheel myself out of here under my own power!"

"Andrew, you need to recover," I said. "And my parents are coming tomorrow, so you won't be here all alone."

"You texted them, didn't you?" he said, his eyes trying to focus on me and failing.

"Guilty," I said.

He visibly sagged.

I turned back to the doctor.

"Just so you know, he is a shapeshifter," I said. "Type O blood is the best for us, or I can donate some if you need it."

The doctor paused for a second. "Is there anything else I should be aware of?"

"No," I said. "Other than that, treat him like you would anyone who's been shot."

He nodded. "We'll let you know if we need you."

They took Andrew in to prep him for surgery, and I was allowed to watch from a corner of the room until he was put under, then I was ushered to the door of the recovery room. D. J. joined me and we talked while we waited for Andrew to come out of surgery. They were faster than I'd imagined, and the whole procedure was completed in just under an hour. Andrew was then wheeled into the recovery room, and I was still sitting there chatting quietly with D. J. when John arrived.

"Tell me everything," he said.

D. J., his mouth set in a grim line, gave John a brief rundown of what had happened. At the end, he sighed.

"Sasha told you he was one of the men who beat you?" he asked, and at John's nod, continued. "We're going to ask you to positively I.D. him and press charges for both the shooting and the assault on you. This has to stop. In no way should it be allowed to stand going forward. Even if the law protecting you folks hasn't passed yet, we will treat these cases as if it has. You have done nothing to deserve this."

"Other than exist," I said. "If Sam and his group hadn't come out, there was little chance most people would have known most of us existed. We'd be like Bigfoot or the Loch Ness Monster. Something the cryptozoologists chased, but most people didn't believe in."

"Even still," said D. J., shaking his head, "there is no way any of you should be treated like this."

Eventually, Andrew awoke and was settled in a room for the night with one of D. J.'s task force set to guard him. John drove me back to get my car at Andrew's office, and then we went home. I was beyond exhausted. John made a couple of burgers, and we sat and watched a few episodes of *Kipo and the Age of Wonderbeasts* before going to bed. I literally had nothing left that night, and after a quiet conversation about what precautions we could think of taking, we sank into the soft mattress, both of us falling asleep almost at once.

26

DINNER WITH THE FOLKS

The next day went by in a blur. I was still tired and was teaching almost by rote by the time school was over. Following a short staff meeting, I headed for the hospital where my parents were visiting Andrew. In spite of his objections, he would be staying at his condo after his release so his doctors could monitor his well-being. For now, he was on forced bed rest, and his arm was going to be in a sling for a while, something that frustrated him greatly.

My mother greeted me as I entered the room and swept me into a giant hug before letting me inside. My dad was sitting on a chair near the bed and greeted me cheerfully as I entered.

"Hi, Kitten, how was work?"

"Exhausting, Dad, but I can't keep calling out, you know?" I smiled wearily.

"I do indeed," he chuckled.

I turned to my uncle, taking off my coat. "How are you, Andrew?"

"Horribly crabby," he said. "I can't do anything! The drugs are making me loopy, and your mother won't let me take this blasted sling off!"

"And I'll be staying to help with business until Martha gets back, so don't think you'll get away with it on my watch," said my mother.

Andrew retreated into a sulky glare, but my father elbowed him in his uninjured shoulder. My uncle grimaced but his mood seemed to improve.

"Well, you've had one adventure after another since you got back from Christmas," said Dad, turning to me. "Think you might want to take a break, get some rest, maybe?"

"That is the plan for this weekend following dress insanity," I said. "I just have to deal with one more perilous adventure tonight. If I can survive John's parents at dinner, we should be in the clear."

"Oh dear," said my mother. "You really do have a challenge waiting for you. I suppose we should meet them eventually. Can you arrange it?"

"Maybe later this weekend," I said. "Remember, not too many adventures?"

"We'll play it by ear," said my mother, smiling.

The conversation shifted from my wedding to Andrew's plans while his office was being restored. He and his assistant would be doing most of their work from Andrew's condo for the next week or so. The police still had to clear the crime scene, and then there was a matter of the blood and the bullet holes. When we talked about it, Andrew just sighed.

"I mean, I did want to change some things around at the office, but I wasn't planning to do it until next year," he said. "I was rather fond of that carpet. Oh well."

At 4:30, I left to go home, beating John to the house by about ten minutes. After cleaning up and changing into jeans and a blouse, I waited for him to join me in the living room. He came down freshly showered wearing a plain black tee shirt under a green plaid flannel and black jeans - his comfort clothing. Neither one of us apparently wanted to feel any less comfortable than we already did.

"Ready?" he asked.

"As I'll ever be. You driving?"

"Yeah," he said. "It's better if I do tonight so we don't get lost. But remember, if I say run, run!"

"Gotcha," I said, donning my coat and snagging my purse.

Their house wasn't that far away, and after about a half an hour fighting traffic, we pulled up to his parents' small, brown ranch.

"Come on," he said, sounding resigned. "Let's go."

I took his hand as we walked to the front door, and I examined the place the where had grown up. It was nowhere near as large as my parents', and I knew John was painfully aware of what his life had been like growing up. I could only imagine how he must feel after everything that had happened recently. I squeezed his hand, and he pressed the bell with the conviction of the condemned.

Footsteps sounded on the other side of the door, and it opened wide to reveal John's adopted father. He was a fairly small man with receding hair and a wispy mustache. He peered at first his son, then at me. No hint of a smile played about his lips, nor did his eyes show any real greeting.

"Hi Dad," said John. "You remember Sasha, yes?"

"Indeed I do," said John's father, George, his manner overly formal. "It's good to see you again."

"Good to see you, too," I replied, forcing a smile on my face that I hoped appeared genuine.

Stepping back, Mr. Arndt ushered us inside, then led the way into a small living room where John's mother was waiting on the sofa. Her expression seemed a bit strained, and she rubbed her hands on her tan slacks nervously.

"Mom, you remember Sasha, right? Sasha, my mom, Hazel."

"Yes, I remember her," she said, eyeing me nervously. "Please sit down. George, take their coats, please. I was just going to check on dinner."

She disappeared from the room as if from a magician's cabinet, leaving no trace of her presence. John and I handed our coats dutifully to George, then sat together on the couch as his father took them out to the hall where a coat rack hung from the wall. He then returned and sat across from us in an armchair.

"You have a lovely home," I said as calmly as I could. "It's charming."

"Thank you," said George, eased a little by the rudiments of civility. "Can I maybe get you a drink?"

"Wine for me, if you have it, Dad," said John. "I meant to bring some, but it slipped my mind."

"For me as well, please," I said.

George rose and went into the dining room, which was just visible beyond the other end of the living room, and came back with an open bottle of red wine and three glasses. He poured us each a glass, and we sipped in silence for a few minutes before George sighed and turned to me.

"Are you still in teaching?" he asked, breaking the silence.

"Yes," I said. "AP Bio, Zoology, and two sections of regular bio this year."

"I suppose biology would be right up your alley."

"Dad!" exclaimed John, glaring at his father.

"Actually, the sciences tend to be where many of my clan end up, yes," I said, turning back to George. "Some of the crow and raven clans get into teaching literature."

"Quoth the raven?" chuckled George.

"Pretty much," I said.

George seemed to relax minutely and took another contemplative sip of his wine. He then looked over at John.

"So how'd you get yourself into this mess?" he asked, not without humor.

"Apparently I was born into it," said John, his tone guarded. "Just came into it a bit later than most."

"Members of the clans have their first change at various times. John isn't the latest we've heard of," I said. "There can be quite a range."

"So your birth mother or father was part of one of these...clans?" asked George, struggling with the terminology.

"It appears that way," said John. "Apparently it sometimes happens."

"What, shapeshifter mothers abandon their children?" George asked me.

"Lone wolves tend to not be social at the best of times," I said. "Usually, the clans keep an eye out for such abandoned infants in order to raise them properly, but we don't find them all."

"Hmm," said George. "Well, do *you* have a proper clan?"

"I do indeed," I said warmly and proceeded to tell him about my family.

Halfway through the explanation, I caught sight of Hazel peering in through the kitchen doorway. She was listening and seemed fascinated by what she was hearing, but I could feel her fear from where I sat. I explained how John had changed and how I'd brought him home to meet my family so that he could get some training and not feel so alone. I described the rescue of Sara and how grateful her parents were. John chimed in a few times about some of his experiences with my family thus far and about our house. George asked a few questions then, and he slowly began to warm up towards us.

Hazel cracked the door open wider as the conversation went on and a little while later, came into the room to sit near George. She still seemed like she might take flight at any moment, but her curiosity was winning over her fear. I snuck a peek at her as John was explaining about the rescue from the dojo and the AP kids banding together, and a small smile crept across her face as she realized that her son had found something he'd always been lacking. Friends.

When the buzzer went off on the oven, Hazel jumped, and then excused herself to go finish preparing dinner. George rose and gestured that we precede him into the dining room. A very short time later, we sat at the table, Hazel sitting between John and George, still unsure of me. Finally, as the potatoes were being passed around, she looked at me directly.

"So John has moved in with you. Do you plan to do the honorable thing?"

John and I smiled at each other.

"Actually, that was what we were going to talk to you about tonight," I said. "John and I have known each other for over ten years, and neither of us is getting any younger. We've already set a date for a June wedding, and of course, we hope you will be involved with the planning."

"June?" asked Hazel, turning to John. "That soon?"

She eyed me, and I could only guess from her expression that she was wondering if I was pregnant and that was the reason for the rush.

"Well, yes," said John. "After Sash gets out of school for the summer."

"Is that enough time to get a venue and a caterer?" asked George. "I would think that they would be all booked up by now."

"We will be having the wedding at my parents' house, and there is a master chef who lives in residence," I said. "We just have to figure out everything else."

"Oh," said Hazel, a little nonplussed. "I suppose that would make it easier. It's just all so fast."

"Tell me about it, Mom," said John. "I had no idea – well, no real idea – what was happening to me that night. Then I get dragged to Wyoming for the weekend, have some very surreal experiences, and come home to everything seeming upside down. Sasha's family was wonderful, but the fact that I am a shapeshifter is something that I'm still trying to get my head around. I don't feel any different, and sometimes, I don't even think about it. But when I do, it's like getting hit with a two by four."

"Or a baseball bat," I said under my breath.

"What was that?" asked Hazel, visibly startled.

John sighed.

"Remember I told you about Sasha's ex Rich and how he or his friends might come around? Well, a couple of weeks ago, they caught me outside of work, and Sasha and some friends had to come and rescue me. I'm fine, I'm fine. I had a black eye and a cracked rib, but I seem to have mostly healed up. Three of them, including Rich and the one that came to talk to you, got arrested, and yes, we are pressing charges.

"Now they've upped the ante. They attached a GPS to Sasha's car and followed her to her Uncle Andrew's work yesterday. The guy shot Andrew in the shoulder, but Andrew managed to get behind him while he was trying to attack Sasha and beaned the guy with a baseball bat. Sasha was attempting to be amusing, but there are people out there who see us as a threat to their way of life. The kicker is the shapeshifting clans have been living here the whole time."

George glanced at Hazel, whose nervous fidgeting was indicative that nothing in her world made sense anymore, but was gamely trying to force it to. George appeared a little better off, possibly due to the wine, and I took a healthy sip from my own glass, feeling a bit helpless in the face of such a statement.

"Well," said George, "I guess congratulations are in order. Will we get to meet your parents sometime soon, Sasha?"

"Actually, they came into town today to help Andrew," I said, glancing at John, then back to George. "My mother was already planning to go dress shopping with me and the bridesmaids tomorrow morning. I'd love it if you would join us, Hazel."

Hazel shook her head, "Perhaps lunch or dinner first?"

"Would Sunday around noon work?" I asked.

"I guess that would be all right," said George, looking to Hazel for confirmation.

At her hesitant nod, I smiled.

"Okay," I said. "I'll ask my parents if that works for them. Do you have a favorite restaurant?

"Via Toscana is nice," said George. "We go there a lot. I can make a reservation if you like."

"That'd be great. I'll go call my parents. Excuse me," I said, getting up and walking into the living room.

A minute-long conversation confirmed that my folks were amenable, and I walked back into the dining room.

"They say that it's fine," I said. "Andrew has an office assistant named Dan who will be staying with him, so my parents can get away for a while."

"I'll make a reservation for six of us, then," said George. "We can meet you all there."

"Sounds wonderful," I said.

"A wedding in June," mused George, a slight smile crossing his face. "We might actually be grandparents yet, Hazel. Is that in the plans for you two?"

"Hopefully," said John.

"And the children?" asked Hazel, hesitantly. "Will they be like you?"

"They might," I said, wincing mentally at the unintentional slight. "It isn't always a sure thing, but almost all of the children get the gift. Three of my brothers have it; the other one doesn't, but his daughter does."

"But why would you want that for them?" said Hazel, suddenly passionate. "Aren't the two of you suffering because of what you are?"

"We don't see it that way," I said. "I count it as a blessing. The freedom of what I am has always been worth it. The fact that groups want to take our freedoms away from us is why the clans decided to come into the open. For thousands of years, no one knew we were even here except the Native tribes."

"Do you want to see?" asked John suddenly. "I can prove to you that shapeshifters are not the monsters everyone thinks they are. Being able to take the form of a wolf has been the most freeing experience I have ever had. Sasha explained all of this to me on the way to Wyoming, and I didn't really understand until I stayed with her family for that weekend and had the opportunity to run and play with others who were like me. So tell me. Do you want to see?"

His parents stared at him for a long moment before his mother shook her head slowly.

"You don't have to show us," she said. "I'm honestly not ready for that. But I love you, John. And you, Sasha, you've been such a good friend to John for all of these years. I would be wrong to ask you to put on a show for our benefit. Maybe someday, John, but not today."

"Thank you," said John, letting out a huge breath. "I'm relieved, honestly, but the offer stands."

There was a pause as everyone gathered their thoughts.

"Thank you for dinner," I finally said. "It was really delicious, Hazel."

"I also made cake for dessert," said Hazel, smiling shyly at the compliment. "Would you care for some?"

"That would be great, Mom," said John.

"Please," I said.

Hazel went out to get the dessert, and George poured us some coffee from a carafe on the sideboard.

"Would you like to come over to dinner at our house next week," I said over dessert. "We aren't great cooks, but we can make some basic foods."

"That sounds lovely," said Hazel, setting the cake on the table. "I'll admit, I have been curious about where you've been living."

"It's a really amazing house," said John, "though it's tiny compared to Sasha's parents' house."

"Is that your family home in Wyoming?" asked George.

"It's the home of the entire clan, though most don't stay there," I said.

"And the wedding is being held there?" asked Hazel, her eyes widening. "It sounds huge."

"Oh, it is!" said John. "There's a pool and a conservatory and a ball room..."

"And way too much space to ramble around in," I laughed. "I think my parents close most of it off normally."

Talk moved on to other topics, such as my teaching and John's lab work, George's firm, and Hazel's bridge club. When we left, Hazel smiled at me, and George had made good on his promise of making a reservation.

As we left, John gave his parents both a huge hug.

"I love you," he said. "See you on Sunday."

They beamed at him, and I couldn't help but wonder if they had thought he might abandon them for his newfound family. They needn't have worried. John was still their son, and if nothing else, his loyalty was solid.

27
WEDDING PLANS AND A CAT

We met for breakfast as planned at the Motherlode Café and Tavern, and then headed over to the bridal shop Mother and I had chosen earlier that week for a ten o'clock appointment. The bridesmaids walked around looking at dresses while my mother and I hunted for the right wedding gown. I felt a thrill of excitement as I looked at dresses ranging in price from so-so to downright outrageous, and we eventually settled on something by Sherri Hill that was not too ridiculous for a dress that I would wear only once for around $1600.

The price made me blanche, but my mother didn't even bat an eye. It had a detachable organza train with faux seed pearls waves rippling across it, multiple layers of soft tulle underneath, and a relatively fitted strapless main dress made of lavishly-beaded satin resembling the swirls of damask florals. The sample was too small, so we handed it to our saleswoman who went to see if she had one I could try on.

My bridesmaids, meanwhile, were having a wonderful time. While the colors of the wedding were muted tones of blue and purple, I had given them the freedom to choose dresses that suited them. I could hear them giggling as they discussed their choices, Nevermore cracking jokes about half of the styles that sent the others into a paroxysm of laughter.

"Well, at least *they* are having a good time," I grumbled.

"And you're not?" said my mother, fondly.

"As long as this dress won't make me into a puff pastry," I said.

The saleswoman returned holding a larger version of the stunning dress we had chosen.

"This is one size larger than you would take," said the woman, "but you can at least get a sense of what it will feel like. Why don't you go try it on, and we'll see how it looks."

I took the dress and, with my mother's help, went into a dressing room to try it on. The satin whispered to the beads, and when I got it on, I was pleased at how lovely I appeared in the single mirror. There was a slight shock as the idea settled like a weight that I was actually going to get married. I felt faint and had to sit down for a moment. My mother smiled sympathetically.

The saleswoman knocked, and when my mother opened the door, the woman came in and gathered the train for me, then guided me out to a pedestal where the she could take a walk all around. In the multitude of mirrors, I could finally see myself.

Mother had only buttoned the top button of the dress, but now the saleswoman was deftly arranging the train so that it fell in a gentle sweep along the ground. The seed pearls whispered over themselves again, and as the saleswoman held the back tightly to give the dress a more fitted look, I stood staring in the mirrors that surrounded the pedestal, gazing at myself in astonishment. The figure looking back at me was a more ephemeral being than I could ever imagine being. The dress accented my figure, and the low décolletage made me seem a much more romantic character than I could ever imagine being.

Nevermore appeared from nowhere to stand next to my mother, and the others materialized soon after. Tanya wolf-whistled at me, and the others applauded.

"Do you like it?" asked my mother.

"It's gorgeous," I said.

"So are you," she smiled, and turned towards the saleswoman. "Let's order it today, so we can get it ready in time for the wedding."

With the saleswoman's help, I extracted myself from the dress, and while Mother went to take care of all the details, I rejoined my friends. They had found, by happy coincidence, a style that had suited all of them and which came in a rainbow of colors. I relented and let them each choose what color they wanted, and we managed to flag down their saleswoman to work with the rambunctious crew. While they were working on their orders, my mother and I discussed shoes, a veil, and all of the other little accessories that go with wedding dresses.

* * *

When all the arrangements were finally made, we were starving.

"Lunch is definitely in order," said Tanya, and we drove to a nearby sushi bar where we ordered way more food than we intended.

"You know," I said to Nevermore over a Mai-Tai, "this is the most fun I've had in days...weeks!"

"Months, even!" she laughed. "We have had almost everything imaginable thrown at us. Sometimes that makes us forget how to actually relax and enjoy ourselves."

"It will be better soon," said my mother. "The legislation will go through, and hopefully, we will see a change in people's perceptions."

"I hope so," said Olivia. "None of us feel safe shapeshifting near home right now, so my family is planning a short vacation to South Dakota in the next few weeks. Maybe see if we can get up into one of the reservations and run on their lands."

"What an excellent idea!" said Tanya, sitting up straighter. "That's it, Sasha. That's what the tribes can do to help!"

Tanya was very excited and it took her a few minutes to calm down enough to explain what she meant.

"My grandmother, she put a charge on my cousin and me to repay a favor to Sasha. But what if I can extend the favor to more of you? She might be able to speak to the other elders, and we could see about providing you with a safe place to change!"

"That would be wonderful!" I said. "I have a place where I go to run sometimes, but not everyone is so lucky."

Everyone seemed cheered by the idea, and we soon finished lunch and went our separate ways in high spirits. My mother rode back to Andrew's condo with me and made plans to come over to the house the next day for breakfast. I drove home in a bit of a daze and spent the rest of the afternoon catching up on my grading, buoyed by the afternoon and the promise of marrying my best friend.

That night after the sun had been down long enough to clear out any late walkers from the canyons, John and I drove out to go for a run. It was supposed to snow again before morning, and both of us had a lot of pent up energy. I, for one, felt far too focused on human concerns. A run would be good for both of us.

During the long drive to where I usually parked, we chatted about small parts of our day. John had spent his time hanging out with the younger groomsmen; they had gotten measured for tuxedos and then spent the rest of the afternoon bonding over pizza and video games.

"It was supremely surreal," said John as we wound our way up into the canyons to my usual parking place. No one was following us, and I had inspected my car with a paranoid fear twice earlier just to be safe. "Suddenly I'm friends with Garrett? How the hell did *that* happen?"

I shrugged, but was secretly pleased that John had people to hang out with. I had no problems being his best friend, but I didn't want to be his *only* friend, especially now. John needed other shapeshifters to talk to. His openness about being a shapeshifter was such an oddity to me. My change in front of Tanya and her grandmother had had spiritual significance. Normally, we don't shift for our human friends.

John's willingness to do so might be dangerous, and the others would reinforce that he needed to be safe. Hearing it from me was one thing. Hearing it from the guys was another thing entirely.

We arrived at my sheltered spot down a back road and parked. No one would see the car there, and soon, we had shed our clothes, storing them quickly. I slipped the collar with its spare key attached over my head and, changing, we trotted out into the moonlit forest to lose ourselves amid the trees.

Unhindered by property bounds or other human impediments, we ran through the trees, dodging around the blue-black shadows where the moonlight never penetrated. Though we wanted to, neither of us gave tongue to the song we both felt. We were too close to civilization.

Being with John, running through the forest, snow crunching under my feet, was bliss. Here, there was no Rich to look out for, no other members of their group hiding in the shadows. There were no frightened parents calling the district, as they still did, though with less frequency. No protestors, no television stories, no Tik Tok Tales of Terror, as Kathy called them. Just us and the moon. It was enough.

With no warning, John slowed; his ears went down, and his hackles rose. Sniffing the air, I caught the scent that had arrested him. It was a cat: a big one. While I would be perfectly happy to exchange playful swats with Garrett at some point, this puma smelled much more wild. No veneer of civilization hung in its scent. If it was one of us, it was not connected to any humans. I nosed John, indicating that we should detour swiftly away. He nodded, and we struck off at a tangential angle, out of the area. The cat's scent fell behind us, and we were soon on our run again.

After a couple of hours, we headed back to the car, and once there, changed and dressed with expedience. Tossing the collar into the back seat, I started the engine, and as the headlights flooded on, they caught two bright circles staring at us out of the darkness. The eyes blinked twice before disappearing, and I shuddered as they faded away.

"It followed us," said John.

"So it would appear," I said dryly. "Maybe running at the farm would be safer after all."

"That would be my guess as well," said John. "I'm not sure that was just a cat, are you?"

"No," I said, "I'm not. Not all of the shapeshifters are happy about us coming out. I tend to forget that sometimes."

I put the car into gear, turning the heat up to full blast. Soon, the chill of both the night and our pursuer faded, but in my mind's eyes, I could see the eyes staring, watching us with uneasy intelligence, and it was a vision that stayed with me until I finally fell asleep.

Contrary to my fears, lunch was not a disaster and went off fairly smoothly with no fireworks and everyone rather more relaxed. My parents spent a while answering every question John's parents could think of, and in the end, his folks even offered to pay for the honeymoon.

Hazel and George had begged off going to see the house due to other commitments, but my parents did, and they seemed excited by Andrew's choice for us. They didn't stay long – both wanted to spend a little more time with Andrew before leaving the next day – but when my dad hugged me and shook John's hand, I found I had a hard time saying goodbye.

My mother also hugged me, and then embraced John, saying, "See you in March."

They departed, and as we stood on the driveway watching them drive off, I caught sight of Ellen waving from her porch. I looked at John with a grin.

"Don't we need a flower girl?"

28

DEEPER CONCERNS

The trip to Montana for the wedding over March break was mostly uneventful, though there had been some difficult moments between the horse and wolf clans when we first arrived. With Sam there to smooth things over, it went better than I'd expected.On the ride home, my parents and I made plans for an early wedding shower in April , and we'd parted ways in Laramie much more relaxed then when we'd first flown out.

When we got home, however, the stress returned in full force. The media had been having a field day. There were protests outside Congress while the debate was going on with the lawmakers. Sam called and said that there was more progress, but it was slow. There was too much fear from constituents whose ministers and priests were pushing the notion of our evil intent to shift the attitudes of some hardcore conservatives.

At least the Catholics seemed to be somewhat sane about it. The Pope had decreed that, as we were animals and counted among God's creatures, we should be viewed as a natural part of the world. Of course the interpretation of that by some priests was that as man had been given dominion over the animals, we should possibly fall into a category somewhere above full animals, but not as high as human beings. The arguments seemed endless.

The Evangelicals made the most direct attack, holding forth that we were demons sent to tempt man to embrace the devil. I could only imagine what the shapeshifters in the South were having to deal with. There had been rumors of houses burning down, of people losing their jobs, of crosses being burned on lawns, and of at least one lynching. Then there were the confirmed news stories of shapeshifter children who had been taken from their homes by social workers when the human grandparents had discovered that their precious darlings were being "corrupted" by the evil monsters. I was so glad, so very, very glad that we lived in Boulder where we had the protection of the local government. Maybe once we became more stabilized, we could help other people going through rough times.

Several weeks had passed since the school board meeting. Life had resumed pretty much the same rhythm it had before Montana, and during this time, I had fallen back into my normal teaching routine. John's work had picked up after a new lab had opened, and he was promoted to run the old lab with a few sympathetic co-workers, which resulted in a pay raise as well as extra hours at work.

When parent-teacher conferences came around for the spring semester, I let John know I'd be home later than normal that evening. He let me know he'd also be late that night due to aligning a new lens on one of their machines and would I be alright by myself? I assured him I would be fine and promised to text the moment I got home.

Parent-teacher conferences were always stressful, and I had more sign-ups this year than normal for a second semester night. Some of the parents attending were those of our shapeshifter students, and they all expressed their gratitude for the work our committee had done in helping their kids and organizing the alliance club.

Others, human parents, came in a bit hesitant to speak with me but warmed up after my unflagging professionalism and solid feedback on their children's progress won them over. A few asked questions about how people were reacting to the news of teachers being shapeshifters, and I replied, with my most generous amount of tact, that overall, people had been very supportive once they realized that we'd always lived among them without incident.

I sent several parents away smiling, relieved to find me more concerned with their child's grades than any secret plot to take over Grandma's house. Still, this was much like eating an elephant. I could convince parents of my good will towards their students, but there were still the forces that spoke out against us. Those were the tougher ones to reassure.

At 8:00 that evening, with the last of the parents gone, my co-workers and I bid each other a good night and headed home. Tomorrow was a Friday, and it was a casual jeans day as a reward for suffering through the endless rounds of anxious parents. As I drove, I mulled over a few emails I would need to write, which students I would have to talk to, and some ideas I wanted to run by Nevermore about improving the relations between the shapeshifter and human parents.

When the car swerved at me, it startled me out of my thoughts, and I reacted by angrily laying on my horn. When it came at me a second time, I realized I was in trouble. The highway was not crowded, and most of the commuters had already made their way home. The car, lit by the intermittent street lamps, was unfamiliar. As he forced my car over towards the next offramp, I realized what he was doing and gunned my car forward, surprising him. I took that moment to dial D.J., routing the call through the Bluetooth in my car.

"Hey, Sasha, what's up?"

"D. J., I'm being chased," I yelled, glancing in my rearview as the driver began to close the distance between us. "I'm on Route 119 near home, and someone is trying to run me off the road."

"Okay, try not to panic. There's a station two exits up. I'll alert them that you're coming. I'm leaving now. Get there, park in front, and stay put, got that? I'll be there in twenty minutes; less if I can."

"Gotcha," I said.

D. J. hung up, and I accelerated even more, my goal now clear. The car pursuing me was keeping pace and trying to come abreast with me. I called John.

"John," I said when he picked up, "I'm being chased. I'm going to meet D. J. at the police station on 116. Can you come?"

"On my way," he said. "I'm leaving now! Bill, I've got to go! Take over. Sasha's in trouble."

I heard calls of "Go!" from somewhere in the room, then John was on the phone with me.

"Any idea who it is?" he said.

"One of the others?" I said, as the car pulled alongside me and swerved at me again, forcing me into the breakdown lane. "Shit! I'm going to have to get off at the next exit. He's not letting me get back on the highway. John! Call D. J. and let him know. I'll have to get off onto 63rd."

"I'll be right back!"

John hung up, and for a few moments, I was alone. The driver wasn't trying to push me over onto the shoulder, but as I saw the exit coming up, he started forcing me right towards it. I had no choice; I took the turn, braking hard to avoid crashing into the Jersey barriers on either side of the offramp. The other car swung in behind me with a squeal of tires and stayed right on my bumper as I continued to slow, trying to stall for a little more time to think. The ramp only went to the right, away from the police station. This was no good. Shit.

The phone rang, and I took the split second to answer.

"Hello?"

"Are you okay?" It was John.

"Yes. I'm off the highway, heading onto 63rd."

"Keep going towards Celestial Seasonings. D. J. said they'll meet you there."

The giant Celestial Seasonings plant was one of the biggest landmarks on my way home. I knew that it would be brightly lit and running even at this hour, but I couldn't see why the building would offer any extra protection until the police arrived. Nevertheless, I was racing toward it when the sedan behind me suddenly slammed into mine. I let out a yelp, and then hit the gas as the vehicle began to advance. John was yelling over the phone, and it was all I could do to hold the wheel as the vehicle slammed the rear end again, this time shoving my car off the road and onto the grass.

Grimly, I held onto the wheel and pressed the accelerator, gaining traction when the wheels found pavement. Behind me, my pursuer was approaching again when I finally decided I had had enough and spun the wheel sharply to the left, turning onto a side street that I prayed would lead to Rt. 116. My car cornered with a shriek of tires, but I was able to gain some distance as the other vehicle slowed.

My intuition was good, and I saw the familiar lighted signs of Rt. 116 ahead. Praying there wouldn't be any oncoming traffic, I swerved right onto the road, barely slowing down, and gunned it onto the straightaway. The other car took the corner behind me and began to put on speed once more. Ahead, I could see the glow of the State Police barrack sign. I reached it and swerved into the parking lot, slamming on the brakes so as not to hit the large brick building that loomed in front of me.

The car following me passed by and raced off down the road. I caught my breath with a sob, and then there were three officers running out of the building toward me.

John was still yelling my name over the phone, and I inhaled sharply before answering.

"They're gone. I'm at the state police barracks. I've got to go."

"I'll be right there," said John and hung up.

The officers helped me from the car, and one of them walked me inside while the others looked over the damage. I shook the entire way.

"We sent several officers over to Celestial Seasonings to catch him," said the man who was assisting me to a seat in the waiting room. "We'll let them know you're here."

Another officer came out and handed me a cup of water, which I drank gratefully.

"Did anyone see the plate?" I asked.

"No, he drove off too quickly," said the first officer. "We'll put out an APB with a description of the car. We'll get him, don't you worry."

"I hope so," I said.

John burst into the lobby and ran over to me, alarming the officers enough that I saw hands drop to their guns for a moment.

"Are you all right?" he asked, sitting next to me.

"I'm fine," I said. "A little shaken up, that's all."

"D. J. just pulled in too," said John. "Nobody got a good description of the car, but they're checking for paint flakes on your trunk. Do you remember what kind of car it was?"

"It was a dark colored sedan...four door, I think," I said.

"We'll get the word out," said the trooper. "Officer Barber said you live near here. We'll put a watch on your house tonight, too, just to be safe. Whoever it was, they may still be nearby."

"Could it have been Rich?" asked John, then turned to the officers. "That's her ex. He was one of the ones who abducted me last month."

"We're checking on him now," said the second officer. "He and his friends are not supposed to be going anywhere near any of you. Their trial is coming up as well, so you would think they would stay clear of you all. If they were smart, that is. They don't seem too bright."

D. J. entered through the doors, spied us, and walked over, his countenance grave.

"The car that hit you matched the color of Todd's Chevy," he said. "Was it a sedan?"

"Yes," I said, rising and turning to the state policeman who had mentioned that they were checking the whereabouts of Rich and his friends.

"I'll see if there are any updates," he said and went inside the offices of the barracks.

"If they're all home, that doesn't rule out their involvement," said D. J.

The other officer returned from the inside of the precinct just then.

"All of them are home," he said. "We asked one of our other officers to swing by their houses anyway. We'll know more by morning, so why don't you all go now and get some rest. Leave your car here. We want to take a closer examination of it."

"I'll follow you back to your house," D. J. said. "Go get what you need from your car, Sasha. I'll arrange to get it towed to a shop after forensics is through."

I thanked the other officers and went out to gather my belongings. I didn't keep a lot of personal effects in my car, so there wasn't much to gather – school bags, a few notebooks, my purse. John helped me get them into his car, and after filling out a rather lengthy incident report, left the station with D. J. following in his unmarked vehicle.

The ride home was blessedly short, and neither John nor I felt like talking. How long would it be before we were safe from the likes of Rich and his friends, I wondered. Why couldn't they just leave us alone?

We pulled into the garage, and D. J. stopped in the driveway behind John's car.

"Let me check the house," he said. "I just want to make sure."

We nodded and let him go in ahead of us, switching on lights as he went. All was quiet except for the low hum of electronics. D. J. searched the rooms from top to bottom, then left after warning us to keep everything locked up tight. We saw him off, shut the garage, and secured the house for the night. Even with everything locked and double-checked, neither of us could relax until I got two glasses of some very potent wine. It was not long after that sleep eventually found us.

29
THE HUNTED

The police confirmed it was Todd's car that had run me off the road, and while Todd had not been behind the wheel, one of the other men who had harassed me and kidnapped John was. The officers had waited in an unmarked car at Todd's house for the driver to pull up, and when Todd came out to get the keys, they arrested both of them. Rich and Gary had apparently not been involved, but D. J. told us that they were keeping an even closer eye on them following the incident. The rest of the group vanished. Life settled down at last.

The remainder of March flew by. Parents stopped protesting at the school board meetings, though there were still some glares directed at myself and Kathy when we stood up to present. We were cautious, and there was a frequent police presence nearby to deter anyone from harassing us. While we appreciated it, their constant presence began to get old. Trips to the Forebear's farm had become almost a necessity, and we managed to get out to run about once a week without being noticed.

Mother, the consummate planner, had not been idle during this time in regards to the wedding, and she called after school on the last day of March to see how our April weekend plans were progressing. When I told her that, no, Nevermore hadn't spoken to me about a bridal shower, she clucked her tongue in displeasure.

"What on earth is she waiting for?" she asked. "The end of June will be here before you know it!"

"Mother, it is essay season! You know she teaches college comp, and those essays tend to take forever."

"Have her call me," my mother said. "We can hold it here. A long weekend away is just what you all need. Invite the young men along too. They could also use a break from all of the recent chaos."

"That's a great idea!" I said, excited at inviting our friends to the house for a weekend of relaxation and, of course, Marseille's cooking. "I'll text John now. I'm sure he'll agree, but I'd rather double check."

John texted back with enthusiasm before we finished talking, and my mother and I finalized plans.

I got in touch with Nevermore next to share the news.

"I completely forgot," she said, sounding contrite, then perked up. "But I think it's a splendid idea! Paul, how do you feel about going up to Wyoming at the end of April? You do? Okay. He's got a conference that weekend, but I am certainly game! What fun! I'll notify the others and make sure they don't have plans."

The rest of the bridesmaids were equally excited when she told them the news. A weekend at my mysterious family home? All of them texted to assure me that even if they had prior commitments, they would move them for such a momentous occasion. A quick call to my mother confirmed that the ladies would be joining us. I would also leave John's parents in her capable hands. On impulse, I contacted Laura, and invited her and Sam to join us as well if they could. She was delighted, and said she would see if Sam could manage the time off.

By the time John got home, he had already called his groomsmen, and all the arrangements had been made. Now all we had to do is make it through the next three weeks without a major eruption on any front, and we'd be more than ready for a weekend away.

Boulder itself had seemed to embrace its new role as the ambassador city to shapeshifters. Although no one was as officially "out" as those of us already visible around the city, the atmosphere towards us was subtly changing. We had several new students enroll in our school, and while this wasn't unusual, all but one was from a shapeshifter family. The parents had made sure to move into neighborhoods that would feed into Viceroy High, and the students found their way to the alliance club within their first week. It certainly appeared that there was a growing sense of pride in both the human and the shapeshifter communities.

Finally, the last week of April came around, and that Friday, I left as fast as I could for home. At twenty minutes to five, Garrett and Olivia pulled into the driveway in what appeared to be a sleeker silver version of a miniature school bus. The van was easily large enough to accommodate all of us with room left over, and Garrett grinned as he hopped out of the driver's seat.

"What do you think?" he asked, patting the hood of the beast now parked in my driveway. "A Chevy Express Passenger Van. Brand new. Rented it dirt cheap from a friend of mine at Budget."

"It probably could carry the entire football team," I said, eyeing it. "How is it in snow?"

Garrett's eyebrows rose and gave me a long look before asking, "Why?"

"Oh, no reason," I said, grinning. "Weather report says we're going to get about six inches of snow Saturday night into Sunday. We might have to handle some tough roads on the way home. John's parents decided not to make the trek because their car isn't up to it."

"I don't know," said Garrett, pretending to think. "I didn't spring for the extra insurance. I already paid a fortune for this thing..."

"Don't let him fool you," laughed Olivia, closing the passenger side door as she came around to join us. "He gave his friend a sob story about impoverished friends getting married. Frank didn't take him too seriously, but he still gave us a good rate. I think it will cost each of us about thirty dollars all told."

I gave Garrett the same kind of skeptical look I had given him ages ago when I was a student teacher and thought he was trying to scam me. He grinned impishly, then went to open up the van while Olivia and I went inside to grab my bags. John pulled into the driveway as I was carrying out my duffle bag and computer, and while he parked his car in the garage, I loaded everything into the storage area, carefully tucking the computer into the cargo net behind the seat. While I called D.J., John loaded his luggage and we piled in to pick up the others from Kathy's house.

"It's all arranged," he said. "The state troopers stationed up near your parents' house will keep an eye out for any out-of-state cars or rental vehicles that seem overly interested in the place. We didn't tell them it was a shapeshifter situation, just that there had been some threats made to a personality who would be there this weekend. We'll keep an eye on your houses here. If Rich and Gary decide to go anywhere, we'll know. Have a good time!"

I was very excited at the prospect of showing off my childhood home to my friends. By the time we got to Nevermore's, Tanya, Kim, Will, and James were waiting. They piled their gear into Garrett's beast and a few minutes later, we were finally heading north out of Boulder.

I sat behind Garrett so I could give him directions if the GPS lost signal and joined in the excited chatter with the rest of the crew. Kathy was telling embarrassing stories of our classes, and John and I were trying not to laugh as she called each of them out for something they had done as students. Then she got to the time John saved a turtle from being run over while he was on the way to school and snuck it into her Freshman English class. The turtle had peed on John while he was trying to keep it from falling off his desk, and while John went to the nurse's office to find a dry set of clothes, a janitor was called to both clean off the desk and relocate the turtle to the pond across the street.

"I never did understand why you didn't put it in the pond before you came in," said Kathy with a chuckle.

"It was really chilly that morning," said John. " I remember being worried it would be too cold for it to do well. Silly of me in retrospect, but I was really scared it would die."

There was a collective silence for a moment, and then James clapped John on the back, and said, "I probably would have done the same thing, man."

"Me too," said Will.

"I remember Kathy telling me about that when I was first hired," I said. "Totally get it."

John smiled, and the conversation moved on to other high school antics. Tanya hadn't gone to Viceroy, but she had a few stories of her own, and even some cool tales from the year she spent living with relatives on the Rez. She took over the storytelling from Kathy, telling myths from her tribe and a number of legends regarding shapeshifters she and her cousin Charles had unearthed at the Reservation Council office where the history of their tribe was stored.

We listened, enthralled, to tales with titles like "The Bear Husband" and "The Two-Toned Possum," which were the tribal equivalents of some of our own stories regarding Native American and shapeshifter encounters. It made me wish that we had invited Charles along for the weekend, and I told Tanya that he was welcome to come up tomorrow morning if he wanted. She texted him my parents' address, and he said he would see what he could do.

The heater hummed to life as Garrett turned up the blower against the falling day, and before long, we crossed the border into Wyoming and were less than an hour from the House. There was more snow on the ground the further we traveled, and the clouds were slowly building far to the west. Drawing ever closer to my home, I felt a sense of disquiet steal over me. Had it only been four months that John and I had been together? Time was becoming distorted; too much had happened too fast. Here we were with people who had become our closest friends in a very short amount of time, driving up to my parents for our wedding shower. Our rather staid lives had been flipped upside down in short order. How does one prepare for everything to no longer make sense?

A short time later, we reached the driveway to my family home, and turned up the long, narrow road that led under the canopy of trees. The pine boughs were thick as ever, casting the road further into shadow. No howl greeted us this time, but when we pulled up into the parking area, Andrew was outside waiting for us by his Mustang.

Garrett parked the van, and as everyone else was gawking at the size of the House, I opened the side door and went to embrace my uncle. Andrew was a little thinner, but otherwise appeared well. There had been other, less visible repercussions to the shooting, though. He was now doing the majority of his work from home, even after the repairs and renovations to the office.

"Welcome!" said Andrew, walking over to me and gingerly gave me a hug, still favoring his arm. He then shook John's hand and as he waited for us to gather our bags, night was beginning to fall in earnest.

"Marseille has prepared a light dinner for us," said Andrew as he led the way into the House. "We'll get everyone settled, then meet in the dining room. Your mother put your guests along the same corridor so they'll have an easier time finding each other."

I looked around at my friends and smiled as I remembered John's first reaction.

"I never imagined your house being this big," said Nevermore. "I knew it was large, but this is a downright manor."

"Remember, it was originally built to hold the whole family. Once we began to branch out into the cities, it was no longer where everyone lived all the time," I said. "It was used during the Civil War when it was not safe for many of the clans to be near the battles. Nowhere to hide."

Kathy nodded, "My people flew north at that time, so a lot of us stayed in Ottawa. Still have a large clan up there that we visit from time to time. Paul's family is from there too."

We crunched our way over the gravel and up to the big front door, which Andrew pushed open with a flourish. The party walked in, the expressions on their faces not unlike John's when he first came to the house only four months prior. Andrew grinned and led the way inside to where my mother waited.

"Welcome in!" she said. "Let me show you all to your rooms, and then please come down and join us."

Mother led the way up the staircase and took my friends to their rooms. John and I were in mine, and once we had tossed our bags on the bed, we made our way downstairs again. John grabbed my hand as we entered the dining room, and we took our seats at the large table. Marseille had made one of his mouth-watering soups and heaped a platter high with a variety of overstuffed sandwiches. I helped myself to a chicken salad roll and bowl of his savory beef and barley, then sat down to watch my friends and family filter in and join the feast.

"Your brothers and their families are coming up tomorrow," said my father, sipping coffee from one of the ubiquitous mugs he'd brought back from his speaking tours. This one was purple and the lettering read "Pacifica Institute" in bright white letters. I knew it was out in California somewhere but had never been there. I vaguely recalled that he'd done a lecture on the mythology of ecological forces there, but I didn't remember the details. Something about glaciers, I thought.

"Awesome!" I said. "It'll be nice to spend some time with them too. Anyone else?"

My mother shook her head. "Sam and Laura won't be coming. Too many political issues. My sister went north with her husband's pack. They aren't coming back."

I thought about Melissa for a moment and found that I didn't have a lot of sympathy for my aunt.

"I can't understand why they want to leave the human world so badly," said Kathy, shaking her head. "It's just going to make it harder on them in the future."

Tanya glanced over first at Kathy and then my mother before asking, "Why are they leaving?"

My mother sighed heavily.

"Not all of the shapeshifters are happy about humans knowing we exist," she said. "They believe it would have been better to remain hidden from the world. Some clans are moving into places where there is still wilderness left, choosing to risk being mistaken for animals rather than integrating. Humans aren't the only ones who are unhappy with Sam and the others for revealing our presence among you."

"And your sister is one of them?" Tanya asked.

"Yes," she replied. "She used to be a lot more sensible, but then she married into another clan, and they are not pleased with the way things have turned out. In any event, she made her choice years ago. I hope she finds happiness."

The mood grew a bit grim for a few moments before conversation resumed. John and James made a bet as to who was faster, and I found myself sucked into refereeing a race after dinner. I knew how fast John was, but James had been a track star back when he was a student, and I found myself curious as to which one was going to win. Garrett and Will started making wagers, and Olivia egged Garrett into joining the race.

"Mountain lions aren't distance runners," said Garrett. "I mean, I'll try to keep up for as long as I can, but you're going to go further than I can even if I am faster in the short sprint!"

"You're on!" said James, fist bumping Garrett.

Will winked at Garrett, and the two of them got back to the business of eating.

"Can I come watch?" asked Tanya shyly, and I remembered that our token human member of the bridal party hadn't had a lot of experience with any of us in animal form. The rest of us looked around at each other, unsure how to reply.

"Absolutely," smiled Kathy. "I'm certainly not going to fly through the snowy woods at night, so you and I can wait for the winner at the finish line."

"Same," said Will. "Bighorn sheep are great at running *at* each other, but in the woods at night, I'd get hung up on a tangle of branches and have to be saved with a chainsaw."

"Won't take long for me," said Garrett. "I am not up for a distance run."

"Out of shape," nodded Olivia, giving me a knowing nod. "Too much pasta."

"Hey!" exclaimed Garrett as Olivia and I tried to cover our laughter. "Not fair!"

"Then it's settled," said James, rising. He gave a small bow to my parents. "My compliments to the chef. That soup was delicious, but I am going to stretch before we run!"

When James returned several minutes later, we trooped downstairs to the little locker rooms. Tanya, Olivia, Will, and Nevermore had gone outside to wait, and Tanya almost literally stopped breathing as three wolves and a puma strode past her into the cool night air. Kathy gently prodded her in the ribs, and Tanya gave a nervous laugh as she walked with us to the edge of the woods.

When Kathy yelled "Go," I bounded out past the tree line, making my way to the border of the property so as to turn them back before they reached the state forest. There were signs, of course, marking the edge of our land, but those were not always easy to see in the dark. I was a much better clue since they could smell me.

The woods were deep in shadow, and there wasn't much of a moon. What little there was rode in silent curvature high overhead and cast no discernible light in the forest below. Not even the stars could penetrate the thick canopy of trees, and I soon found myself deep within the burgeoning woodlands already growing thick and verdant with new leaves.

Scents overtook my concentration, and I used them to tell me many things about the land around me. Rabbits were mating and preparing their warrens, fox pups were being reared in dens along the ridge and near the brook, and a little further away, a moose calf had just been born and its mother's milk come in. All the new signs of life in the spring presented their abundance to me as I ran, and I was soon lost in the midst of my senses.

It wasn't long before I heard the thundering of paws upon the earth and turned in the direction they were coming from. James and John were approaching, and as soon as they caught sight and scent of me, they pivoted back towards the House. Neither one seemed to be taking the lead, though if James held true to his track training, he might keep something in reserve for the final push, a trick John might not know how to do. Once they passed, I bounded back to the House, eager to see the finale of the race.

It was then that my nose caught something on the breeze. It smelled like the oil Marseille used to clean his pistols, and it had a very distinctive scent. There were always hunters in the Medicine-Bow forest at this time of the year for turkey hunting season, but it alarmed me that there were armed men so close to our land. I raced for home and bolted into the clearing to find everyone applauding James as the winner. Both he and John were panting into the cold air, and Garrett lay nearby on the ground, tongue lolling as he breathed in soft chuffs.

"It was close," said Kathy as I sat down next to her, panting. "John was about four steps behind James as they entered the clearing."

"That was amazing!" said Tanya. "I'm so glad I got to see you all run."

James sat just a little bit taller, preening under her praise. I glanced up at Kathy and saw a smile creeping across her face. It was clear to me that she had the same thoughts I did. Weddings had a way of sparking new relationships, and it looked like mine was no exception.

"Okay, it's getting colder out here, and I'm not part of the fuzzy contingency at the moment," said Will. "Shall we head in for the night?"

We trooped inside and those of us who needed to changed and dressed again before joining the rest. As the others headed for the living room, I locked the back door and decided to tell my mother about what I'd smelled in the woods. It might be residual from some hunter hiding in a blind, but something about it felt off.

When I got upstairs, I called my mother to her study.

"We've had to turn back a few hunters recently," she said, mulling over my news. "People don't respect the signs, so we like to hike loudly, effectively scaring all the game away. They get a bit cranky with us until we point out that they are on private property. There have been some very surly people the last few years, but most of them did not require an escort off the land."

"So I shouldn't worry about it?" I asked.

"Well, be cautious, but with the storm coming, I would think that the hunters won't be a problem after the snow comes in tomorrow."

We returned to the gathering, grabbed some bowls of Marseille's kettle corn, and settled down to listen to the chatter. I watched with some amusement as Tanya and James slowly moved closer to each other as the night progressed. He was being unusually attentive, which, for the former aloof track star who ignored almost every girl in high school, was highly irregular. If they weren't an item by the end of the weekend, I would be very surprised.

It wasn't much later when the hour and the events of the day began to assert themselves and before long, one by one, we bade each other good night and straggled off to bed.

By nine o'clock the next morning, the number of people in the house had grown exponentially. My brothers and their families had descended on the house in spite of the pending snowstorm. None of us have ever been afraid of the snow; we had ridden through enough April blizzards to know that this would be short-lived and the accumulation would melt quickly. Most of us had spent decades living there, and we knew that the weather wasn't nearly as strong as the House. In any event, Marseille could cook enough on the old gas stove to feed a small army, and no one would go hungry no matter how long the snow lasted.

The day was full of games and races, though we stayed in the vicinity of the House as a precaution. There were flurries off and on all morning, and when the snow began to fall in earnest around three 'o clock, we pulled everyone inside for some downtime. John and I headed for the pool, and some of the other former students joined us. I won't say that we had an epic pool noodle fight that caused a lot of water to slosh out over the sides, but I won't say that we didn't either.

It was the most fun John and I had had in ages, and it was a well-needed reprieve.

After one of Marseille's famous feasts, we gathered in the living room to open presents. The storm had picked up in intensity, and we could hear it howling around the eaves and testing the window casements. Curtains of snow lashed against the windowpanes and hissed like a cat as they scraped across the glass. We ignored it, though, and left it to rage its impotence at the solidity of the walls enclosing us.

John had just opened a joke gift from Bobby which included a small robot vacuum that was guaranteed to "pick up all pet fur," when a loud CRACK from outside caused everyone to jump. A second later, the lights went out. Several of us turned on the flashlight apps on our phones to light the room and make sure everyone was okay.

"Just a falling branch," said my father. "Hold on a sec. The generator should kick in."

A minute went by and nothing happened. From the doorway, Marseille motioned to my father. Together they left the room while the guys began to crack jokes and make silly shadow puppets on the walls to amuse the kids. Mother's expression was very focused, however, and I could tell she was straining to hear over the howling winds outside. For a long moment, no one moved as we stood between breaths, waiting to see what would come next. From the darkness beyond, Marseille and my dad returned, the lights from their phones extinguished.

"The line for the generator has been cut," said my father. My mother moved for the phone, but he shook his head. "We tried the extension in the kitchen. It's out. Someone has cut us off."

My mother nodded, "Marseille, is the kitchen still clear?"

"Seems to be, yes," he said, his accent more pronounced than usual. His normally jovial expression was gone, his lips tight.

"Alright," she said. "We'll take the kids and humans to the safe room. The rest of us will go out the long tunnel. It's been a long time since we've had to use it."

"Wait!" I said, as my siblings and I all looked around at each other in astonishment. "Safe room? Long tunnel?"

"I'll explain once we're there," said my father. "Let's move. Take the kids by the hand so they don't get separated on the way, and turn off the lights. Whoever is out there is counting on seeing us through the windows."

Those of us with good night sight led those without into the foyer and down to the kitchen. As Marseille closed the door behind him, we heard glass shatter somewhere up above.

My mother took us across to the pantry, opened it, and ushered us inside. She felt around the top of one of the tallest shelves, and we heard a slight click. The back wall swung out slightly to reveal a narrow passage. Turning on her phone light, she led the way down into the tunnel. Marseille closed the pantry door and waited until the rest of us were through before pulling the secret panel closed behind him.

We walked in silence down the long corridor as it led deeper into the earth. The lighting came from fluorescent bulbs overhead, which, given the situation, made the tunnel feel like something out of a horror movie.

"Why didn't you tell me about this?" I asked my mother.

"Yeah," said Stephen. "This is the kind of thing you tell your kids in case you have an accident or something like this happens."

"Your father and Marseille know, and whoever takes over the family would be told at the proper time," my mother said.

"I knew too," said Andrew, "but I always was too nosy for my own good. I spied on your mother one day when she kept disappearing to the kitchen. I knew Marseille was in Laramie finding some of his secret ingredients, so I couldn't imagine what she was doing."

"I check the tunnels once a month," said my mother. "Andrew was actually a big help in getting the safe room up-to-date a few years back. It has its own water supply now instead of just bottles of water and a small generator to run the pumps and the fans. There are lots of battery-powered lanterns and food supplies, cots, bedding. You will be secure there."

"And the rest of us?" asked David.

"Your father and I are going out the tunnel to protect our home," said my mother. "Anyone who wants to come with us is welcome to do so."

We reached a steel door in the wall, and my mother produced a small remote control with two buttons on it. She pushed one, and the portal swung open. Several small emergency lights came on around the room, and when she hit a recessed switch on the wall, a number of larger lights flickered overhead.

"Okay," I said, turning to my father. "So tell."

"Remember what I said about hiding up here during the Civil War?" he asked. "There wasn't much in the way of the House at that point, just a small log cabin and a barn. Fort Laramie is quite a ways away, as you know, and we weren't on any of the trade routes, so we were safe. We also had good relations with the local tribes and helped each other as colonists moved west. It wasn't a good time for any of us.

"Even still, with all of the new settlers and army battalions around, the family decided that it would be helpful to have an escape route out of the House in case of anyone trying to attack us. There's a cave system under the foundation that was originally used, but it was deemed too dangerous after several small earthquakes caused part of it to collapse in the early 1900s. Your great-grandfather had this tunnel built, and my father added a safe room during the 1960s in response to the nuclear threat from Russia.

"This is where you folks who aren't up for the fight can stay and be safe. Tanya, Kathy, Mark and the children must stay here. Andrew, Marseille, I want the two of you to remain and guard them. There's a satellite phone on the counter hooked up to an antenna on the roof. Use it to alert the authorities and let them know we're in trouble."

"I'm going," said John. Garrett, James, and my three brothers who could shape-shift indicated their agreement as well. Bobby's wife

Angie moved to stand by his side, as did Stephen's girlfriend Theresa. Olivia seemed torn.

"I'm not going to be useful out there," she said to Garrett. "I don't want to let you go without me, but I am just not able to hide or move as well as you all are."

"Stay here. Help guard the children," said Garrett, coming over to kiss her on the forehead. She reached up to hug him, and they embraced for a long moment, kissing again before parting.

My other two brothers made their farewells to their families, and we swiftly slipped out and continued down the passage. I heard the latch snick closed behind us, and then we were moving down the corridor at a jog. We went along silently for about ten minutes before the way turned, and we found ourselves at another door, this one fastened with a deadbolt. My mother unlocked it and led the way into what must have been part of the original cavern. An opening at the far end was white with driven snow, and it was bitter cold. I looked to see my mother close the door most of the way and was hard-pressed to see the outline in the wall.

"It's wonderful what a bit of fake rock can do," said my father with a grim smile.

With unspoken accord, we stripped, putting our clothes in a waterproof bag which my mother placed inside the passageway before closing the door.

The freezing temperature didn't encourage any of us to stay human for long, and soon, our small pack of wolves and one lone puma stepped out into the night. Snow lashed my eyes as soon as I left the shelter of the cave. The storm was much fiercer than the one John and I had run in when we found Sara. Winds howled through the treetops, making the boughs scrape together in an eerie symphony. Snowflakes blew like a myriad of tiny needles into my muzzle and sensitive nose. I squinted through the gusts at my mother who was waiting for everyone to orient themselves. When she was sure all of us were focused on her, she and my father led us back towards the House.

The wind rendered our noses mostly useless, and the snow stung our eyes as we made our way through the woods with careful precision. Would the invaders be expecting an attack from outside? Likely not. They had timed their assault for when we were all in the living room, and while there was no direct access into that room from outside, they probably could have seen just enough through the window to know when there was a large gathering there.

The dark bulk of the House loomed out of the curtain of white like some monster lying in wait for its prey. No light shone from inside, and there was little way of knowing if anyone was peeking out through the windows at the woods. My mother gave a low growl and eased up to the door with the foot press, but it wouldn't budge; the lock had engaged automatically when the power went out. We'd need to find another way in.

She took the lead as we made a circuitous route around the perimeter of the House, sticking close to the woods and using the swirling powder as cover. As we approached the wing with the conservatory, I saw that one of the big windows had been smashed. Large swaths of white broke up the darkness within, and I could only imagine the palm trees and other tropical plants withering under the assault of the cold. Angie and David, the two lightest-colored wolves, slunk closer to the broken window but soon straightened, turning back to the rest of us, tails raised. The way was safe for now; we crept into the building, careful not to step on the broken glass that littered the floor.

I looked around, feeling like I was in some sort of dystopia where people return home only to find it abandoned or maybe even the haunted feel of the Overlook Hotel in the film version of *Doctor Sleep*. The giant planters and their contents created bizarre shapes that loomed in the darkness, and several of the more delicate specimens had already begun to freeze, twisting and curling into themselves. I shook myself to get rid of the thoughts, and then John cocked his head towards the double doors. A slight movement betrayed the presence of at least one of the intruders, and I chuffed softly to get Mother's attention, using my nose to indicate the entryway to the House. Garrett moved up next to John, his long tail lashing side to side in agitation. The way in was closed; how could we take the man down?

As the figure started to turn, we scattered to the sides, my mother and father taking the sentry stations on either side of the entrance. The rest of us crouched down behind the planters and watched as the stranger strode into the conservatory and lit up a smoke. A radio at his belt crackled and spat out some sort of instruction for checking the third floor. Cupping his hand around the match to light the cigarette, he inhaled deeply and scanned the room. He didn't see my dad become human behind him and bring a pot down on his head. The heavy ceramic smashed into the back of his skull, and he fell to the floor, dropping everything as he collapsed.

My brother David grabbed the gun by the strap and dragged it behind a group of pots while my father shifted back. We crouched, listening intently and hoping that no one had heard the commotion. No one came, and my mother nosed open the door, leading all of us down the cold, still hallway towards the foyer. There was a crackle of static ahead, and we instantly crouched low as one of the men paced past the entrance to the corridor. He didn't glance around, and we were able to continue our progress after a few tense moments.

Ahead the radio crackled to life again. We all moved to the sides of the corridor and crouched down, listening.

"No, I haven't seen anything. They must have gotten outside somehow," came the voice of the intruder. His footsteps were drawing nearer.

"Impossible," said the voice on the other end. "We had all of the entrances blocked. They're here somewhere. Keep searching."

The speaker sounded familiar, but I couldn't quite place him. The static of the radio was messing with my perception of the voice, and I shook my head, irritated that I couldn't recognize it.

The man paused and peered into the gloom. We were shadows in shadows, but he was wearing some sort of thermal vision goggles. The only thing that saved us was that we were still cold and wet from the snow, and it was obviously not high grade equipment. He stared in our direction, took the goggles off, tapped them, and then shook his head. Slipping the headgear back on, he returned to his pacing, heading away from us. I breathed a silent sigh of relief, and Garrett stalked towards the foyer, John at his heels. The rest of us followed.

Garrett made it to the corner, peered around the doorframe, then leapt forward, pouncing on the man and knocking the radio from his grip. Garrett's fangs at his throat rendered him speechless, though we could hear low whimpering sounds as he fought his terror. John retrieved the radio, and we wrestled the intruder into the darkness of the pool room. Once inside, Garrett released him, and my father changed, staring down at our captive.

"How many," growled my father, his anger palpable. "How many of you have invaded our home?"

"I'm not telling you, animal," said the man, spitting on the ground by my father's feet.

Garrett let out an angry hiss that rumbled to a low yowl at the end, and the sharp smell of urine filled the air.

"Ten," said the captive, a look of panic on his face. "There are ten but more are on the way."

"How did you find us?" asked my father, grabbing him by the front of his jacket. "We aren't listed in the local directory."

"One of the guys is an officer in Boulder," said the man, flinching as David bared his teeth and growled. "And one of the others knew how to get here."

I exchanged a glance with John, and it suddenly dawned on me where I knew the voice from. His brow furrowed in concern, and I knew we'd had the same thought. It could only be Cloverly. But who else was with him? Rich and company hadn't come near us since the car incident. Could one of them have slipped out of Boulder without anyone noticing? There was no way to call and be sure.

I shifted back, ignoring the cold and my state of undress.

"Who sent you?" I said.

"No one sent us," he said, looking away. "You creatures are dangerous and need to be killed or controlled. We tried to expose you all, but a few of you got to the government first. You're probably all running it at this point anyway."

"Well, if you can believe there's a child pornography ring being run in a basement of a pizza shop, then I guess you can believe anything." said my father, disgusted. "Hold him here while I find a gag and something to tie him up with."

My father rose and came back with the long cord from the pool skimmer. He dragged the man over to one of the cement pillars at the far end of the room and tied him while Garrett and David made sure he didn't try to run. Lastly, he took one of the towels and shoved one end of it into the captive's mouth.

"You should be glad we're *not* some lawless animals. Not like you," he said. "We'll let the police take care of you later."

He made his way back over to the rest of us and crouched down.

"David, you, Bobby, and Stephen go back and bring the other man here. If we're going to prove that we are better than they are, we can't let him freeze. Tie him up with something: twine, zip ties, anything. We'll wait here."

My brothers slipped out of the room and we waited for them to get the man we'd left unconscious in the conservatory. The air by the pool was still comfortably warm from the water, and I was happy to be out of the numbing chill of the wind. The boys returned in human form carrying the still-unconscious man now trussed like a chicken. We wedged him among the chairs so he wouldn't roll into the pool and drown, then everyone except my father resumed our wolf forms.

"I wish I kept spare clothing in here," he said. "You go on ahead. Marseille or Andrew will have already called for help, but I'm going to try to get to them and let the authorities know the full lay of the land. You split up and find the rest of the intruders. Take them out one at a time if you can."

He shifted back, and we cautiously left the pool room, slinking towards the foyer. The House was still under the noise of the storm, but very faintly, I could hear the occasional burst of static upstairs from one of the walkie talkies carried by the intruders. They had not ordered radio silence, which was going to make our job of finding them before they found us that much easier.

We slipped downstairs into the kitchen, taking care not to let our claws click on the flooring. It was deserted, though there were some pots and pans strewn about. Drawers and cabinets were left open, and the pantry door was ajar. My father changed back and walked inside to open the passageway again. With a nod to the rest of us, he slipped in, shutting the secret panel behind him, and we turned, going back upstairs to continue our hunt.

In the foyer, John and I glided up towards the guest rooms, listening for any hint of men ahead of us. The rest of our group had also paired off, with Bobby and Angie heading towards the ballroom, Stephen and David making their way downstairs, and James and Garrett going up the opposite staircase towards the other wing. Only my mother remained in the foyer, becoming one with the shadows beneath the stairs.

We passed my bedroom, noting the door was wide open. Inside, closets were ajar and my bureaus had been toppled, the drawers strewn about. The other rooms in the hall were the same, but there was no evidence of anyone within. There were lingering traces of scents, though, and I recognized Cloverly's right away. One of the others, however, stopped me in my tracks, and I whined almost imperceptibly. John eyed me, puzzled. He didn't recognize the scent because his exposure to it was limited to the one bad night at the dojo, and no one could blame him for not remembering. I knew it, however. Somewhere, Rich was in the House.

I ducked back into the last room we'd checked and shifted back. John stayed in wolf form, his head cocked.

"It's Rich," I said, my voice as low as I could make it. "I don't know how he did it, but he's here."

John shifted back, his anger plain. "What about the others?"

"I don't smell them," I said. "The only other scent I recognize is Cloverly."

Looking at me in the dim light, John nodded.

"If it comes down to fighting Rich, I'll do it," he said. "I don't want that on your conscience."

"We'll figure it out when the time comes," I said and shifted back.

John did the same, and we padded out into the corridor. The howling winds were louder now, as the storm found new vigor, but the faint footfalls upstairs told us what we needed to know. Somewhere on the floor above were four to six intruders bent on finding and likely killing us if the men downstairs were any indication.

We reached the servant's stair to the third floor and listened intently to the area above. Only faint sounds gave away that anyone was there, and even those were slow and measured. A few of the men likely had some hunting skills, I thought. Unlike Rich. In the entire time I had known him, charts and graphs were the only thing he had pursued. Cloverly had weapons training, and I had to assume the rest had at least some practice as well.

A sudden spate of gunfire on the floor above us spurred us into action, and we leapt up the stairs. There were a lot of footsteps heading away from us, and when we reached the third floor, we could see the bright flashes from guns across in the other wing. Fearing for James and Garrett, we bolted down the hallway, ducking into the little sewing room we'd watched anime in what felt like so long ago.

The shots continued, and then we heard a man screaming along with the yowl of a large cat, closely followed by the bellow of an enraged bear. Olivia had come up out of the safe room, which meant that my dad had gotten through. She might not have good eyesight, but her nose was second to none, and she had joined in the fight with no hesitation.

We peeked out of the room; the action was all the way down the end of the other wing. We could see five men standing, brandishing their empty firearms at the bear, while three wolves darted in and around them, snapping at their legs. Another man lay on the ground, holding his leg as he rolled back and forth in agony.

John and I lost no time in racing up behind the men, all of whom were trying to get new magazines into their weapons, but unable to because of the wolves lunging at them, snapping viciously at their hands. I saw Garrett crouching and bleeding from several wounds to his flank. He was still snarling and slashing at the men whenever they came close enough for him to reach.

As we got closer, I picked out Cloverly and bowled into him, knocking him to the ground. He drew a knife as he fell and stabbed at me, grazing my shoulder. It was a clumsy strike, however, and it only scored a thin cut through my fur. I snarled at him, stalking forward, and he pushed himself back into the wall, where he sat, waving the knife at me ineffectually. I contented myself with baring my fangs at him, holding him at bay.

Behind me, the fight continued. One of the men had finally gotten a cartridge into his rifle and was taking aim at Olivia. Before he could fire, my father leapt at him, teeth grinding into the bones of his wrist. He dropped the gun, screaming, and my father grabbed the weapon in his jaws, dragging it backwards. There was a deafening bang from a firearm, and everyone froze where they were.

D. J. stood behind Olivia, his gun smoking in his hand. With him swarmed several members of a S.W.A.T. team, the officers pointed their rifles directly at the men.

"Weapons down!" shouted one of the S.W.A.T. members. "Shapeshifters, stand down! We'll take it from here!"

One of the men hesitated, then put his gun down, eyes never leaving James whose teeth were bared in the rictus of a snarl as he slowly backed away. The black armored officers wasted no time in collecting the weapons and cuffing the attackers. As they read them their rights, I looked over to see Charles peeking out from behind D. J.'s shoulder. Tanya's cousin shrugged disarmingly.

"Grandmama had a vision," he called. "It was strong enough that she forced my cousin Enoch to drive twenty miles to the nearest phone. Tanya had texted me the address yesterday, but I hadn't heard from her. I checked around at Boulder police stations until I found your man, here, D. J., and he called the state police. When he checked on his cousin, who was supposed to have been watching Rich, he couldn't reach him, and no one knew where he was. We got up here as fast as we could. Got to Laramie just before the blizzard hit. Let me tell you, that driveway of yours is one hell of a ride in a Bearcat. That beast can tackle just about anything!"

D. J. stepped around us, checking to see who was injured. Olivia had gone over to Garrett, her sudden movement causing a slight panic among the officers. D. J. stepped in to quell their concern, and they resumed processing the invaders. When my mother was escorted upstairs by a S.W.A.T. team member a few minutes later carrying a bag of clothing, Olivia and Garrett limped into a nearby bedroom to get changed. They emerged clothed except for shoes, Garrett leaning on Olivia's shoulder. He had to be set gently on the floor until one of the officers who doubled as a medic could tend to him.

James and my father also went in to change, leaving John and me the only ones in wolf form for the moment. I sniffed the air. Something was wrong. Rich was not with the group. So where was he? As soon as James and my father came out of the room, I went inside, changed, and dressed. John had elected to stay in wolf form and continued to keep Cloverly in his place, growling deep in his chest. When I came out, I spotted D. J. giving Cloverly hell a safe distance from the angry wolf. When he saw me, John backed off and let D. J. close enough to his cousin to really let loose.

"...going to give your mother an aneurysm, you know that?" he yelled as Cloverly cringed on the floor. "Of all the hare-brained things to get involved with..."

"D. J.," I said. "Rich was here. I smelled him. Did anyone find him downstairs?"

D. J. looked up in surprise, then turned back to Cloverly.

"Are you out of your mind?" he asked. "You brought her ex here as well? What has gotten into your head?"

"They're animals, Deej!" Cloverly said, trying to get to his feet and staring defiantly at his cousin. "Rich had as much a right as anyone to hunt them, especially since they humiliated him!"

"Boy, did you buy their line. You know you'll be fired for this, and serve jail time for breaking and entering, not to mention assault and battery and attempted murder. Did any of that occur to you?" D. J. said, hauling Cloverly to his feet and held him while a member of the S.W.A.T. team cuffed him. "You know your rights better than any of these other yahoos, but I'm going to tell them to Mirandize you anyway so some slimy lawyer can't get you off on a technicality!"

"Fine," said Cloverly, his face showing his utter contempt. "Animals don't have the same rights as humans, Deej. Any judge will see things our way, wait and see!"

D. J. handed his cousin off to one of the other policemen, and then turned to us. He gazed at us, a little wary, but when John wagged his tail and gave a goofy dog grin, D. J.'s shoulders relaxed.

"They'll find Rich," he said. "Don't worry."

"He might have been by the back door," I said. "It's downstairs past the kitchen. My brothers were headed there. Have they come back, Dad?"

"Not to my knowledge," said my father. "Olivia and I came straight up here."

"The troopers are searching the entire house right now from top to bottom," said D. J. "We should stay up here till they are through."

I stooped to see how Garrett was feeling as his wounds were bandaged.

"How's he doing?" I asked

"The injury's mostly superficial," said the medic. "The shotgun was loaded with birdshot of all things." He turned to Garrett. "You're going to have to have surgery to get as many of the pellets removed as possible. The docs won't likely be able to get them all, and going through a metal detector will be a bitch from here on out. There's an ambulance on the way, and as soon as the area has been cleared, we'll send you out."

"What about me?" yelled the man who was holding his lacerated leg. "Don't I get an ambulance? I was mauled by a vicious beast!"

The medic scowled at him.

"Sir, you're lucky you're not dead. You'll have to wait your turn. If this man had wanted to kill you, there would be no need for an ambulance, now would there?"

The man subsided, and after the medic was done dressing Garrett's leg, he turned his other patient. He was not nearly as gentle with him. Across the room, another officer was tending to the man my father had bitten as he moaned and cradled what remained of his hand.

About ten minutes passed, and the officers got a call that the House had been cleared. We followed D. J. downstairs and found my mother speaking to one of the troopers. Bobby and Angie were with her, but neither Stephen nor David were to be seen.

"No one was below," said the trooper. "We looked outside and saw wolf tracks leading off into the woods. Some of the men are gearing up to go after them now."

My mother glanced at me, and I felt her silent command to help my brothers. Angie and Bobby also caught her message. We trotted towards the stairs leading down while my mother continued talking with the officer.

By the back door, we found six troopers donning lighter colored camo they'd brought in from their vehicle.

"We'd like to help," I said, noting their alarm as John came towards them. "We know the woods better than anyone, and we don't need night vision goggles to help us see. Just don't shoot us."

Several of them hesitated, then one man nodded, and the group continued their own preparations. After changing in the little room, Angie and I met Bobby and John in the foyer. The officers watched us warily as we shouldered the lower door open; with the electricity still out, the magnetic lock wasn't working and required the force of two of us to move it. One by one, we stepped back out into the storm.

The tracks were still visible, though they were rapidly being erased by the blowing snow. The four of us trotted into the wood line, fanning out a bit to see if there was any variation where the trail went. There was nothing. One line of tracks, boot prints overlaid by at least one set of wolf tracks, led off into the forest.

It was still snowing heavily, and the wind growing in intensity, rather than lessening. I couldn't smell wolf or human anywhere nearby, though with the driving air, I wasn't surprised. John head-butted me and veered off the trail. When Bobby indicated that he and Angie would stay the course, I followed John off into the woods, wondering what he'd picked up that I'd missed.

A few minutes later, I heard a whining coming from the brush, and we almost fell over David and Theresa where they lay curled around Stephen, sheltering him from the worst of the cold. They were still in wolf form, and I knew that something was wrong when I nudged Stephen with my nose, and he didn't move. In the dark, it was hard to see the pool of blood under Stephen's body and staining his silver pelt, but the smell was unmistakable. My lip curled when I found the cause. He had been shot in the chest with something a lot heavier than birdshot. We'd have to move fast.

David shifted back, shivering in the cold.

"There were two of them. One was your buddy Rich - I remember his smell - but I'm not sure who was with him. Whoever it is, he's one hell of a shot. We're going to need help for Stephen and quickly."

He shifted back, and I howled for Bobby and Angie to find us, adding my warmth to David and Theresa's; John stood watch until the others arrived. While Angie ran for help, Bobby took my place, and I looked over at John when he whined. He nodded at the woods, and we set off through the brush again. Staying in the shadows, we ran parallel to the tracks, and John gave a low growl as he peered ahead, scenting the air. I walked over to him and sniffed the wind, closing my eyes to better focus on only what my nose could tell me. It was a mixed scent; Rich's odor was present, though tinged with vivid fear, and there was another that I couldn't place. It was someone who used guns frequently enough, though, that the scent of metal and oil was part of his odor. Unlike Rich, however, he had no tinge of fear to him. I nodded to John, and we faded into the depths of the forest once more.

Every sense I had was on high alert, more so now that I knew for certain our quarry was ahead of us. We were downwind from them, which certainly gave us the advantage, but they had the choice of position and could be on the ground or up in a tree for all we knew. Going around to try to approach them from behind might work, but we would have to find them first. While we crept along, I worried about Stephen and prayed he would be alright. The amount of blood he had lost coupled with the cold could kill him if the others weren't fast enough. I whined deep in my throat and pressed on.

Pushing through the brush tangles as quietly as possible, I paused, listening to every tree moan and every branch that broke in the relentless wind. The scent we had been following grew stronger; if only we could see them!

John stopped ahead of me, dropping low to the ground. I followed suit, and spotted the two bundled figures huddling near a giant pine tree. A large branch had fallen, and its base was propped against the trunk, the broad spray of needles giving the men a modicum of shelter from the snow. Both men had rifles, but one of them seemed ill-at-ease holding his; I would bet that it was Rich. The other was handling the weapon with practiced ease, and he was peering into the storm through thermal glasses more technical than those worn by the men inside. We were still a significant distance from him, and although I knew their glasses range would be impacted, I didn't want to give him an easy shot at us either.

I gave John a shoulder nudge, and we backed away, working a wide circumference around the tree. Both of them were facing the direction of the House, glancing around at the woods nearest them. The pace we were setting was painstakingly slow, but every moment they sat there made them colder and hopefully slower. We reached the back of the tree and waited while the gun guy opened a thermos and poured two cups of some steaming beverage. He handed one to Rich, and they resumed their watch.

There was still plenty of cover between us and the tree, so we turned and made our way towards the men, crouching flat whenever one of them turned. We got within about twenty feet of them before the cover petered out, and John and I braced ourselves to run across the intervening space. My basic plan was to disarm Rich and pin him until the cavalry arrived. I could only hope John would manage to do the same to the gunman. Neither of us wanted human deaths on our conscience; it wouldn't go over well with the humans if we took lives in wolf form. The media would have a field day with that and would go out of their way to spin it to make us look like blood-thirsty killers.

We slipped from our cover, making a final, desperate sprint across the snow. The gunman heard us coming and had just started to swing around when John slammed into him. The gun went off, and the bullet tore great chunks from the trunk of the tree. Rich had just staggered to his feet when I bowled him over, snatched the weapon from his limp fingers, and then planted my front paws solidly on his chest. Out of the corner of my eye, I could see John standing on the man's back, growling ferociously, jaws inches from his neck. The man had the sense not to move, though I could see him glancing wildly around for any weapon to use on the ninety pound animal crushing his spine. Nothing lay in reach, however, and he eventually dropped his head to the ground in defeat.

I found myself staring down at Rich, the smell of anger and fear coming off him in waves. I bared my teeth and growled low and long. Saliva dripped from my jaws onto his upturned face, causing him to flinch away in disgust. He had tried to kill my brother, him and this monster beside him. It was all I could do not to rip out his throat and be done with it. Why couldn't he just leave us alone? What was so damned important about our relationship that he had turned into a stalker and potential murderer? His eyes sought mine, and I stared right back at him, furious. The acrid smell of urine hit my nostrils, and it made me growl deeper. He'd earned that little bit of humiliation, I thought, that and a thousand times more.

"Do you hate me, Sash," he whispered. "Good. I hate you too. You lied to me for years about what you are. Now your brother might be dead and others too. You know what? You deserved this. You had it coming."

I snarled at him, snapping my teeth a hair's breadth from his nose and leaned my weight harder into his chest, digging in my claws. He closed his eyes and turned his face away, refusing to make eye contact with me again. I continued growling at him, waiting impatiently for help to arrive.

A relatively short time later, Bobby and James led the six snow-proofed troopers right to our location, and both John and I stepped back to let them take our captives. The officers approached us cautiously, but we made it clear by adopting less threatening postures that the men were more than welcome to take them. As Rich was pulled to his feet, he gave me one last angry glare, then submitted to the police. Apparently, they were a lesser threat than we were.

Bobby and James led the way back to the House, breaking a clear trail for the men to follow, John and I trailing behind in case Rich or the gunman tried to escape. The fight had gone out of the two attackers, though, and they walked in sullen defeat before us.

Once back in the house, we all changed and joined my family as fast as we could. Everyone assembled in the foyer, and there seemed to be more troopers in the house than before. Kerosene lanterns had been placed around the room, giving it a cheerful glow. The rest of the family had come up from the safe room, and Kathy had already whisked the children away to the conservatory to "save as many of the plants as they could." We all felt better with them out of the chaos.

By the time we arrived, Stephen and Garrett had already been bundled off in ambulances to the nearest hospital. Olivia had gone with them, as had Bobby and Angie. The rest of us stood watching the invaders who sat handcuffed and bloodied on the floor. Several troopers guarded them with rifles ready, and none of the prisoners were seeming too good at this point.

"We'll be taking them to headquarters just as soon as we can get a large enough vehicle up here, Ma'am," said one of the troopers to my mother.

She nodded and walked off to check on the rest of the family, arms wrapped around herself to ward off the chill. Mark and David had gone to seal up windows or close off the rooms that had been broken into, while Marseille and my father worked to get the power back on.

Tanya and Charles beckoned John and myself to come sit with them, and Charles took my hands, his expression more serious than I had ever seen him.

"I need to find a better way to be a warrior for you," he said. "I think I'll be getting Grandmama her own phone for her upcoming birthday, as well as getting your number from Tanya here. We need better communication if I am to help you and your people."

"You did just fine this time around," I said, then turned to Tanya. "Your Grandmama won't always be around, Tanya. Time to get your prophesy motor tuned."

"Actually, I wonder if it isn't already kicking in," she said. "Remember when I felt I had to text Chuck your address?"

"Tans, I thought you agreed to stop calling me Chuck."

"I never said when!" she shot back, laughing, then gathered her composure. "Anyway, the impulse to do that might just be the beginning of my gift kicking in. I never would have thought to do it before, and Charles here isn't exactly a party guy. I just felt like I had to invite him."

"Hopefully, it will give you a bit more advanced notice than that next time, though twenty-four hours isn't bad." I said. "Now we just need for you to learn to pay attention to it more."

"I have a vacation coming up this summer," said Tanya. "Maybe I'll go visit Grandmama. Wanna come?"

"Nope," I said. "She said we wouldn't meet again. I'm not going to force the hand of fate at this point, believe me!"

A half an hour later, the transport van arrived, and the prisoners were escorted out. D. J. accompanied the state trooper as his cousin was taken to the waiting vehicle, then he returned just as the lights came on. Below, the furnace rumbled to life, and there was a collective sigh of relief from the gathered crowd.

My mother went into her office and was gone long enough for Kathy to enter the foyer with the children in tow, exhausted and covered in potting soil. When my father and Marseille emerged from the cellar and the office still remained closed, I knew that something important was going on.

D. J. came over to me and John, his face drawn and filled with sorrow. He ran a hand through his hair and gave a big sigh before meeting our eyes. The betrayal of his cousin must have devastated him, and I felt very sorry for our friend.

"I have to leave now to deal with Rich and my cousin. Can the two of you stop into the station when you get back, either Monday or Tuesday, whichever is better? I need to get some formal statements from you, though Sasha's parents have already given us a good idea of what went down here tonight."

"Sure, D. J.," said John, and I nodded.

"Thank you," he said. "The troopers will talk to your parents more tomorrow. For now, we all just want to let you all get some rest tonight. There's some more state troopers coming out to guard you all once the storm dies down. I got Clover to state that the rumor of other members coming was a lie; no one else would drive out in this weather, so you don't have to worry about another attack tonight. Oh, and that guy with Rich? Apparently, the group paid him quite the sum of money to come out here tonight. He's a sharpshooter from some paramilitary outfit over in Utah. He's wanted in about ten states and will be going away for a long, long time."

He turned and made his way out, hat in hand and head lowered as he walked. It isn't everyday one's cousin commits the level of betrayal Cloverly had. John and I watched him pass through the front door and out into the night, then turned our attention back to the rest of the family. They were slowly drifting into the comfort of the living room where someone had laid a fire.

Marseille appeared with long skewers, marshmallows, and other s'mores fixings, and I could see him helping weary parents make comfort treats with their children. I was far too wired to sit still, so I beckoned to John and made a circuit of the house. All of the broken doors and windows had been solidly latched and boarded over as needed. No one would be able to get in without alerting someone.

By the time we got back, my mother was just emerging from the office, and I gave her a quizzical look.

"I just got off the phone. I spoke first with Susan, and then we asked Sam and some of his colleagues to join us on the Zoom call," she said. "They were very interested to hear about the invasion. This is evidence that we all need protection, when a simple family gathering can turn into a nightmare. The members of the committee are going to play up the fact that there were children present, and that if it was not for the safe room, the younger members of the family would have been in terrible danger.

"A special hearing is being set up for Monday with members of Congress, and we will be asked to testify over Zoom," she continued. "They may call you too, Sasha, because of Rich's involvement."

"Sure," I said and glanced tiredly at the grandfather clock. It was after ten, and I felt myself wilting.

"I'm going upstairs, tidy enough of my room to find the bed, and crash," I said. "John?"

"I'm with you," he said. "I've had enough "fun" for one day. Let's go up and call it a night. We can unwrap presents tomorrow if people really still want us to."

"I'll pass the word," smiled my mother. "I'll see you two in the morning."

John and I went upstairs, and I stood sighing at the mess. I held back tears as we pushed bureaus into place and closed closet doors. As I put the drawers into one dresser, I felt a wave of sorrow wash over me, and I sat down on the edge of my bed to cry. It was intense and so violent, it hurt my chest. John sat down next to me and held me, letting me weep myself out.

"How can they be so hateful?" I sobbed. "A few months ago, they had no idea we even existed! Now they want to kill us, and for what?"

"Rich hasn't been right in the head for a while," said John, stroking my hair. "He and Todd and Gary just fed into each other until they imploded. Hate can only breed more hate. You know that."

I leaned against him, the tears slowing, the exhaustion that comes from a storm of emotions beginning to overtake me. I knew from experience that I was likely to wake tomorrow with a killer headache, but for the moment, I just wanted to be held.

"It'll be okay," he said, resting his head gently on mine. "It will all be okay."

I wanted to believe him with all of my heart, but we would have to see what the next few months would bring. If the government didn't take this invasion seriously, what would have to happen before they did? Something like a massacre? Would that be the only catalyst they would pay attention to? I fervently hoped it wouldn't come to that.

30
RESOLUTIONS

We arrived at the station on Monday afternoon and were promptly ushered into D. J.'s office. It wasn't long before he entered, his complexion peakéd. An aura of sadness surrounded him like a shroud, and he gave us a tired, strained smile that never quite reached his eyes.

"How are you holding up?" John asked him.

"I spent my morning reporting all the gory details the little twerp confessed to me when they put him in lock up at the Laramie State Police Barracks. He's been working with a group called Humans First for a number of months. Turns out, one of Gary's friends recruited him not long after you left Rich, and he got himself assigned to my team solely to spy on you and your associates. I figured I could trust him, being blood and all. When the shooter showed up at your uncle's work, he and his partner were already stationed nearby to keep any other patrols from coming too close. Your call to 911 derailed his plan, and he had to play the dutiful watchdog and alert me."

He stared at the floor for a moment and shook his head.

"Stupid kid," he said, looking back up at us. "He bought their line of 'shapeshifter world domination' hook, line, and sinker. He even admits it, much good that will do him. I don't think he knew how crazy Rich and his pals are. His parents are beside themselves over this, and I have a sneaking feeling that they're blaming me somehow. It's going to be a rough time in my family for a while."

I nodded with sympathy, feeling bad that he had to go through so much for our sake. John put a hand on D. J.'s shoulder, and our friend flinched slightly before relaxing under John's worried gaze.

"Sorry, man," said D. J., meeting John's eyes. He laughed, a bitter laugh. "Would you believe that until Saturday night, I had never seen any of you folks up close in animal form? You scared the hell out of me, John. You, the most human of all the shapeshifters I've met, scared tough ol' me with your wolf form."

"I'm so sorry, D. J., I had no idea...," said John, removing his hand like he'd been burned.

D. J. cut him off.

"Shit, it's okay. It's not like they started our unit and had anyone come in to prepare us. We were told it was taboo to ask, so we just accepted it. Maybe we should find a few shapeshifters who feel comfortable with the idea of showing themselves to us. Last night, I knew...*knew*... you wouldn't hurt me, John. You even wagged your tail, for Christ's sake! But I still felt a deep-seated fear of you until you came back as a human, and I've been stewing over it ever since. I'm not as prepared for this assignment as I thought. If we're to protect your people, we need to have trust between us."

He stopped and then regarded both of us seriously.

"Could you ask a few of your friends if they'd be willing to come to a training session and show my team what you are? I know, I know it's taboo, but if we are going to help you, the other members of the team need to see what you really are."

"We'll ask the APkids," said John, glancing at me for confirmation. "They've been raised in the city and are as near to my level of human that you're likely to get. One of their mothers is a lawyer and can probably be convinced to come speak to your people as well. Would that help?"

"Oh," said D. J., sounding relieved, "You have no idea how much that would help."

"I'll get back to you after we talk to them," I said.

D. J. gave us a tired smile and shook our hands without further hesitation, a weight obviously lifted from him.

"I wish things had gone better regarding Rich," he said. "Do relationships between humans and shapeshifters usually end badly?"

"Sometimes," I said leaning into John's chest. "A lot of the time, shapeshifters never tell their partners because they are afraid they won't accept them. Most of them eventually drift apart. It takes a special couple to make the relationship work. Like Sam and Laura."

"I can see where that would be difficult," said D. J. "Well, Rich has not done anything to deserve your sympathies – nothing, Sasha. He's going to go to jail for a long time, not in the least for breaking his bail conditions. What I don't understand is why you didn't attack him, John. I would have bitten him somewhere tender if I were you."

"I was taught by a very wise teacher that what separates us from the regular animals is our humanity and a promise made long ago to help people, not hurt them," said John, glancing at me. "Biting Rich in anger would not have helped anyone."

"True," said D. J. and grinned. "Though it might have made you feel just a tiny bit better."

John laughed, and my mood lightened. Rich and his friends' days of lurking in the shadows were over, and I would be able to move forward with my own life. There was a wedding to get ready for and a myriad of experiences with other shapeshifters to explore. We still had work with the governor and the mayor, Nevermore and I had our hands full with the kids and the school board, and who knew what would come next? Life had been all about change of late, and perhaps, just perhaps, the greatest changes were still yet to come.

Post Script 1

Two weeks later on a Thursday night, the phone rang while John and I were preparing dinner. Putting down the knife I was chopping salad with, I answered, hearing my mother's excited voice on the other end.

"Turn on the news! It's happening!"

John and I rushed to the Theater and put on the local news channel. A very formally dressed man was standing at a podium and behind him stood Sam Winston and the other members of the shapeshifter delegation.

"...and so, it has been decided that, as of today, all members of the shapeshifter clans in America shall be given the same designation of protected status as any other citizen and shall be hereby included under anti-discriminatory laws as with those members of religions, the LGBTQ+ communities, and racial minorities.

"This governmental body has spent several months now with the delegation you see behind me. They are as much members of this country and our communities as any human and shall be accorded the same protections and rights under the Constitution as any other citizen living in this country. Thank you."

The man stepped aside as the press began to barrage him for information, and the delegates stepped forward to respond. A sharply dressed black man, who introduced himself as Ekene Alaneme, a serval, fielded the questions the press bombarded them with, deferring occasionally to other members who could better respond. Sam only spoke once or twice. As I sat on the couch holding my cell phone still pressed to my ear, I felt a sense of exhilaration at what we were witnessing. My mother was talking to my father in the background, and then came back on the line with me.

"This is a proud day," she said. "Not that I expect anything to change overnight, but at least there is legal protection for us now."

"No," I said, my eyes still glued to the TV, watching the reporters ask the delegates what their future plans would be. "I should think that letting the furor settle for a little while would be the best thing for everyone. Let people see that there is nothing different, even with the protections, and then everyone should calm down."

"I should hope so," said my mother. "I'll call you back later, Sasha. Andrew is calling."

I hung up the phone and continued to stare at the television with a sense of relief and not a little trepidation. I knew that not all shapeshifters were as cautious as we were, and some would use this as license to make a spectacle of themselves. I hoped that it would not be the case, but some just were a bit more incorrigible than others.

I made calls to the former students, and to Kathy and Paul. They had all seen the broadcast and knew what it meant. A short time later, they all descended on our house, and who were we to tell them no? A little while later, pizza, love, and merriment filled our house as we celebrated our new freedom as one people together.

Post Script 2

The dress was lovely, the reception exquisite, and Marseille's pink *petit-fours* tasty beyond compare and a little *extra* pink. The groom glowed with pride as we danced to our chosen song, "The Luckiest" by Ben Folds in the ballroom of the House. Staring into each other's eyes, both John and I felt the weight of our future together and that of our family-to-be. In the crowd of our friends, I saw Sam and Laura, Susan and Meredith, the APkids, Kathy and Paul, John's parents, the badgers, and my entire family watching us with all the love one could imagine. Whatever the future held, whatever came our way, our journey together had just begun. What lay ahead for the future of man and shapeshifter remained undetermined, but here, in the magnificence of the House, with this galaxy of people, we were all one for this little time and space.

And that was enough for now.

ABOUT THE AUTHOR

Deborah Jarvis has been writing for a long while and has been an advocate for all things greyhound for slightly less time than that. She teaches high school and college literature and writing, and lives in New Hampshire with her husband Rob, her son Will, a Greyhound, a European Village Dog, a Lab cross, and three magnificent cats. Her daughter Rosalynde lives nearby. *Wolves Running* is the first book in *The Shapeshifter Symposium*.

For more information, including social media, email, and the author's website, visit: linktr.ee/the_rael_coyote

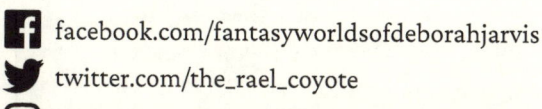

  facebook.com/fantasyworldsofdeborahjarvis
  twitter.com/the_rael_coyote
  instagram.com/the_keyralithian_chronicles

THE KEYRALITHIAN CHRONICLES - BOOK 1

The Crystal Pawn

Deirdre Hawes had never thought of her life as extraordinary until one day she met the father she never knew and thus began the adventure of a lifetime. Armed only with the knowledge that she is heir to magical gifts that would allow her to call on the aid of the long-vanished dragons, she finds herself drawn into a web of intrigue and murder where the powers behind the throne are aligning to make sure she doesn't succeed, no matter the cost. Deirdre soon finds her life in the hands of those she's been told not to trust, but trust them she must if she is to have any hope of not only completing her quest but surviving to make the journey home.

THE KEYRALITHIAN CHRONICLES - BOOK 2

The Ivory Queen

On the run from the forces attempting to take over the country, Deirdre and her companions must cross the desert and enter the jungle to find a lost tribe of her kinsmen who hold the key to her being able to call the dragons and end the war. Along the way, she also has to master her burgeoning powers and find a way to succeed as the ever-increasing forces ally against her while she races the clock to save what has become her home.

FORTHCOMING

The Ebon King - The Keyralithian Chronicles - Book 3

Cut off from the people she loves the most, Deirdre must devise a plan to rescue her love and find a way to bring the Ebon King to the southern lands as only he can unite the country against the invading forces threatening their homeland from within and without. Only with the help of some unexpected friends will she accomplish her goals to finally save Keyralithsmus and restore peace to all in habitants human and magical.

Forever Demond

For Marcy Collins, being at a dig in a previously undiscovered catacomb in Rome should have been the highlight of her career, and it was until late one night, when an uninvited figure enters the dig site. When the man disappears right in front of her, Marcy finds herself on the edge of unravelling an ancient story, one that is connected to the very catacombs she is helping to excavate.

When she meets the man again within the Hall of the Animals at the Musei Vaticani, Marcy realizes that there is much more at stake than a mere chance encounter and begins to research the mysterious Francis De Mond. As she uncovers more of his background, she begins to realize that De Mond and a tragic figure within the archives of the monastery may just be one and the same person. As others begin to make the same connections, Marcy becomes the one person De Mond can turn to for help, and when his enemies finally reveal their true intentions, she may be the only person who can save him.

Made in the USA
Columbia, SC
01 September 2024